THE ISLAND OF LOST SOULS

THE ISLAND OF LOST SOULS

MARTYN BEDFORD

BLOOMSBURY

For my daughters, Josie and Polly

First published 2006

Copyright © 2006 by Martyn Bedford

The moral right of the author has been asserted

Bloomsbury Publishing Plc, 36 Soho Square, London W1D 3QY

A CIP catalogue record for this book is available from the British Library

ISBN 0 7475 8223 8
ISBN 13: 9780747582236

10 9 8 7 6 5 4 3 2 1

Typeset by Hewer Text UK Ltd, Edinburgh
Printed by Clays Ltd, St Ives Plc

The paper this book is printed on is certified by the © 1996 Forest Stewardship Council A.C.
(FSC). It is ancient-forest friendly. The printer holds FSC chain of custody
SGS-COC-2061

FSC
Mixed Sources
Product group from well-managed
forests and other controlled sources
Cert no. SGS-COC-2061
www.fsc.org
© 1996 Forest Stewardship Council

1ST SGT. WELSH

'In this world a man himself is nothing.

And there ain't no world but this one.'

PRIVATE WITT

'You're wrong there, Tom. I seen another world.

Sometimes I think it was just my imagination.'

The Thin Red Line
Dir. Terrence Malick

'Then Ludwig realised that, whatever Aesop's vision of violence was, it still encompassed heroism.'

The Nudist Colony
Sarah May

PART ONE

Call-up

It was hot in the club. Suffocating. Finn's face felt as if it was made of glue, his T-shirt so damp the hairs in his armpits stuck to the fabric, tugging whenever he moved. He looked around. Where was Lila? She'd headed off to the bar a few minutes ago and he'd lost sight of her. He needed another beer. He needed the pill she'd promised to bring back for him; his *leaving present*. The music was piling up all around him, hassling him with spiky points of noise, burrowing into his head until he wanted to tear off his ears. What *was* this shite? Then, like a light going off, the music stopped. The DJ resumed his spiel. Finn calmed himself, took a last suck on his cigarette and sent the butt sparking into the gloom. Leaning against the wall in an alcove, acting cool, his black gear camou-flaging him against matt, blackwashed brick. All anyone could see of him, he imagined, was a luminous face, and arms severed at the biceps, floating. The wall chilled his ribs through the sweat-saturated cotton. He felt special.

Draft Nite.

Every Friday night was a draft night, these days – a weekly ritual, his office emptying out to the pub *en masse*, then the club, to piss it up with the latest batch of draftees. With 240 people working in an open-plan the size of a football field, there was always at least one leaving the company to go off and fight. Three this week, including Finn, so all this wasn't just for him; but he'd seen people – guys and girls – pointing him out, casting him glances, noticing him. Like he was the birthday boy. Like he was some kind of hero. It felt good, but it also felt hollow and meaningless. Who were these people? Like suddenly he mattered to them because he was about to be strapped into a uniform. Two years, he had worked there; after tonight he'd probably never see any of them again . . . and he (and they) couldn't have cared less. It was like throwing a party and having a bunch of strangers gatecrash.

Finn wondered what Kurt was doing right now.

What time was it out there? No idea. If Kurt was here, he'd be out on the floor – dancing, mixing it, giving it plenty – not snuck away by himself in some dark nook.

There was a reek of spliff. He'd got some himself, stashed away for later, back at his place, but just now he wanted to shift himself up, not down. Jolt himself out of the sour mood he had been in all day. All week, all year. You could kid yourself it started when things with Lila deteriorated. But things with Lila deteriorated because he was already turning into this – 'You're so cynical, Finn, so pissed off all the time' – and she couldn't take much more of being a repository for his shit. Repository, that's what she'd said. Finn told her he'd need to look it up, or was she planning on taking the dictionary with her when she left?

He didn't used to be like this.

The letter had come on Monday morning. Finn had just finished shaving. The heating had fouled up again and he'd had to make do with cold water. His throat was blotchy. He was inspecting the skin in a mirror when there was a knock at the door. He half-expected it to be the nutter in B–block, fussing about the window. Paladin Mansions' twin towers had been built so close together that if you opened your kitchen window too wide the folk in the flat opposite couldn't open theirs at all. Not without smashing it. Most tenants in Paladin kept their windows locked shut in case someone climbed out of their window and into yours to rape you or rob you or kill you. It happened. Then there was the constant gloom. Finn and Lila had to switch on the light in their kitchen, whatever the time of day. And if the nutter happened to be cooking at the same time, you'd lower the blind so you didn't have to watch each other, like food-show chefs performing for a live studio audience of one.

A second knock, louder. Lila had left for work already, so if Finn didn't open the door then the door didn't get opened.

He recalled her opening the kitchen window to let out the odour of last night's takeaway. Had she shut it again? Oh, who gave a shit? He massaged moisturiser into his neck, ignoring the knocking. Fuck him, fucking weirdo. There was another knock, the voice of the mailman.

That was it.

One minute you're thinking of cold showers, shaving rash, windows and piss-you-off neighbours; the next, you're sitting on the bed not opening a letter.

The envelope bore the national crest. He'd had to sign for it. They'd been working their way through the alphabet for months, so he had a good idea what it was. Usually, Finn read his mail right away; or on the subway, if there was room. If it was running. But that morning he stowed the letter, unopened, in his jacket pocket. He felt it against his shirt in the juddering, pissy elevator that dumped him at the ground floor of A-block. He felt it in the street, in the push and shove of the platform, in the press of the train. At the office he took off his jacket, shawled it over his chair and worked as normal (i.e. doing fuck all, busily). But, all morning, he thought about the letter, even when he was thinking about other things. He didn't open it, though. So long as he didn't open it he had one last decision to make for himself before the system made them all for him.

How many days could he get away with that?

He pictured them, rat-a-tatting at the door of the flat, or striding into the office. And suddenly you're like an escaped con who sees the uniforms closing in and knows it's over. It's over and something else is beginning.

For now, though, Finn was on the loose. He liked to think of it in that way. So long as the letter remained unread, he wasn't drafted.

He should phone someone. Mum? No. Dad? Yeah, right.

Lila? But he knew better than to call Lila at work, even about something like this. He wanted to go round the shop, wait outside in the street till she saw him; make her come outside, or catch her on a cig break. Maybe Lila would love him again if she knew he was going off to fight. Finn shook that notion out of his head right away. Pathetic. His capacity to become a teenager again, where women were involved. But he wanted to tell her, he wanted her to be the first to know, for her to be there with him when he opened the letter. If you were a couple, you shared the big stuff that happened to one of you.

He wanted to tell Kurt.

But his brother was already out there; beyond reach. He'd volunteered a year ago, in the war's second year, when the 'theatre of operations' had expanded and the allies needed more troops but hadn't yet resorted to conscription. Well, the theatre of operations was wide open now. Kurt was eighteen months older than Finn. Divorced, already. Officially, he had signed up out of patriotic duty at a time of international crisis. Unofficially, he reckoned he'd be better paid, fed and clothed in the Army than he was living on the dole and hustling poker games. Also, he'd see a

6

few places, learn new skills; if he ever made it back in one piece, he could start all over again.

In his latest letter home, after the 18–25 draft had been announced, Kurt wrote: 'When your turn comes, bro, don't think about being killed or about killing. Just learn your job – and do it.'

Finn shouldn't have signed for the papers. Should've ripped them up, there on the doorstep. Or set them alight, publicly, in front of the media, like others had done. Except most of them were in jail now. Or dead. *Cowards. Traitors. Scum.* Stashed away in labour camps or on isolation wings, along with the grasses and paedos. For their own protection, was the official line. Even so, there were beatings. And some – more than some – had 'committed suicide' in their cells. The Government made sure you knew this. Resistance, evasion, desertion, it made no odds: you got twenty-five years, minimum; only no one expected you to last anything like that long.

Finn had felt sick as he shut the door on the mailman. In his throat, his chest, his stomach, his gut. In the muscles of his legs and the palms of his hands. Not until he'd sat down on the bed and the shock had begun to subside did the first thoughts surface.

Who *were* they? Who the *fuck* were they to order him to fight? He hadn't even voted for the bastards. Hadn't voted for anyone.

Didn't agree with the war (or the 'war' from which this one had evolved, way back when this was – supposedly – all about the preservation of democracy).

Didn't agree with conscription.

Didn't want to die. Not for his country. Not at all.

He was twenty-four. You don't die at twenty-four.

Finn skipped breakfast. When he'd done with sitting on the bed holding the unopened letter, he went through to the kitchen and started to make coffee, to put bread under the grill, because these were the things he did automatically each morning. He stopped. Switched off the kettle and binned the half-cooked bread, unable to stand the smell, let alone the thought of eating, of swallowing, of digesting.

He dressed. He put on the radio, then turned it off again.

He moved about the flat as if it didn't belong to him. As if he was staying with a friend who hadn't woken yet and, until they did, Finn didn't know what to do with himself or where to sit or where anything was kept. Every ordinary thing he did, or looked at, had the amplified quality of something significant.

Why wasn't Lila here? He wanted her to be here.

Li, it's come.

Oh, Finn.

It would've been easy to phone in sick. But the thought of being trapped in this place all day by himself, restless and useless . . . and you couldn't just go out and walk the streets for hours, with the rain coming down like this. Finn gazed out across the new day, first-hacking-cough-of-the-morning cityscape. Glazed, angular. The vast grey-black slabs of construction like so many blocks in a stonemason's yard, waiting to be chiselled into sculpture. You push one over, they would all topple.

So he went to work, like any other day.

A woman left her flat as he emerged from his. Out of necessity, they walked along the corridor together. Neither spoke, letting the briefest eye-contact pass for hello. Finn recognised her, but didn't know her name or anything about her, even though they'd been neighbours for however long. Fat; fortyish; dyed red hair. The sandals and tights combo. As they passed the last apartment before the elevator vestibule, the woman nodded at the flowers held in a scrollwork iron ring screwed to the door. Orange and yellow blooms, like a flaming torch.

'There's another one,' the woman said. A heavy accent. 'God bless them.'

She was talking to herself, not him; muttering the words as

though they were an incantation, a private prayer. Finn wouldn't have been surprised if she'd crossed herself. The flowers looked fresh, and he didn't recall seeing any there the previous evening when he'd come home. But you saw so many these days it was hard to be sure. There were no bouquets at the foot of the door, though. So it *was* a new death, then. Another Lost Soul, claimed by the war. The occupant of the flat – the parents? grandparents? wife? girlfriend? brother? sister? – would have fixed the flowers to the door, according to custom, to identify this as a home in mourning. Within hours, neighbours would lay their own wreaths on the step as a mark of respect. You didn't need to be a friend, or even know them – it was just something you did.

Something other people did.

Finn would only do it for someone he knew, and he didn't know anyone in this dump. Even if he did, he'd sooner knock on their door and say to their face whatever it was the bouquet was meant to express.

There was nothing ominous in Finn seeing those flowers on the morning his call-up papers came; it wasn't even much of a coincidence. For months now, it had been rare to leave the building or walk to the subway station without passing at least one door dressed like that, as well as others whose bouquets had withered and faded or begun to decompose. Everywhere you went these days there was the fragrance, the staleness, the stink of flowers.

In the elevator, the woman spoke again.

'They should do something about the passage before we all burn,' she said.

The 'passage' was the narrow alleyway separating A- and B-blocks at Paladin Mansions. Tenants used it as a tip, habitually dropping stuff out of their windows and down into the passage below. Litter, old newspapers and magazines, food scrapings, empty bottles, cans and packets, broken toys, vacuum-cleaner bags, old clothes, nappy sacks, empty cardboard boxes, polystyrene packaging, bubble wrap, as well as bigger items like mattresses, curtains, furniture, TV sets, fridges, rugs. Dead pets, sometimes. If it was damaged or useless or unwanted, out it went. Periodically, the city authorities cleared away whatever hadn't been salvaged by street scavenger gangs or rats. But this hadn't been done for weeks and, in places, the accumulated debris reached the window ledges of the ground-floor flats. It was only a matter of time before a tossed match or cigarette butt or a bunch of kids set the whole lot alight.

Finn glanced at the woman, her frizz of fake-red hair backdropped by lurid graffiti. She was foreign. She looked like she might come from one of the countries the allies were at war with; except, if she was, she'd have been interned by now. She wouldn't be here, moaning about rubbish. And, she'd said: 'God.' 'God bless them.'

'Yeah,' he said. 'If it ever stops raining long enough for the stuff to dry out.'

'Crash, crash, crash.' The woman covered her ears. 'All day, all night.'

Finn and Lila usually bagged their trash and hauled it down to the communal bins, like you were supposed to, and it didn't bother him what the rest did. That was their problem. One time, though, he'd hurled a broken CD-player out of his kitchen window just to hear how it sounded, smashing into the junk thirteen floors below. But it must've landed on something soft because it hardly made a noise.

Was it the elevator, or was she the source of the reek of piss?

She had brown freckles the size of coins at the base of her throat. He imagined telling her he'd been drafted. *I just got my call-up papers. I'm off to fight in the war. Yeah, they came this morning, actually. My brother's already out there. Infantry. He volunteered.* What would she say? What did she think of the

10

war, of the draft? She wasn't even born here, though, so what would she care?

Anyway, he couldn't see himself ever talking to her about any of that.

She turned away from him, facing the doors.

They didn't speak again. When the elevator halted at the ground floor, Finn and the woman got out and went their separate ways.

At lunchtime, he tried Lila's mobile. It was on voicemail. He left a message for her to call him, but he knew she wouldn't get a chance. Probably, she wouldn't even get a break. At his place you only got twenty minutes, and most people worked through anyway, stuffing down home-made sandwiches or vending-machine crap at their desks. The idea was they'd get away earlier at the end of the day, except no one ever did. Finn always took his break. He had to get out, clear his head; even if, like today, he copped for a soaking as he scuttled along to his regular café. On dry days, he sometimes took a carry-out to a bench in the civic gardens; only, if you sat there too long, you were sure to be hassled by a wino or a junkie, or cottaged by some guy. So, mostly, he came here, with its green plastic seats, white plastic tables, and green-and-white-striped walls. It made him think of peppermint toothpaste.

He had the letter with him, unopened still.

Still, no one knew. There was nobody at the office he'd have confided in. Some mornings – some days – he'd make it through without a snatch of conversation that wasn't work-related. So keeping this to himself was no big deal. You just sit there staring at a screen, tapping keys; or you stand at a coffee machine, tapping buttons. Or you take a leak. Or you take a call, or make one. A guy in his team had taken to photocopying pages from a novel and reading them at his desk, like they were work papers; but they caught him and sacked him. Finn used to talk to him, sometimes.

No music; the CD juke was necklaced with an 'out of order' sign. The air con in the café was too high so he kept his jacket on, but he was still cold. Shivery. Like he was sickening for something. When his order arrived, he took out the envelope and placed it on the table. White and neat, like a serviette.

He thought of leaving the letter there when he returned to work. Just leaving it.

He thought of not returning to work. What could they do?

Not until he'd finished eating did he open the envelope. Using a clean knife from the cutlery stand on his table, he slit the flap. He slipped the papers out and, moving his empty plate to one side, set them down in front of him and smoothed the folds flat.

There.

Next Monday, at 10 a.m., he would undergo a medical. At that examination, he would be informed of the date on which he was to report to his designated unit for military induction. Failure to attend either the medical or the induction would result in the issue of a warrant for his arrest as a deserter. Desertion, the letter reminded him, carried a mandatory minimum sentence of twenty-five years' imprisonment with hard labour. The Department of External Affairs took this opportunity to thank him in anticipation of his contribution to the efforts of the Alliance of Democratic Nations towards restoring international peace and security.

This last word was translucent, thumb-printed with grease.

Finn scoped the nightclub again, peering into the throng for Lila. Nothing. Must be having trouble sorting the pills. There were dozens of familiar faces, but none of them was hers. Most of data processing was here tonight, by the looks; purpled by cigarette smog in a sinuous slick that captured the illumination from a bank of tinted spots. The national flag hung above the dance floor, agitated by warm air from the shimmying mass of bodies. Directly beneath it, a group of seven or eight guys were circled, pints raised, letting rip with one of the chants you heard just lately, wherever boozy lads gathered. About how we were going to kill the scum, kill the scum, kill kill kill the scum. Another of the new draftees from Finn's section – what was his name? – stood to attention in the middle of the ring, saluting. When the song finished, they doused him in beer to a chorus of whoops and whistles. He looked about eighteen.

'Got a light, pal?'

Finn focused on the face suddenly looming at him out of a corona of dance-floor haze. Droopy eyelids; he didn't know him. How did anyone's skin get so pale, so papery? He was holding a cigarette out in front of him and studying the tip minutely, as if this might cause it to combust spontaneously, saving him the trouble of blagging a flame. Long, tapering fingers, the nails bitten right down so you felt the pain in your own fingertips just to look at them. Finn produced his matches. He was about to hand over the box when the guy leaned in for Finn to spark him up. So he did. The bloke inhaled, careful to expel the first mouthful of smoke away from Finn.

'Thanks,' he said.

He offered the cigarettes. Finn helped himself. They smoked together without speaking for a moment, gazing towards the dance floor. The pulse of music was immense. Situation over, as far as Finn was concerned. The guy would just drift away, blend back into the crowd in the same way that he'd materialised, as if from nowhere. That was what he'd do. But he didn't. Pressing his lips close to Finn's ear to make himself heard, he said:

'You with that lot?'

'Kind of.'

'Work's party, or something?'

'Yeah.'

'Draft night, yeah?'

Finn nodded. The guy asked which company they worked for, so Finn told him.

'Never heard of it.'

'No one has.'

The guy smiled. He pulled at his shirt front a couple of times, for ventilation; smoked, took a slug of whatever he was drinking. A short of some sort, mixed with orange, though it was hard to tell in that lighting. There was ice in there. Finn thought about dipping his fingers in the glass to fish out one of the cubes, running it across his own forehead, his neck. Dropping it into his mouth.

'So what d'you do, then?' the bloke said at last.

What was this? Was he being perved on? Or was the guy setting him up for a scrap? He starts off with the friendly chit-chat, then takes offence at some innocent remark you make and away you go: push, punch, glass in the face. The guy was edgy enough for it, beneath the mateyness; there was a tension in him that was almost, but not quite, antagonistic. Though he was the one pushing the conversation, he seemed more defensive than aggressive. Scared, even.

'Sorry?' Finn said. But that only made the guy lean in closer, louder.

'Your job – what is it?'

'Data processing.'

'What is that, exactly?'

'I process data.'

'Right.'

They both laughed. This was better. 'Anyway,' Finn said, 'technically, I don't have a job. Not any more.'

The guy's lips were at his ear again. 'Yeah?'

Finn made like he had a semi-automatic rifle in his hands, spraying imaginary ammunition in the direction of the packed dance floor. He watched for the realisation to surface in the other guy's face, but he remained expressionless. Nodding away to himself, as if the information didn't surprise him. Finn dropped his hands to his side, feeling foolish for having done the gun thing.

They both smoked some more.

'So how come you're not out there?' the guy said, after a moment. 'Getting soaked with beer.'

The question came with a smile, like he was teasing, but his eyes were serious, locked on Finn's. Searching there for something. The look of a lonely man in need of a friend, was how it seemed at that moment. Finn took in the scene playing itself out before them. All those bodies. If you stared long enough, the swathe of animation ceased to be made up of individual figures, dancing, but growths from one grotesque, leviathan creature, its skin bristling with countless humanoid polyps.

Finn shook his head. 'Not me.'

The other guy went to speak but, before he got the chance, Lila was back.

She looked at Finn, then at the guy, as though puzzling out whether she knew him. The guy shifted his weight from one foot to the other, easing away, dropping the half-spent cigarette on the floor and treading it out. He went to clasp Finn's shoulder, but aborted, turning the gesture into an ineffectual wave. He nodded again, told Finn it had been good talking to him. Then he left. Just like that.

Lila laughed. 'Do I smell, or what?'

'Weird bloke,' Finn said, watching the guy go. 'Forget about him.'

He was done with this place. Sooner be at home, with Li, just talking into the small hours, like they didn't seem to do any more. You couldn't talk here. Couldn't make yourself heard or understood, not properly, not about anything that mattered. It was Draft Nite – *his* night – but so what? Why couldn't you walk out on your own party? They'd talked already, the evening of the day the call-up papers came, once Lila was home from work and he

15

was able to show her the letter at last. He hadn't expected her to be upset, but she was. So maybe they weren't as washed-up as he'd imagined. Or maybe the fact of Finn going – *leaving her*, he guessed – had shocked her, with its reality, its definiteness, in a way that the gradual, to him seemingly inevitable, slide towards *her* leaving *him* hadn't.

'God.' She'd not spoken for a while after he handed her the papers. Then, her eyes, filling up, that was all she managed. *God.*

'Well, it was always coming,' he said. 'Wasn't it?'

'Yeah, I know. But.'

Finn had sighed. 'Yeah. But.'

'How are you about it?' She looked at him. Held his hand. 'Are you OK?'

'I'm OK.'

'You're not.'

'No, I'm not. I'm fucking scared, if you want to know the truth.'

They'd laughed, then. Awkwardly. Sadly. They might have hugged – she might've hugged him – but they didn't; she didn't. What she did was read the letter again, as if for confirmation. She let go of his hand to hold the letter in both of hers, and looked it over a second time.

'Next *Monday*?' she said.

'That's just the medical. It'll be a week or two after that before I have to, you know . . . *report for duty.*'

'Even so.'

After a pause, he said: 'I don't want to go, Li.'

'I don't want you to go.'

There was resignation in both their voices, yet Finn sensed – or was looking for – a subtle distinction between hers and his; as though Lila's was a less equivocal acceptance of the inevitable. A door was closing on them, and it wasn't of their doing, and it was beyond either of their control, he knew – but, all the same, Finn

16

felt like she had been the one to close it. Perhaps she'd been conscious of this too. Because, when she spoke again, her tone was different. Conciliatory: as if she'd hurt him and wanted to make it better.

'You'll get leave,' she said. 'And we can write. Phone, even. If they let you.'

They'd talked some more, without getting anywhere. Where else was there to get? Then, the next evening, it was the practicalities. Lila would have to move out of the flat once he left (he'd raised this, not her); the tenancy was in his name and, legally, she shouldn't even have been living there. And there was the furniture, all his gear. Thirty-six hours after his call-up and they were discussing storage.

Now, it was his party and Lila was bent on giving him a good time. But he didn't want a good time. He wanted to be at home, alone with her, in the quiet.

Just to lie together on the bed and hold one another, would be good.

She handed him a fresh bottle and, grinning, disguising the movement as a kiss, slipped a pill into his mouth on the end of her tongue. He chased it down with a swill of lager. In this light, his own skin became paler, almost translucent, while Lila's became darker still, from coffee to chocolate. It was as if their relative substantiality was being tested: her solidity, his diminishment. Finn felt himself, almost literally, to be fading away in her presence. The pill was lodged in his throat. He took another swig of beer. By the look in Lila's eyes, her own pill was already in the system. She kissed him again, properly, her beaded braids gently chafing his cheeks. When they'd finished he asked if she wanted to head home as soon as these drinks were dead.

Lila made a face, her long bare arms looped round his neck. Nodding towards the dance floor, she said: 'We haven't even been up yet.'

'Li, I'm wrecked.'

She was smiling, doing a little dance move against him. 'Come on.'

Later. An hour, maybe two.

Finn sat on the toilet. Even down here, the music followed you, fibrillating the thin cubicle walls. He lowered his face into his cupped palms and made washing motions, but closing his eyes caused his head to swim, as though he was on board a ship and the floor, the whole toilet stall, was rolling and pitching with the sea. His mouth filled with a watery flush of saliva.

He opened his eyes. Better. But there was no erasing the pictures in his mind, or the sounds flooding his ears with each pulse of blood. The pill wasn't helping, it was making him worse. He wondered, panicking, if Lila had sorted him something hallucinogenic by mistake. He was in no fit state for tripping.

Only, this wasn't his imagination, it was a memory.

Finn had seen the police making an arrest on his way to work that morning. A girl – fourteen, fifteen – snatched a woman's handbag outside the subway station and was legging it, right past him, when two cops who'd seen the whole thing from across the street intercepted her. Finn was barged aside in the scuffle. And then – when the girl wouldn't let go of the bag, when she spat and bit and and kicked and swore, when she broke free and tried to run off – one of them finally wrestled her to the ground, pinning her down while the other used his truncheon on her leg, like an axe, again and again and again, until the girl's ankle fractured with an audible crack. The sound of a road-worker's pick splitting a paving slab.

The incident had left Finn shaky for a while afterwards, for most of the day. If he was like that over a kid in the street, how would he hack it out there, where Kurt was? Fuck sake. Even now, the scene replaying in his head, he was trembling, close to tears, to hoiking his guts over the floor. Sitting on the toilet, the backs of his thighs numb with pins and needles. The muffled wash of music from upstairs breaking over him, as if the policemen's coital grunts, the crack of bone breaking, the appalling shriek of pain, had been synthesised in the mix – as if the soundtrack of the whole sickening tableau of brutality was being pumped out through the speakers along with the drum and bass.

Finn had to get out of there. He stood up, steadying himself.

Slipped the bolt and went to step out of the stall. But the door opened in on him, suddenly, pushed from the other side, and before he knew what was happening he was locked in again. The cigarette guy, with the papery face and chewed-to-fuck finger-nails, was in there with him. He made it clear to Finn to be quiet.

Finn was too spaced to think straight or to do anything.

He leaned against the cubicle wall, concentrating on keeping his eyes open. Whatever he did, he mustn't close his eyes.

The guy reached into a pocket. So maybe it was drugs, then. Finn couldn't help laughing. What he really needed right now was more drugs inside him. Or it was a blade. A robbery. But the guy pulled out a lemon-coloured calling card, holding it in front of Finn's face so he could see what was printed there. Waiting for Finn's gaze to lock on to it, to register the inscription. Finn nodded. He felt the guy frisk him with those long, bony fingers until he'd located his wallet. After slotting the card into one of the button-down compartments, the guy folded the wallet shut and put it back where he'd found it. Then he let himself out of the stall. And Finn was alone again.

Medical

Age: 24
Height: 1.85m
Weight: 72.59kg
Hair colour: brown(ish)
Eye colour: hazel

That kind of crap. Alongside 'distinguishing features', Finn had written 'chest hair in the shape of a jester's hat'; for 'chronic illnesses and/or medical conditions', he'd put 'anomie'. One of Lila's words. They gave you half an hour to fill in the form; he had completed his in fifteen minutes and was enjoying a cigarette when a nurse (she must have spotted him on CCTV) came in to remind him that smoking wasn't permitted. The others in the room, still hunched over their forms, had looked up at him like he was some kind of freak. Finn had found it comical at the time, but now – striding away from the clinic in a deluge, dodging the taxi touts, pushing burger and fries into his mouth – it pissed him off. This sheeplike obedience to authority; like life was one vast classroom and you were lost unless there was someone standing out front barking at you, telling you when to sit, when to stand, to come in, go out, when to be quiet, when to speak up, telling you what to do and think and say. Telling you what to know and what not to know. Telling you to do as you're fucking told.

'I won't last five minutes in the Army,' he'd told the mail-order catalogue model of a doctor who'd examined him. No white coat, but the patterned V-neck, the check slacks, the sculpted plastic-looking hair that was more wig-like than a wig. He even moved in the staccato poses of the menswear section.

'Why not?'

'I don't like taking orders.'

The doctor had false teeth, for sure. 'You say that, but once you're in I think you'll find that you learn to take orders, irrespective of whether you, ah, *like* it.' A spread of the hands. 'You put your cigarette out when you were told to, didn't you?'

In the early weeks of conscription, you could say you were gay and they'd have to fail you, because they didn't want queers in the forces. But that loophole had closed long before they reached the surnames in Finn's section of the alphabet. He'd also heard of draftees feigning insanity at their medicals. Now, though, it wasn't enough to sit there gibbering, or rocking back and forth on your chair, or acting like you were a beetle – you had to supply proof of treatment for a psychiatric disorder prior to call-up. And if you claimed to be a user, and took something beforehand so your samples tested positive, that no longer disqualified you. Junkie or not, you'd be packed off to the war regardless. The failure rate at draft medicals was down to four per cent.

Finn had passed, no problem. He'd been told the name of his unit (infantry, same as Kurt), and the place and date, seven days from now, when he would report for duty. He'd been issued with a 'tag' number. In his unit, the Medical Examinations Officer had explained, that number would be tagged on to his name whenever he was spoken to, or whenever he had to identify himself.

21

'The tag is part of who you are now, son.' It was printed on the form he'd filled in. It was printed on him, too. Before they'd done with him at the clinic, Finn had been made to queue with all the other draftees to have the number tattooed on his chest. It was sore. As he walked, he felt the bloodied digits sticking to the gauze patch they'd fixed there.

'Taxi! Taxi, mister!'

A kid. Nine or ten. Finn shouldered past, ignoring him.

'You gonna get wet, mister!'

He didn't respond. You don't respond; once you respond they've got you.

Touts, everywhere. Since soaring fuel prices, then rationing, then the ban on the private use of cars, hardly anyone drove. You still saw trucks and vans, though not so many; the police, military and Internal Security vehicles, along with fire rigs and ambulances. But the people walked or cycled. Or took the subway. Sidewalks were infested with pedestrians. As for the roads, they'd been taken over by public transport. Taxis, buses, minibuses. Auto-rickshaws, customised from just about anything with wheels. The system was a free-for-all; with so much demand, anyone laying their hands on a vehicle could set up in business. And for every vehicle, there was a tout, hassling you to jump on. The boy hassling Finn now was touting for a guy driving an open-sided milk float, with seats installed where the crates used to stack.

Finn walked. He walked a lot nowadays. He'd lived all his life in the Capital, but he'd never been so immersed in it. The touts. The beggars. The street-vendors. The litter. Graffiti. Pigeon shit. The checkpoints. Food-stink. Diesel-stink and the throaty din of traffic. The cancelled expressions on the faces. And the weather, a round-the-clock monsoon. It was how he imagined a Third-World city to be: the entire population taking to the streets in a vast urban pinball game. If you stopped to think about it, you hated the place. But you didn't stop to think. You just got on with it; head down, and off you go, day after day. Irritated by every-thing. Jumpy as fuck. The sudden blare of a klaxon – a taxi driver papping at some guy on a bike – set Finn on edge; as if a kid had snuck up behind him and popped a balloon. Walking the city, these days, you always felt like, at any moment, you might burst into tears or lash out at someone or be on the receiving end of a beating.

The rain was gusting in from the side, so that his left arm and leg were soaked to the skin while the rest of him was just plain wet. Umbrellas were useless among the tall buildings, with their perpetual winds, and he hadn't bothered with waterproofs that morning for the fuckwit reason that it wasn't raining when he left the flat. Not even a hood. The rain was in among the roots of his hair, rivering into his ears, his eyes, his mouth. Up ahead, a homeless bloke in a transparent plastic poncho emerged from the doorway of a closed-down insurance company. He'd left his sleeping bag there, along with a small dog that could've been asleep or dead. Finn thought: *Yeah, plastic poncho. Nice one.* He couldn't help smiling to himself. Even some guy living rough in a doorway wasn't as wet as him. Finn watched poncho-guy cut right across the stream of pedestrians and make for a trash bin at the kerb side. He lowered his trousers, gathered up the poncho, positioned himself on the bin and crapped into it.

'Hey,' he said, grinning, catching Finn's eye. 'Fucken outside toilet, man!'

Finn laughed. He gave the thumbs-up and walked on by. Poncho-guy looked draft age, though how could they draft someone with no fixed address? Maybe they toured the city with a truck and rounded them up, like stray dogs.

He finished off the fries, swallowed a last chunk of burger and binned the wrapper. In his head, he re-scripted the dialogue with the doctor, writing in new lines for himself – things he wished he'd said, but hadn't. Psychological profiling, the man called it, though it hadn't been much more than a cosy chat while Finn slipped his clothes back on after the physical. No point saying you were afraid of dying and of killing, that you lacked the aggression or nous to fight effectively; the training officers in your unit would take care of that. No point, either, in declaring opposition to the war or to conscription; these were 'topics of political discourse, not medical grounds for exemption'. Besides, the doctor added, displaying those synthetic teeth, the Government was democratically accountable and we were all bound by its laws . . . wasn't that one of the things we were fighting for? And if you raised a moral objection, you had to specify the recognised religion you adhered to, along with the reference number of the application for Conscientious Objector Status, which you'd lodged, hadn't you?, when the draft was introduced.

'Perhaps your sense of patriotic duty will be restored once you come under enemy fire?' the doctor had said, as Finn stooped to refasten his laces.

That was when Finn should've come back at him with the difference between patriotism and xenophobia. And with the different types of duty. Duty to the concept of what it is to be a human being; duty to the underlying principles of a nation; duty to the Government of the day and whoever that Government chooses as its friends. Where is the dividing line between loyalty to the State and loyalty to yourself? And what of individual freedom? The freedom to choose whether or not to die for your country. Or maybe the individual is already dead, and we're just cogs in some fucked-up machine of community. Maybe your life doesn't belong to you, but to the country you happen to have been born in. Is that citizenship? Is that what we're fighting to preserve?

Well, fuck that.

But all he said, when the doctor spoke of patriotic duty, was: 'Yeah, right.'

24

At the next block, Finn had to cross the street. A section of sidewalk in front of Government offices was cordoned off by police tape; there had been a fire a couple of days ago; he recalled hearing about it. The building's street-level windows gaped either side of the entrance like blackened and empty eye sockets. Incendiary device, probably; anti-war protesters. Officially, though, it was a gas leak. From the level of security in the Capital just lately, they must've been anticipating a whole epidemic of gas leaks. You couldn't travel from one district to another without being frisked and ID-checked a couple of times. Gaining admission to the clinic had been like entering a top secret military installation.

There was another checkpoint here, just beyond the damaged building. Finn submitted to the search, showed his photocard. When the officer asked the purpose of his journey, he said he was on his way home from a draft medical. The guy pumped his hand. He pumped Finn's hand like they were comrades; like he wished for all the world he was young enough to be going out there, too, instead of doing this.

Seven days. A week from now, he would be a soldier.

He thought about the calling card. It was in his wallet; Finn had taken it out the morning after the night at the club, just to look at it. To be sure the whole episode hadn't been part of the trip. Lemon yellow. It was the colour of the fly-posters you saw, if you managed to see them before they were torn down again; the colour of the stickers on subway trains, lampposts and phone booths. The colour of the background field of the website whose address was printed on these posters and stickers, beneath the slogan: 'Shaft the Draft'. Finn had logged on to the site a while back, when the draft was announced and the subversive material started appearing. But he'd closed the home page the moment it filled his screen, suddenly nervous. Paranoid that the site might be

25

monitored. You didn't want to be tracked reading anti-draft stuff. And, even though he'd downloaded nothing, he made sure to delete his cookies, clear his history, and wipe the temporary Internet files from his hard disk. Was that enough? He didn't know. He stayed away from the site after that. Probably, it was closed down by now in any case. Unless the whole thing was a set-up, a way of smoking out the dissidents and dodgers.

The card he'd been slipped in the toilets contained the familiar slogan. There was a mobile phone number scribbled on the reverse, and what looked like 'Leander'. Finn had no idea if this was a name or a code word. Maybe the pseudonym of the guy who'd given him the card, or of the person he was meant to ask for if he dialled the number. There was no way of knowing. You couldn't even be sure that, if you called the number, you wouldn't be lured to some rendezvous where a couple of IS officers lay in wait. In the nightclub, the weirdo had seemed genuinely scared of being caught making the approach; but, then, a skilled entrapment operator would do, wouldn't he?

So Finn hadn't called.

Even keeping the card, stowed in his wallet like a wrap of coke, felt like an act of sedition. He should get rid. If he wasn't going to make the call, he should lose the card. What could these people do to help, anyway? 'Shaft the Draft.' How could you do that? You couldn't. You fucking couldn't.

'Would you come with me?' he asked Lila.

'You serious?'

'Would you?'

'They'd catch you,' she said. 'Every night, on the news, there's another one.'

She was right. You couldn't switch on the TV bulletins without the mugshot of the latest captured evader filling the screen, or coverage of the sentencing (without trial) of one who'd

26

been caught before. Just last week, there was footage of a draft-dodger – nineteen, fresh out of college – who had been hiding out in his cousin's basement. The local Support the Troops group had got to him before the IS did – hauled him out into the street, beat him half-dead and strung him up from a lamppost; the cousin, too. The pair of them dangling side-by-side till the police finally got round to breaking through the mob to cut them down.

'I'm not talking about being caught,' Finn said. 'I'm asking if you'd come.'

It was a hypothetical question, Lila told him. And life was complicated enough without having to get your head round things that weren't going to happen. OK, so that was a no, was it? No, she wouldn't come with him. 'Finn, don't.'

Don't make this any harder than it needs to be, he took her to mean. Don't let's end on a quarrel. Not *end*. Separate. An enforced separation. Whatever, it was the evening of the medical and they were at the apartment at Paladin Mansions, putting gear into boxes. His and Hers. By the time Finn reported to his unit, the place would be cleared and Lila would be installed in a sublet room above the shop where she worked.

'You're bleeding,' she said.

He looked at his shirt front, where the leakage from his ID tattoo had seeped through the dressing. Lila made him take off the shirt, cleaned him up and re-dressed the damaged skin. She had tattoos of her own. She told him it would be sore for a few days and he should keep it clean and dry and check it for infection.

'I'm going to miss you,' he said.

Lila fixed the tape over the new dressing. Kissed him. 'Two weeks, every six months,' she said. 'Six months is nothing. You'll be home again before you know it.'

With his shirt off, and her touching his chest, kissing him, it was easy for them to leave the packing for a while and go to bed. In bed, making love, the uncertainties over what would happen to them, and how each of them felt about that, simplified, became irrelevant for the moment. In bed, Finn could convince himself they loved one another equally and that these weren't their last days together.

The Incomer

Bryher told herself she'd gone down to The Strand to await the arrival of the Incomer. Even though she'd been there since sunrise, at low tide, when she knew no boat could dock at the pontoon for hours. Even though she had spent that time on a ritual patrol of the shoreline, searching the shallows and the newly exposed strip of beach, seldom lifting her gaze to the ocean itself or to the horizon, from where the vessel would eventually materialise. The Incomer was days overdue but, for Bryher, the waiting had lasted much longer. Sometimes it seemed as if her entire life – her life as it had become, at least – was reduced to this solitary coastal vigil. Of late, anticipating the new arrival on the island, she'd grown confused, uncertain exactly who or what it was she was searching for. It even occurred to her that Roop himself might be on the boat, though she realised this was impossible. All the same, there was a knot of exhilaration and dread in her stomach; and, even though she understood the boat to be the source of her expectancy, she scoured The Strand with renewed hope, that morning, that she might at last find what she sought among the debris that had washed ashore overnight. A body. It wasn't that much to ask for: a body. By the time Qway and Tye came down, her footprints would have tracked the sand back and forth as far as the eye could see, if the waters hadn't returned to conceal them. The boat was in the offing now. It was such an everyday sight, yet Bryher found herself transfixed, as though she had never seen a boat before. She was still staring at it when the two men greeted her. Qway asked how long she'd been waiting and she said: 'A little while', seeing from the effect of her answer that both men regretted the question.

'He's coming,' Qway said, unnecessarily, out of awkwardness.

She looked out across the surface of the sea. 'Yes,' she said. 'He's coming.'

The two men – Qway at one end of the makeshift stretcher, Tye at the other – carried him from the pontoon, across the beach and along the dirt track that led to her cottage. The Incomer was delirious with fever and pain, each jolt sending him into a bout of writhing that, once or twice, threatened to pitch him to the ground. But, at last, they manoeuvred him through the doorway and up the steep, narrow stairs to the bedroom. *I must not resent him for being alive*, Bryher said, to herself, as soon as Qway and Tye had gone, leaving her alone with her patient. He had calmed a little, now that he was still. She composed herself, paying attention to the muffled shush of the sea beyond the closed window, and to nothing but this. As near to silence as it was possible for sound to be, it reached her at some, almost sub-audible, level. Then she set to work. His clothes were filthy. She removed his boots and socks, then cut off the shirt and trousers with scissors, to disturb him as little as possible. He lay there, naked on the bed, except for a pair of bright orange boxers. He stank. It was anyone's guess how long he had gone without bathing. But, even allowing for the debilitating impact of the infected wound, he looked in good physical shape. This surprised her. He was a

30

mainlander, after all – from the Capital, so she'd been told – with their toxicity levels, their diet, their sedentary habits. But he was well-toned, if somewhat slender, though she suspected he hadn't eaten for days and that any weight-loss was recent rather than chronic. Naturally he looked ill from the pain inscribed, even during sleep, on his face. There were odd concentrations of colour and pallidness on the surface of his body, as if (though she knew this not to be the case) his blood – his *life*blood – was pooling where it was most needed, leaving other areas depleted. All the same, she had expected his condition to be poorer. If the Incomer appeared this robust now, his prospects for a full recovery were encouraging. So long as septicaemia didn't develop.

This was Bryher's chief concern as she peeled off the rudimentary dressing Mr Skins, or his wife, had applied to the wound with strips of parcel-tape. A temporary drain should have been fitted, but hadn't been; or perhaps it had, only to be removed prematurely. It was hard to tell. The area immediately around the wound was red and swollen, the paler skin beyond this streaked with pinkish-mauve filaments. As for the injury itself, several of the stitches had ruptured; bloated gouts of pus nestled in there, like maggots, spilling watery fluid down his side and on to the sheet. Bryher's gaze strayed to his chest, drawn by a smudge in among the fine hairs. A tattoo. Directly over his heart, a series of black digits had been etched into the skin: KD150/468C.

Probing with her fingers, she tried to assess the extent of the infection. This brought him thrashing from the fitful slumber he had lapsed into. The noise was far worse than when he was being bumped along on the stretcher. More bestial than human. The Incomer's face and torso were drenched; every pore, it seemed, oozing globules of sweat as fat as raindrops. Bryher mopped his brow, stroking the spiky fringe from his forehead and drawing a damp cloth slowly back and forth until he quietened again. His hair, where it wasn't darkened with moisture, was the colour of nutmeg and cinnamon. Their flavours suggested themselves in her mouth.

Withdrawing abruptly from the bed – her bed – she let the facecloth drop to the floor and went over to the window.

Bryher would tend to the Incomer, everyone agreed.

It had been easier for them to accept that than to agree to allowing him on to the island in the first place. None of them knew for sure how seriously he was wounded, but Bryher would take responsibility for his treatment. She had trained and worked as a nurse, for one thing, though that hardly mattered here, where tasks were so interchangeable. But the Incomer was hers. Hers to care for. For all that the Gathering had reached consensus (a reluctant, qualified consensus, strained with mis-givings, but a consensus even so) it was Bryher who'd persuaded them. She would be the one to make him well. Then they would talk once more about whether to let him stay longer than was required for his recovery. The islanders had discussed it in those terms, despite the fact – she was only too aware – that it was the prospect of *her* recovery which underlay their decision to allow him ashore at all.

The Incomer.

What else could they call him, for now? For all that there was a name ready for him, it didn't fit him yet, didn't properly belong to him. She supposed that, for him, it wouldn't do until he regained some sense of awareness of himself and of his surroundings. Of the transformation in his circumstances. In the meantime, how could a partially conscious man assume a new identity, or have one conferred upon him? All that could wait. The initial task was to save him from dying, then to make him better; for Bryher, alone, to nurse him, along with her own grief. At the Gathering, and as she waited for the boat, and even when he was being stretchered, whimpering, along the track, this had seemed attainable. She could do this. Now, seeing this strange figure in the bed – touching him, smelling him, tasting him – she wasn't so sure.

Bryher didn't begin to weep until she saw the cormorant. It was little more than a stone's throw away, where the garden petered out into the shallow incline abutting the cove. The irregular line of rocks along this ridge was decorated with the kelp she'd strewn there early that morning to dry. Perched upon one of these rocks was the bird, stark against the sky, facing out to sea with its wings spread wide; its feathers were ruffled by an onshore breeze, but otherwise the creature was utterly motionless. Like a totem pole, she thought. At another time, she might have barely registered such a common sight. Or she might have found it pleasing. Uplifting. But at that moment Bryher looked at the solitary cormorant and, before she knew it, she had to brace herself against the window sill to stop her shoulders from trembling.

When she had finished crying, she busied herself. She'd noticed that the bottle of water she kept on the sill needed replenishing. A scum-line of evaporation scored the blue glass. It startled her to discover a daily task so long neglected. Taking the bottle down to the kitchen, she rinsed and refilled it before restoring it to its usual place. There, it sparkled with captured light from the window, distributing geometric blue shapes about the walls of the bedroom and across the bed. With that done, Bryher made a second trip to the kitchen for a bowl of warm, soapy water. Then she set about washing the Incomer. Once he was clean, she could re-dress the wound.

With word having reached the island that, at last, he was on his way, she had spent the previous day preparing the honey. As much of the pollen as possible had been filtered out in case of allergic reaction and, dependent on guesswork until she could examine the wound for herself, she'd made up a large batch. Better to have too much than too little. On seeing the volume of discharge from the wound, Bryher knew she'd done right. With little or no leakage, a change of dressing every few days was possible; with a real weeper like this, the honey's rapid dilution would require a fresh application each day, perhaps more often. She dried him, tilted him on to his good side and – braced against his paroxysms of pain – began cleaning the wound. When he had calmed again, she applied the honey. Holding the spatula above the ragged opening, she let gravity tease the mixture into the deeper cavities. The honey was viscous, unravelling from the blade in a sluggish cord of amber; in among the traumatised flesh, warmed by the Incomer's body, it would become fluid. She ladled in plenty. The work was soothing – to her, if not to him; he writhed and murmured in his sleep and she had to steady him with her free hand to keep him in position. Bryher relaxed. The methodical action of treating him helped her to detach herself from the man, from his presence, and to focus on that inflamed area of torso. At first she was conscious of this shift in concentration, and that it was deliberate. But, gradually, she ceased to be aware of absorbing herself in her task and became simply absorbed. Trance-like. She might have been cooking, measuring an ingredient into a sauce. He was a patient, that was all. Delirious, shored up by pillows, and with a gash that had to be healed . . . a patient. He was less, even, than that: just a wound, an elongated volcano of infection, its crater acting as a reservoir for the thick trickle from her spatula.

What were they expecting?

That the Incomer would become a substitute, no doubt. That his body (hadn't she asked for, longed for, pleaded for a body?) would occupy the space where Roop's should have been.

There was no Roop. No body.

It was this absence which, in the early weeks, had made it toughest for her to accept that he was dead. Actually, physically, dead. She'd hated herself for wanting it, but – almost as much as she wished Roop was still alive, still with her – Bryher had craved

34

the certainty of his corpse. Now, the sense of absence was more abstract; she no longer wanted literal confirmation of his death so much as a tangible outlet for her grief. Some remains. A home-coming for whatever was left of him. A grave to visit, to tend. Without these she'd become stuck; embedded in her desire for a body. Uselessly scanning the island's shores for a glimpse of something that might be him. There was no nursing him back to life, and she hadn't been able to hold him in death, or even bury him; now, instead of Roop, she was offered this other man – this *substitute* – carried to her home like a piece of salvaged jetsam, just as she had asked them to do.

To the islanders, it must have seemed so simple.

Bryher nursed the Incomer. His body. The laying of her hands on the skin of a sick, possibly dying, man in a bed that was hers and had once been hers and Roop's – and, even as those associations came to her, she shut them out. Concentrated on the task, the nursing. Detached, clinical, efficient. When the wound was filled, Bryher prepared the dressing. Diluting some more of the honey with water, she spread it over the rectangle of absorbent pad, like butter on bread. She let the first coatings soak into the fabric, then smeared on the last, thickest, layer so that the highest concentration was at the surface. As the honey in direct contact with the wound diffused into the damaged tissues, reaching the sites of deepest infection, the reserves within the saturated pad would be drawn into play. The work was messy. Her fingertips were tacky, accumulating fragments of lint, and the aroma was so sickly sweet as to be unpleasant. Going over to the window, she opened it as wide as it would go. The sound of the sea became more distinct – a heavy curtain being opened and closed, opened and closed – and the thin aluminium chimes suspended from the window frame clinked tunelessly, prettily.

Bryher returned to the bedside. She placed the dressing over the wound and covered it with a second, non-absorbent, one – a

35

piece of polyurethane film cut from the roll in her medical kit. She fixed it all in place with strips of surgical tape. The dressing extended beyond the centre of inflammation, in case of underlying infection at the margins. So far as she could tell, the sepsis was localised, for now. Certainly, the Incomer was feverish, his temperature raised; but his pulse was normal, he wasn't breathing rapidly and there was no sign of him progressing into cold shock. But she could leave nothing to chance. If he developed septicaemia, they did not have the antibiotics here to treat him, nor any way of getting them urgently. It was bad enough that they didn't have the means to set up a drip to give him proper pain relief. And there was no sending him back to the mainland, if his condition deteriorated. As soon as any hospital saw the ID tattoo they would become suspicious. They would report him. His counterfeit identity would be exposed, along with the islanders' – with *her* – complicity in harbouring him. They were committed now. Whatever happened, the Incomer would be cared for here, by her. If he got worse, he would die. Simple as that. He'd die. Here in her bed. Bryher doubted whether she could take another death right now.

Waiting for Pizza

Lila was on her way out, which was an odd moment for her to start up a conversation about him being drafted. She was standing in the doorway of the apartment; the door was open, she had one hand on the handle, a yoga mat rolled up under the other arm. When she turned to say something, he thought she was simply going to remind him of the party at Steff's after class, that she wouldn't be back till late and he wasn't to wait up, or something. But what she said was:

'Finn, maybe it'll do you good. You know?'

He switched his attention from the TV to Lila. 'What will?'

'You've been unhappy for so long,' she said, '. . . I guess, I'm just wondering if you need something like this to break you out of that spiral.'

'Like getting shot. That would do it.'

'*Finn.*'

'You seriously think being called up is what I need right now?' He faked a laugh, raised a can to his lips and swallowed down some beer. Then, he turned one of her own familiar phrases back at her: ' "Looking for the positive in the negative," yeah? It's easy for you to say that.'

37

Lila was letting the door butt against her foot. He wished she would come in and sit down so they could talk properly, but wondered if she'd – consciously or not – chosen this point, this place, because it would be easier for her to step away from him when he (as he was doing) responded badly. What he wished was, given it was his last week, she wouldn't go to yoga at all, or to the party, but would spend the evening here with him. But they'd already discussed that. Now they were discussing this.

'Anyway, I'm not unhappy,' he said.

Lila nudged the door open wider and let it come to rest once more against her foot. 'Is that true? *Really?*'

No, of course it wasn't. How could you be happy when you weren't sure what you'd done to make someone else create a space between the two of you – couldn't even say for sure that this had happened, only it seemed that way to you? And you'd figured maybe it wasn't anything you had done or said, but just the fact of how you were. That, somehow, you were no longer the person she'd fallen for; or – after nearly two years – whatever you'd had between you had run its course. Two years. Fuck. He remembered thinking, in the early days with Lila, that he'd never felt so good about himself as when he was with her. Once, just a week after they'd met, she'd come back to Paladin Mansions for the first time, to see where he lived, and the elevator had got stuck between floors. An hour and a half, they were there, just the two of them, before an engineer sorted it. They didn't shag or anything like that, they just sat down in that filthy fucking lift and smoked and talked . . . and when the thing started up again and the doors opened, he saw his own disappointment reflected in her face. Finn wouldn't have cared if they'd been stranded in there for days. Thinking back, he couldn't even recall what they'd talked about – just that they had, and how good that had felt. If they were stuck in the elevator now, he didn't know if they would have anything much to say to one another. Nothing new or interesting or surprising, anyway. Perhaps that was it: some-where along the way, he'd lost the capacity to surprise her.

'I'd like to get to choose my life-changing experiences for myself,' he said, at last, ignoring her question.

Lila's tone eased into sympathetic. 'I know. I know you would.'

'Go,' he said, smiling, with a wave of the hand. 'Have a good time.'

'You could come, if you wanted,' she said. 'To Steff's.'

Finn suspected she didn't mean it. He thought about saying: *OK; great, I'll see you there*; but he didn't. He shook his head, told her thanks but no thanks. Lila left then. First, she came over to kiss him goodbye again and to give him a hug, then she left and the door clicked shut behind her.

Finn stretched out on the sofa in front of the TV, the third of a four-pack just opened and a carton of twenty smokes on the go. He hadn't showered or shaved, or changed out of the clothes he'd worn the previous two days, since the medical. He hadn't left the flat in that time. This was the last of the beer and cigarettes, so he'd have to do something about that. Should've asked Lila to bring some back. Fuck it. Drinking, smoking, channel surfing, picking absent-mindedly at his tattoo scab, waiting for pizza to arrive. Trying not to think about her. The class would be over by now, she'd be on her way to the party. Finn considered calling her, but decided not to. His hair was oily, his skin itched. His own odour was beginning to revolt him. He should take a shower before going to bed, except Lila had probably used up the last of the hot water, getting ready to go out. There was no food in the place fit to eat.

This was like being a student again.

Only, students didn't have to fight. Unless you failed to hit eighty per cent attendance, or your grade average dipped under sixty; then, they'd draft you as an exemption defaulter. Finn was always OK on grades, but his attendance record . . . well, he had no idea, but it hadn't been eighty per cent, that was for sure.

Anyway, he wasn't one. He wasn't anything just now.

Finn fixed on the screen. Shite. He zapped channels. More shite. What were the chances of them getting back together when he came out?

He'd read somewhere that sometimes people who are terminally ill give up on life even before they know they're dying. They become depressed, lose all motivation to do anything or go anyplace; nothing has any point any more. Getting out of bed is an effort. This carries on for a while, then they find out that, all along, some cancer or other has been taking hold in there, slowly killing them. It's as if their unconscious intuits that the body is done for, and starts shutting the whole system down.

The lager was sour tasting, it made his eyes water if he gulped it too fast. How long would you have to lie on the sofa like this before you got bedsores?

Finn killed his cigarette.

A movement at the window startled him. Pigeon. The bird had settled clumsily on the ledge, a wing pressed against the pane so that the white under-feathers showed through the grey. It loosed off some shit. The creature was skinny, scruffy; it limped as it shuffled for position, seemingly observing Finn through the glass with one eye aimed his way. It pecked at the window, and Finn saw that the other eye was missing. A hole, a ragged indentation, still moist and pink. Cat, airgun pellet, disease; could've been anything. He thought about shoving the window open to dislodge the bird but, instead, went over and shut it from sight with the curtain.

There was an old boy on the fifth, apparently, who trapped them for food.

Finn slumped back on to the sofa.

The state of this place. Jesus. But the prospect of tidying, vacuuming, washing up, emptying ashtrays. One of the cans on the coffee table was stuck there.

Zap. A nature documentary. Zap. A convoy of armoured personnel-carriers, at speed, plumed in the dust of their own making. VO: . . . 'final push into the outskirts of the enemy-held city of' . . . Zap.

Jumping was an option. Thirteen floors. It wouldn't be any big deal: at Paladin one a month was the average, if you added A- and B-blocks together. He'd heard one smack the sidewalk a few weeks ago, when he was in the lobby. *A jumper.* Hearing that sound for the first time, there was no mistaking it. According to the janitor, you could calculate the floor by the quality of the impact. That time it was a single mother from the twenty-first, Finn found out later. She'd had a baby harnessed to her chest in a sling when she took the dive.

He couldn't do that, jump. Didn't have the courage, or the desperation. How bad must the alternative be, before you'd choose to leap from a high window?

It wasn't despair, with him, it was self-pity. Afraid to fight, afraid to resist, afraid (either way) of losing Lila . . . and feeling sorry for himself. Sometimes he was so pathetic, so fucking pathetic, he made himself fucking puke.

He aimed the remote again. Zap. Zap.

Another beer, another smoke. He was ravenous; where was the pizza for fuck sake? He considered porn on toll-TV, but porn invariably depressed him, however exciting it seemed in anticipation. Zap. Zap. Zap. He switched off the TV. Instantly, the clutter of sounds from other flats and from the street intruded, as though activated by the remote control. A siren, a car alarm. The trundle and clatter of skateboards on concrete drifting up from way below. A wailing baby. The wind, testing the building's superstructure. You could imagine Paladin's towers to be the passenger decks of a vast cruise liner, waves breaking incessantly against the hull, gulls calling, engines thrumming above the hellish cries of the men labouring to keep the ship going.

What did Finn know? He'd never been on a ship. Never been outside the city.

When the pizza came, it would be lukewarm and taste of padded envelope.

Not drunk, but heading there. He closed his eyes, feet lolling over one armrest, head propped against the other, and listened to the lives being lived all around him.

He must've drifted off.

It was – what time was it? Jesus, ten-thirty. The phone was ringing. He'd been dreaming about a phone ringing. He needed a piss. Finn hauled himself off the sofa and went to the phone. *Lila?* No. A woman, but not Lila. At first he didn't recognise the voice – he was too sleepy, still, too beery – then he began to tune in. Mum. His mum was on the phone. What was she saying? Something about Kurt. Finn snapped awake now, got her to start again from the beginning.

'It's Kurt,' she said. Finn waited for her to say he was dead. But she didn't. She said: 'Kurt's home. They sent him home.'

Kurt's Foot

Finn's brother was sitting, reading a newspaper. The old standard lamp stood behind the armchair, its tasselled burgundy shade looking – from the doorway – like a hat perched on Kurt's head. His face, toplit by the low-wattage bulb, dropped dark blots across its own bleached planes. Ink stains, Finn thought. A mask of yellow parchment patched with navy-blue. His hair was shaved to stubble, like black pepper scattered across his scalp. On seeing Finn, he lowered the paper to his lap and placed his hands on it, palms down, as if anxious that a sudden gust of wind might tear it away. Mum, having led Finn into the house, had finessed it so that he was first to the living room. He sensed her at his shoulder; then, as he went in, he heard her move away, towards the kitchen. Allowing them a moment of privacy. As though him and Kurt were an estranged couple she'd brought together for a reconciliation.

The brothers looked at one another across the room. Kurt was beaming. He wore a T-shirt, football shorts. When did his legs get so hairy? One leg made a right angle; the other – the one without the foot – was stretched out, supported by a stool under the knee, the stump of his shin encased in bandage and flesh-tone strapping.

43

Finn's gaze settled there. 'Mum told me,' he said.

'She tells people I lost it. "Kurt lost his foot."' Kurt gave a laugh. 'I didn't lose it – I knew where it was all along, it just wasn't attached any more.' They were both staring at the stump now. It might've been an unusual object one of them had found in the street and they were trying to guess its function. 'I could've put it in my pack and brought it home, if I'd wanted. So don't let her tell you I lost it.'

This wasn't like Kurt, talking about it, all chatty and smiling. Effusive, almost. You'd have thought he was bragging – unable to contain his excitement – about some achievement at school. Like they were kids again. The house could do that to you; this room, looking as it always had, for as long as Finn could remember. Same chintzy wallpaper, same patterned carpet, same suite with its flock covers, same heavy, floral curtains. Same clashes of swirls, circles and stripes, turquoises and oranges, mauves and chocolate-browns. The framed print above the mantelpiece: 'Chrysanthemums in Vase, with Tortoiseshell Kitten'. And, along the mantelpiece itself, the painted plaster figurines: hedgehog, badger, squirrel, rabbit, and others from the Woodland Creatures series their mother had collected. It was as though you'd never left. Or as though an entire family had been tragically killed many years ago and, as a mark of respect, a neighbour had preserved their living room exactly as it was on the day they died. But what neighbour would do that, round here? The last lot had been done for removing breeze blocks in the connecting wall of the loft so they could sneak in and burgle the place while Finn's mum was out.

Anyway, feeling like a kid again cos you'd come home didn't explain Kurt.

Finn had expected awkwardness, evasiveness. That was how it had always been with Kurt, when shit happened – expulsion from school, the failed driving test, divorce, losing his job. He schtummed up, and you crept around him. Not tonight.

He was off again.

'What I lost was about ten centimetres of shin.' Kurt calibrated the amount in the air with his thumb and index finger. 'Otherwise they could've maybe stitched it back on. The foot. Microsurgery.' Looking up at Finn again, the shadows cast by the lamp shifting about his face so that his features seemed to be flickering, adrift. 'I've no idea what happened to that piece of shin. The bone and muscle and stuff – it just went. Fat. Ligaments. Tendons. Skin. It all just went. But the foot . . . OK, this is me, here, yeah?' he gestured at himself, then at some point across the carpet, 'and over there's my foot. Still in its boot.' He grinned at Finn. 'Eh?'

'Kurt –'

'I was undoing the laces when they found me.'

As he mimed the unlacing, Kurt became distracted by his hands. They were stained with newsprint. He stared at his palms in apparent fascination for a moment, then licked them – lapping at each in turn – and wiped them vigorously on the chair before inspecting them again. A bottle of pills on one of the arms fell to the floor.

Painkillers, Finn assumed. When he saw Kurt struggling for them, he went over and picked them up. Put them back. It was this that made him realise he'd been standing rigidly in the doorway the whole time. His joints – knuckles, elbows, knees – were stiff with tension. He noticed the crutches, then; modern ones, made of aluminium tubing, propped against the sideboard within Kurt's reach.

'RPG,' Kurt said.

'What?'

'Rocket-propelled grenade.'

'Oh, right.'

They should hug. But how do you hug someone who's sitting down? How do you hug Kurt at all, for that matter? He didn't recall him and his brother ever hugging one another. If it'd been him, sat there, Kurt would've ruffled his hair. But that was out of the question for Finn; too intimate. Just plain wrong. He considered giving his brother's shoulder a squeeze but, in thinking about it, the moment was gone.

Finn sat down on the sofa, at the end nearest Kurt. Kurt was in Dad's chair. The chair their dad had always sat in, when he'd still lived here.

Dad would've been in the kitchen at this time of the evening, listening to the radio. Finn could imagine its muted burble. Could picture him at the table, drinking piss-weak tea, studying the newspaper with the perspex magnifying sheet he used for reading. He didn't need glasses; it was the poxy papers, with their type size. The smell of scorched toast, melted cheese and steamed-up windows. And whisky. The whisky he dashed in his tea, like no one would know.

'Does Dad know?' he said.

Kurt's smile went. 'I told her not to tell him.'

'You can't not tell him.'

Kurt ignored this. He scratched at the side of the chair arm, then raised the middle finger. 'Dried snot,' he said, turning the finger this way and that so the light caught the fragment trapped in the nail. Yellowy white. Desiccated. 'Remember how he'd sit here, picking away and wiping it off on the chair?' Another grin. 'What is it? Ten years? Ten-year-old nose pickings. The fucking chair's covered with his DNA.'

Kurt sent the piece of encrustation spiralling on to the carpet. He looked at Finn, asked if he'd been drinking.

'Few cans, that's all,' Finn said.

'You look a right fucking state.'

Finn's hand went to his unshaven jaw. 'Yeah, well.'

He didn't want to tell him about being drafted just yet. They fell silent. Kurt seemed to withdraw into himself, staring into space. Fiddling with the newspaper on his lap, but not reading it.

He looked to be in discomfort. Finn found himself staring again at the fucked leg. He thought of the girl, the young mugger, and the policeman hacking away at her ankle; as the image recurred, he wondered, even as he dismissed the idea, if it'd been an omen for what had happened to his brother. No. You look for connections. When big stuff goes down, you try to make a pattern out of it; otherwise it's just random, meaningless. But it doesn't mean any more than the little stuff.

Mum came in with mugs of tea. Biscuits, cake. Her slippers were trodden down at the heels, making flapping sounds as she walked. Her finger joints looked swollen, veiny. No rings, but the mark where one had been was still discernible after all this time. She set the tray down on an occasional table between her two sons. A smile for each of them. *There.* As she straightened she hesitated, cast a glance at Kurt.

He nodded. You'd think he was about to cry.

'Come on,' she said, suddenly businesslike, sorting the crutches out for him. Helping him up. 'Let's get you upstairs.'

Finn didn't know what was going on. He shifted, uselessly, to the edge of his seat; Kurt was already up, supporting himself, poling himself across the room. Mum held the door open and followed him out, sending Finn a brief smile of reassurance. *Wait there*, her expression seemed to say. Later, in the bathroom, Finn would notice the incontinence pads. Somewhere between a sanitary towel and an oversized nappy. The shelf was stacked with them. But, just then, the only clue to what had happened came with the closure of the living-room door behind his mother and Kurt, its backdraught distributing a faint but unmistakable whiff of shit.

They'd hardly played war when they were growing up. Hardly played with toy guns or toy soldiers; hadn't been in street-gang battles. Though Finn did recall one time, in the scrap of back

47

garden, when they arranged plastic commandos in trenches they'd dug in the mud. And the birds – jackdaws, or crows – crawking, flapping about above the boys' heads, dive-bombing, pecking at the soldiers or trying to pick them up with their feet.

What they were into, him and Kurt, was adventure.

Sitting on the angled roof of Dad's shed, pretending it was a space rocket, a boat, a hot-air balloon; spinning stories between themselves about their voyage. Then, crashed or wrecked, leaping off into the garden – their moon, their jungle, their desert island – and more tales of hazard and hardship and heroic deeds. Sometimes they'd carry guns or knives, and there would be killing to be done for food or self-protection; but, mostly, the games – as Finn remembered them – were about endurance. Survival against the odds. A battered, weary, triumphant homecoming to the joyous tears and embraces of those who'd written them off for dead. Stuff like that.

Reflecting on it, now, Finn supposed they might've been acting out some kind of unconscious yearning for their father's return. Except that, no. No, of course not. Dad didn't leave till Finn was fourteen and Kurt nearly sixteen, and these would've been the make-believe dramas of boyhood, not adolescence. (So where did *that* idea spring from?) Maybe the games were to do with their own dreams of leaving. Finn didn't know. All he knew was that, once they'd grown up, neither brother made any voyage more adventurous than abandoning the family home – Mum's home, by then – for flats in other districts of the city they had always lived in. Until Kurt volunteered.

'D'you remember that time we tried to hitch-hike out of the city?' Finn said.

Kurt shook his head. They were at the kitchen table, eating egg and chips.

'You must do.'

'I don't remember fuck all.'

Since he'd returned downstairs from being cleaned up, Kurt's mood had deteriorated. No more grinning talkativeness; he was sullen, laconic. Irritable. Mum had knocked up some dinner for them. As he started eating, Finn realised how hungry he was. The pizza had never arrived. No explanation. Probably, it was the elevators. They were out of order when Finn, having slung on some clothes after Mum's phone call, hurried out of the apartment to catch the subway over here. It had taken him five minutes to descend thirteen flights of stairs, and it would've been longer coming up. No pizza boy would do that. Ate the pizza himself, most likely. Or binned it. Or been mugged for it. Finn shovelled in egg, chips, wedges of white sliced bread thick with marge. Gulped from a fresh mug of tea. Kurt fussed at his food, barely interested.

He looked at Kurt. Kurt remembered. You couldn't forget stuff like that.

They were about nine, ten; they'd studied the map, packed up some food, some cash they'd stolen from Mum's purse, then taken a bus out to the end of one of the routes, right in the suburbs. There, they'd walked to the start of the motorway and begun hitching. Got nicked, thumbing lifts on the hard shoulder. Had a ride home in a police car. But, in the hour at the roadside before the cops pitched up – breathing in exhaust fumes, feeling the kick of sidewind from vast artics. – Finn had fucking loved it. Hair all dishevelled. T-shirts pasted to them with sweat. The taut threads of muscle in Kurt's forearm as he thumbed the traffic, tracking each vehicle with a sweep of the arm like a matador drawing the bull safely past.

'We were heading for the coast,' Finn said.

Kurt shrugged.

'You said we'd build a beach hut. Get a boat, catch fish and that.'

Another shrug. 'Yeah, whatever.'

49

Finn let it go. Concentrated on eating. Their mother watched her sons, drawing occasionally on a cigarette. Her eyes never left them. It was like they were competing in an eating contest and she was one of the judges. As boys, they would sit like this, tucking into whatever she'd cooked for them while she sat silently across the table from them, smoking, no food in front of her. Listening to their talk without joining in. Studying them intently. You'd have thought she didn't trust them to eat at all if she wasn't there to invigilate; that was her duty, as a mother, to ensure her sons were fed. The instant they were finished, she would clear their plates away and, even as they got down from the table, she'd be making a start on the washing up. How many years was it since they'd sat like this, the three of them, in the kitchen's relentless, unforgiving wash of white from the neon strip?

'So, how's Lila?' Kurt said. Then, unsmiling: 'She dumped you yet?'

In the silence, the question was like a rupture.

'She's at a party. I left a message on her mobile.'

'I don't want her here.' Seeing him like this, Finn took Kurt to mean.

Finn reassured his brother. He'd just told her he'd gone over to his mum's for the night and for her to call him, soon as. Kurt had crashed with him and Lila in the weeks before he was assigned to a unit; he always asked after her in his letters home. A couple of months back, Finn wrote to him about how the relationship was on the slide, how he loved her and couldn't bear to lose her, but didn't know what to do to keep her. Kurt's reply was six pages instead of the usual six lines. All about Finn and Lila, but mostly about Finn and about love and the loss of it. Finn had read the letter so often he knew much of it by heart. Which was why he was still in shock from the pointed remark of a moment ago. 'She dumped you yet?'

'State of you,' Kurt said, 'no wonder she goes to parties by herself.'

Finn looked at him. 'Can we get off Lila's fucking case, d'you suppose?'

Kurt's fork was poised in front of his mouth as though he was puzzling over what Finn had just said. Then he gave a shrug, like it was no big deal. Kurt pulled the chip from the fork with his teeth and chewed thoughtfully before swallowing, Finn watching him the whole time. Waiting for him to say something conciliatory. But he didn't. He just ate another mouthful, then pushed the rest away. Lining up the cutlery just so among the leftovers in the centre of his plate. Intricately, painstakingly. He could've been a child attaching the final component of a kit airplane.

Their mother got up, her chair scraping the floor. She left the room.

Finn found her outside, where the kitchen window placed a rectangle of light on the weed-fractured cement she called a patio. She was staring into the darkness, her back to him, though she'd have heard the door. Finn drew up beside her. He bent to ignite his own cigarette from hers; her hand was cold in his, the skin shiny as an onion's. She smelled of cooking. They stood and smoked and didn't talk about Kurt.

Kurt was already in bed by the time Finn was done shaving and showering. Kurt had claimed his old bed, under the window, leaving Finn to his. Bunks, they'd been, until Dad dismantled them into twin singles. The curtains were closed. The lamp at Finn's bedside was on, Kurt's off. The mattress gave too easily as Finn sat down, roughing his hair with a towel. The wanks he'd had in this bed. He smiled.

'You asleep?' he asked.

'No.'

'This is so fucking weird.'

51

'I found my old cum hanky under the mattress,' Kurt said.

'Seriously?'

'What do you think?'

They laughed at the same time; great girlish snorts. This was good, laughing. All the affection he felt for Kurt surfaced in that moment, suppressing the sourness of their earlier exchange. Finn draped the towel over a radiator. Too warm in here. He got into bed and killed the lamp. On their backs in the blue-grey, they aimed hushed words at the ceiling, Kurt back in the zone again. They talked of how old their mum was looking; Kurt's story of how she'd been, when he got out the taxi. Like she was cross with him. Like he'd ruined a pair of shoes first time he'd worn them.

That was three days ago. Kurt hadn't wanted anyone to know he was home, till now. Not even his brother. Finn didn't make an issue of that. One minute you're fighting in a war, the next you're back at your mum's, minus the bottom of your leg; you'd want time. Finn would've been the same. He didn't know how he'd have been.

'What was it like out there?' he said, quietly.

'The war?'

'You never said. In your letters.'

'I tell you what it was. It was boring. Most of the time, you're just sitting around waiting for something to kick off. Or going out on patrols where fuck all happens.' He was silent a moment. 'There's a lot of fuck all.'

'You get to kill anyone?'

'What are you, twelve all of a sudden?'

'I'm just asking.'

Kurt exhaled. 'I never even loosed off a single round.'

The hush settled on them again. Finn wanted more. He wanted to know what to expect. He wanted to *know*. At last, he said: 'You see it on the TV –'

'Stuff goes overhead. You hear it hit somewhere.'

'What about when . . . you know, when it happened.'

Kurt didn't answer for a while. Then, matter-of-factly, he said: 'Someone shouted: "Incoming!" Then it came in. Quick as that. Didn't see anything, didn't feel anything – I'm just up, then I'm down, and it's like a thirty-second chunk of your life never happened.' After a pause, he added: 'Two guys died. I didn't see it. I got told.'

Finn didn't ask any more questions. He heard Kurt drink, then settle himself again. Finn's own bed felt too small, too narrow, too short. It was so stuffy in here.

Kurt was talking again. They were making him a new foot. A *prosthetic*. 'I'll get some compo as well. A few thou. So I'm set up, basically.'

Finn doubted that; everyone knew you got fuck all, or you'd spend years in the courts fighting for a pittance. Kurt would know it too. He wanted to ask about the incontinence – was it physical or mental, or both? Was it permanent? He saw how that could be as tough on Kurt as losing the foot. Finn kept the thoughts to himself, in case his brother flipped again. The way he was tonight, his moods were contained in a set of boxes and you had to take care which ones you opened. So, mostly, Finn listened. It was OK, talking in the gloom like this. If he thought of them growing up together, the associations were as much aural as visual. Disembodied voices in a dark room. A sniff. A scratch. A fart. The click of a bed frame, the shush of cotton. Like this, he could imagine telling Kurt his own news. A secret to share with big bruv. But Kurt was the one with secrets right now. Tonight belonged to him, and Finn decided not to say anything about being called up. He'd tell him in the morning.

'What I want to know is how they make sure it's the right length?' Kurt said.

'I don't know.' Finn was wondering how it felt, with a duvet

53

weighing down on your legs when you've only the one foot there. He shifted his own feet. 'They must work it out. The . . . you know, the difference.'

'Maybe you have to make do. You're gonna limp anyway, so what's half a centimetre? I don't suppose anyone gives a toss.' Neither of them spoke for a while. Then, Kurt said: 'You got anything?'

Drugs, he meant. 'No,' Finn said. 'Not on me.'

'These things they gave me are fucking useless.'

'I can sort you something tomorrow.'

There was the rattle of a pill bottle, of Kurt swallowing once, then again. The sound of a glass being replaced on a bedside table.

'D'you know what it is?' Kurt said.

'What what is?'

'The *difference*. The fucking difference.' He answered the question himself. 'Thirty-one centimetres. Give or take. Cos there's the bandages and that. But thirty-one centimetres, stump-to-ground. I measured it.'

Finn didn't have anything to say to that. He wanted a smoke, but his cigarettes were downstairs. He could hear their mother using the bathroom, then the crick-crick of floorboards on the landing. There was a pause – he imagined her, listening at their door – before the sound of her shutting herself into her bedroom. It occurred to him that if Kurt crapped himself during the night, he'd have to help him clean up. Change him. Change his twenty-five going on twenty-six-year-old brother's fucking nappy. Finn shut his mouth, pinched his nostrils tight, so Kurt wouldn't hear him crying.

'You know you're supposed to be able to feel it?' Kurt said. 'Like a phantom foot. Leg, whatever.' Finn composed himself. Said, yeah, he'd heard that. 'Well, I can't,' Kurt said. 'I can't feel fuck all. I can't even feel the foot I've still got. It's like this one's died with the other one. Just given up and died.'

This time they were quiet for so long Finn thought Kurt must've fallen asleep. He was drifting himself, embryonic dreams forming and dissipating – incoherent and disorientating – so that it startled him when Kurt broke the silence.

'Did it freak you?' His brother's tone was calmer now; less agitated.

'What?' Finn knew what.

'Seeing me like this.'

'No.'

'Yeah, right. Should've seen yourself, stood in that doorway like a dummy.'

'So I'm just going to breeze in? "Hey bro, how's it going?" '

'Eh?' A smile in Kurt's voice. 'I thought you were gonna throw up.'

'Yeah, well, it's easy for you,' Finn said.

'How d'you work that out?'

'You're not the one with a brother who's lost a foot.'

They laughed again, like before. Only, this time, the laughter went on longer, clutching at them in spasms each time they thought they were through with it.

Finn believed he was in his bed at the flat. But the door wasn't where it should have been. Someone had moved his bedroom door for fuck sake. There it was. And as he stepped out on to a landing that wasn't his, and found a light switch that wasn't in the right place, he remembered where he was. He went to the bathroom and pissed. Two forty-five, according to the clock in there. Finn yawned; a real jaw-cracker, Jesus. The house was dead quiet. His mouth tasted of egg and stale beer and stale tobacco.

Back in the bedroom doorway, with the light from the landing making a bright gash across Kurt's bed, Finn saw that his brother was gone.

Mum had warned him about this: Kurt's habit, since he'd returned home, of waking in the night and hobbling downstairs to sit in front of the TV. The first night, roused from sleep herself by the sound of him moving about, she'd gone down to see if he was OK. But he'd sent her away, irritated with her, wanting to be left alone.

Finn went to the top of the stairs. No TV noise. No glimmer of light.

He descended. All was silent and dark down there. Kurt wasn't in the living room, or the kitchen. The front door was chained, bolted, deadlocked. Finn went through to the kitchen again and tried the patio door. It opened. Finn retrieved his coat from the banister post and – barefoot, bare-legged – let himself into the back garden. Cold, wet cement gritty beneath his soles; drizzle, like flecks of spit on his face. His skin was goosebumped. Had an urge to piss again, even though he'd just been. The dark wasn't total, what with the background patina of sodium yellow from unseen street lights, but it was dark enough. As his eyes adapted he moved tentatively on to the spongy oblong of lawn. Shapes started to form: a tree, shrubs, a clothes-line pole, a fence, the blocky mass of the shed with its window so black it might have been a sheet of solidified ink. Finn saw the shed in the moment before he registered the noise that came – that could only be coming – from inside it. The sort of noise that made you think of rats. There was nothing to be afraid of. It was just a dark garden in the middle of the night, and his brother was scrabbling about in Dad's old shed.

Hesitating at the door, Finn detected an alteration in the quality of the noise. A slowing down, a cessation. Kurt might've heard something and stopped to listen. But Finn didn't think so. It was the sound of activity coming to a natural conclusion; as if Kurt was oblivious to Finn's approach and had stopped what he was doing because he was finished. There was a grunt. Animal-like. Almost of satisfaction. Finn considered knocking, then how ridiculous that would be.

He tugged open the door.

'Kurt?' No response. Not even the sudden shuffle of someone surprised by an intruder. Finn felt for the light switch, unsure if it still worked. 'You in here, Kurt?'

The light snapped on. A bare bulb suspended from the main roof beam. There was a stink of burned dust. Finn was dazzled. When he was able to look around, he saw his brother sitting on a stack of beer crates against the farthest wall. A spaced, druggy look in his eyes. Looking at nothing. His head lolled like it was too heavy for his neck muscles; like it would pitch him forward face-first on to the floor at any moment. In Kurt's right hand was a hacksaw. There was blood on his knuckles and in the dense wrist hairs, and Finn's first thought was that he'd cut his hand somehow. He tried to make sense of how Kurt could have done that. Of how he could've cut the hand that held the hacksaw by its looped-steel handle.

'Kurt.'

Kurt wasn't for talking. Finn took a step closer. There was more blood. On the floor. Puddled, pooling on the rough boards like someone had tipped up a whole can of crimson paint. The metallic smell was nauseating. Finn wanted to shake Kurt, jolt him awake, sitting there like a fucking drongo. He couldn't have taken anything. He didn't have anything. He'd asked for gear, so how could he have got himself into this state? The painkillers. Jesus, he must've taken all the painkillers. Finn hurried now, moving in on his brother, taking care where he trod – thinking about the phone call he'd have to make. What to do before that. Thinking about all this fucking blood and where it was coming from and what it had to do with anything. About making Kurt puke the pills up, and not sure if you were meant to do that. But you had to find the empty bottle, because they'd need to know exactly what . . .

57

He saw the foot.

The foot, the ankle, some shin. Like a joint of pork on the potting table beside Kurt. The jagged stick of bone in the middle. The yellowy-white toenails. He looked at his brother's legs. His hairy legs. One bandaged, the other not. One dripping, the other not. They dangled in front of him like the legs of a child, both of them too short to reach the floor – both the same length, now.

The Bench She Made

Bryher sat on the bench in the garden while, inside, the Incomer slept. The front of the cottage was a suntrap at this hour and she could easily have drifted off herself. Eyes closed, she tilted her face towards the warmth, listening to the gulls and filling her lungs with salty air. It was good to be free of him for a while and from the odour of sickness. She had built the bench herself. An asymmetrical, uncomfortable thing; it wasn't a good bench, but it was hers and she liked to sit there whenever she could. Building it, she had learned the names and functions of the tools she'd seen Roop use so often. It was Roop's ability to make things that led her to make something herself. Never having made anything, she wanted to know how it felt. How Roop felt when he did that. Creating something, looking at it once it was finished and thinking: *I did that . . . without me that wouldn't exist.*

When the bench was finished, and Roop had helped her haul it into place, he'd said: 'You're a carpenter now, Bry.'

'Even though I don't swear while I'm doing it?'

'That'll come,' Roop had said, laughing. 'You have to give yourself time.'

Bryher told him she'd loved the complexity of the wood in her hands and the peppery, wood-dust smell and, best of all, the minuscule sounds of a screw being sunk flush and tight into soft pine. Was that how it was, for him? He'd smiled and said he imagined it was never the same for any two people. She'd liked that answer. With the curls of swarf from the planing of the slats, she'd fashioned a brightly painted mobile that dangled lopsidedly in the kitchen. 'Swarf' was Bryher's favourite word now. Roop wondered if she would make other things, now she had the taste; she'd told him no. The bench was enough.

Roop.

It was odd that this bench, which she had made, reminded her of him more than the many things Roop himself had made, and with which she was surrounded.

If they hadn't come to the island he would still be alive. But, then, if it wasn't for *her* he would still be alive — because although the idea of living here had been his, the decision had been a joint one. Roop would not have come here without her, she knew. There was no end to ifs where untimely death was concerned; from the small, specific ifs of the coincident time, place and chance of the moment itself, to the larger ifs of life's patterns that brought someone into alignment with their death in the first place. The ways in which a person might not have died at that instant, in that location, in that manner were incalculable. To think about it was torment. Yet the notion of death — of accidental death, of any death — being 'untimely' troubled her; people died when they died, that was all. Bryher had always believed this before, when she'd worked as a nurse. Now, she was less certain. Less prone to cold logic.

When she pictured Roop, most often she saw him on the boat that had carried them from the mainland. Perhaps if he had been recovered she would've pictured that version of him: his inert body, his lifeless face. As it was, the image she seemed to fix on was of him at the prow of the small fishing smack, watching for the island to pull into view. The dishevelled hair, the buffeting of his jacket. He'd beckoned to her to join him there, clamouring at the first sight of land. As she left the shelter of the cabin, the wind sucked her breath away; took his words away too, so that she saw his mouth open and close but caught just a fragment of disconnected sound that seemed to issue from the wind itself. He'd hugged her to him, their faces turned into the spray.

'This is it,' Roop said, yelling into her ear. 'This is fucking it.'

She recalled laughing, kissing him, saying: 'No going back now.'

It struck her as an odd remark at the time and, even now, she didn't know why – of all the things she could have said – she'd said that. Bryher hadn't hesitated about the move, other than to consider the practicalities, the logistics, of them quitting their jobs, their homes, their loved ones, to start anew in a place they had never seen and where they would know no one. From the moment they'd decided, she'd only looked forwards. Leaving the mainland was such a perfect idea she wondered why they hadn't thought of it before. And there they were, seeing these shores materialise across the chop of the strait dividing the island from Mr Skins' place.

They'd brought no camera with them, so they took no photographs during the crossing, or of their disembarkation, or of their new home as they stood outside for the first time – its garden overgrown, its stone walls unwhitewashed, back then, and its roof in urgent need of repair. Until now, Bryher had never felt the lack of pictures to record their transition from one life to another. And, even though the image of a windswept, boyishly excited Roop at the prow of that boat was blazed on her memory clearer than any photographic print, she'd have liked to have something tangible of him – captured in that moment – to hold and to take out and look at from time to time.

Footsteps approached along the path that led down to the cove. Two men, talking.

Bryher hurriedly dried her tears. She identified the visitors by their voices before she saw them. Nudge and Zess. As they came into view she noticed that Orr was following them – scuttling along like a puppy, though he was seventy-five and looked a hundred. Even in this weather he wore the coarse, flappy hat he had made from sackcloth, fastened beneath the chin with twine. She smiled at them. Her smiles felt fake these days, even if – as now – they were meant. But she made a glad-to-see-you face, and the men returned the greeting; in Orr's case, with an extravagant wave, as if signalling from a distant hilltop. Nudge managed only a nod. From the clothes they wore and the things they carried, she realised they hadn't come to visit her, as she'd thought, but were on their way to where the boat was moored.

Zess was first to speak. 'Fishing,' he said, unnecessarily, gesturing at their kit and nodding in the direction they were headed.

Bryher indicated the bench. 'Sitting.'

Zess laughed when he saw she'd intended him to; even Nudge lifted his head, then lowered it. Zess adjusted the haversack looped by one strap over his shoulder, seemingly at a loss for what to say next. She imagined him rummaging in the pack for a handful of words stored there for just such an emergency. The three men had drawn to a halt; with the sun behind them, it was hard to make out their features. Bryher had to squint. She hoped Nudge would say something, but he simply stared silently at the ground. Orr was gazing off in all directions, mumbling to himself. He might begin shouting at any moment, and Bryher was anxious to let her patient rest.

'How is our friend?' Zess said, serious again, glancing towards

62

the cottage. At the Gathering, Zess had been among those needing to be convinced. So Bryher was heartened to hear him inquire after the Incomer's health, and to call him 'friend'.

'It's disgusting,' she said, 'the state they let him get into.'

Zess nodded but made no comment.

'He could've died. Still could.'

'There'll be something in it for Skins,' Zess said. 'There always is.'

Bryher exhaled. Implicitly or explicitly, the taint of the mainland, she knew, would inform everything that was said about the Incomer; whatever the degrees of sympathy towards him, he would have to remain on the island a long time before this connection was broken, if it ever was, in the minds of the people here. He lay upstairs, wounded, but – to some of them – he might as easily have been festering with plague.

She let Zess's remark go.

A wasp, attracted by her honey-sticky fingers, made abstract patterns in front of her face; Bryher brushed it away. She looked at Nudge, motionless, expressionless beside Zess; a tethered beast waiting patiently for the herdsman to unhitch him and lead him away. Before, if she'd encountered Nudge and Zess like this, Nudge would have done the talking. But he had exchanged no more than a handful of words with her since the accident; or, at least, since the retelling of the accident in the days that followed. The story of what happened, the answers to her persistent questions about how Roop died, and how Nudge had been unable to save him, the description of every last detail. His version was hers now. It was all she had of Roop's last moments, even though she tortured herself nightly, daily, hourly, with the images Nudge had painted in her head at her insistence.

The cost, to Nudge, hadn't concerned her at the time.

And if the intimacy of these outpourings might have been expected to draw them closer together – to unite them in grief – well, it hadn't happened.

63

As she watched him – willing him to speak, but unsure what to say herself – she remembered that this trip would be his first on the boat since that day, and how tough that would be for him. And it struck her that, for the first time in weeks, she'd thought of the boat in relation to someone other than Roop or herself.

On impulse, she raised herself and went to where the men stood. She offered her hands to Nudge. They might have been bloody stumps, the way he looked at them. But, at last, he reached out and held them in his, her own small hands fragile in his meaty fists. Bryher drew him closer and they hugged clumsily across the low wall. He had been the first to support her, when she asked for the Incomer to be admitted. She hadn't spoken to him about this. The embrace could have been construed as a belated thank you, but she knew – and suspected Nudge did, too – that it was more than that. When he was done with being held, he released himself. The gesture was complete. A small gesture, for now, and by no means a definitive one; but the simple act of contact signified a *rapprochement* between them that, with no need for words, was mutually understood. That was how it felt, to Bryher. Later, it would occur to her that by using this route to the mooring, when there were others, Nudge had made a gesture of his own. Or, at any rate, created the possibility for hers. It was chance, of course, that she'd been outside on the bench when they passed. But, then, it had been chance that Roop was the one to drown, not Nudge.

The Birdmen

What was he doing there, in the café?

What he was doing, was waiting for Mr Findlay – whoever Mr Findlay was – to make himself known. What he was doing was sipping now and then at a tall iced coffee, nibbling now and then at the (stale) complimentary wafer. What he was doing was trying not to look like he was searching every face for one that might belong to this Mr Findlay; or like he was cacking himself in case 'Mr Findlay' turned out to be a couple of plain-clothes IS men. Findlay? No, he didn't know anyone by that name. Or Leander, for that matter. Phone call? What phone call? He hadn't called anyone about anything. Yeah, it would be cool. There was no way they could have traced the call to him. So, cool. Everything was cool. Finn was just a guy on his own in a café, a draftee chilling out in the final days before joining his unit.

But what in the name of fuck was he *doing*?

Less than four hours ago he'd been at the hospital. At the bedside, holding his brother's hand; their mum holding the other. Looking at Kurt's face, his eyelids. That jaw. All those machines; like something off the TV, only silent.

Now he was in the café, trying to erase pictures of Kurt from his head.

Finn sat at a window table, as 'Leander' had instructed. Angled into a corner so he could keep an eye on the street and the interior. It wasn't noon yet, so the place should've been quiet, doldrummed between the breakfast crowd and the lunchtime crush. But it was filling up. Busy enough for Finn to be inconspicuous. He'd asked the waitress how come and she'd said everyone was waiting for the birdmen, like she expected him to go: *Oh, right, yeah.* But he had no idea what she was talking about. It could've been another cryptic message for all he knew. He didn't ask who they were, the birdmen; thinking about it, he shouldn't have spoken to her at all. He should have played Joe Ordinary. Joe Ordinary with a backpack stashed under the table; if this was a set-up, he'd have trouble explaining that away. Off visiting family. Friends. Say his goodbyes, and that. He made sure not to look at the waitress again. Another sip. Iced coffee disgusted him. But they'd told him to order a tall iced coffee.

He should be with his mum, now; helping sort things.

He should've heard Kurt get up during the night. Gone to him sooner. How could you let yourself sleep so deeply you didn't get woken by a guy with one foot – not a guy, your brother, your so-sick-he-shat-himself *fucking brother* – stumbling about your bedroom, the landing, the stairs?

Finn hadn't been to this place before, or to this district. A dumpy area – all graffiti, blocked drains, chipboard shopfronts; there'd been a spate of piss-bombings round here; he'd read about them. Kids zooming by on electric mopeds, pelting pedestrians with polythene bags of urine. The café itself was the colour of piss. Done out in easy-wipe surfaces – formica counter, glass and chrome display case, tile-effect lino, pine-effect laminate on the walls, waxy tablecloths, plastic seats. Even the drapes looked like they were made from the same material as shower curtains. Once all the punters left you could just hose the whole place down. Maybe they did. Outside, there were more tables – all empty, tagged with 'reserved' signs – arranged under a canvas canopy. For the birdmen, he guessed. He pictured them, costumed in feathers. Rain drained unevenly from the perimeter of the canopy, but underneath it was dry. Finn watched the water splash on the paving flags. He was staring out the window because he'd scoped everyone inside the café at least three times, seeking Mr Findlay, and had to stop himself doing that. A cigarette would've been good, but there was no smoking. He'd already been told to put one out. What he should do was think up more ways of drawing attention to himself.

He thought about trying Lila, but if they trawled his mobile records they might be able to locate the call and pick up his trail from there; make a connection.

They had spoken earlier, when he called her from a payphone at the hospital; it was breakfast time, she was at the apartment getting ready for work. At the sound of his voice she'd started to ask how come he'd gone over to his mum's, but he cut in. Told her what had happened. She cried. He couldn't hear her, but he knew.

'Jesus, Finn.'

'I'm going back with Mum.'

'D'you want me to come round?'

'No, it's OK.'

'I can phone in sick.'

'It's all right, Li. It's best, just me and Mum.'

'OK.' Silence. She was crying again.

They said their goodbyes and Finn hung up. If she had offered, once more, to come over – if she'd insisted – he would've said yes. *Please, Li, come.* He needed her. Needed to be comforted, not doing the comforting. But Lila didn't insist, and he knew that there'd been a time when she'd have come over as a matter of course.

He was so fucking *tired*; a couple of hours' sleep he'd had last night, that was all – then Kurt, and everything that followed from that. Kurt was unconscious before the ambulance arrived. They were worried about his blood pressure even as they readied him for the gurney. They didn't want to know too much about the pills just then; it was the state of his leg, the BP. The BP scared them. You could see it. You could hear it. They tucked it away behind unafraid faces and unafraid voices, but it was there. The BP was 'through the floor', one of them told the other; it made Finn think of Kurt's actual blood, soaking through the floor of the shed. They loaded him into the ambulance, and Finn and Mum climbed aboard as well, and they were nee-nawing along the road that would take them to A & E and the guy in the back was doing whatever needed to be done to Kurt and the driver was radio-ing ahead . . . when Kurt's heart stopped. VF, the paramedic called it. 'Cal, he's gone into VF.' By the time he was being trolleyed through plastic flap doors and along a corridor, they were on their second go with the shock paddles. After the third, they gave it up.

It was Finn's first dead body. First real one.

The jaw was the thing. Slack. Sunken. Lips sucked apart to make him buck-toothed. On TV, dead faces were either mangled, or sleep-like. Actors holding their breath. The whole time at his brother's bedside, Finn's gaze fixated on that jaw.

They'd gone home, eventually. Dawn broke while they were in with Kurt and they came out to find the sky had shifted from yellowy city-black to shades of chalk dust and smoke. What Lila called a 'ghost sky'. Mum was telling the auto-rickshaw driver how her son was a war hero, how he'd lost a foot fighting for his country and that was why they'd been at the hospital – babbling away; Finn couldn't bear to listen. He caught the driver sussing him in the mirror, like he'd assumed Finn was the son and wondered where his stick, his crutches, were; like he wanted to turn round and check his feet out. All the way home, Mum kept up her monologue; once they were indoors, and it was just the two of them, she quietened down.

Finn made tea in mugs. They sat in the kitchen and smoked.

It had been like this between them for as long as he could remember. They'd never had much to say to one another; or maybe they had, but the search for a route out of the silence was just too much effort. It'd been the same with Dad. And it wasn't like they'd been any more communicative with Kurt; there was no favoured-son thing going on here. Theirs had always been a house of the unsaid.

Mum went to speak, then had to start again. 'The shed needs seeing to.'

'I'll burn it down,' Finn said. He was the last man, now. 'You don't use it.'

After a long pause, she said: 'Did they take it away?'

She meant the foot. He couldn't recall the ambulance crew doing anything about that; they were way too preoccupied. Jesus it must still be out there, on the potting table. He couldn't tell her that. Not with how she'd been: pestering them to switch on the life-support for her dead son, then banging on like that in the taxi.

'Yeah, they took it.' He gave her a nod. 'I saw them. It's gone.'

Finn didn't want her getting ideas about the foot. Bringing it into the house; some kind of cherished memento. He'd have to see to it.

She looked at him. 'Why did they take so long?'

'I don't know.'

'That can't be right, can it?'

An hour, nearly. Fifty-five minutes for the paramedics to get there. Maybe they should immerse themselves in complaining about that, suing the shit out of the ambulance company, like that was the real issue, the thing they needed to think about instead of thinking about Kurt or why he'd done that to himself in the first place. But Mum was already moving on, picking over another

69

part of the rubble of unanswered questions that death piles up all about you.

'I didn't hear him,' she said.

'Me neither.'

'The previous couple of nights, I heard him go down.'

'I know, Mum.'

She was sobbing now. Sitting at the kitchen table, still in her coat, sobbing. One hand cupped at her mouth. Finn hesitated, then reached for her other hand across the table and gripped it, as he'd gripped Kurt's. She didn't return the pressure; just sat with her arm outstretched, her fingers misshapen by his. By the time she was through, her face was flushed and puffy and her eyes seemed the wrong size for their sockets, as if she'd had reconstructive surgery after an accident.

It was raining. The shed was damp inside and out and there was no paraffin or petrol to be had. The shed wouldn't burn. So he broke it apart with the tools he found in there and reduced it to planks and junk and broken glass and roofing felt.

The foot, he buried in the border like a dead pet.

When he went back inside, drenched and dirt-smeared and tingling from the exertion, he found his mum in the hall. She'd evidently been out while he was seeing to the shed and bought a flower holder; she was fixing it to the front door, showing no sign of registering him as he stood watching her. There was a bunch of red carnations, trimmed and ready to be slotted into the scroll-work ring. A house in mourning for its war dead. When the neighbours got to hear how Kurt died, Finn wondered if they'd place their own flowers outside or whether Mum's would be left to rot by themselves.

'I can't handle this,' he said.

She looked at him, now. 'Handle what?'

'Any of it.'

★   ★   ★

70

In the café, Finn shut his eyes.

He wished that when he reopened them it would be six months, a year, five years from now, and he wouldn't know precisely how many hours ago his brother had died. And every other thought in his head wouldn't be about Kurt, Kurt's jaw, Kurt's foot. Or that, opening them again, he would see Mr Findlay standing there beside the table, smiling, ready to put an arm round him and usher him away from all this; take him somewhere safe and kind and deathless.

What Finn saw, though, when he opened his eyes, was the first of the birdmen.

An old boy with scabs on his bald scalp and a too-big quilted coat, so that only his fingers showed beyond the cuffs. The coat was cerise, rain spotted. In one hand he held a brass cage in the shape of a bell jar, the ring at its apex looped over the crook of his middle finger. Inside was a speckled bird Finn couldn't name. Thumb sized. It sat right at one end of its perch, head cocked – leaning a little – as if compensating for the tilt of the cage. The man nabbed a chair from one of the outside tables and stepped on to it with care, then straightened, raising the cage above his head and securing it on a hook set into the canopy framework. Finn hadn't noticed these hooks, but saw now that there were several along each joist. The man got down, wiped the chair with his cuff and sat on it. A waitress appeared at his side. By the time she returned with his order – coffee, and an aperitif of some kind – two more birdmen had arrived. Each hooked their cages above the same table and joined the first man; others came – all men, all old, some doing a shuffle-walk – and, before long, the outside tables were full. Twenty or so birds were arranged over the men's heads, by now, one or two of the cages swaying slightly where they had yet to settle. Like lanterns, Finn thought. When the last of them was up and their owners all had drinks in front of them, the punters who'd been inside the café began to file out – taking their cups and glasses with them – to stand wherever there was room beneath the canopy. Finn joined them, mesmerised by the spectacle, the ritual of it all. The air reverent as the murmurs of conversation ebbed away to the sort of hush that heralds a sacred ceremony.

'What birds are these?' he whispered to a woman as they went out.

'Songbirds,' the woman said, and that was all.

Outside in the fresh, damp air, he huddled in among the others. Nobody spoke, everyone stood as still as they could, so as not to jostle the birdmen at their tables amid the throng – sipping their drinks, smiling fondly at one another, at faces in the crowd and, most of all, at their birds in the cages above their heads. The birds sang. An ululating chorus of trills, chirrups and warbles, each one so idiosyncratic, so dissociated from the rest, that the result should've been discordant but was, instead, sweetly melodic. Harmonious as any concert orchestra. As the comparison struck him, Finn saw one birdman patterning the air with a spoon as though conducting. Scattered spores of bird-song permeated the space beneath the canopy – surround-sound, each cage a speaker issuing its own notes into the mix; blocking out interference. Filling your ears, your head. You heard nothing but the music, yet you strained for every nuance, as if the melody might be drowned out at any moment and lost for ever. The café, though, sat in a little-used street, so there was no traffic noise for the birds to compete against; even the spatter of rain-water and an occasional chink of cup against saucer acted as a percussive accompaniment. Finn had never heard anything like it.

The concert – for that's what it was, he decided – lasted until the birdmen had finished their drinks. To Finn it seemed a long time, but also too short. Too abruptly ended. Singly, or in pairs, as they drained their coffees and their aperitifs, the old men stood on their chairs to retrieve the cages and – after a few handshakes here and there – they dispersed. No bills for them to settle, Finn noticed. The waitresses simply stood smiling at the café doors and watched them leave. Even before the last of the men had departed, their audience began to go their separate ways along the rainswept street. A sense of strangers sharing in something magical had developed while the birds sang; now it was over, the drawing together quickly became a drifting apart. But Finn felt sure that each of them took a fragment of the togetherness with them; he saw it in their faces. This, now he thought about it, was almost as magical as what they'd just witnessed. It was cold again with the thinning of the crowd. He realised that he hadn't moved from the spot where he'd stood during the bird-song. Beyond the café's glass frontage he registered his pack, still stashed under the table. The unfinished iced coffee. Finn was making his way back there when the last of the birdmen put a hand on his shoulder to steady himself as he lowered his cage from its hook.

'Thank you,' the man said, stepping down from the chair. Smiling, he added: 'Did you enjoy the birds?'

'Yes.'

'Good. Good.'

Finn wanted to say something about the music and how it had affected him, but all he managed was to ask how often the concerts took place.

'Concerts?' The birdman smiled again. 'Is that what this was?'

'Seemed like one to me,' Finn said.

'Bird concerts. I like that idea.'

He could've been any age between seventy and ninety. A threadbare head, and jowly sagging skin mapped with liver spots and capillary deltas and odd tufts of silver stubble. His nose, broken at some point, kinked to the right. But the eyes, for all that the whites were clotted with yellowish jelly, seemed lively, interested. Taking note of Finn, absorbing detail, so that Finn had the impression of standing where the old boy stood, scrutinising himself. Finding himself wanting in some way, though he couldn't suss where that came from because the other man's gaze was anything but harsh. The birdman appeared tired, suddenly. Weary. He transferred the cage from one hand to the other, his fingers so disfigured by arthritis they looked as if they'd been removed, disassembled bone by bone, knuckle by knuckle, and put back together any old how. The cage appeared heavy, too cumbersome for him to manoeuvre through the clutter of tables, chairs and the few stragglers who had lingered under the canopy to talk, or to order more drinks, or to shelter a moment longer before heading off.

'I don't suppose you could help me with this, could you?' the birdman said. 'I only live just round the corner.'

Finn looked at the cage. 'I . . . sorry, I'm waiting . . . I'm meeting someone.'

'It really is only a short distance. Five minutes, there and back.'

'Sorry, I can't.'

'Looks like it's just you and me, then,' the old man said, raising the cage to eye level. The bird skittered from side to side along the perch. Deep chocolate brown, almost black, with a dull yellow beak; the feathers, where they caught the light, had a bronze, oily sheen. A blackbird. Finn knew that much at least. Addressing Finn again, the birdman said: 'I'm glad you appreciated the, um, *concert.*'

Finn noticed something about the bird. 'Is it injured?'

'Broken wing. Unfortunately the little chap met my cat a moment or so before he met me.' Then, to the bird. 'You don't like living in there very much, do you? But believe me you'd like it a lot less on the outside.'

The blackbird whistled, as if by way of reply.

The old man smiled at Finn. Two of his front bottom teeth were gone. 'He's a he, by the way, not an it.'

'Right.'

'Very spoilt, I'm afraid. Aren't you? Yes, you *are.*'

'What's his name?' Finn said.

The birdman paused to survey those few customers still loitering beneath the canopy. Then, leaning closer to Finn, he lowered his voice. 'I call him Mr Findlay.'

Going into Hiding

'Leander' was waiting for them at the birdman's flat. Finn recognised him right off as the guy who'd blagged a light at the club on Draft Nite; the guy who slipped a yellow calling card into his wallet and which he never got round to binning. He seemed more relaxed this time; this time, Finn was the one on edge. They shook hands.

'Good to see you again, Finn.' He pointed at the sofa. 'Sit down.'

Brisk, businesslike. With his leather attaché case, sharp suit and tie and shiny shoes, you'd have thought they were there to discuss personal finance or double glazing. Unmistakably the same guy – same droopy eyelids and pale, parchment skin, same tapering fingers and bitten nails – but, since their first encounter, he might've had an attitude makeover. Finn was reassured. He wanted the confident, the impersonal, the efficient; what he did not want was some nervy, geeky amateur or, worse, a mad-eyed revolutionary hugging him like they were comrades. It was as if Finn making contact had snapped him into action. Every word, gesture and expression seemed to say: *OK, let's get on with it.* Finn dumped his backpack and sat on the sofa. Leander lowered himself into one of the armchairs.

'When's your call-up?' he said.

'Four days.'

Leander made a kissing sound, tongue against teeth. 'Got your ID with you?'

Finn patted his jacket. 'Yeah.'

'Anyone likely to suspect you're doing this?'

He hesitated, thinking of Lila. 'No. I didn't know I was doing it myself until this morning.'

The guy looked to be giving that plenty of consideration. Then: 'You quit your job already, didn't you?'

'Uh-huh.'

'What about your girlfriend? The one at the club. She know anything about this?'

'She knows about the calling card.'

'That's all?'

'Yeah, that's all.' It was true, it was all Lila knew. She had no idea where he was or what he was doing, or that she would come home to an abandoned apartment.

Finn zoned out for a moment, distracted by the birdman setting Mr Findlay's cage on a stand by the window, murmuring to the bird the whole time. The old boy joined them on the battered suite, its chairs and sofa set so close together the men's knees almost touched. The light in the room was the colour of cider, as if the sepia décor had leached into the air. Cold enough to see your breath.

Lila. What would she make of him, now?

She opposed the war, and the draft . . . but, the way she saw it, they were facts. The war was a fact. The draft was a fact. *Finn's call-up* was a fact. From the day that 18–25 conscription was announced, Lila's take on the draft had been caught between antipathy and resignation. You hated it, you protested it, but what could you do about it? 'When your turn comes' hadn't been a proper topic of discussion because, for want of a viable alternative, they both knew too well what would happen when his turn came. All the same, it had hung over them these past months. And, though they agreed about the politics, there was a tension between them in relation to the war. It was rooted, back before the draft was introduced, in something that happened – or seemed to happen – when Kurt stayed with them that time, waiting to join his unit. Lila had asked Finn if he would ever volunteer, even though she must've expected, and *wanted*, him to say no. Yet, despite her own anti-war views – and the fact that Kurt was going off to fight, by choice, and Finn wasn't – Lila's treatment of the two brothers altered in those few days. As though her respect for Kurt, to whom she'd never shown much fondness, had shifted up a notch, while her respect for Finn had shifted down. It was so subtle a shift you'd hardly have noticed it. And you certainly couldn't have mentioned it to her without appearing paranoid. But it was there.

Leander was talking again, asking if his girlfriend was *secure*. 'Once she realises what you've done, will she . . . compromise you?'

Finn shook his head. Whatever uncertainties he had about Lila, he was sure she would never do that.

'And your mates?'

'No.' *What mates?* he should've said. Finn spent most of his life not fitting in with how other people thought he should be as a colleague, a mate, a boyfriend, a son, a brother. 'There's a couple of lads I see for a beer now and then . . . I haven't spoken to them since that night.' He tapped the side of his head. 'I've been all over the place.'

'Sure,' Leander said. Like he understood. Like he'd been there himself. But he looked too old to have been drafted; maybe thirty, thirty-one. Older than twenty-five, anyway. 'How about your folks? You spoken to them?'

78

'Dad's out the picture. Mum's . . . she doesn't even know I've been drafted.'

Leander nodded. 'So, inadvertently or otherwise, no one's going to fuck you over. I'm talking about between now and your report-for-duty date.'

'No,' Finn said. 'No one's going to fuck me over.'

Finn was thinking of the people he'd fucked over. Mum's face, as he'd walked out. Leaving her, fixing flowers to the door. He'd told her he couldn't handle it, then left – just like that, without another word. For all she knew, he'd gone off on one – dipped out of dealing with what Kurt had done to himself and slunk away to be on his own for a bit. She'd be thinking: *He'll show up when he's ready; he'll show up for his brother's funeral.* Whatever, she could have no idea about any of this. No idea that, from her place, he'd gone straight to a payphone a few streets away to dial the number on the card. Then he'd hit the cashpoint, headed home to pack, and set off for the bird café. It'd had to be this abrupt, this decisive, or he might not have seen it through.

There had been just the one detour: he'd gone to the book store, to wait in a doorway just along the road from the staff entrance. Squatting there in the shadows with his backpack, like a beggar – hoping, willing that Lila would show in the hour and a half before he had to leave for the rendezvous. No idea what he would say to her, or what he *could* say to her, just that he had to see her one last time. What if he asked her, right there and then, to come with him? Finn pictured her doing that: just walking away from her job, her own life, and heading off with him. Thirty minutes, forty-five, sixty, seventy. Watching that jaded red door, waiting. A couple of smokers let themselves out – he recognised one of them – but not Lila. When she finally came Finn was almost out of time. She didn't spot him along the street, in a doorway of his own; didn't even glance up, just rummaged in her bag for a cigarette, a lighter, and lit up. That way she had of

79

holding the cig with her right and lighting with her left, even though she was right-handed; always, it looked as if she was igniting a cigarette for the first time in her life. The way, on the first exhalation, she invariably released the smoke through her nostrils, not her mouth. Observing Lila in these simple acts, Finn was struck by the familiarity and the oddness – it was like watching a stranger playing a cameo of someone you knew intimately. He'd been anxious that, when she took her smoke break, one of the other sales staff might join her, making it difficult for him to approach or to speak to her privately. But seeing her by herself, spying on her like this – unguarded, unaware that she was under surveillance, content in her own company – he witnessed a Lila he'd never seen before. The Lila she was when he wasn't around. She looked the same but, also, utterly different. This was a version of Lila that didn't need him, that would do just fine without him – not only now, at that moment, but the next day and every day from now on. You could emerge from your doorway, cross the street and make her aware of you, snap her out of that version of herself. Or you could stay hidden, watching her minutely, memorising each detail, pushing the tears from your face with your sleeve, until she finished her cigarette, trod the stub out on the sidewalk and let herself back into the shop to carry on with her day, oblivious to you. So that was what Finn did. He could have pretended to himself that the less she knew about what he was doing the better it was for both of them; or that a goodbye without words would be more eloquent than anything either of them could say. But he knew these weren't the reasons he'd let their parting go unmarked.

'OK, here's how it shapes up.' Leander was nodding, intense. We've got four days before anyone starts looking for you. So, first thing tomorrow, we shift you out of the Capital to another safe house while it's still all right for you to travel. You can hole up there till we sort the documents you'll need after that. Tonight, you stay here.'

Finn took in the surroundings properly for the first time. The whole place was crowded with furniture, ornaments, picture frames – ancient gear, all of it, but junkshop rather than antique. An L-shaped room with a double bed and matching bedside tables at one end and a kitchen area at the other. In between, a dining table and chairs, sideboard, TV cabinet, coffee table, dresser, dressing table, wardrobes, bookcases, a large wooden trunk, a couple of footstools, two chests of drawers and the suite they sat on. It could've been the stockroom of a second-hand furniture store. The home, he supposed, of an old man who had moved from a house to a bedsit and taken the entire contents with him, unable to bring himself to chuck any of it. Photos, everywhere, on every wall and spare surface. Tacky ornaments. For all Finn knew, the guy had been widowed and this was all he had left of his dead wife. The smell was a mix of mildew, wood polish, bird crap and cat food. The cat itself was nowhere to be seen, though its silvery hairs gave the sofa's ribbed brown upholstery the appearance of a sugar-dusted chocolate log. Finn reckoned this would most likely be his bed for the night.

'How come I have to be moved out of the city?'

'You've got two options,' Leander said, slipping into his double-glazing sales spiel again. 'The first is, you spend the rest of the war in an attic, or tucked away behind a false wall. No going out. No being seen at windows. No noise in case the neighbours get suspicious. Someone brings you food and takes your shit and piss away in a bucket. We've got guys living like that. Hundreds of them.' He paused, seemingly to let this register. 'Or, we fix you up with false papers and a new ID – move you out to some place where no one knows you, where you can go out into the street and no one's gonna recognise you or point the finger.'

'Live a normal life?'

'Well, not normal exactly. But, yeah, a relative . . . freedom of movement.'

'What about emigrating?' Finn said.

'Where? The only countries we can travel to just now are ones in the Alliance, and they're extraditing deserters. You'd still be in hiding. And, if you don't speak the language, how d'you blend in?' Leander paused. 'Besides, we don't have access to a network anywhere else. No contacts, no documents, no safe routes, nothing.'

'OK.' Finn nodded. 'OK, so.'

They talked some more about the technicalities, Leander fielding his questions with patience; he gave the impression that – if Finn had wanted – they could have discussed the whole thing for the rest of the afternoon. When they'd done talking, Finn handed over his documents. They disappeared into the attaché case, along with the cash he'd been instructed to bring. Even after Leander had split off a portion and handed it back, for 'travel expenses', it was still a shitload; not so much that the withdrawal would arouse curiosity at Finn's bank, but enough to make him uneasy at seeing this guy zip most of it away. But he was in their hands; he either trusted them, or walked out.

The birdman was studying him again, the way he'd done at the café. A still, silent presence in his chair, his knuckly hands resting on the worn fabric, fretting at the film of cat hairs, working them into small, white furballs which, periodically, he would let drop to the floor. It occurred to Finn that the old boy might not even live here; that when Finn left in the morning, the birdman would leave too; that all this furniture, the cat, even Mr Findlay were props in an elaborate subterfuge. That, once Finn was in hiding, there would be no trace of him or of the people who'd helped him.

'Where's the cat?' Finn said.

'She's shy,' the birdman said. 'I expect she'll be in one of the cupboards.'

Finn glanced at the clutter of furniture, as if the cat might emerge from a door at any moment. He thought of his own flat, of Lila returning to his absence. The twin blocks of Paladin Mansions were a few kilometres away, but right now they might as well have been on the other side of the globe. He imagined IS officers hammering on his door, four days from now; breaking it down. Finn had a fleeting panic about the police coming round sooner than that to question him some more about Kurt. But, no. Why would they? The cops had already interviewed him at the hospital, and they'd said the coroner's office would be in touch 'in due course' for a formal statement. He'd be called as a witness at the inquest, if one ever took place. As one cop put it: 'Trauma Drives War Hero to Gruesome Suicide' wasn't a headline the Government wanted its electorate to read at their breakfast tables just now.

Fuck sake.

Finn let his chin drop on to his chest. Let all his breath out at once.

'What is it?' Leander said.

'Nothing.'

'You're not tied into this, yet, Finn.' The guy gestured at the window. At the city outside, waiting to take him back again. 'You can just walk away from us and turn up for duty like none of this ever happened.'

'You haven't asked me *why*,' Finn said. 'Why I'm doing this.'

Leander shrugged. 'I don't really care. You don't want to be drafted. That's all I need to know.'

'You don't care if I'm a dodger or a resister . . . or what my reasons are? The "politics of protest" and all that. What if I'm just a fucking coward? Shouldn't I be out there, on the marches?

Chanting: "We won't go!" Throwing bottles at the cops? Getting tear-gassed? Going to jail for my principles?'

'You think that would be more heroic?'

'Who's talking about heroic?' Finn said.

'You could join up if you want to be a fucking hero.'

Finn looked at him, but didn't respond.

'You're not fighting,' Leander said, with another shrug. 'What you are, is one more soldier they can't call on.'

Finn hesitated. Some of the agitation left him. 'I don't know what I am.'

'Look, Finn, you are being ordered to fight against your will. And – whatever your reasons, whatever you want to call yourself – the moment you refuse to obey that order, you become an activist.'

Finn let that remark settle. He no longer had the energy to argue. The room hushed, apart from the chik-chik-chik of an unseen clock and the scuffling of Mr Findlay on his perch. The bird's activities sharpened the room's musty, feral odour. Finn, who'd been leaning forward, slumped back in his seat, suddenly weary. Dizzy. There was a lightness in his head and in the pit of his stomach; his hands trembled slightly. The palms were damp. If he stood up, he would faint for sure. Finn realised that, as well as being exhausted, he was hungry. All he'd had since last night's fry-up at Mum's was the wafer that came with his iced coffee. At the hospital, and after, the idea of food – if it entered his head at all – had nauseated him. Now, though, he was ravenous; he imagined eating and eating, bloating his stomach and easing blood sugar into his system; like threads of warmth worming through his veins. He craved food almost as much as he craved sleep, just to curl up right there on the sofa and shut his eyes and have them lay a blanket over him as if he was a small, sick child.

Addressing the birdman, Leander said: 'You OK with this?'

Finn noticed that the two men never referred to one another by name.

'Long as he doesn't snore.' The birdman offered Finn a solemn face. 'The last young chap snored like a bandsaw. So,' he shrugged, 'I'm afraid I had no option but to hand him over to Internal Security.'

It was part of their routine, Finn suspected; put the new draft-dodger at ease. Even so, he smiled. Living with the birdman for one night wouldn't be so bad.

Mr Findlay sang again. Finn looked over at the cage. His brother wouldn't have appreciated the bird concert. It was one of the differences between them, the things they found beautiful. In some ways, he felt, this was as significant a difference as the fact that Kurt fought and he wouldn't, or that Kurt was dead and he was alive.

Without planning to say it, Finn said: 'My brother died this morning.'

The whole story came out, then, and the two men listened.

'My wife lost a brother in the last war,' the birdman said. 'Bomber pilot. That's how I met her. We were in the same squadron, me and him, and he introduced us at a dance.' The birdman smiled. 'I thought she was his girl, at first.'

Finn looked at him. 'You were a *bomber pilot*?'

The birdman nodded. 'Two years.'

Finn and the old boy were sitting at the dining table, plates of food in front of them. Leander had left. He'd checklisted the contents of Finn's pack and promised to return later with one or two extra items, as well as details of the train Finn would be taking the next day. Once he'd gone, the birdman had made sandwiches: fish paste and cheese spread on white; paper-thin discs of cucumber. They washed the meal down with strong black tea from a china pot the birdman had to pour using both hands – one on

85

the handle, one on the spout – on account of his arthritic grip. The revelation that he'd served in the Air Force came out of nowhere; they'd been talking some more about Kurt, initially. Finn had wondered if his death might offer him a way out of the draft. Defer it at least. The bereaved brother seeking compassionate leave. He felt ashamed of the idea almost as soon as he'd suggested it. In any case, the birdman had shaken his head.

'You play that game, son, you're in the system. And once you're in the system they won't let you out of their sight.'

They'd switched subjects after that. The roof of the old boy's block was leaking rain-water down the stairwell; the tap water wasn't safe to drink unless you boiled it or used purifying tablets; no heating, *again*. Then, somehow, the stuff about bomber pilots.

'Why does that surprise you?' the birdman said. 'You didn't think I was old enough?'

'No, it's not that.'

Finn didn't know how old the birdman was, but he looked plenty old enough to have been conscripted last time round. It seemed obvious, now, that he would've fought, or would've been eligible to fight. 'You weren't a conchie, then?' Finn said.

The birdman sipped his tea. 'Because I'm helping you?'

'Yeah, I guess.'

'No, I wasn't a conchie.'

'Right.'

Finn ate, eyes on his plate the whole time. A radio, tuned to a classical music station, was playing quietly at the other end of the bedsit. For Mr Findlay's benefit, apparently. The melodies helped the bird to settle. Finn wondered about the birdman's opinion of him; of dodgers in general, but mainly of him. The story about his wife's brother, maybe he'd invented that to imply there was a bond between them; but it sounded authentic. The birdman didn't come across as someone who'd make up something like that. He was helping him, that was all that mattered. Whatever his

86

reasons, he was sheltering Finn, feeding him, listening to what he had to say about Kurt and about himself. Not judging him. Being here, with him, you were made to feel as though evading the draft – *running away* – was the most reasonable, natural thing to do, even though the birdman himself, in his youth, had done the opposite.

Finn watched him. Just getting a sandwich from plate to mouth was tough.

Jesus, the tea was worse than the iced coffee. He set his mug back down. Just as he'd asked Kurt about fighting, he wanted to ask the birdman. He'd felt awkward with his brother; he felt awkward now. Ashamed. When you were afraid to fight, how could you pump a guy for his war stories without him taking you for an asshole?

What's it like to drop bombs, then?
How does it feel to come under anti-aircraft fire?
What's it like when the guys you serve with get killed and you don't?
And how does that feel now, all these years later?

Yeah, right. Like you ever could ask any of that. So he didn't.

Later, when the sandwiches were long finished and they were sat on the suite and talking about not very much, the birdman – his gaze on Mr Findlay's cage, as it caught the thin gleam from the window beyond it – came as close as he ever would to offering Finn a reason for sheltering him; for wanting Finn to make a different choice to the one he himself had made all those years ago.

'My father reckoned the war would make a man of me.' Then, turning to look at Finn, he said: 'What he didn't say was what kind of a man.'

Safe

The land beyond the city limits was flat, featureless. Farming country: meadows of chequered cattle, and dull yellow blocks of stubble; he had no idea what crop had grown there. Some fields were partially flooded. A river, thin as a snake, was disfigured with growths of overspill. So it rained here, too. Somehow, he'd had the idea it only rained in the Capital, the sprawl of buildings pulling down their own pissy weather system. It was raining now, streaking the window. The train was an hour late leaving and had stopped twice for no apparent reason, but at last it had brought his first sight of the countryside. Sodden, dead level. Even so, he couldn't take his eyes from the scene as it bled past. He was safe, for now – travelling under his own name, with his own ID, three days away from being hunted down as a deserter. He was committing no offence, yet. All the same, when the ticket inspector came by, or others in the crowded carriage glanced Finn's way, he half-believed they could see 'draft-dodger' tat-tooed across his forehead.

The guy next to him was taking a call on a translucent turquoise cellphone the size of a matchbox, pecking away at a laptop with his free hand. Figures, some kind of spreadsheet. 'Today, not tomorrow,' he was saying. 'I don't care . . . No . . . Tell him it's today or it doesn't happen . . . I don't care . . . Tell him to look at the contract . . . No . . . No . . . I don't care . . . That's his problem.' The guy snapped the phone shut.

Work. Finn wouldn't be doing any more of that for a while, thank fuck.

They were passing a conifer planation, bar codes of daylight among the neat rows. Zip zip zip. He imagined walking there; the smell of pine. He had no idea where he was going or what would happen, but he knew what he'd left behind. Not just the job – his flat and the city, too. All of it, peeling away. Far from the claustrophobia of the fugitive seeing his options close in on him, Finn felt oddly liberated.

Or he would've done, if it hadn't been for leaving Lila.

So far he'd held out against calling her, even from a payphone. Even though he ached with the regret of letting her go that time, outside the book store.

Just to have held her. To be able to hold her now.

He stopped a vendor and bought a sandwich and a can of soda, reaching for them through the press of bodies. Rail services had been cut right back to save energy. The few trains that still ran were always packed. This one was. People stood all along the aisles and in between the carriages. Soldiers, some of them. In uniform. The haircuts. No way of telling if they were heading home on leave or on their way to rejoin their units. A couple of tables along, four squaddies had set up a card school; Finn could hear them laughing, taking the piss. At each station the vendors came aboard, jostling through the throng so they could do their trade and jump off again before the doors shut. Before the war, minorities had sewn up this business. But the internments and deportations had seen to those who originated from enemy states, and harassment, hostility, abuse and a spate of assaults on anyone who looked like they *might* had driven off the rest. The pack working Finn's train were caucasian. The two women opposite were discussing this. Biddies. Spooning pasta salad from Tupperware tubs. Just before, one had shown the other pictures of her grandchildren. They thought it was good. One of the best things to come out of the war: hearing your own language more often, seeing fewer faces that were unlike yours. Finn wondered what they'd have made of Lila. What they'd have had to say about the café in the basement arcade at Paladin that was torched one night, wiping out the mother, father and four kids who lived in rooms at the back.

Another delay.

In this part of the country, the plains gave way to hills; low and blunt, like folds in an unmade bedspread. The train had halted alongside a lake, with a small island in its centre. Just a ragged mound of mud and scrub. A colony of white birds – gulls, of some sort – had settled on the island. Motionless, watchful. As if they'd been stranded there and, suddenly unable or unwilling to fly, were waiting to be rescued.

Finn scrunched up the sandwich wrapper, took a long pull on the soda.

He could've done with something. But Leander had said no. 'You get searched at a checkpoint and they find any shit on you, you're fucked.' He'd been made to flush away the stuff he'd had on him, the stash in his pack, the lot. All he had was booze – the bottle of vod the birdman had handed him as he left, but that was stowed in his pack in the overhead rack. Or cigarettes. Only there was no smoking in this compartment. Finn closed his eyes. Thinking of the vodka-hazy conversation they'd had last night, him and the birdman, before he'd finally crashed out on the couch covered with the hairs of a cat he never got to see.

The old boy had spoken of revenge. When he saw what they'd

done to Kurt, hadn't he wanted to go out there in his brother's place and shoot as many of them as he could?

Finn shook his head. 'What does that say about me?'

The birdman shrugged. He said you couldn't choose your instincts, you could only choose what to do about them. Which made a kind of sense to Finn at the same time as it made no sense at all. Revenge against who, anyway? The enemy troops who'd blown away Kurt's foot and fucked his head? Or the Government that packed him off to die in its name?

Take your pick.

'Some lads in your situation would've gone.'

Finn had withdrawn into himself. 'So, I'm not some lads.'

'I'm not having a pop at you, son. I'm just curious.'

'I'm pissed off with *him*, too, if you want the truth.'

'Your brother?'

In his imaginings, Finn reaches Kurt in time, stops the bleeding, saves him; or Kurt's lying there dead, no feet, and Finn's punching him, swearing, yelling, beating him about the head until you can't see the slack jaw, the dropped chin, the buck-teeth, for all the gore. Or Finn's sawing through his own shin.

'Yeah, my brother. My poxy brother. Fucking doing that to himself.'

'You get angry with them,' the birdman said. 'My wife spent fifty-odd years smoking herself to death, and there's not a day when I don't blame her for that.'

Finn didn't want to talk about the birdman's wife again. His wife died, his wife's brother died, your brother died. So what? The trouble with olds was they acted like they knew everything, like there was nothing you'd done or were going to do that they hadn't already done, like experience was this great gift they were handing down to you. Sometimes you just couldn't listen to that. But, looking at him . . . Jesus. Finn was drunk, tired. Tetchy.

91

After a moment, he'd yawned and said: 'I need to turn in. I'm knackered.'

The birdman had set his drink down and gone off to sort some bedding.

Now, on the train, Finn wished they'd talked for longer. Wished he hadn't blanked the guy like that. They'd barely exchanged a handful of words afterwards. In the morning Leander had pitched up before either of them was moving and, in no time at all, Finn had been washed and dressed and lugging his pack into the station. Even the bottle had been handed over without comment. No ceremony. Just pressed into his hands, and that was that.

The card school was still going. Seven-card stud, by the looks. Kurt's game.

In his youth he'd wanted to be like Kurt – have his looks, his build. Down to the smallest details: the pattern of the hairs on his forearms; the creases either side of his mouth when he smiled; the shape of his biceps. If you were at a party with Kurt, or in a bar or club, or walking along the street, there'd be some girl, watching him, her eyes saying: *Notice me*. Finn had wanted that. He'd wanted to tan like Kurt. Move like him. Make people laugh like him – guys, too, not just girls. Be tough like him. For a long time, he'd thought of Kurt's toughness as physical, to do with the heft of his limbs and his handiness with a punch, his speed and power. One time, after a night out with a couple of Kurt's mates, they got jumped outside a burger place. No reason, just boozy lads up for a scrap; four v. four. The fight hardly got started before Kurt took two of them out, swinging one headlong into railings and decking the other with a single blow. The other pair legged it after seeing their pals go down. Finn hit no one. Threw a carton of milkshake at one lad and saw it explode on his shoulder, that was all. The scene was over in less than a minute, yet they talked about it the rest of the way home; Finn as hyper as anyone, on the surface, yet conscious that he'd done the least possible, without actually running away. In the confusion, Kurt's friends and Kurt himself – cheek swollen, knuckles bruised – hadn't noticed Finn's part in the fight. Or if they had, they didn't say so.

'You OK?' Kurt had said, massaging Finn's neck with his unhurt hand.

'Yeah,' Finn said. 'I'm fine.'

Around then, in their late teens, Finn had realised his brother's strength was not just physical. He was stronger in his head. Hard, decisive, certain of himself. He had a raw aggression, an assertiveness, that Finn had secretly coveted, even after he came to understand what crap all that was. Even after they'd grown up and the age difference didn't seem so great and he'd discovered enough of his brother's inadequacies – his weaknesses, out in the world of adults – that he no longer idolised him.

But, still.

The reduction of him, at the end, was what got to Finn. That Kurt could've been so *reduced*. If Finn had died like that, his brother would have sought revenge. For sure. But he couldn't conceive of how things might've happened that way round.

A backpack is the last thing you want when you're making your way from train to platform to concourse to street, with all the push and crush, the taxi touts and hotel touts, the ticket barriers, the people coming from all directions. Finn shouldered a path to a bay out front where luggage trolleys were parked nose-to-tail. Space. Standing the pack at his feet, he took his bearings, lit a cigarette. Dusk, already. A stench of scorched oil from the food stalls ranged across the way. One displayed a goat's head, complete with horns, eyes, hair and grinning teeth. He told a hotel tout he'd already got a place to stay; when the boy persisted, Finn told him to fuck off.

'Yeah, fuck you too mister. Fuck you in the shit-pipe you motherfucking asshole.'

'*Shit-pipe?*' Finn couldn't help laughing. 'Since when is that a word?'

'Since now.'

The boy was about nine. He moved away, giving Finn the finger.

The safe house was only fifteen minutes' walk, according to Leander, but the directions were complex and the sodium-lit rain beyond the station awning resembled the special-effects deluge in a B-movie. And his stash of money, the travel expenses he'd been allocated, was in a zipped belt beneath the waistband of his trousers. Which was another reason for staying off the streets. So, he'd take a cab. But before you got to the cab rank – before you could leave the station at all – you had to pass through a checkpoint. Finn had supposed there would be one but, all the same, the sight of it up ahead jolted him. Typical set-up: metal barriers funnelling folk into the exit past three men and a woman in uniform – one pair checking ID, the other watching for anyone trying to slip through. Avoid checkpoints, Leander had said. They logged your details, and you didn't want to leave a trail for them to plot once you were officially missing. Finn retreated into the station proper and scouted for another way out, but couldn't see one that didn't involve scaling four-metre railings. He headed back to the main exit. Fuck it, he'd go through, he'd have to.

Then he spotted 'shit-pipe' boy again.

'Hey, c'mere a minute,' Finn said. The boy came. The same sullen, fuck-you face but curious now, sensing an angle for him to work. Finn made like he was giving the boy a smoke. 'I need you to get me out of here. Get me to a cab, yeah?'

He saw that the young tout caught his meaning. The cash changed hands in among the lighting of the lad's cigarette and was tucked away out of sight so quick and neat that, even though Finn had palmed him the notes himself, he couldn't have sworn that the boy ever touched them. Five minutes later, Finn was out.

Following the lad through a staff-only door, down a flight of stairs and across a delivery yard, busy with mail vans, that gave straight on to a cobbled side-street. The boy even led him to a place, away from the station plaza, where he could flag down a taxi with no hassle.

'You ever say "shit-pipe" to anyone,' the boy said, as they parted, 'make sure to tell 'em where you heard it first.'

'Yeah, where to?' the cabbie said.

Finn told him the neighbourhood.

'Got an address, or do I mind-read? A street, even, would be good.'

Finn named a street. The cabbie popped the door locks once Finn was inside. The pack was on the rear seat, beside Finn, due to the trunk-jackings. At lights, or wherever traffic jammed up, a gang would appear from nowhere, jemmy a trunk and rip off the contents. This cabbie had been done twice in a month and had finally removed the trunk lid altogether to avoid the damage. He twisted in his seat as he spoke, lobbing words over his shoulder, voice raised above the engine's throaty rattle. At first Finn wondered how he could afford the diesel, or even obtain any; then he caught the smell. Vegetable oil. Drivers in the Capital were using it too, so that you walked around with a taste of fried breakfast in your mouth. The questions came. How long was he in town, where was he staying, was it business or pleasure or what? Finn told him lies.

The station occupied a hill above the town, an elevated freeway drawing cars down into the centre as though by pulley. You could see the entire town from there; you could see where it ended, scribbling out into nothing. Low-rise cubes – factory units, warehousing, retail parks – then terraced homes, then a huddled core of office towers, patterned asymmetrically with rectangles of illumination. An industrial town, he knew that much;

95

ex-industrial, anyway. Metal or glass or something. Whatever, he wasn't sure they made it here any more. When the cab left the freeway and blended into the flow along a boulevard flanked by shops, Finn became aware of the gloom – more blue-grey than the usual, pervasive yellow, even allowing for the fact that most of the shops were shut by now. Moody, seedy. Third World urban dilapidation meets metropolitan chic. As if the neighbourhood was being shot in monochrome. It took a moment to figure out the cause. Then he saw that just one street light in three was turned on.

They stopped at an intersection. There were women in the doorways, more or less naked under the long coats they allowed to flap open.

Looking where Finn was looking, the cabbie said: 'Like some of that?'

'Nah.'

'I can fix you. Younger, you like? Fourteen, fifteen.'

Finn ignored him.

The driver was studying him in the mirror. 'Whatever you want, I can bring. Girls, boys, whatever. Shemales?'

'Just drive, yeah?'

The cabbie laughed. 'Mr Cool Kid.' Then, taking a right into the street Finn had named, still smiling, he said: 'Maybe, OK, pussy's not your thing tonight, but – don't mind me saying – you look like the man who needs *something*.'

A bedsit, two floors up. Finn got into the block, the flat itself, no problem, by keying in the codes he'd been made to memorise. He shut and bolted the door and set down his pack and the carrier of food he'd bought at a twenty-four-hour store along the street. The lights didn't work. He noseyed around as best he could in the semi-dark. Two rooms: lounge, bedroom and kitchen in one, with a separate bathroom. Empty. No carpets, curtains, cooker, fridge, TV, furniture. Blank walls, rough floorboards. No bed, except for a single mattress in one corner. The radiators were cold. The air was chilly, musty and, as he moved about, he smelled dust. But the bedsit was otherwise odourless. He tried to picture the previous occupant. A dodger, like him, probably – clomping about, settling himself, wondering at the drag of hours ahead. The apprehension. You could believe you were part of a procession of individuals who'd passed through this place and there was a kind of reassurance to be had from that. But the bedsit itself – more like a cell, a holding pen – seemed to have been rinsed of all traces, physical or imaginary. Even the mattress was new, still in its polythene wrapper. Each arrival and departure was distinct, unconnected. Finn saw that he wasn't a part of anything; that, when his turn came to move on, he too would leave no impression.

There was no shower. He tried the taps in the sink, the wash basin, the bath. Nothing. Just the clunk of airlocks being released in the plumbing. In the kitchen, though, in a neat line on the draining board, stood six one-litre bottles of uncarbonated mineral water. Along with the mattress, they were the only signs of arrangement. Finn had the place to himself, that was the plan. He wasn't to go out; wasn't to answer the door to anyone. Leander had given him a mobile. He was to wait for a call. That was all, just wait. It could be a day or two. At the window, he sparked up one of the spliffs the cab driver had sold him, ready made, from a stash in his glovebox. A long draw. He looked down into the street, his breath misting the glass. An amusement arcade spilled reds and yellows into the evening, along with the bass beat of music, artificial voices, synthesised explosions. Kids gathered outside. Above the arcade, the windows of the building opposite were boarded up, 'TO LET' sashes pasted across the panels. If he kept back from the window, he would be invisible. He ate by the dregs of the day's light, standing at the breakfast bar. Sardines,

97

scooped from the tin with crackers; water, straight from the bottle; chocolate. He smoked. He considered the difference between alone and lonely. This was alone. How long did you have to be alone before loneliness set in? He wasn't sure that it hadn't begun to take hold already.

A day, two days. He could do this. He could find it within himself to do this.

He said his name aloud – 'Finn, Finn' – just to hear the shrill snap of its echo.

The Incomer's First Visitor

From her bedroom window Bryher watched the boat manoeuvre out to sea, trailing an entourage of gulls. She could make out two figures – one fore, one aft – although she was unable to tell them apart. Neither of them was Orr; he would have stayed ashore, ready to help – be indulged in the belief that he was helping – when the boat returned with its catch. She wondered if Nudge was the one in the cabin, steering, as he had been on the evening of the accident. There would have been no saving Roop, even if Nudge had been on deck with him; Nudge would simply have been swept overboard as well. Afterwards, he had vowed never to set foot on the boat again. But, at each Gathering since then, others had urged him to reconsider. Not to haul the burden of the past with him into the future, as Sholo had phrased it. And now, finally, there he was (if it was him), at the wheel, facing out towards a swathe of sea where weed-drifts sketched dark streaks across the bluish-green shimmer.

How often Roop had set out in the same boat. How often she'd watched him from this window – in the early weeks, when he was new to fishing and she was new to seeing him out there. As

99

the novelty wore off, she'd get on with work of her own while he was at sea. Today, though, she watched that boat. Like so many things of late it was both a comfort and a painful reminder. At this hour, in the crystalline glare of the sun and with the sky unbroken by cloud, the fret was no more than a spectre at the edge of her thoughts. Yet even the clearest seascape carried its trace for Bryher, these days. If she returned to this window at dusk it would be out there: solid-looking, indisputable; a long thick tongue of smoky-grey on the horizon. Apparently motionless, but rolling in by nightfall to the island's periphery, sending glaciers of mist along its clefts and engulfing any vessel whose crew was incautious enough to remain offshore after dark.

An avalanche, she thought. As if it had been the fret itself which claimed him.

This morning, as she watched Nudge and Zess set off, Bryher spotted a second craft further out. A patrol launch, broaching the swell at an acute angle and leaving streamers of foam in its wake, the sunlight brilliant on its white flank. She felt a pull of apprehension. But the launch was some way off, cruising parallel to the shore, and showed no sign of altering course towards the fishing boat or towards the island. In a moment it would have negotiated Gibbet Point and moved out of sight.

Any number of things might have drawn her away from the window: she was hungry; there was her patient to attend to; there were household chores. But it was Amver's voice, calling from downstairs, which distracted her. The Incomer stirred at the girl's breezy 'hello-up-there', the clump–clump of her feet.

Bryher intercepted her on the stairs. 'He's sleeping,' she whispered.

'Oh, right . . . sorry.'

Amver retreated, Bryher following her into the living room and pulling the door to. There was an aroma of hot food: lentils, onions, fresh-baked bread. Yué's cooking rather than Amver's,

Bryher hoped. The girl had done her hair differently, her long inky-black curls shored up with a scaffold of clips, slides and spikes that would have looked ridiculous on anyone else.

Bryher smiled. 'Hello, Amv.'

The girl indicated a basket on the table; a casual gesture, as though the food had magicked its way there and was nothing to do with her. 'Mum sent this for you.'

'Smells good.'

'Usual slop.' Amver laughed at her own remark. 'Don't tell her I said that.'

She resembled her father so closely – at least, a prettier, feminine version of him – that it always surprised Bryher to see amusement in those features when Mor's expression had been typically so serious. She wondered if Amver missed him, still. It was a year since Mor had left the island, and his family. Did the missing of someone cease that soon? Did it even begin to fade?

Bryher made an effort to be affable, welcoming, even though the girl's sudden appearance had thrown her a little, left her feeling intruded upon.

'Your hair looks fantastic.'

Lowering her voice, the girl said: 'There's a pair of Mum's chopsticks in here somewhere, holding it all together. Don't tell her *that*, either.'

Bryher laughed. The age gap was just five years – Amver's seventeen, to Bryher's twenty-two – yet, whenever she was with her, Bryher felt about forty. The difference was more mental than physical. She *thought* old. Older, anyway. Since Roop. She and Amver were almost close enough in years to be friends, but Bryher was a widow and, for all that she'd 'lost' her father, Amver wasn't. Also, she had been fifteen – still a child – when Bryher and Roop had first come here, and Bryher hadn't yet adjusted to her flourish into womanhood and the attitude that came with it. Even so, she liked the girl. Right after Roop died, Amver was the only one to act normally with her; the only one not to treat her like a piece of precious porcelain that might break if it was handled. Bryher would always remember her fondly for that.

The girl glanced at the door to the stairs. 'So, what's he like?'

Bryher smiled, shaking her head. 'Poor Yué.'

'What?'

'She has to cook my lunch just so you can have an excuse to come down here and have a nosy at the Incomer.'

Amver seemed about to protest, then checked herself. With a laugh, she said: 'Am I that transparent?'

Bryher went to the table, removed the dish from the basket and set it down.

'Actually,' Amver said, 'the food *was* Mum's idea.'

'There's enough here for all of us.'

The girl said no, thanks; she'd already eaten. Bryher fetched cutlery, bowls, plates and butter for the bread. A half-loaf, still warm and pliable. She filled one of the bowls for herself and broke off a hunk of bread. The rest would keep until later, in case the Incomer woke and was ready for some food. Yué must have made this with him in mind, because it would be easy to eat and digest. His first meal since the Skins had finished with him.

'He comes from the Capital, doesn't he?' Amver said.

Bryher smiled. 'Apparently.'

'Have you spoken to him?'

'He's not regained consciousness yet.'

Amver frowned.

'He'll be all right,' Bryher said.

The girl had approached the table and picked at the loaf, tearing off a strip of crust and chewing one end. Bryher watched her: the litheness, the casual certainty of her own sexiness. Why had she said the Incomer would be all right? She couldn't be sure of that yet. Probably, she wanted to reassure herself as much as Amver, but all she had done was to make herself anxious again. She should check on him before she ate; take his temperature, at least. Steam was rising off the soup. Amver held her hand over the bowl, as if to test her capacity to endure the heat, then – after a moment – withdrew it. She inspected her palm.

'Can I see him?' she said.

Bryher shook her head. 'I don't want him disturbed.'

'What's his scar like?'

'It's not a scar, yet. It's still a wound.'

Amver popped the piece of crust in her mouth. Holding her hands apart, still chewing, she said: 'Qway reckoned it was *this* long.'

'That's his knob.'

'*Bry!*'

Both women burst out laughing, then. Amver's interest in the Incomer was understandable. She had been born on the island, lived here all her life and never left. Never been to the mainland, let alone the Capital; apart from *émigrés* like Bryher and Roop, the only mainlanders she'd met in seventeen years were the Skins and their men, the occasional local official and, since the war began, the men from the coastal patrols on their routine landings. And now her own father lived there. Why wouldn't she be eager to see the young mainlander, newly come among them? Even so, Bryher hardened towards the girl. The idea of letting her watch him while he slept, making a curiosity of him. She was aware, too, of feeling proprietorial; of wanting to keep him to herself. This *wasn't* how she felt towards him, not really, but a sense of ownership flared in her for a moment, before she extinguished it. Became kind again.

'D'you ever think about your dad?' she said.

Amver looked surprised. 'My *dad*?'

'Uh-huh.' Bryher picked at the bread herself now. The smell of the soup was sharpening her hunger. 'It's a year now, isn't it?'

'Sometimes it's like he was never here at all,' Amver said. She shrugged. 'I dunno. Yeah, I guess I think about him a lot. What he's doing, does he ever think of me . . . that kind of thing. Jad misses him the most – not that he'd ever admit it.'

Amver's brother was eleven when Mor left. He'd taken it hard, it was true, but Bryher wasn't convinced that he missed his father any more than Amver did. At least, their missing of him manifested itself differently. There had been a marked change in Amver, these past twelve months – a loss of innocence, a coarsening – that couldn't entirely be attributed to her shift through the gears of adolescence. She and Jad shared an aura of semi-detachment from the rest of the community; but, whereas her brother seemed to be immersing himself in the island's physicality, a space for him to explore his solitude, Amver gave the impression of wanting to sever the ties altogether – with people and place alike. But, then, the girl *would* be gone soon, in just a few months, so perhaps the dissociation was inevitable and had nothing to do with Mor.

The two women had that in common, at least: a sense of dissociation. Almost, but not quite, a disaffection. Like Bryher, of late, the girl had taken to referring to the community as 'they', instead of 'we'. She did so now, shifting the conversation back to the subject of the Incomer once more.

'Will they let him stay, d'you think?'

She meant would he be allowed to remain once he had recovered from his injury; allowed to live here – on the island, in this cottage, with Bryher – not just as Roop had done, but *as Roop*.

'I don't know,' Bryher said.

'I hope so.'

'You don't know him. None of us do.' Smiling, she said: 'Maybe, when we know him, we won't want him to stay here any more than some of the others do.'

Amver evidently had nothing to say to that. She had moved

towards the door and Bryher went too, to see her off, their movements oddly stilted, as if synchronised; Bryher was put in mind of two dancers practising the choreography for a new routine. A momentary awkwardness at the end of the girl's visit. Bryher kissed her lightly on the cheek, thanked her for the food. Up close, Amver smelled of peaches and mint.

'Qway's at the hives today, if you need more honey. I can call in.'

'Mm, yeah. Couple of the big jars. He's . . . there's a lot of infection.'

'I'll bring some down.'

'Thanks.' Bryher gave her a grin, teasing her. 'You never know, he might be awake next time you come.'

She looked in on the patient, unsure if their conversation had disturbed him. It hadn't. He was still asleep, his bedding dishevelled. She checked his temperature, then tidied the sheet. Watching him, Bryher reflected on what Amver had said about him being allowed to remain here. There were some – Tye, Hobb, Zess, Liddy, Effie – who felt the community had been railroaded into taking him in. Hurried into it, anyway. The islanders opposed the war, and conscription, and there had been talk of supporting the anti-draft movement. But nothing material had come of it. Then, Roop's accident. It was Bryher who'd persuaded them not to report him as missing – initially, in the belief (the hope) that he would be found alive; then, because to notify the authorities of his disappearance at sea would invite official recognition – and, along with it, her own admission – that he was dead. So, nothing had been said. The idea that, with Roop gone, there was now a 'vacancy' on the island hadn't even occurred to Bryher or, so far as she was aware, to any of the others. Not until word reached them that the network was seeking *safe berths* with sympathetic communities in the region. That was it. Bryher saw

105

fate at work, that it had been *meant* for them not to report what had happened to Roop. They wouldn't even have to hide a deserter, with all the difficulty that entailed; instead, at less risk of discovery, they could let him live amid them, passing him off as one of their own, with a new, ready-made identity. One life had been lost, but now another might be spared. These were her arguments to the Gathering. How could they refuse? They couldn't. At least, they didn't. But things had moved quickly, at the end – more quickly than the islanders were used to – and some of them feared a consensus had been reached in haste. That, as Tye put it, the weight of Bryher's grief might have 'tilted the scales of reason', not just for her but for all of them.

Seeing the Incomer in that bed – a real, live, breathing man, not some abstract, hypothetical construct – Bryher was as sure as she could be that they'd done the right thing, regardless of the outcome. *Look at him.* The thought came to her that she should talk to him, or read aloud to him – as if he weren't simply asleep and confused with pain but in a coma. As if the sound of her voice might bring him round, back from the dead. The idea was bizarre. And, as she considered it, Bryher knew she wouldn't. Even if the words were out of a book, she couldn't begin to imagine how she'd contrive the intimacy to speak to this stranger as he slept in her bed. She talked to Roop; had talked to him each day since he'd gone. A word or two, sometimes a monologue: telling him of her day, of some small thing that had happened. Perhaps that was where the notion of talking to the Incomer originated. But, if she spoke to him, she feared she wouldn't be able to stop herself from slipping into the voice she used with Roop, or that she might stop talking to Roop altogether and speak to this man instead. So, no.

Bryher stood at his bedside a moment longer, studying him. Then she returned downstairs, to the lunch Amver had brought.

A Bus Journey

A monsoon they called it, in these parts. Whatever it was, the rain beat down hard on the asphalt, sending a slick brown river along each gutter and threatening to flood the road altogether. Finn had taken shelter in one of several concrete pipes, a metre or so in diameter, laid side by side on the muddy verge. Each tube was occupied – others, like him, waiting for the bus. The rain's reverberation on the concrete was deafening. Finn had been there an hour. Squatting on his haunches at first; then, as his muscles cramped, sitting cross-legged. Peering out at the deluge. The meet was to take place on the bus, whenever that finally showed up, but no one had said Finn had to keep watch for it at the stop in a fucking monsoon. All he'd been told was: make sure you catch the afternoon bus (there were only two a day, from this place); wait for the contact to reveal herself; when she gets off, you get off too. Piece of piss.

He'd been on the move since dawn, after the call came. Three nights alone in that flat; eating sardines, corned beef, crackers and canned peaches; drinking mineral water – washing, brushing his teeth, with it. Nowhere to go. Nothing to do, once he'd finished

107

the paperback he'd brought, except read it again. And drink vodka, sleep and smoke the rest of the spliffs. Finn rationed these activities, spreading them through the day to mark time. Read-smoke-sleep-wash-eat-read-smoke-read-sleep-eat.   Exercises: squat-jumps, push-ups, sit-ups, the yoga poses Lila had taught him. Gawping out the window, careful not to be seen. Conversations in his head with Lila, Kurt, Mum. With himself. Or repeatedly checking the mobile, worried the battery would drain before Leander phoned. Once, on day two, he tried to meditate – for the first time in months – in an uncomfortable half-lotus on the mattress. But his mind was too active with sawn-off feet, and Kurt, and Lila's voice ('inhale the smile, exhale the frown'), and imagining that every thud and creak in the block was the IS, come for him.

Then, at last, the call. Followed by a walk to the station – in the wet, getting lost – sneaking in, to beat the checkpoint, the way the shit-pipe boy had sneaked him out. Another train ride that somehow took six hours to fetch him a further two-fifty K away from the Capital. And, as he'd disembarked, they'd done him. Three teenagers. A slick operation: a kid asks for a light, Finn sets the backpack down while he sorts his matches; a second kid barges into him from the side; a third shoulders the pack, and is away into the tide of people. Kid two vanishes as well but, as Finn is about to chase after his gear, the first kid – the one wanting a light – is right there, obstructing him, drawing lines in the air with a knife in front of Finn's face. Slowly backing off. Smirking. Perfect white teeth. He's not even shaving yet. Talking to Finn the whole time:

'Come on, then. Eh? Come on, you cunt.'

Finn, peripherally aware of the other travellers – moving clear, rubbernecking, doing nothing; there's a knife, some jerk getting done over, so why would they? Why would anyone get involved? Another fake pass with the blade. Swift, graceful. As if he's razoring a gauze scarf as it floats to the floor.

'Fancy this? Fancy some of this, then?'

And the kid turns, and is gone.

All he possessed, now, were the clothes he wore, his watch, the money in its belt, his cigs and the phone, down to one charge-bar and, in any case, a credit of zero for outgoing calls. He had his ID card, too, though this might've become a liability, seeing as how, at ten that morning, he'd failed to report for induction. How long till they officially declared him a deserter, circulated his details? Hours? A day, two? He didn't know. He needed new ID, he knew that much. He could've binned the card, but there was the risk of a security check, and – as long as his no-show hadn't been processed into an APB – he was safer with *some* ID, however big a gamble, than none at all. With no card, you'd be held pending inquiries. Which meant you'd had it.

Finn watched the rain on the road. It was cold, in the pipe; he could've done with a sweater. He couldn't believe how *fucking stupid* he'd been, getting scammed like that. 'Got a light?' Fuck sake. What you needed in those situations was a handgun. The kid pulls a knife on you, and you let him enjoy himself for a moment before you produce the gun. Then he's the cunt. He is, not you. You're the one smirking, telling him: *Come on then.* Does he fancy this? Eh? Does he? And just when he thinks you won't use it, you shoot him straight in the fucking teeth.

The bus was a single-decker, a beat-up diesel converted to electric; liveried in silver with cream-and-maroon chevrons and old, old, old. As he headed towards a vacant seat, Finn searched the faces of the women. It could've been any of them. After Mr Findlay, anything was possible. That child with plaits, clutching her granddad's hand. The old girl, dozing, so frail-looking you wondered if she'd survive the journey. That mum, breastfeeding. Or one of the schoolgirls, loud and amused, passing a cellphone between them in the back row. The driver was female; it could have been her, for all Finn knew. Anyway, whoever the contact was, he wouldn't find her, she'd find him. He sat next to a bald guy reading a tabloid. The usual: war stories, war pictures. A vertical plume of flame against night sky filled the front page, bisecting the headline: 'HELL FIRE'. Finn dreaded him starting a conversation about the war, or anything at all. Even after three days' solitary confinement he didn't want to talk to anyone. He'd feigned sleep for much of the train ride and he'd do the same on the bus if he had to.

A youth was at their window. Naked except for filthy boxers with a cartoon motif, restraining an obvious erection; the kid butted his forehead repeatedly against the pane. In the rain, his skin looked as if it had been oiled. Cross-eyed, his chin livid with eczema from the drool that leaked from his fat lower lip. He eased a bony hand through the vent along the top of the window. 'Coins,' he said. 'Please, some coins.' The bus pulled off just then, but he made no attempt to step clear and, as the driver swung hard away from the kerb, the kid was dumped on his ass in the road. Finn waited for the bump as the rear wheels went over his legs, but it never came. The guy with the newspaper hadn't even looked up.

The route took them from the interior into a coastal region. The transition was marked by a series of climbs through wooded mountains to a high pass, above the treeline, where the clouds separated briefly and a first, distant, glimpse of the ocean panned unexpectedly into view and, just as rapidly, disappeared. Like you'd imagined it. Then the slow, grinding descent to a belt of lowland that carried the road parallel to the coast through scrub and salt flats and, eventually, the beginnings of a rainforest. It was humid here, although still raining hard – the downpour seeming not to cool the inside of the bus, but to accentuate its warmth, as if the sweaty air outside had been compressed into the vehicle and become trapped. With it came the pungent odour of vegetation from the thickening jungle that flanked the road; a smell of semen and rotten cauliflower. It recalled the stench that, on a rare warm day back home, rose off the rubbish dumped in the passage between A- and B-blocks at Paladin Mansions. Bizarre that thoughts of the city should surface in this wild, remote spot. Awash with growth and, for endless kilometres, nothing but the road itself to show people had ever been here. To discover that such places existed in his country was a revelation. But the early start, the travelling, the humidity, the rhythm of the bus, were lulling his attention away from the window. He drifted. Chin dipping on to his chest, eyelids flickering; he wasn't quite asleep, nor quite alert – though when he was finally jolted awake by a sharp tug of the brakes he had no idea if he'd been out for hours or just a few minutes. Panicky. Heart racing. He'd been in the throes of a bad dream: he was on a plane in heavy turbulence, the whine of the engine cutting out intermittently as the aircraft – vibrating, on the point of stalling – strained to maintain altitude. The juddery deceleration of the bus coincided with the plane's plunge and, snapping from his nightmare, Finn found himself braced for impact.

The driver was stopping to let off passengers, that was all; a couple more came aboard. Finn relaxed his grip on the armrests. He felt foolish. Also, gummy mouthed and headachy. The bottle of water he'd bought at a roadside stall at the last rest-stop was already lukewarm and stale tasting, but he downed some all the same. The first of the newcomers settled himself. Moving along the aisle behind him was a woman, distributing leaflets about Jesus; beaming, insistent, forcing them on people whether they wanted one or not. 'Thank you, Jesus loves you. Thank you, Jesus loves you.' She wore a hat made from woven strips of palm leaf, by the looks, that had been bleached by time. The bus was already in motion, and she swayed with it, as if the

111

vehicle itself was propelling her between the rows of seats, shifting her weight from right to left with each outstretched arm. Finn's turn. He shook his head but the woman pressed a leaflet into his hand all the same. 'Thank you, Jesus loves you.' The leaflet was thicker in the centre. He opened it. Tucked inside was an identity card.

He folded the leaflet shut again immediately and slipped it into his pocket.

She must've sat down towards the rear. Finn wanted to turn round to get a proper look, but knew not to. He'd still been half asleep when she got on and hadn't paid her close attention. A long patterned dress of some sort – green? blue? – and bare freckly arms and that home-made hat. She had seemed young – about his age – but maybe this was just an impression. To do with the way she'd sashayed along the aisle. And her wrist, as she'd made him take the leaflet, was knuckly as an adolescent boy's.

Later, while the guy next to him slept, Finn retrieved the leaflet and opened it so he could inspect the identity card while appearing to read about Jesus.

Finn's photo, sealed beneath the laminate – the same mugshot as on his old ID card; and it was his thumb print, probably. It would have to be. The same official stamp, but a different validation date; different serial number, too. The address meant nothing to him; he'd never heard of the place and could barely pronounce it. Where 'status' had said 'single', it now said 'married'. He smiled. OK, they'd got him out of the war, and now they'd found him a wife. The woman with the hat, maybe? The Jesus-freak. A *wife*, though. Fuck sake. Finn wondered when he'd get to meet her, what she looked like, her name, her age. As for his own age, Finn saw that he wasn't twenty-four any longer, but twenty-six. Too old to be called up. That was the thing, the clincher: close enough to his own age for him to pass himself off as twenty-six, but . . . too old to be drafted. Finn let his breath

112

escape in a long exhalation, gazing out the window for a moment. It was for real, all of this. The realisation centred itself in his diaphragm, like a weight, drawing his lungs down to his stomach. If the bus stopped, if he made the driver pull over, he could just vanish into the rainforest, where it would be green and gloomy, full of hiding places, makeshift shelters, wild creatures to trap, fruit and leaves and nuts to eat, streams to drink from. He could live alone, he could survive, learn to exist like that if he had to. Even as he imagined such a life – the romance, the adventure – the fact struck him that he was already running away, and that this would be running away too. That if you ran away from running away there'd be no end to it.

Finn looked at his ID again. The name. This card, of course, bore a different signature to his own – a crazy, looping scrawl that spilled out from the confines of the designated strip and might have spelled 'Boof' or 'Poel' or 'Keuej', with the actual name printed above it in a neat black typeface: 'Roop'.

Roop. He tried it out, under his breath. Roop. Roop.

That's who he was, now: *Roop*. What kind of a fucking name was that?

'Hi, I'm Mrs Finch.'

Finn nodded. 'That your real name?'

She tipped the hat back a little. Her eyes were such a light brown they were closer to yellow; he'd never seen anyone with yellow eyes. 'What do *you* think?'

'OK, I guess my name's Roop, then.'

They shook hands, almost formally. 'So . . . where's your gear?'

Finn told her what had happened.

'Hey, bummer.' She shrugged, though, like it wasn't a big deal to her. The bus had gone and the other passengers who'd got off

113

had moved away, leaving Finn and the Jesus lady alone at the bus stand. 'When are you due to join up?' she said.

Finn checked his watch. 'About five and a half hours ago.'

She made a face. 'Wow, you've cut it fine!'

'*Me?* Yeah, like, I thought I'd hang around in an empty flat for a few days – take it right to the edge, you know? I get off on that.'

'Oh, right.'

He gave her a look. 'Yeah, right.'

Mrs Finch shook her head. 'Tell you what, of all the anti-draft networks, ours must be *the most* unreliable. You ought to write a complaint. I would.'

They got on better after that. As well as they needed to, at least. They were on the outskirts of a small town which they soon left behind as Mrs Finch led the way on foot along the highway the bus had taken. Ordinarily, they would've remained on the bus a while longer, but security had been tightened along this stretch of coast – 'drug smuggling', she said – and there was no point putting yourself through checkpoints if you didn't have to. So she hoped he was up for a couple of days' hiking. Finn said yeah, he guessed he could do that. After a few hundred metres, they turned on to a broad dirt track treacherous with mud and water-filled potholes. To either side, fields of crop sprawled in tall rows into the mid-distance. Sugar cane, the woman told him. That's what folk did round here – worked in the fields or the processing mill in town, which explained the sickly-sweet smell he'd detected when they left the bus.

'What's the noise?' Finn said.

'Cicadas.' Mrs Finch gestured at the fields. 'There's thousands of them out there. You walk in, you'd have them in your hair, your clothes, your mouth.'

The fields spoke with one voice, made up of many. Shrill, vibrant, relentless, metronomic; so loud you had to talk over it. A vast pulse of sound. It was as if the sugar cane was alive, the swathe of crop beating out the percussion of its own growth. The cicadas usually started up at dusk, Mrs Finch told him, but the afternoon was dark with impending rain and the false twilight had set them off.

'All this land has been reclaimed from the rainforest for cultivation,' she said.

'You're from round here?'

'No, I came with my husband. He used to run a charity mission in the town.'

'Used to?'

'He's a CO.'

That made sense. Mr Finch, the conchie; Mrs Finch, the draft-dodgers' mate.

'Where is he?' Finn said.

'Compulsory employment.'

The euphemism for hard labour. She named an internment centre – a boot camp – in a distant region of the country, and Finn knew, to be sent there, he must have refused even a non-combat posting. He also suspected, as Mrs Finch must've done – though neither of them said so – that she wouldn't see her husband alive again. If the work or the internment regime didn't kill him, the conchie-bashers would.

'They offered him a military chaplaincy,' she said. Finn sensed from her tone that she was finding it the hardest thing not to wish he'd accepted.

Finn didn't respond. What was there to say to this woman that would make it any different? They fell silent, walking side by side to the accompanying, enveloping din of the cicadas. When they'd been going for a while, Mrs Finch stopped and asked for Finn's old ID. He gave it to her, along with the redundant mobile. She went into a stand of bushes away from the track. She set the card alight, holding it by one corner until it was melted and blackened

115

beyond recognition, just a deformed piece of sooty plastic. The phone she smashed with a large stone, scattering the pieces in the dense scrub.

'Right, that's seen to.'

They were off again. Mrs Finch walked, as before, with one hand on her palm-leaf hat, as though it might blow off at any moment, and the other thumbed under the strap of a string shoulder-bag. She had long legs and a brisk, loping stride and, even though he carried nothing, Finn was pushed to keep pace with her. He felt easier now that the last items connecting him with his true identity and Leander had been destroyed. There was the looming sense of a destination.

'Where are we headed?'

'Some outlying villages have been flooded,' Mrs Finch said. 'Hundreds of homes are uninhabitable, if they haven't been swept away altogether. It's dreadful.'

Finn waited to see where he fitted into this.

She pointed ahead along the track. 'There's an emergency encampment for the displaced another half hour from here – Tent City, they call it. We'll put you up there tonight while we find you a guide.'

'A guide?'

'We don't lack sympathisers round here. The Government has syphoned off regional aid for so long they've created two gen-erations of the disaffected.' Then, as if alarmed by a sudden thought, she said: 'Did they take your money?'

He caught on to what she meant. 'No, just the pack. Clothes and that.'

'Only, you'll need to pay.'

'This isn't where I'm staying, then? I mean, long-term.'

'We have to sneak you another few kilometres up the coast,' Mrs Finch said. The only safe way was by foot, but the jungle kicked in again after the cane plantation and he would need

116

someone with local knowledge – one of the resettled villagers – to escort him. 'It's only a day's walk, if you don't get lost. Maybe a day and a half. And then, a boat ride.'

'A boat? To where?'

'To the island.'

Walking with Hano

The guide was eating breakfast with his family outside the tent. The woman and the two children paused at Finn's approach, but the man went on. Bowl raised to his chin, scooping gloop into his mouth with a plastic spoon. Some kind of fish porridge, by the smell. It looked like wallpaper paste. There was an odour of wood smoke from the embers of a fire. A pot hung above the fire, and an oilskin canopy had been rigged up to keep the rain off. It was wide enough for them all to shelter while they ate. The air was musty, moist, freighted with sacks of slate-black cloud; dawn had broken, though you wouldn't have known. It was cool, now, but soon the humidity would kick in. At a gesture from the man, his wife filled a bowl for Finn; he thanked her and said no, he wasn't hungry. They seemed offended and he wondered if he should've accepted; but he'd already breakfasted with Mrs Finch and, besides, the thought of eating that stuff . . . The woman divided the extra helping between the children and her husband. Hano, he was called. They'd been introduced the previous evening by Mrs Finch. She'd urged them to set off right away, but it had been close to nightfall by the time they tracked down someone willing to guide Finn into the rainforest for the sum on offer. Also, the man had been drinking. 'Come back in the morning,' he'd said.

Finn ached from a night on the floor of Mrs Finch's tent, just a groundsheet beneath him. No roll-mat, no sleeping bag, no pillow, nothing. His contact had fed him last night and again this morning, and then she'd gone. She hadn't said where or why, just wished him luck, then left. He felt abandoned and nervous among these people. There were hundreds of tents. It'd taken Finn a while to find his way back to Hano's and there had been a moment when he'd begun to panic, to wander, lost, among the columns of identical shelters as though trapped in a maze. In the end he had paid a boy to bring him here. Fuck sake, he needed to be guided to his guide. It was almost funny. Finn squatted under the canopy with the family. Hano asked for a cigarette. Finn gave him one from the pack and tapped out another for himself; they took turns to light up with a stick from the fire. The man finished his breakfast in silence. He put his bowl down. He said he wanted paying up front. Finn counted out the notes on to the straw matting by Hano's feet, though the man seemed entirely in-different to the fact. Smoking, watching his children eat. At another gesture from her husband, the woman gathered the cash, folding it into a pouch she wore on a beaded cord round her neck.

The silences were getting to Finn. He smiled at the children. They looked back at him with no expression. 'How old are they?'

Their mother pointed at the boy and girl in turn. 'Six, four.'

He noticed, then, that the woman was pregnant. She drew her shawl – actually a coarse brown blanket – tighter around her shoulders.

'Did you lose your home?' Finn said.

'This is our home.'

'I mean before. In the floods.'

Now it was Hano's turn to speak. 'The floods were six months ago.'

119

Finn thought about them, living in the tent for that long. He already knew from Mrs Finch that the man had no work – that he'd been employed in the cane fields but had been sacked for drunkenness, for brawling. He looked too small for that. Short and stringy and round-shouldered, his limbs out of proportion to his torso; the build of a chimpanzee. Hunched over the fire, pale faced, his chocolate-brown hair pasted back from his forehead. He too wore a blanket, but with a hole cut out so that it fitted over him like a poncho. Finn recalled the street guy, in his plastic poncho, taking a crap into a kerb-side bin the day of the medical. Was that really just – what? – two weeks ago? Less. It was as if a year had been condensed into a few days. There was a surreal quality to his life just now; each day, each stage of his journey, making less sense than the last and yet, added together, they somehow achieved their own logic.

'Come on,' Hano said. 'We must go.'

Finn was to be taken through the forest to a beach – a natural landing-point – where he would be met by one of the islanders and ferried across the strait. 'Smuggled across', was the phrase Mrs Finch had used. She'd set aside his questions about the island. 'One step at a time', she had told him. 'First, you have to get yourself to the beach.'

They walked all morning, him and Hano. The going was level, to begin with, as they skirted the last of the sugar plantations, then the track descended to a wooded creek before following it upstream. The steepening sequence of climbs hauled them up through dense overhanging scrub – rhododendron, Hano said – that protected the two men from the worst of the rain but soaked them in their own sweat. Finn's thighs were sore. On the tougher sections his breath came in jagged rips, like cloth being torn; Hano seemed less troubled, though now and then he'd cough and turn his head aside to fire a pellet of phlegm into the undergrowth. They paused only to share water from the canister the guide had brought, or to smoke Finn's cigarettes. They barely spoke. If Hano said anything, it was usually to name a plant or shrub or tree they passed, like this was a nature walk. He carried their provisions in a haversack, as well as a pair of binoculars round his neck; in his right hand, he held a machete. He used it as a walking stick on the steeper inclines, or to lop off any encroaching flora. Trailing along behind, Finn picked his way through the puddles, bogs and exposed tree roots. His boots were soon clogged with mud and he lost his footing repeatedly. Cursing, each time. Stumbling along the track in a series of fucks and shits. He was glad, now, not to have the burden of his backpack. Inside an hour, the path diminished almost to nothing, indiscernible from the animal runs that made a lattice in the rainforest's thick carpet. From time to time they startled small creatures or birds; Finn only caught a glimpse, a blur, the scuffle of their escape into the foliage, but his guide always put a name to whatever it was. The two men left the stream. Hano led them on a route so complex that, within minutes, Finn couldn't have retraced their steps to the point where they'd branched off. Here, the ground levelled again and they cranked up the pace. Then the descent; an hour, two. Punishing on the knees, the ankles. Finn was dumped on his arse a couple of times. At the foot of the decline, Hano called a halt beside a river – fifteen metres or so wide, greeny black with the reflection of the branches arched above. A distance downstream the current broke over rocks, but it moved slowly here and the surface was calm. Hot and aching and drenched in sweat, Finn imagined plunging in, clothes and all. He made do with kneeling at the edge, scooping water on to his face and neck.

The guide eased the haversack off. 'Let's eat.'

'We have to cross that?' Finn said.

'We'll eat first. Take a rest.' Hano sat on a rock and opened the bag, pulling out hard-boiled eggs, a thick gourd of pepperoni, and two lengths of raw sugar cane. He sliced up the sausage with a knife that he wore in a sheath at his waist.

'What do we do, swim? Build a fucking raft?'

The man handed Finn his share of lunch, and a hip flask of fluid that tasted of rum and burned your throat like ignited lighter fuel. 'It's not so deep,' he said.

They ate, they drank, they chewed on the cane till it was splintered and sucked dry of sweetness. They smoked. The pack was almost empty, but Finn hadn't supplied any of the food so he couldn't complain about doling out smokes to Hano. This was almost enjoyable, once you stopped; so long as you forgot about the walking still to come, and so long as you forgot that you didn't much care for the company. They lay on their backs on the damp earth, blowing smoke into a scrawl of midges above their faces. The moment was shared, intimate, though there was no intimacy between them; nothing Finn wanted to say to the other man or, it seemed, that he wanted to say to Finn. 'You act like you're this mysterious loner,' Lila had once told him. 'Like you have such low expectations of everyone else that you're happier with your own company – but what it is, is you have low expectations of yourself.'

Looking back, he saw that Lila had hung around way beyond the point where she'd begun to give up on him. Finn calculated the days since he'd left. She'd have moved out of Paladin by now. Had she twigged what he'd done? Had the IS tracked her down, questioned her? He wondered whether she was missing him, what she thought of him going on the run like that, and without telling her. Whether she'd be thinking about him all that much. Probably, she would. Two years was a big deal, no matter how bad things had got. You didn't just draw a line under someone. Probably, Finn had surprised her. Doing this. Lila would be in her new bedsit, or at work, or on a smoke break, thinking how Finn had managed to surprise her one last time. It was weird, the idea of Lila going on with her life back there – minus Finn, but otherwise pretty much as before. Living in the city. Working. Seeing her friends. Doing the things she did. Just days ago, he'd been with her. Now, they were so removed from one another he might've imagined her.

Fuck sake, and here he was with chimp-man.

He studied Hano: his red T-shirt, translucent with sweat; his perfectly hairless forearms, satiny, as if they'd been waxed or the skin itself was made of wax. His fuck-off expression. What was there between them? Two strangers shoved together by circumstance. Cash changes hands, they hike off into the jungle. Finn finished his cigarette. Jesus. Someone had to say something eventually or it would do his head in.

'How d'you know this forest so well?' Finn said.

Hano took a while to respond. 'Used to work for Mr Skins. Trapping.'

'Mr Skins?'

'Crocodile farmer.' The guide aimed a hand in the rough direction they were headed. 'His place is a few K from here.'

'And, what? You trapped *crocodiles*?' Finn sat up and looked around. He thought maybe they shouldn't be resting up beside a river.

The guide laughed. A piss-take laugh. 'Trapping for pelts. Meat. There's no crocs in the wild out here these days, just what Mr Skins raises in his pens.'

'Right.'

Finn watched a slick of algae drift downstream, towing debris in its tail: leaves, twigs, flower petals, the upturned husk of a beetle as big as a thumb, its legs busy in the air. A splash and the beetle was gone, taken by a fish.

Another long pause. 'I don't work for him no more.'

'How come?'

'The man picks you up, he drops you. Way he is.' Crocs

weren't the half of what Mr Skins was into, Hano said. His 'trading portfolio'. This was his domain, his jungle. 'You take a crap anywhere on this stretch of coast, Skins gets word before it hits the pan.' The guide spat. 'Probly, he knows what you ate that's in the crap.'

'Will he know about me?' Finn said. 'About you and me?'

'We better hope he doesn't.'

The time came to wade across. The water was thigh-deep but sluggish, easy underfoot. As soon as they reached the opposite bank, the guide removed his trousers, boots and socks and made Finn do the same. 'Leeches,' he said. On their legs, feet. Finn had one in the webbing between his biggest toes. Hano burned the things off one by one with a cigarette, leaving dots of pink skin where they'd attached themselves.

They made camp at dusk after a full afternoon's hike. It was only another hour or two to the landing place but night fell quickly here, Hano said, and this rainforest was no place to be trekking in the dark. Besides, the launch wouldn't be there till the next morning. Finn didn't care if the rendezvous was five minutes away, he was done in; he'd been half-asleep on his feet in the final stages of the walk and just wanted to stop. The guide brought out his poncho from the haversack, along with a blanket for Finn, and an oilskin sheet like the one they'd sheltered under at breakfast. This he fixed over a low branch as a simple tent, staked to the ground along the sides and open at both ends. He harvested ferns with the machete and spread them thickly on the floor of the makeshift shelter. They ate more of the eggs and pepperoni and shared the rum. Finn's legs twitched uncontrollably as he sat, shoving food into his mouth faster than he could swallow.

After they'd eaten, Hano took Finn to a lookout point on a ridge just along the trail from their camp. He pointed out the beach where Finn would be collected; it was dimly visible, way down below, in the gathering gloom. The only place accessible to a launch anywhere along this coastline, the guide said. Apart from Mr Skins' place. And *there* was the crocodile farm. Hano's outstretched arm drew Finn's gaze some distance to the north of the beach. Finn aimed the binoculars. The settlement gave up little detail; no sign of crocs, or people, or of any activity – just the vague grey blocks of buildings pinpricked with brightness. Huddled in a clearing, at the point where the forested slopes thinned and flattened out to meet the sea. The *ocean*. Finn refocused the binoculars. In the last light of the day, the water was the mauvey blue of a bruise, edged with white where it frayed against the shoreline. He hadn't reached the coast with Kurt, that time they ran away as kids, but he'd almost made it now. The thought would've choked him up, if he'd let it.

'Where's the island?' he said.

Hano showed him where to look. But there was nothing to see. Out to sea, a long, thick strand of mist obscured everything.

'In the morning, when that lifts,' Hano said. 'Then you'll see the island.'

All the same, Finn trained the bins in the direction where the island lay. He tried to imagine what awaited him out there. His new life, for however long he was to remain a fugitive. His *wife*. His new identity. Finn wanted to ask if Hano had known the guy, but to talk of Roop was to reveal too much. He hadn't told the guide his real name, let alone the false one. Mrs Finch had disclosed next to nothing; just that the real Roop was dead and Finn should get himself to the beach and let the islanders handle the rest. The network hadn't used them before, but they were good people.

It hadn't occurred to him that 'Roop' would be dead; that he would be taking the place of a dead man. It should've been obvious but, until now, he hadn't given the man much thought, except in relation to himself. Dead at twenty-six. Same as Kurt.

A final night in the jungle, a hike downhill at daybreak. He wished he could make out the place through the fog, but there was nothing, not the shadow or hint of land. It had stopped raining at last. Finn's sweat-soaked shirt, and his trousers – still damp from the river crossing – clung cold to his skin. The sky had cleared and was already filling with stars, but the moon was still low, a shred of clipped thumbnail.

'We'll catch some sleep,' Hano said, 'then I'll take you down.'

Finn woke with rain on his face, cold and stiff, itching from the leech wounds and from where he'd been bitten to fuck by mosquitoes, and to a mixed-up looseness in his guts. In his still-sleepy state, it was these things that seemed to have woken him. Only, someone was tugging at his waist, trying to turn him on his side. How could it be time to get up when it was still dark, pitch-black, and why was Hano pulling at him like this? And how come it was raining directly on to his face? The tugging stopped. Finn tried to wake properly, to make his brain work. Pushed himself up to a sitting position. No blanket. He reached out a hand, but the place beside him on the bed of ferns was empty. A sound of movement nearby.

'Hano?'

There was a torch. Where was the torch? He heard more sounds, saw a flicker of light a little way off and managed to stumble to his feet and move towards it. Shaky legs. No tent. The oilskin canopy was gone. He called Hano's name again but got no reply. Then, as he closed in on the light, he collided with something, someone, and the light shifted and he saw that the shape was Hano. Hano, packing up the gear.

'Hano.'

That was when Finn saw the glint from the blade of a knife. He didn't see the man's hand move or feel the knife go in, though both must've happened, because Finn took a blow to the side of his stomach and, as he doubled up on the ground, clutching at himself, his shirt was already wet.

126

Life without Roop

After eating her share of the lunch Amver had brought, Bryher set the rest aside for her patient, then went back upstairs to change his dressing. He didn't seem in as much discomfort, so she worked less tentatively. He appeared more settled altogether. There was no evidence that the infection was easing, though. Perhaps he had simply slipped into a deeper phase of sleep, where the pain couldn't quite reach him. An awkward, messy job, even so, and by the end she wondered if she had more honey on her hands than he had in his wound. She rolled him on to his back once more and saw that he had the beginnings of an erection. Bryher glanced at it before replacing the sheet. The sight of his cock, stirring and twitching beneath the thin white cotton, made her smile. Once, when she had found Roop spark out on his back like this, she had fondled him, then taken him in her mouth while he continued to sleep (or pretended to; when she'd raised her head she saw that, although his eyes were shut, he was trying not to betray a grin). For a while after this, they would take turns to feign sleep during the other's love-making.

Bryher left the Incomer and went to the bathroom to wash her hands.

It was good to be nursing again. Good simply to be busy, to have a framework of tasks to complete through the day and, along with that, a sense of purpose. The others had exempted her from communal work in the weeks after Roop's accident; nothing had been said, but she was conscious of being given time: time to mourn, and to be by herself. She had been grateful, at first. But Bryher had begun to feel that time – and how she filled it – was part of the problem. There must be more to life without Roop than this cycle of grieving and introspection. She would have preferred to work in the flower fields, but the picking season was still a way off. So, lately, she had assumed responsibility for the kelping. Working alone, at her own insistence. Each day, in the week before the Incomer came, Bryher had gathered the weed that washed up at Gibbet Cove, just across from the cottage, then, ranging further afield, at The Strand and Long Strand. She'd spread her harvest in the sun and, once it was dry, hauled it in batches across the island to be burned in the stone-lined pit on Whin Hill. Strenuous toil that left her tired, filthy, foul-smelling and aching all over. Her palms were chafed red by the salt. But Bryher relished the work. Especially, she loved being on Whin Hill, despite the stench of smouldering kelp that would hang a pall over the place for days. Tending to the fire, sitting in the sunshine among the heather and brightly flowering gorse, the breeze in her face, watching the magnificent ocean rollers crash on to the rocks below. The waves, with their immense fetch, had journeyed 3,000 kilometres before striking this land where she lived. Given how Roop died, the scene might have been tough to bear; but, as she had always done, she found it hypnotic, exhilarating. And, sometimes, she'd almost forget to scan each incoming wave for a glimpse of something that might be him.

Whin Hill had been one of their places. Whin Hill, the beach at South Bay, the flat, sun-baked rocks above The Shoot. Gibbet

Cove, of course. Back on the mainland they'd lived in the interior, in a small town that served as a commuter dormitory for a much larger city. They'd worked in that city: she, at the hospital; he, at a timber yard. The nearest coast was a day's journey away and, though they'd both had fondly remembered childhood holidays at the seaside, Bryher and Roop had never been there together. In their early weeks here, it was like being children all over again: the sand, the rocks, the sea, the long days of sunshine. When they weren't making the cottage habitable, or learning the working routines of the community, the pair of them would take off, exploring the island. Finding discreet places to make love, mostly.

'Isn't this all you ever dreamed of?' Roop said to her, one time on Whin Hill, in their first week, when they'd gone there for sex and then stayed to watch the sunset.

'Yes,' she said.

She supposed it was. At least, the island was so different, so much better, than anything she had known in her life up to that point that Bryher had to believe it was what she would have dreamed of for herself, if she'd dreamed of anything. But Roop was the true dreamer. While Bryher had always been open to new experiences, to movement rather than stasis, she hadn't come here in pursuit of an idyll but in search of one. On Whin Hill, on the beach at South Bay, with Roop, it was quite possible to believe she'd found just that. Now that she could only visit these places without Roop, Bryher had expected them to be ruined for her – desolate, desperately sad, lonely spots, too painful with memories for her to tolerate them. That the whole island would be tainted in this way. But that hadn't happened. Whenever she revisited the places that were special to her and Roop, they remained so for her; she loved them, still. Idealised them, still. Her desolation was located elsewhere; it was located in the void which Roop had once filled.

Today, Liddy was burning the kelp. Even from this side of the island, with Whin Hill obscured from view, Bryher could see the smoke accumulating in the air high above the pit. As she recalled it, the sunset up there that time with Roop hadn't been all that spectacular or beautiful; it was just that, in their previous lives, neither of them had ever made a point of watching the sun go down . . . and here they had done.

To go on here without him. She wasn't sure she could.

Until the news of the Incomer's imminent arrival, Bryher had more or less decided to give up. To quit. She'd confided this to Sholo, late one evening – leaving her cottage for the first time in many days to walk to the white house on the point beneath South Hill, where Hobb and Sholo had made their home these past thirty years. In fact, it had been the middle of the night. Bryher had apologised; she'd had no idea of the hour.

'Come in,' Sholo had said; smiling, sleepy and rumpled in her nightgown.

The older woman made tea and they sat on the veranda, talking by the light of a candle-lamp. Sholo was a first settler, a matriarch, a woman who might have been born the age she was now. Bryher had known not to expect some platitude about grief being no state in which to make a life-altering decision; known, too, that Sholo would do more listening than speaking. She tended to pose questions, rather than supply answers, in the belief that the solution to a problem was often already there, within you, if only it could be brought out. As a result, the islanders believed her to be wise; or believed themselves to be wiser for her company, which Bryher thought amounted to pretty much the same thing.

'Do you want to leave?' Sholo had asked. 'Or do you want to give up?'

Of course, that was the essence. Without Roop, a pointlessness had set in – a weary lethargy in which nothing held any meaning or interest for her, so that Bryher succumbed to a sense of giving up. Giving up on the island, specifically. For what was the point of loving this place without him? But a more general giving up, too – a giving up on *everything*; in her lowest moments, even her own life. Not that she wanted, actually, to kill herself . . . just not to have to endure the act of living, getting through the hours and the days. Somehow, and despite the lack of any desire to return to the mainland, this 'giving up' had mutated into the thought of leaving the island. Then, talking to Sholo – considering Sholo's question – Bryher saw that giving up on the island wasn't the same as leaving it, any more than giving up on life was the same as suicide. Giving up was a state of mind, a gradual process; whereas departure was an abrupt physical act. Sometimes, for a while, a person's existence settled uneasily and, seemingly, irreconcilably between the two. Until they left. Or until they found a reason to stay.

The night Bryher sat on the veranda with Sholo, neither woman had known about the Incomer, or even that the island would offer itself up as a refuge – that turn of events wouldn't be set in motion for another week. So, in deciding to wait, to allow her thoughts to settle, Bryher hadn't changed her mind because of the Incomer. But, now he was here, dependent on her, his presence was a timely diversion. Not a reason to stay, as such, but a reason to stay a little longer. In doing so, she might come to feel less like giving up. She didn't know. But it was possible. In the meantime she would keep busy, assemble blocks of distraction to span the gap between Roop and no-Roop. There had been the kelping, now a patient to care for. There was a new boat to build and, if she was still here by then, the flower-picking. There were the rest of the islanders to reacquaint herself with, or not, now that she was 'Bryher' rather than one half of 'Bryher-and-Roop'. There would be other work; maybe other places and people one day. But these were external factors. Roop was internal. One of the things nursing had taught her was that physical wounds, like emotional ones, heal from the inside out.

★   ★   ★

Amver returned in the afternoon with the extra jars of honey. Once the girl had gone, Bryher set about making up a bed for herself on the living-room floor, using cushions and spare bedding. It would do. She slept poorly enough in her own bed these days so it made little difference where she lay herself down. In any case, it would be hours before she would be exhausted enough at least to attempt to sleep. She considered what she might do between now and then. There was the usual work to do about the cottage, her supper to be made and eaten, clothes to be mended, a book to read, if she managed to concentrate. Her routine. A list of activities to prolong the point where she would have to go to bed. Night-times were the worst – the long, dark hours when the lack of Roop was most acute, dragging her in and out of sleep and breaking up the night into hallucinatory fragments of wakeful and stupefied disturbance. Since his death, she had been reduced to a near-constant daze of fatigue in which she craved sleep all day long only to fail to sleep for more than a few hours each night. But it wasn't even dusk yet and she had to find the energy from somewhere to get herself through the evening.

With her makeshift bed in place, Bryher decided to run herself a bath. She reeked of honey and the thought of a long soak appealed to her. As a girl she'd always preferred baths to showers, loving to be enveloped in water so deep it lapped at the rim of the tub and as hot as she could bear it. She had loved to close her eyes and set herself afloat. Yes, she would do that. She would bathe like she used to when she was a child. But she never made it as far as the bathroom. Halfway up the stairs – perhaps it was the tread of her footsteps that brought this about – she heard something from the bedroom. Bryher paused, unsure what it was at first and listening for the sound to come again. When it did, she was sure: it was his voice. The Incomer had woken and was calling out.

Mr Skins

If he could just make it to the beach, he'd be all right. If he made it to the beach, the launch would come and he'd be taken to the island and they'd fix him up. He hadn't lost too much blood. Not as much as he might've done. His clothes were soaked, but most of that happened right afterwards; once he'd patched himself up, the bleeding had slowed. Some seepage, that was all. What he'd done, initially, was rip his T-shirt into strips, pack one piece into the wound and hold it there with his hand. But as soon as he started walking he couldn't maintain the pressure. So he plugged it with mud, instead, used longer strips of the T-shirt round his midriff as a bandage and kept the whole thing tight with the belt from his trousers. The mud gradually dried and, held fast by the makeshift strapping, it reduced the blood loss almost to nothing. All Finn had to do, then, was find his way down through the jungle to the landing place.

The beach had been obvious from the lookout point the night before. But, at first light, as soon as he began the descent he lost sight of the coast, the ocean, the sky itself at times, so dense was the canopy of branches. In some places there were too many tracks to choose from, in others none at all and he would have to wade through the undergrowth as best he could until he came upon another trail. Other times, Finn had to retrace his steps: one path ended at a steep gorge; a second had been obliterated by a landslip. All the while, the pain in his side; no food, no water, tired, weak from the blood he'd lost, no guide, no sense of direction in a landscape without streets, no sense of time (his watch was gone, peeled from his wrist in the night). No cigarettes, even; Hano had taken those too. Finn stumbled on, figuring he'd be OK so long as he kept heading downhill. Sooner or later, this would bring him to the coast. Whether the boat would be there, whether it would've waited for him, he had no idea. But he had to get to the beach. If he stayed here, in the rainforest, he would die. If he tried to retrace the route back to the refugee camp, he would get lost and die; and even if he made it, what then? Confront Hano? Fight him? Force him to hand back the money? Hano had fucked him over. Finn was alone now and if he didn't make it to the beach, to the island, he was fucked altogether.

It must have taken him more than half a day to reach the ocean. Finn emerged at last from the forest into an inlet where a narrow river oozed into the sea across an expanse of mudflats. The wound had reopened and blood drained into his trousers. All he wanted was to stop, to rest a while. But this wasn't the place, the landing point. This wasn't the beach he'd seen from the ridge. He must've over-shot, or undershot, and now he'd have to set off again along the shore, if that was possible, except he had no idea which direction, or how far it was, or whether he'd even manage another step – because, right now, it was all he could do to remain upright. Then Finn heard a shout behind him. He turned to see two men a hundred metres or so along a track that led inland beside the creek. Both wore blue waterproofs that gleamed with the rain. One was talking into a radio handset. The other was aiming a rifle in Finn's direction.

★   ★   ★

There was a collection of A-frame buildings, huts and sheds around an open area of dirt and worn grass. The main structures were roofed with palm-thatch; two of them, Finn saw, stood on stilts at the marshy edges of the compound, joined to the central clearing by boardwalks. One building looked unfinished. The reptile enclosures – five in all – were side by side along the rear perimeter, hard up against the high chain-link fence. The pens were sunken behind log barricades that kept the crocodiles from view as Finn was escorted into the heart of the settlement; but he heard them, thrashing in the water, and their pig-like grunts and snorts. And he could smell them: a feral stench of fish, blood and excrement that even the steady rain failed to flush away.

Two mongrel dogs fell in step beside him, as though he was taking them for a walk. Across the clearing a pack of children, ranging from toddlers to nearly-teens, stopped what they were doing and watched him in silence. Shorts, T-shirts, bare feet. One of them – a girl in a sleeveless top smeared taut over the beginnings of a pair of breasts – was holding a stick; she'd been scoring lines in the dirt to form a grid, each child standing quite still in its own square. Apart from the youngest, a boy of maybe two or three. He was squatting, crapping on to the ground near her feet. The girl gave him a crack on the shoulder with her stick that set him howling, then returned her attention to Finn as if nothing had happened. Eleven, twelve. Hard to tell. Her naked arms were sleek with rain. She flashed him a look that, from a girl a few years older, would've been a come-on, though with no guarantee you'd get to have her. On her young face, the expression was more like a petulant smirk of disdain.

Finn was the first to look away.

He was taken to the biggest of the buildings. Dizzy, clutching at his side; so nauseous he thought he might puke. He just wanted to sit down, to do anything other than walk. The escort, the one with the radio, showed him into a huge lounge that resounded with their footsteps on the bare floorboards. The man wore shades, despite the weather, and, beneath his cagoule, a yellow vest bearing the crest of a basketball team. He was tall enough to play, but had the build of a weightlifter. He looked bigger for being indoors, clumsier. Finn took in the room. Wicker chairs, wicker couch. Bare whitewashed walls that, even with no sunlight, were too bright to look at. A ceiling fan the size of an aircraft propeller distressed the foliage of a dozen or more potted plants positioned around the room and chilled Finn with his own sweat.

'Sit down,' the man said. 'I'll go fetch the boss.'

Finn sat in one of the chairs and closed his eyes. When he reopened them two people were sitting opposite him, side by side on the couch, as though they had been there all along. Older man, younger woman; mid-fifties and early thirties, so far as Finn could tell. The escort was standing guard over by the window.

'Thank you, Rudy,' the older man said. Rudy made to leave, but was stayed in the doorway. 'Oh, and next time,' his boss said, 'a plastic sheet, please.'

He indicated the chair where Finn sat, already stained with blood.

'Yes, sir. I should've thought.'

'Even a couple of towels would have been better than nothing.'

The escort apologised a second time and was allowed to go. Once the door was pulled to, the boss returned his attention to Finn. He started to remark on the difficulty of removing bloodstains from wicker furniture, then – correcting himself, excusing his manners – broke off to perform the introductions. 'Mr Skins, Mrs Skins.' They were nothing like he'd imagined them, from what Hano had told him of the crocodile farmer. He hadn't imagined a Mrs Skins at all. As for her husband, he'd pictured – well, he wasn't sure . . . someone big, brutish; someone shabby and tough, coarsened by the farming of crocodiles and a life hemmed in by jungle and the ocean-battered coast. Someone more like Rudy, the escort. Not a man, a couple, like this. So slender. So elegant. Two slender, elegant people. Mr Skins in a cream-coloured linen suit, clean and neatly pressed, a white shirt unfastened at the throat, beige moccasins and straw panama. He smoked a cigarette as thin and black as a strip of liquorice and which smelled of perfume, each bluish exhalation feathered to nothing by the fan's downdraught. Mrs Skins – tanned, artificially blonde, smoking a regular cigarette – sat beside her husband, her candy-striped cotton dress ridden right up. Her legs were the colour of caramel. Unshaven. Not as hairy as a man's, but patterned with dark-blonde down all the same. Their hirsuteness was surprising, in a context of studied perfection. Finn looked at them, then took care not to look again. Her legs were ruptures in the fancy-dress-ball picture of colonial impeccability the couple presented.

'And *you* are?'

Mr Skins' question made him start. Of course, he should introduce himself. Finn gave his name as Roop. At least he still had the fake ID card, tucked away in a compartment of his otherwise empty money-belt. No one spoke for a moment. Skins allowed himself a small, neat smile.

No longer smiling, the crocodile farmer said: 'Let's start again, will we?'

Finn looked at him. 'What?'

'You are wounded.' The man gestured at Finn. 'Quite possibly seriously. I imagine you're anxious to have that attended to. So,' Mr Skins drew on the thin black cigarette, exhaled, 'we resume at the point in the conversation where I say "And *you* are?", and you say . . . well, something other than "Roop".'

Finn opened up the pocket on the money-belt. 'Look, here's my . . .'

'Please.' Mr Skins raised a hand. 'The chair is ruined – there is nothing we can do to save the chair – but while you are still

137

bleeding it makes no sense for us to waste time passing a dead man's identity card back and forth between us. Does it?'

Finn stowed the card away again. Fell silent.

'You don't wish to divulge your name,' Mr Skins said at last. 'I respect that. How about this, then: instead of your name, you tell me how you came to be here?'

How much to tell, was the problem. Finn recalled what Hano had said about the crocodile farmer knowing who crapped where on his territory; and, the way he'd seen through the Roop thing, you had to be careful what you told him. This was the last place he'd wanted to end up, but here he was. Stranded. Cleaned out. Injured, like the man said. He didn't have any choice but to seek his help. For sure, he didn't want to antagonise him – make an enemy of him – by being caught out in another lie. But he didn't want to compromise the network, or the people who were waiting to shelter him, any more than he had to. So, he told Skins this: he was a draft-dodger; he was heading through the rainforest to meet a boat; his guide robbed him, knifed him, and left him for dead; he'd managed to haul himself here.

'Your guide,' Mr Skins said, when Finn had finished. 'Who was he?'

Finn hesitated, but saw no harm in revealing his name. He certainly owed the bastard nothing. 'Hano,' Finn said. 'He told me he used to work for you.'

'That would be an overly generous description of his contribution while he was with us.' Mr Skins finished his cigarette. Even though an ashtray rested at his elbow on the arm of the couch, he passed his wife the stub – carefully, so that neither of them would burn their fingers – and she extinguished it for him in her own ashtray. Still, she hadn't spoken. Mr Skins, again: 'You referred to a boat, I believe.'

'A launch, yeah. It was meant to pick me up along the coast from here.'

138

'And take you where?'

'I don't know.'

'And. Take. You. Where?' Mr Skins had leaned forward a little. His voice was calm, not noticeably harder than the first time he asked the question. It was the way he spaced the words.

'An island,' Finn said.

'An island.' The man reclined again, with another of those small smiles. He tipped the hat back on his head. He might have been mocking himself for failing to work this out sooner; but, from his tone, Skins seemed to be congratulating Finn for avoiding another, futile, evasion. '*Of course*, an island. Roop lived on an island . . . you are passing yourself off as Roop. A simple enough deduction.'

Finn eased back into his own chair, shivering yet sticky with sweat.

'The poor man is *ill*, darling.' This was Mrs Skins, her first words.

Her husband said: 'You're quite right, we should have that injury looked at. What am I thinking of?' Then, to Finn: 'My wife has an eye for the – what would you call it? – the *human dynamics* of a situation, whereas I'm afraid I tend to be distracted by the logistics. The practicalities. Would you say that was true?'

The question was addressed to Mrs Skins. She agreed that it was true.

'We complement one another,' Skins said. 'Don't we?'

'Yes.'

'That dress is rather fetching on you, my dear.'

Mrs Skins smiled. Twelve years of marriage, Mr Skins said, and he still had the capacity to amuse his wife. Throughout this exchange they hadn't so much as glanced at one another or taken their eyes from Finn. Skins continued to study him, as he drew his wife's hand on to his lap and held it. 'Don't ever assume, *Roop*, that this essential difference in our natures makes one of us more or less stupid than the other.'

139

It was a double act. Finn, spaced out and close to fainting, was the one-man audience at a bizarre piece of experimental theatre. The Skins chose this moment to sip simultaneously from glasses of what looked like iced lime cordial that Finn hadn't even noticed were there. Then, as if synchronised, they set the drinks back down on their respective occasional tables. Mrs Skins' armpits were unshaven, too, Finn saw. The hairs were tacky with perspiration. Darker than the hair on her legs; almost black. Finn shut his eyes, then opened them again. They poured him a drink as well from a large jug (where had the jug appeared from?) but, despite his thirst, one tentative sip – along with the acidic scent of the lime – and he felt nauseous. What he craved more than anything was a cigarette. But they hadn't offered him one.

Finn's injury, the need to attend to it, had already been forgotten it seemed. A lull settled on the conversation, punctuated by the creak of wicker, the fan's rhythmic clatter and the sounds of children playing outside. One of the dogs barked excitedly, then there was a yelp followed by a diminishing sequence of whimpers. An image of the girl came to Finn; her sulky expression. She was the Skins' daughter, he realised – the resemblance between the girl and her mother was unmistakable. Not just in their looks. They shared an air of performance – a sense of their watchability – along with a couldn't-give-a-fuck attitude to the fact of being watched. Fake or genuine, it was hard to tell. Different from the man himself. With Skins, you – not him – were the one under scrutiny. Under his gaze, you felt knowable; that you'd never know him as well as he'd know you. There was something almost paternal in his manner that scared Finn and, at the same time, made him feel safe. Cold and warm, like the room. Like his own skin. He had detected this, too, in Hano, when the guide spoke of his former boss: respect and fear, both in the mix. He had seen it in Rudy, when the escort was reprimanded for letting Finn bleed on the chair.

'You would like me to get you across to the island, I imagine?' Skins said.

Finn swayed in his seat under a sudden wave of exhaustion. With the glare from the walls, he could barely keep his eyes open. His trousers were so wet now he might've pissed himself. Spreading his hands in a gesture of surrender, he said: 'I'm cleaned out, Mr Skins. I've no way of paying you.'

The man clicked his tongue, as if Finn had disappointed him with a crude or inappropriate remark. 'What do I say about money, my dear?'

'You say it's for buying me clothes, shoes and perfume. And for having my hair stylist helicoptered in when required.'

Mr Skins gave his wife a sideways glance; beaming, affectionate. He might've been interviewing her on a daytime-TV talkshow. 'What *else* do I say about money?'

She unlocked her gaze from Finn's, at last, to look at her husband. 'You say: "Money is life-sustaining, but should never be mistaken for life itself."'

'For life itself. Exactly. For life itself, Roop.'

The compound's medic cleaned his wound, put stitches in. Then they let him sleep for a while. Finn had reckoned on a guest room, but Mr Skins got his wife to show him to another of the buildings – the unfinished one Finn had noticed earlier. It was to be a suite of offices, she told him. The outside was done, but for the veranda and the steps down to the boardwalk. Cinder-blocks were stacked up to the door for now. Inside, the lights and ceiling fan worked, and there was a basin to wash in, only no hot water just yet. At least the toilet had been plumbed. Desks, PCs, chairs and filing cabinets, still flat-packed, boxed or bubble-wrapped, were stacked against the walls. Reminders of Finn's old job. Which wasn't so old, but could've been from another lifetime or from another person's life. It smelled of dust, in here, and of packaging. There were bars at the windows, as there were in all the buildings. His bed was a rectangle of yellowish foam insulation sheet, left over from the build.

He was woken after what could only have been a couple of hours. Mrs Skins, again. She'd brought him food: a bowl of boiled rice, bananas, green tea. A change of clothes too. Lurid orange boxers, socks, T-shirt, jeans. None of them especially clean, or quite his size, but an improvement on the bloodstained ones he was wearing and which the crocodile farmer's wife would arrange to be taken away and burned.

'I'm sorry about what happened earlier,' she said.

'What did happen?'

'My husband.'

At the time Mrs Skins had seemed integral to whatever game her husband was playing, so she surprised him by distancing herself from that. He didn't want to get drawn into taking sides. 'You're feeding me,' Finn said. 'I've had my wound treated, and I've got somewhere to rest up. You and Mr Skins have nothing to apologise for.'

'And the wasp trapped in a jar is grateful for the smear of jelly.'

Finn looked at her. 'I'm sorry, Mrs Skins, I don't know what that means.'

'Ignore me. I'm unused to visitors.' The woman lit a cigarette and, taking in the room with the sweep of an arm, said she hoped he wouldn't be too uncomfortable. Without waiting for an answer, she said: 'Yesterday you were in the rainforest, today you're here, tomorrow – who knows? – you might be some-where totally different.'

From her delivery, she might've added: *I do envy you that.* But she didn't, she simply let the words trail off on an out-breath of smoke. His food, his tea, were going cold. He wished she'd leave so he could eat, then sleep some more; Mrs Skins, though, showed no sign of going. It was as if she was prolonging their encounter. Maybe he was sport to her: a new plaything for her to toy with; but something in her manner, her mood, told him different. She seemed sad. Sad for him, but also sad for herself. Not that staying here with him appeared to be cheering her up – if anything, the woman was making herself more miserable. She took another deep draw on her cigarette.

'Hano stole my smokes, too,' Finn said, as the fumes reached him.

She shook her head. 'He tests me.'

'What?'

'Why we're here. He wants to see if I'll fuck you.' She'd moved over to the window and was standing with her back to him, staring out in the direction of the main dwelling. 'He has convinced himself that's what I do to entertain myself in this place: fuck people. Men. The men who work for him. Men like you.'

'I don't work for him,' Finn said.

She turned to face him. 'Everyone works for Mr Skins.'

Finn scratched his throat. Sweat rash. He hadn't shaved since – when? – since the morning of the day those kids stole his pack. He chanced a wisecrack.

'If we're going to fuck, Mrs Skins, I could use a shower first.'

She looked like she was deciding whether to be amused or insulted. In the end she chose to ignore the remark. Withdrawing from the window, the crocodile farmer's wife patrolled the periphery of the room, smoking, slowly circling Finn at its centre, as if defining the space that was to be allocated to him. Moving like a catwalk model, or like her idea of one. Finn stifled a yawn. He needed to eat, to sleep, to be alone. To smoke, for fuck sake. The effort of talking, sparring like this, was doing him in.

'Where are you from?'

'The Capital,' he said.

She made a face. 'And you're . . . what? A politico? A coward?

143

What?' She drew on the cigarette again. 'We have a couple of our chaps serving out there just now,' she said. 'My husband may well arrange for you to be introduced to their wives. The little children they've left behind.'

Finn said nothing, unsure if her note of disapproval was for him or Mr Skins.

'He imagines the dirt wouldn't bother me,' Mrs Skins said, after a pause. 'The *stink*. When I go back, he'll kiss me – just to see if he can smell you on me.'

'Look . . .'

Gesturing at the door to the restroom, Mrs Skins said: 'Anyway, there's just the washstand, here.'

She seemed genuinely puzzled by the need to spell this out. She'd shown him the basin, hadn't she? What didn't he understand about the washing facilities? As if, from the moment he'd made his remark about needing a shower, they had discussed nothing else. Finn let it slide.

'I'm afraid I can't let you have one,' Mrs Skins said.

A cigarette, she meant. She drew a shape in the air with hers. He was aware that he'd been watching her smoke as she circled the room. 'Why not?' Finn said.

'Under strict orders. "No cigarettes for our guest." '

The woman had stopped now and was standing in the middle of the room, close to Finn, facing him. He asked why Mr Skins would do that, and she said it was 'another of his little tests'. A test for her: would she let him have a cigarette?; a test for him: how would he cope without one? She hooked a loose strand of hair behind one ear. All the while she'd been in the room, Finn had been aware – they both had, for sure – that he was trying hard not to stare at her armpits, trying not to imagine what it would be like to push his tongue into the hairs there. This awareness settled on them now that Mrs Skins had drawn to a halt. No more than a step apart, they studied each other in silence for what seemed like minutes but could've been only a few seconds. She might have been daring him to touch her, or daring herself to touch him.

'I'll do what I can for you,' the woman said, finally, stepping away from him and moving towards the door. The breaking of a spell. Before he had time to respond, she added: 'But, essentially, you have two options in this place: you can contradict my husband . . . or you can do as he says.'

He was woken, the second time, by one of the security team. Mr Skins wanted to see him, the man said. It was late afternoon, Finn reckoned. The light in the compound softened by the easing of the rain; chalky, tinged with green from the encroaching jungle. Looking at the sky – more white than grey – it was possible to believe in a sun behind all that cloud. The puddles were the colour of aluminium foil. Now that the downpour had ceased a treacly heat had moved in; Finn, his side aching, groggy with unspent sleep, sweated as he was taken to meet his host.

The crocodile farmer was standing on an elevated walkway at the front of the reptile enclosures, two men at work alongside him. The men were naked apart from shorts and flip-flops; Skins was still in his cream linen suit, but wore a plastic sack over each foot, gripped beneath the knee with rubber bands. One of the workers was hauling baskets of fish on to the walkway from a trailer; the other, lifting each new basket in turn on to the balustrade and tossing the fish in handfuls into the first of the pens. Finn recognised him now, this second man: Rudy, minus the basketball vest but still wearing the shades. The two dogs were skulking around the trailer, lapping at the blood that spilled from the baskets; no sign of the girl, or the other children. Finn saw that one of the dogs was pregnant. He climbed the steps. Skins also had plastic bags fastened over his hands, like the protective gloves of a burns victim. Now and then, at some unspoken signal, Rudy would pass a single fish to his boss, who'd spin it over the log barricade much as a knife-thrower might flick a blade.

'They live to die,' Mr Skins said, beckoning Finn to join him. 'They're born in captivity, they breed in captivity, they live in captivity, they are killed in captivity.'

Finn looked down into the pen, and across at the adjoining ones. So many crocodiles in one place seemed impossible. Hundreds. Still as sculptures, except for where a cluster of fish detonated a small blast of activity. You could walk from one end of the enclosure to the other without touching the ground, stepping from croc to croc as though they were logs, if they would let you. Each pen had been landscaped along similar lines: a large central pond fed by a stream from a miniature waterfall, slabs of rock, earth mounds, patches of grass, a few trees, shrubs, some felled trunks, a strip of shingle beach and, in the water, a narrow sandbar, an island or two. The scene put Finn in mind of a prehistoric swamp. The crocodiles were strewn wherever there was space, or where there wasn't – overlapping, half-mounted on one another. They looked ancient. Extinct creatures restored to life in some zoological experiment. Arranged according to size, it seemed, with the biggest in the first enclosure and the smallest – babies, like overgrown lizards – in the furthest pen. Because of the fish, all the creatures in the first pen faced the front, their slotted yellow eyes fixed intently on the men on the viewing platform, as if in anticipation of an important announcement.

'How many are there?' Finn said.

'Two thousand,' Mr Skins said. 'Give or take.' He launched another fish; it disappeared into the pond, the water boiling briefly as the two nearest crocs disputed its retrieval. 'I don't let them get much beyond three years old.'

The quality of the skins deteriorated after that, he explained. You were paid by belly-width and suppleness, so you wanted them young and plump; the shooting and skinning was done here, he said, then the skins were shipped to a processing plant in the interior and on to specialist manufacturers. Handbags, purses, shoes, belts, boots, jackets, watch straps. He didn't wear crocodile himself; it brought him out in a rash.

'The meat, we feed to the ones who remain.' Mr Skins produced one of his smiles. It pushed creases into his cheeks, like brackets enclosing his mouth. 'They rather like it. A welcome change from fish, I imagine.' Anyone else would've looked ridiculous, his hands and feet bagged up, but not Mr Skins. He studied Finn. 'So tell me, what was your line of work before you vanished from the Government's radar?'

'Computers. Data processing.'

'I'm afraid I haven't the faintest idea what that is.'

'Me neither.'

They both laughed. Another volley of fish hit the back fence and dropped into the pen. 'Even their eating is geared to death,' Mr Skins said. 'They can't know that, naturally – and, even if they did, they would continue to eat. But how fortunate to live without the certainty of one's own death.'

Finn thought of Kurt. He wondered if his brother – at the end, in the shed, in the minutes before he lost consciousness – was certain of death; if there was a point when a background awareness of mortality, of a dateless, placeless, unnamed death, hardened to specific, imminent fact. *It's happening here. Now. Like this.*

Mr Skins' voice startled him. 'Do you have an urge to live, Roop? Or an urge not to die? Which is the stronger, would you say?'

'Aren't they the same thing?' Finn said.

'Ah, consequentially, yes. But surely you would agree that one is an impulse towards that which we desire, while the other is an impulse away from that which we dread.' They might've been discussing the type of music Finn preferred. 'In this *great escapade* of

147

yours . . . are you moving towards something or away from something?'

'It's more complicated than that,' Finn said, after some thought.

'Of course, of course.' Mr Skins nodded. 'We live in complex times.'

'Moving away, I guess.' Finn shrugged. 'The war, the draft. This Government. This fucking country.' More, even, than that: his job, his flat, the city. His mum. Kurt. Lila. Himself. He wasn't even 'Finn' any more. He pictured himself: a solitary figure on a road, running – but running backwards, looking only at what he'd left behind. 'If I'm moving towards something,' he said, 'I don't know what it is yet.'

Finn had to shift his weight from one foot to the other to ease the pain from the knife wound. He could feel the stitches tugging at his flesh.

'They're not like us.' Mr Skins gestured at the enclosure. 'The crocodile does not concern himself with the past, or the future – his preoccupation is the immediate present. Feeding, copulating, sleeping. Living for the moment. In many respects, it is an enviably uncomplicated mentality.'

'I saw something happen to someone,' Finn said. 'Someone who fought.' He felt childlike beside Mr Skins and the two men. His own voice sounded small – the voice of a young boy. 'It . . . freaked me. What it did to him.'

Mr Skins placed a hand in the centre of Finn's back, where the shoulder blades met; the plastic bag rustled as he massaged the spine, the ribs, the neck, the hard knots of muscle. Finn steadied himself against the pressure.

'My wife believes we should help you.'

Finn nodded.

'The *human dynamic*,' Mr Skins said. The massage ended; Skins took his hand away, let it hang at his side. 'Mrs Skins is a compassionate woman and I usually defer to her in matters of the heart. But, you see, I have little doubt that you tried to seduce her.' He nodded in the direction of the unfinished office suite. 'Tried to fuck her.'

Finn felt the jolt of what the other man said. Something physical, like a small electric shock. He looked back across the compound, as though he might catch sight of himself and Mrs Skins through the windows of the building, re-enacting the scene they'd played out there earlier in the afternoon.

'That isn't what happened,' he said.

'That's her position, too,' Skins said. 'But you must agree that my wife holds a particular appeal. No one can blame a man for failing to resist such a temptation.'

'I didn't hit on her, Mr Skins.'

'In any event, there is the whole question of the war and your act of desertion.' Skins seemed suddenly irritated by Finn's denial. 'For every young man who evades the draft, another is sent to die in his place.' He half-turned towards Finn. 'Of course, it isn't a simple matter of statistics – but you take my point?'

Finn searched for something else to say; something that wasn't pleading and pathetic and hard done by, or filled with his sudden flush of hatred for this man.

Skins cut in. 'As it happens, Rudy's brother is out there. Isn't that so, Rudy?'

The man paused in his work. 'Yes, sir. Marine Corps.'

'What do you think we ought to do with a draft-dodger, Rudy?'

Without waiting for a reply, the crocodile farmer signalled to the man hauling the baskets of fish out of the trailer. He stopped what he was doing and, with a snap of the fingers, coaxed one of the mongrels to heel. Grabbing it by the collar and one rear foot, he lifted it on to the walkway. Rudy took the dog and, quick and easy as tossing a sack of trash into a skip, flung it over the barricade. Finn went to shout: 'No', but the only sound he made was a gasp.

149

The dog landed on one of the crocodiles, splayed across its back, and the croc thrashed to one side to dislodge it. The mongrel stumbled to the ground, shook itself. Both creatures seemed unsure what had happened or what to do next. The dog, lean and mean-looking in the compound, appeared puny in there. A rack of skin, fur and stick-thin limbs. Its legs trembled and it started to whimper. But the crocodile – and the others near enough to catch on to the dog's sudden arrival – settled down again, indifferent. A half-turn of the head, a snort, a shifting of feet. Then, calm. But they were watching the dog, now, not the place where the fish came from. Finn, Mr Skins and Rudy watched as well; hushed, motionless. Finn, sick with something like excitement – so engrossed in seeing how things turned out that, even if he could've saved the dog, he wasn't sure he would've done. Slouching, mewing like a kitten, it picked its way to the barrier. Unmolested.

'They are baffled,' Mr Skins said. 'Since birth, they've eaten nothing but dead things. They have never had to kill for food. So this dog, this living creature, confuses them – their instinct, the genetic legacy of their species, tells them to kill . . . but the conditioned habits of their captivity tell them otherwise.' He placed his bagged hands on the balustrade, leaning forward to gaze down at the dog, directly beneath him. 'So, which message will win, d'you imagine? Hn, *Roop*?'

Finn didn't answer. But he began to believe the dog might escape.

The animal looked up – judging the height of the barricade, it seemed – then yapped, twice, as if asking the men for help. Maybe the barking did it, or the first, useless, jump – the frantic scuffle of claws against the logs. Maybe the crocs would have left the dog alone, if it hadn't made a fuss. Whatever. In a snarling explosion of ferocity the two closest to the dog attacked, catching it between them as it descended from a second leap. A set of jaws clamped

150

shut at either end, pulling the animal apart like a party cracker. Each crocodile withdrew with its spoils – a head, the hind legs – while the trunk and forelegs and paint splashes of blood and shit and viscera popped on to the ground. Momentarily, the forelegs pawed at the dirt, as if trying to drag the headless, partially amputated torso into one last jump. Then they stopped and twitched and became still. Other crocs moved in. When they'd finished, all that remained of the dog was a dull stain that the next rain would erase.

'You see, characteristically, my wife misses the bigger picture,' Mr Skins said. 'The practicalities.' Finn turned away to retch. 'You're upset. A little disgusted. But, and please forgive me for making such an assumption . . . but I suspect that, like me, once the dog was in there you longed to see it ripped asunder. A dog in a crocodile pit: that's a plot with one acceptable denouement. To have seen it escape unharmed – to have been denied violence – well, we'd have felt cheated, wouldn't we?'

Finn lifted his head, mopped his mouth on his sleeve. Deep breaths.

'Your situation is less straightforward, of course,' Mr Skins said. Rudy and his mate, meanwhile, resumed the feeding of the crocodiles as if the incident with the dog hadn't occurred. 'Come,' Skins said, 'I'll take you back.' The man continued his spiel as they descended from the walkway and crossed the compound. Finn's legs, like the mongrel's, shook with each step. 'The plot, in your case, is: draftee goes on the run. The resolution, in dramatic terms, requires that you succeed. You *escape*.'

'You talk like this is a movie,' Finn said. 'Like it's scripted.'

'My very point: the next page of your script is ours to write. You and me. Just a boat ride from here, there's a place for you: new home, new life. I have boats. I can have you taken there. I can make your new life possible.'

'Or you can have me killed.'

151

'Well, *killed*. You see, you're placing a literal interpretation on what happened back there in that pen. My little tableau.' Mr Skins had an arm round Finn's shoulders now and it was all he could do not to lean into the man for support. 'Let me suggest a metaphorical reading: the dog – domesticated, *safe* – being returned to the wild from whence it came.'

Finn saw then that Skins – a trader – would look to cash in on his good fortune at having a fugitive turn up on his doorstep. To keep Finn alive so that he could hand him over to Internal Security in return for the hefty reward on offer for the capture of deserters. The crocodile pit, for Finn, was the mainland; then jail, or the front line.

'If you turn me in,' he said, 'I'm as good as dead anyway.'

'Believe me, it isn't an ending I contemplate with relish,' Mr Skins said. 'Hero caught. Hero brutalised. Hero dies. Plot-wise, it is vastly inferior to the one I outlined just now – our tale of the hero's flight. So.' He sighed. 'What to do?'

They were back at the new office building. Finn couldn't wipe the image of the dog. He sat on the cinder-block stoop, head bowed, Skins standing beside him. He tried to picture the place, the island, just a boat ride away. But, at the point when it'd been dangled before him, this new life seemed more unattainable than ever.

'Don't help me,' Finn said, after a moment. 'Just let me walk away from here and fend for myself. Take my chances on the mainland.'

'Trouble is, I already have helped you. Provided you with shelter, medical aid, a place to recover from your ordeal in the jungle. And, look, more food.' Finn glanced up. The girl – the Skins' daughter – was approaching from the main house with a tray. 'Just by your presence here you have compromised me,' Mr Skins said, quieter now. 'Harbouring a wanted felon. A traitor, at that.'

Finn thought of the perimeter fence, the armed sentry; of what activities – besides croc farming – must be going on here to warrant such security. Sheltering a draft-dodger for a couple of days surely wasn't a big deal for an operator like Skins, he figured. But Finn didn't get to decide what was or wasn't a big deal just now.

The man was talking again. 'But the script – *our script* – says you escape. So that's what we must work towards. I'm going to need your help with this one, Roop. Between us, we have to come up with a happy ending.'

The girl was with them. She wore a bikini top and filmy batik sarong, her hair beaded and in braids. Despite her appearance, she didn't seem prematurely sexy to him, now. She seemed gawky. Uncertain of herself. A skinny, androgynous child dressed as a young woman, that was all. The girl, who'd stared him out when he first arrived, avoided his gaze this time, tilting her chin down so that the weighted cords of her hair screened her face. She bent to set the tray on the step. Fish soup, a thermos, a bowl of plain white rice with steam rising from it. As she straightened up again, he saw that she'd been crying.

'My eldest. Have you met?'

Finn said nothing, neither did the girl. She dipped her head again.

'The bitch is expecting her first litter,' Mr Skins said, watching his daughter rub angrily at her eyes as more tears came. For one appalling moment Finn thought he was referring to the girl. Then, with the sensation of iced water coursing through his stomach, he realised that he meant the second of the mongrels. And that the first – the one torn to pieces – had belonged to the crocodile farmer's daughter.

'So, don't be too upset on her account,' Skins said to Finn. 'She will have her choice of the puppies, and that little episode back there will soon be forgotten.'

*　　*　　*

Finn ate alone in his quarters, staring out through the bars at the window. The rain fell again. He had no appetite. His wound hurt like fuck; something was wrong in there – it was bulging, sore, the stitches weren't holding and he felt sweaty and feverish most of the time. Setting the food aside, he tried not to think about the pain. Or the dog. Or about this fucking place, or the girl, or what would happen to him.

He could die here.

Whatever Skins said about happy endings. What was to stop the man turning him in dead? The number on his chest would confirm it as the corpse of a dodger, and the crocodile farmer would have his bounty just the same. Or, if his wound got worse, became infected – probably, it already was – he could die anyway, stranded here, or in some prison cell where no fucker gave a shit whether he got treatment. Once Finn started to think like that, he couldn't stop himself. He imagined all kinds of things.

He imagined a policewoman calling on his mother, informing her that her son is dead. His mother is confused. Of course Kurt's dead, didn't the woman notice the flowers on the door? *No, not Kurt – your other son. Finn.* He was on the run from the draft and got shot by bounty hunters in a distant region of the country. She asks Finn's mother to come with her to identify the body. Finn pictured his mother, sobbing. *Not Finn as well. Not both of them.*

Fuck sake. Finn pushed away his own tears.

They kept him locked in. At daybreak and at dusk, he would be brought his rations. Usually one of the men brought his meals, but one morning the girl came and, the next evening, Mrs Skins. Neither of them said a word to Finn, or replied when he spoke to them. Mrs Skins' right eye was swollen and reddened, and – despite a layer of blusher – he saw the bruise on her cheek. The look she gave him when he asked if she was OK, you'd have thought he'd been the one to hit her. He didn't see her again after that, or the girl. He hoped to talk to the girl most of all. In her, he saw Mrs Skins as she might once have been. It struck Finn that, in different ways, they were trapped here, dependent on Mr Skins, just as he was. 'Wasps in a jar', as Mrs Skins had put it. He understood what she meant, now. And yet he got no sense of a common cause or a shared enemy. His arrival at the crocodile farm had made life tougher still for them; and, alive or dead, he'd be leaving, while they would have to remain. Maybe mother and daughter hated him for that. Or maybe they were too afraid to be seen showing him the slightest sign of friendship.

Nothing to do all day but sleep or watch the goings on outside. Mostly, not much happened. Just Skins' men moving about the place, or the children playing, or the pregnant dog waddling about, sniffing and pissing, barking for minutes at a time for no apparent reason. Once, a helicopter landed, was loaded up with boxes, and took off again. Finn would sit and stare at all of this. Waiting. Willing Mr Skins to come. If only Skins came, he'd discover what was to happen to him; what he would have to do to buy his release, to reach the new life that had been revealed to him but which felt, now, like something Finn had misheard or invented. But days passed and there was no visit from the crocodile farmer. And, hour after hour, Finn continued to keep watch. More baskets of fish being hauled over to the pens; truckloads of supplies arriving; hundreds of oblong cartons – cut flowers, he assumed from the logo; occasionally, a few crocodile carcasses being transferred to one of the sheds. Short bursts of activity that kept him at the window for ages in the hope of the next one, or of a glimpse of the man himself, so that he might call out to him. One afternoon, Finn saw a young woman cross the compound. Slim, coffee-coloured skin, shorn black hair. She had her back to him, but – the look of her, the way she walked – he saw right away that it was Lila. Somehow, she had come searching for him. He pressed his face to the bars and called out:

'Lila! Here I am! I'm in here! Lila!'

The woman half-turned at the sound of his voice. It wasn't Lila. Finn watched her enter one of the buildings, pausing in the doorway. A man stood there, one of Mr Skins' gang. They looked in Finn's direction for a moment then closed the door.

Even though it wasn't Lila, he convinced himself it was and that she'd gone in there to fuck that man. Most of that day, he went on thinking it. Drifting in and out of sleep, sweating, thrashing about, dreaming the weirdest dreams, losing blood and pus from his wound, talking aloud to himself and to an imagined Lila.

He would die, here, or he would go fucking crazy.

Or (and Skins fucking *knew* this) he would do whatever was asked of him.

He took to killing cockroaches, ants, flies, mosquitoes. There were mice, too, but they were too quick. Finn was too ill. Weak. Barely eating. Thinner than he'd ever been and sapped of the mental and physical strength to put up any kind of fight. He craved cigarettes, but they wouldn't give him any. Not even a shave or shower; his body was a patchwork of sores, sweat rashes and insect bites, and his ID tattoo had become reinfected. His clothes were disgusting. The wound, he couldn't bring himself to look at any longer; each time they brought food, he pleaded for the medic, but the medic never came. Despite having little to do but rest or sleep, he was tired most of the time. Exhausted. At night, he hardly slept – on account of napping during the day, but also because the dark made him more nervy and tense than ever. His mind became overactive; he'd wake with a start at his own thoughts or at the slightest sound. Then lie there, unable to get back off. At night, the insect noise from the jungle kicked in – like a thousand whistles being blown at once, incessantly, right outside his room. Or he'd be disturbed by a power cut. Every couple of hours through the night the power would go off. And, once the ceiling fan stopped, it grew too hot and humid to sleep; the mosquitoes, no longer kept at bay by the wash of air, would move in to feast. So he would give in. Get up and stand at the window, watching the ghostly scenes out to sea. Beyond the fence, where the creek led down to the shore, the powerful arc lamps of the fishing boats bathed the ocean with a bluish-white glare. Mr Skins' men, luring fish to the surface. He could see figures in silhouette as they hauled in their catch. If the wind was in the right direction, voices reached him. Disembodied and watery. One night, there was a different boat, different cargo, though Finn couldn't make out what. That time, the men on the dock carried rifles and semi-automatic weapons.

He imagined trying to escape, and how far he would get.

At night, if he slept, Finn dreamed.

The fifth night, he dreamed it was morning and that he'd woken up in the flat at Paladin Mansions, in his own bed, even though he'd gone to sleep on the sheet of insulating foam in the Skins' unfinished offices. Disorientated, confused. Then, when he realised he was at home, the momentary euphoria gave way to dismay and anxiety. He shouldn't have been there, he should've been at the crocodile farm. Jesus, if he didn't get back there before he was missed he would be in such fucking shit with Mr Skins. But he couldn't find his clothes, or his shoes and, fuck!, the front door was locked and there was no key, he looked everywhere, but there was no fucking key. To leave, he had to jump. Out of the window, into the debris in the alley thirteen floors below. He clambered on to the ledge. He jumped. The falling went on and on and on.

That was the lead-in to the lowest point. Days six and seven, Finn just lay on the foam bed staring into space, mumbling. Slipping in and out of consciousness.

Skins came. After a week, Skins came.

He spoke of many things. Then, finally, he said he wished to reveal the *happy ending*. Because, yes, there was one. Did Finn

157

want a happy ending? the man asked. Yes, he did. More than anything, he wanted that. It would involve them getting Finn to his feet, somehow, Skins told him; it would mean helping him outside, across the compound and down to the dock, so that he could be put on board a boat to the island. The boat was there, waiting for him. Over on the island, people would be waiting too, to receive him; to shelter him and make him well again.

'And, once you're well,' the man said, 'you can start working for me.'

Finn raised himself a little on his makeshift bed, forcing himself to focus on the crocodile farmer, to concentrate. 'Doing what?'

And then Mr Skins explained.

PART TWO

Waking Up

He awoke to the smell of sweetness and a metallic *tink-tink-tink*.

No idea where he was. The last thing he recalled was being helped to his feet by two of Skins' men . . . then, nothing. The metal sound must be the ceiling fan, only there was no draught. How could that be? He opened his eyes a little, just a slit. It hurt, it was so bright in here; he thought for a moment he was back in the white-walls-and-wicker lounge. Brighter than that, though; as bright as he remembered sunshine to be. Finn's eyes stung, like they'd been squirted with something; so filled with fluid that the shapes and colours of the room fractured on the surface of his eyeballs.

He let the lids close again.

What *was* that smell? So sugary and . . . he knew it, he knew it, he could taste it in the wash of saliva, but he couldn't put a name to it.

The pain in his side. Fuck sake.

Even just lying here, not moving. The thought of moving, of even trying to lift his head – he'd black out, for sure. He would puke. It was as if every part of him – every last centimetre, from the perspiration pinpricking his scalp to the tensed, tight-curled toes – was connected to one point of pain. As if his entire being centred there.

Too gentle to be a ceiling fan. Too tinkly, too random. Wind chimes. It was the sound of wind chimes. Maybe they'd moved him from the office building to the main house after all, installing him in one of their bedrooms, just until he was well enough for the crossing. Going on a boat, Jesus. Being lifted from where he lay, taken down to the jetty, loaded on board and bounced out there on to the fucking ocean.

How long ago had Skins come to see him? An hour, a day, a week?

It felt like Hano's knife was still in there, cutting away. He couldn't face going on any fucking boat. Oh, fuck. Fuck. Fucking Jesus.

He let his breath find its way back to normal.

Honey! That was the smell. Overwhelming. Like falling asleep in a meadow full of flowers, with pollen clogging the air and bees drumming about and no oxygen to be had, just the too-sticky sweetness being drawn into your nose, your throat, the pores of your skin. Not drawn in, pushed out. Like you're exhaling honey, sweating the stuff. He imagined a hunk of coarse brown bread, layered thickly with butter and clear golden honey; biting into it, chewing, swallowing.

He was thirsty, more than hungry, he realised. Raging for water, for something cold to gulp down.

When had he ever slept in a meadow full of flowers?

It was a bed, this. Not a spongy roll of foam on the floor. This was a real bed: pillows, a sheet beneath him, another draped over him and tucked in tight.

He needed a leak.

The idea of pissing, though. It would hurt, do some damage. In any case, he was going nowhere. He'd have to do it right here in the bed, on these smooth sheets.

It would kill him to piss; it was killing him, holding it in.

Noises were coming from somewhere. Close, but not in this room. Footsteps on wood, on stairs. Someone was walking up a flight of wooden stairs.

The sound he made wasn't a word so much as a grunt, a bestial exclamation – he wasn't even sure he'd had a specific word in mind when he opened his mouth, just the need, the panicky desperation, to cry out before it was too late. But the shout did for him. The warm gush spread over and beneath him, as if triggered by the effort he put into calling for help. But painless, just a sense of release. Of relief. It was the most wonderful, joyous piss, and he almost laughed to think he'd been so afraid. There, it was out of him. To hell with the bed, the sheets – it was out of him, and he was fine. Even the pain in his side seemed to relent a little.

Just then, softer footsteps. In the room. Finn rolled his head to one side, in the direction of the sound, and tried once more to open his eyes, blinking away the tears.

He'd never seen her before. Kind of blonde. Plain white T-shirt, faded toffee-coloured cords. Her face was so lemony white in the glare he thought, for a moment, that she might be translucent – that the whiteness was the wall behind her. That she had materialised like a spectre from within the wall itself.

'I've wet the bed,' he said.

She told him it wasn't a problem.

The woman. He thought of her as 'the ghost woman', and would continue to do so for a while even after he'd discovered her name. Would continue to associate her with a watercolour wash of whites and yellows and browns, long after he'd seen her in other lights, in other clothes. When she'd finished changing the bed, wiping the waterproof undersheet, cleaning him; when he had recovered from the pain of being manoeuvred through all of that and was able to speak again, he asked where he was. She told him the name and he remembered it from the fake ID card.

'This is the place?' he said.

'Uh-huh. You're on the island now.'

'I'm here already?' He was on the island. He was on the fucking *island*.

'The Skins sent you across,' the ghost woman said. 'You were out of it.' She was bundling up the spoiled sheets, concentrating on that.

Finn's eyes were coping better with the light. 'It's so bright.'

'The sun comes right in here, this late in the afternoon.'

He thought she'd offer to close the curtains; but, when he glanced over at the window, he saw that there weren't any. The wind chimes dangled from the frame. On the ledge, there was a small blue bottle filled with water, a pebble and an odd, globe-shaped ornament. He couldn't look there for long without his eyes filling up again.

The woman was watching him. When he caught her, she dropped her gaze; made some adjustments to the sheets she held by the scruff, like a sack.

'Is there any water?' Finn said. 'I'm dying of thirst here.'

She went away and came back with a jug and a glass. The sheets were gone. She set the jug and glass down on the bedside table and, sorting the pillows, eased his head and shoulders up a little and helped him swallow some of the water.

'Steady,' she said. 'Just small sips.'

The water was ice cold, delicious. If she'd let him, Finn would've downed it all at once without pausing for breath. Close up, she smelled of honey, too. He looked at her. Tomboyish. Hair chopped short, unkempt; between yellowy blonde and light brown and, when she pushed her fingers through it, it spiked up on her scalp. In the sunlight, her eyes were the only points of

164

contrast in the bleached oval of her face; deep, burned sockets of shade, with smudges like tobacco stains beneath each lower eyelid. Even her lips were so colourless they blended into the surrounding skin. She was anaemic. Maybe even a little jaundiced. But, as Finn looked at her, he thought, for some reason, of butterscotch. As if suddenly conscious of his scrutiny, she took the glass from his lips, stood up and stepped back from the bed.

'So I'm *Roop* now, I guess,' he said.

She nodded.

'And you are . . . what are you? *Who* are you, I mean?'

'My name's Bryher.'

'Briar?'

She spelled it for him.

'You're . . . are you the one who's my wife?'

She hesitated. Did the thing with her fingers through her hair again. 'If anyone comes snooping, that's who I am, yeah.'

She wasn't the sort of woman Finn would've chosen for a wife, or imagined for himself, if ever he imagined things like that. Which wasn't often. He tried not to feel disappointed, or to let it show. If he'd learned anything from his time on the run, and from Mr Skins in particular, it was the fact that his 'liberation' – if that's what this was – had narrowed, not broadened, so many of his options.

And none of that was her fault.

Smiling, he said: 'And we live in a house made entirely of honeycomb?'

The woman seemed on the verge of smiling, too.

Roop, Bryher. Didn't anyone have a normal name any more? He was taken by another spasm of pain.

The woman's face showed concern. 'We should get you sitting upright.'

'Yeah, right.' He more or less gasped the words. 'You can seriously fuck off.'

'In case of complications,' she said. 'So, actually, *you* can fuck off.'

Finn had to laugh at that. Laughing was a serious mistake. He found himself weeping and laughing all at once. She'd cleaned him up after he'd wet himself, now she was watching him cry.

'You were lucky the blade missed your kidneys,' she said.

'Lucky. Right.'

'Who stabbed you?'

'Guy called Hano. He was meant to be taking me to the beach.'

The ghost woman nodded. 'The wound's infected. Whoever cleaned it up and put the stitches in . . . well, anyway. You're here now.'

She explained about the size of the wound, the extent of the infection – 'sepsis', she called it – and about the honey. OK, so he'd gone however many days with no treatment at all, and now he was being packed full of fucking honey. But, this Bryher, she seemed to know what she was talking about. She seemed cool with all of this.

'What are you, a doctor or something?'

'I used to be a nurse,' she said.

Finn pressed his head back hard into the pillow and bit down on his bottom lip to try to make that hurt more than the place where the real hurt was. He pictured the pain as solid, a lump, a tumour of pain; he imagined taking a knife to it – a scalpel – and cutting it out, so there'd just be a hollow. An inert, painless hollow in his side.

He felt her fingertips trail water across his forehead; heard her voice: 'Go with it. Don't resist, just let it pick you up, like a river, and float along on the surface.'

She told him to keep breathing, counting each breath for him up to ten and then starting over again at one, two, three . . . When the spasm ended, Finn lay there panting. Sweating. He tried to smile.

'And the honey is making me *better*, is it?'

'We don't have powerful enough painkillers here. They should've dripped you up with some. Or given you pills.'

'None of that happened.'

'Typical Mr Skins,' Bryher said. Then she announced that she was going to fetch a chair from downstairs. 'And you're going to sit in it.'

'This is weird, isn't it?' Finn said. Serious. He wanted to be serious now.

She frowned. 'What is?'

'You and me. *This*. Don't you think it's the weirdest, maddest fucking thing?'

'We share a house,' Bryher said. 'It's no big deal.'

'Yeah, but . . .' Finn looked at her. Once more, she'd retreated a little from his bedside. Evidently, she didn't want to be his wife any more than he wanted her to be. He thought about this for a moment. 'My real name's Finn,' he said. 'Finn.'

'OK. It would've been best for me not to know that . . . but, OK.'

'I wanted to tell you.'

The ghost woman, Bryher, nodded. Then she went off to fetch the chair.

He must've drifted back off to sleep, because when she came to him again the room was gloomy, illuminated by a candle in a holder at his bedside and another on the windowsill. The flame at the window was contained within the strange, spherical ornament he'd noticed earlier. It glowed bright pink at the centre, deepening to mauve at the edges, and cast a rose-coloured sheen. The woman saw where he was looking. It was the shell of a sea urchin she'd found on the beach, she said.

The air smelled of wax and smoke. 'How long was I out for?'

'Couple of hours.' She was sitting in a rattan chair, bolstered with cushions.

167

He looked at the chair. 'Is that for me?'

'Come on.' She stood up and moved the chair to the side of the bed, next to the table. 'Thirty seconds of pain, then it's done with.'

She got him into a dressing gown, then helped him from the bed into the chair. It was easier than he had expected; and she was right, the pain didn't last. Sitting up wasn't so bad – better than lying down, once he'd found a comfortable position. Also, he felt at less of a disadvantage, now that he was no longer flat on his back.

She brought him a tray of food. A thick soup – lentils and onions – and wedges of bread. He managed to feed himself, after a fashion. The food was good.

'I can't believe I'm actually here,' Finn said. 'That I've made it.'

'Uh-huh. Well, you have.'

The ghost woman watched him eat. There was a glass of what looked like fruit juice but was, she said, a herbal infusion. For the pain. It wasn't strong enough, but it would help; it was better than nothing. Even the drink didn't taste too bad. It was only when he started eating that he realised just how hungry he was. He continued the meal in silence, Bryher busying herself about the room – tidying, remaking the bed, putting fresh dressings and supplies of honey on the bedside table.

'I thought they were going to kill me,' Finn said. 'Or turn me in.'

The woman was a little tired in her movements now, but less ill-looking in the candlelight. She shrugged. 'If you're more valuable to Mr Skins alive than dead, then he'll keep you alive. That's how he is.'

Finn didn't say anything.

'He knows where you are,' Bryher said, 'and he knows what you are.' *What you are.* A dodger. The way she said it wasn't harsh; she wasn't judging him, merely stating a fact. 'Skins will bide his time. Then, one day, sooner or later, he'll be able to put a price on that knowledge.'

Finn looked at her. It was as though she knew of the pact he'd made with the crocodile farmer. But she couldn't have done; she knew Skins for the type of man he was, that was all. The man she didn't yet know, he realised, was Finn himself.

Roop's Clothes

There were reasons why she might have slept poorly: her make-shift bed on the living-room floor; her confused thoughts as she reflected on the day's events. Her mind, so full of him, should've been too active for her to settle. Yet she'd slept for seven hours. Her best night in weeks. In the morning, fresh and well-rested, she was more relaxed with the Incomer – with Finn – than she'd been the previous evening. More generous-spirited towards him. After all, he had survived a knifing, and a week with the Skins, to wake up in a strange place, on the cusp of a new life – to be lived in the shadow of capture. It was no surprise that he was preoccupied with himself.

They talked again after breakfast. She gave him a bed bath, checked his pulse and temperature, changed his dressing – the wound was noticeably less inflamed – and transferred him into his chair. Efficient, clinical, impersonal; if the nurse was unembarrassed, the patient would be. She fetched toast, water and a herbal infusion; he requested honey, for the toast, joking that he might be developing an addiction. He wanted cigarettes too. 'Smokes.' Bryher said there were none and saw, in his face, an immediate dip in his mood. When Finn had eaten, she rooted out pyjamas for him to wear underneath the dressing gown and helped him on with them.

'Where are my clothes?'

'I had to cut them off you,' she said. 'Besides, they were disgusting.'

'Actually, they weren't even mine. The Skins burned mine.'

'Just be grateful you weren't wearing them at the time.'

Finn liked that. He told her he'd been robbed of his pack, then his money, his watch, his smokes; now his clothes were gone. Everything. He had no possessions, apart from an ID card which, in any case, was fake. He said it was like being reborn.

'How's the pain this morning?' she said.

'D'you mean relative to yesterday, or relative to a state of total painlessness?'

'Relative to yesterday would be more useful. Medically speaking.'

'Then, it's a little better.' He held a thumb and index finger fractionally apart. 'A little less fucking appalling, anyway.'

'Good.'

The pyjamas were on. He drew the bathrobe round himself. She looked at him, in those clothes. Once he regained some weight the fit would be more exact.

As if reading her thoughts, Finn said: 'These were Roop's, weren't they?'

'Uh-huh.' She didn't want to discuss Roop with this man. But he wasn't done with the topic and she supposed she should be grateful he'd at least thought to ask her about herself; to recognise that his wasn't the only life affected by all of this.

His voice quietened. 'When did he die?'

'Two months ago,' she said.

'Twenty-six, though.' Finn exhaled. 'Jesus.'

'Uh-huh.'

171

'How did it happen?'

'He was out fishing. They got caught in the fret and strayed into the path of an aircraft carrier. The bow wave swept him overboard.'

The words came out matter-of-factly; even to her they sounded rehearsed – like something she'd had to recount so often that the explanation of Roop's death had become technical, emotionless. As it was, she hadn't needed to describe it to anyone, until now. She had practised it in her mind often enough. Turning the accident into a set of words that could be stored in a compartment of her brain, and rationalised; or pulled out like this, when required, without unravelling everything else.

'The *fret*?'

'It's a sea fog.'

The Incomer fell silent. It was as if her definition of a fret had saddened him more than what happened. She might have said more, at this point, but he didn't push it and she was glad; glad that he'd asked about Roop, glad that he had stopped asking. She was aware of him watching her; her own gaze settled on his bare feet resting on the carpet. One of his big toenails was blackened. It would become detached, in time.

'You've still got your boots,' she said. Her statement seemed to puzzle him. 'You said you'd lost everything you owned; well, you haven't – you've still got the boots you were wearing. I didn't throw those away.'

Finn gestured at his wasted, invalided condition. 'That's good. I'm thinking of going for a long hike this morning.'

Bryher brought a basin of hot water, shaving soap, a small towel and Roop's razor and set them on a tray on Finn's lap. There were no mirrors in the cottage, she told him, so he would have to manage without. The razor was a cut-throat. The Incomer said he'd not used one before and she suggested he take care, in that

172

case, because the nearest blood-transfusion facilities were seventy-five kilometres away. She left him to shave while she washed up the breakfast things. After that, she took a selection of books from the shelves downstairs and placed them on the bedside table. It would be a few days before he was able to move about; he was going to have a lot of time to kill. Pain relief might be his main concern, just now, but soon it would be the boredom of confinement to a chair and a bed in one small room.

'Isn't there a TV you could bring up?' Finn said.

Bryher smiled. 'There isn't a TV set anywhere on the island. Or a radio.'

'You're kidding?'

'Some of the cottages don't even have electricity.'

'This is the fucking Stone Age, right?' Finn was smiling too now. 'I've passed through a time portal and emerged among a community of Neolithic man.'

Bryher didn't rise to this. When she had nursed on the mainland, she'd always enjoyed the banter with patients – the flirtatiousness. It lifted morale, hers and theirs, and lightened the job's darker moments. Nursing the Incomer – here, in the cottage, with him in Roop's clothes, in Roop's *place* – the playful levity seemed inappropriate. She had slipped into it automatically already, once or twice, and now that she caught on to what she was doing she stopped herself. Retreated inside herself a little, a knot of unease and self-reproach in her chest. Something close to guilt.

'We need to set some ground rules,' Bryher said, aware of the hardness in her tone. Surprising herself with talk of rules. 'If we're going to make this work.'

Finn sobered up. 'OK. Yeah, sure.'

'When it's just us . . . when there are no outsiders on the island, you and I live together like two friends sharing a house. All right? Everyone who lives here, we can trust. There's no need for pretence in front of the islanders.'

'They all know who I am?' he said. 'Our . . . arrangement?'

'Yes.' She hesitated. 'It was a communal decision.'

Finn appeared to be digesting the information, or registering her hesitation; it was hard to be sure which. 'How many of you live here?'

'Seventeen,' Bryher said. She went to correct herself, to say sixteen, then she remembered that the Incomer had made it seventeen again. 'Seventeen, including you. Twelve adults and five children. Well, one of them's not a child any more.'

'And Roop – your husband . . . his death hasn't been re-ported?'

'No.'

'Mr Skins knew.'

'One of his boats put in here the next morning, while we were out searching.'

There was a pause, then Finn said: 'Tell me about outsiders.'

'We hardly get any. The occasional coastal patrol, or a boat that's off course or needing repairs. Mr Skins' men – Skins himself, sometimes – but his men must know about you, anyway, and wouldn't dare betray you without his say so. Once a year we get a census official. And that's about it.'

'What if someone does come sniffing?'

'We act like we're married.'

'You mean we fight and shout and throw things at each other.'

'This is serious.'

'OK. Sorry.'

'We . . . what I'm trying to say is, we have to put on a . . . a credible show of intimacy in front of strangers. That's all. The rest of the time, we're cool.'

Finn frowned. 'A credible show of intimacy. How do we do that, exactly?'

Bryher wished she hadn't started this line of conversation. Then, noticing his failure to contain his amusement, she couldn't

174

help but let out a laugh. 'Oh, I don't *know*.' Quickly, she became cross again. 'Look, to be honest, I thought I could handle this – but, now you've woken up and we're talking . . . I'm struggling.'

'You want me to go back to sleep?'

She paused. 'I want it to be uncomplicated. As uncomplicated as possible.'

Neither of them spoke for a while. Finn stared in the direction of the window. Then he picked up the books she'd brought and began reading the jacket blurbs. All the time they'd been talking, Bryher had been standing with the tray of shaving gear, poised to take it away. She decided to do that now.

'You've kept all his things,' Finn said, stalling her in the doorway. She didn't look at him. 'For me? I mean, for someone like me. Someone on the run.'

'I kept them for myself.'

Leaving him alone in the cottage, she headed up the lane to Yué's, to return the dish. It could have waited, but she wanted the exercise. This was her excuse to herself for taking the hilly inland route rather than the quicker coastal path; it was nothing to do with forcing herself to avoid the beaches. As it happened, no one was home. She left the dish on the step, placing rhododendron petals and a shiny pebble inside to signify thanks. Bryher was relieved to find they were out; she wasn't ready for company, with the inevitable questions about the Incomer. Once news circulated that he had regained consciousness, he would be an object of even greater curiosity. The sunlight glistered and a breeze blew in from the sea, perfumed with wild garlic, honeysuckle. Outside Yué's, Bryher paused to take in the view above the treetops and windbreaks to South Hill, iridescent yellow with gorse. Below, cradled in the curve of Long Strand, the water was closer to green than blue. As she stood there, the telltale noise of sawing distracted her. It would be coming from the chandlery.

175

The building of the boat had started. She couldn't see the yard for the trees beyond Zess and Effie's place, but the rhythmic rasp of wood being worked carried to her in the quiet. Roop's sound. Bryher listened for a moment, then retraced her route to the cottage.

The Naming of Things

The window gave Finn his first glimpse of the island. He'd got the ghost woman to set his chair there so he had something other than the room to gawp at. In the long days, he sat. Gazing out. Or snoozing, or reading, or talking to Bryher, if she was about. At the window, his eyes – conditioned to see rainy grey – adjusted each morning to bright blues, yellows and greens. The bedroom looked on to a beach, then water, then an islet, then more water to the horizon. The beach was Gibbet Cove. The craggy islet – volcano-shaped, twin peaks – was Gibbet Rock. Bryher named these sights for him. She said mutinous sailors were hung from the rock in olden times; probably her idea of a joke. Gulls congregated on the outcrop, or spiralled above it, cries chipping at the air. This, and the waves, were almost the only sounds. At night, if pain didn't tug Finn awake, the silence did – as if his city-soaked mind couldn't still itself without noise.

Bryher named other things for him . . .

The varieties of gull and seabird.

Tye and Qway, who lived in the one building visible from the window – a whitewashed stone cottage, above the rocks at the end of the beach. The men who'd carried Finn from the quay. They kept hens, a goat. In their garden was a see-saw, a climbing frame, a tractor tyre dangling from the branch of a tree.

The kids who sometimes played there. Jad, Peef, Kags, Jafe. All of them born on the island. Jad was the eldest, the one who could climb to the top of the tree.

The cage-like contraptions Bryher mended on the low dry-stone wall out front as he gazed down. Lobster pots. Salt flaked off them, powdering in the breeze. For all that the work was rough, she handled the pots as though playing a harp.

She named the island for him; at least, taught him to pronounce the name he already knew. In the ancient language it meant 'the isle of the lasting sun'; over time, this had been corrupted. Now, its closest translation was: 'the island of lost souls'.

'We just call it "the island",' she said.

Bryher had been here for two years, the community for thirty; just six settlers, initially. Before then, the island was owned and occupied by a reclusive billionaire. She named him, as well: Purgo. His money had laid the submarine cable that brought electricity to the island, and had installed abstraction pipes and a pumping system at the natural reservoir at Great Pool. When Purgo died he bequeathed the island, and a part of his fortune, to a community in the Capital. Not really a community, just a few people squatting a dilapidated mansion in the months before demolition. His only granddaughter was one of them. Sholo. Twenty-two at the time; the age Bryher was now. Sholo and her man, Hobb, were among the first settlers.

'Purgo's money ran out years ago,' Bryher said.

'How do you live?' Finn was on his side, trying to concentrate on anything but the penetrating ache where she was seeing to his wound. The talking helped.

'We produce most of what we need. Fruit, vegetables, milk, cheese, butter, eggs, fish. Flour, for bread. *Honey.*' Finn sensed the

178

smile in her voice as she said this. 'Other stuff, Mr Skins brings us – in trade for fish or flowers. And kelp. They use it to make soap and glass and iodine pills . . . dietary supplements.'

'Flowers?'

'We grow them. Daffodils. Narcissi.'

'Yeah, I saw boxes of flowers being shipped in and out of his place.'

'They wouldn't have been from here. Ours won't be through for a while yet,' Bryher said. 'He has people growing for him all along this coast.'

'What would Skins want with flowers?'

She was taping up the fresh dressing and didn't reply right away. In that pause Finn worked out the answer for himself. Saw the doors of mainland homes, festooned with wreaths for their war dead; saw his mother, fixing one to her door for Kurt.

'You're happy to trade with him, then?' Even as he spoke, Finn was conscious of his own trade-off with the man. But he was curious, recalling something Skins had told him: 'These people operate by a different set of morals to the likes of you and me.'

'I don't know about happy, but we do it.' Then echoing the crocodile farmer's wife, Bryher said: 'One way or another, everyone in these parts works for Mr Skins.'

In these early days on the island the relief of being away from Skins' place, of being alive and on the loose, had worn off. Giving way to unease about what he was doing here, with these folk. With Bryher. Being cared for like this, you could imagine yourself to be a wounded soldier in a military hospital, a nurse coaxing you back from the dead. The gentle and the strong. But as Finn lay there, or sat there, he was the one without strength. So shit scared of dying he'd almost got himself killed evading a war where other men his age were dying for real. Even then, allowing himself to fantasise that this was an act of bravery. That he had endured his own ordeal in escaping – like fighting your way back from behind enemy lines.

Kurt had lost a foot. Both feet. His life.

What had Finn lost? A girl, a litre of blood, a few kilos in weight.

What deepened his shame was that not once did Bryher treat him as though he had reason to be ashamed. He would have to find a way to live with her – to live *here*, mainlander among islanders, waiting for Skins to call in his debt. 'The proposition' the crocodile farmer had called it. Like he was giving Finn a choice.

Skins had pulled up one of the new office chairs, still sheathed in its plastic wrapper, and sat himself down alongside the foam sheet where Finn lay.

Finn's task was simple: Delivery. Collection.

First, the delivery. A boat puts ashore on the island, with a consignment of goods. Finn safeguards the goods until such time as Mr Skins can safely come to claim them. This, the collection. That was all he had to do. Finn, adrift on a wave of pain, had struggled to make sense of anything the man said; he might've been hearing this language for the first time.

'Goods,' Finn said.

'Yes, goods.'

'Why not just bring them in here? Last night . . .' Was it last night, or several nights ago? He slipped into sleep; but, no, he was still speaking. What about? *Goods*. The boat. The men with guns. That was it. 'One night, I saw a boat come in.'

'Regrettably, that particular shipment was intercepted after it left us,' Skins said. 'No proof it came from here . . . but, nevertheless, I received a visit.'

So the explanation went on, Finn dipping in and out. He had to listen. Skins kept telling him that, and he tried, really tried to stay awake, to take it all in. As far as he could tell, it broke down to this: Mr Skins' operations had been compromised. All goods entering or leaving the crocodile farm would be suspect, subject to inspection without notice – to raids – by customs officials. Officials who were now themselves under close scrutiny from above and, therefore, no longer 'open to influence'.

'So, you see, until they tire of this game I must make other arrangements.'

'I'm not a drug-runner,' Finn said.

'Merchandise passes through you, that's all.' Skins gave a shrug. 'Is a river bed responsible for the fish that swim in its waters?'

'And if I refuse?'

Skins let that go; the answer, in any case, was obvious to both of them.

Day seven, Finn's first walk.

He was managing about the cottage by then, cruising the furniture and walls and doorways; a couple of times Bry had helped him out into the garden. This time he headed down to Gibbet Cove, solo. Had to use a stick, shuffling along like a geriatric, pausing for breath, sweating; but he made it.

The tide was out. A small launch, afloat on its mooring when he'd looked out his window earlier, sat stranded in the shallows. The beach was the colour of milky tea, striped with bands of rust-red shingle; rocks and boulders piled up at either end like builders' rubble. At the shoreline tiny birds skittered, dispersed by each wave, as if playing dare. Finn sat on a rock, tilting his face sunwards. It was always sunny here, though there'd been regular night-time downpours that left the ground damp in the mornings. Bryher said it was a characteristic of the island. Its microclimate. Sunshine by day, rain at night. Hence, 'the isle of the lasting sun'. Finn didn't know if this was true, or if the run of fine days since his arrival was coincidence. It was as illogical as the landscape –

moorland, heather, bracken, gorse – just a few K across a strait from the rainforest that shrouded Skins' place. Whatever, it was good. Unlike the mainland coast, where the heat was humid and oppressive, this was a clean, dry warmth. Finn was sticky, even so, from his exertions. His clothes – an old sweatshirt and joggers of Roop's – smelled musty. Bryher hadn't fussed about letting him have them; after all, he had no gear of his own. This was mostly how she'd been with him: friendly, but practical and sensible. Carer and patient, landlady and lodger.

Finn was fine with that. He'd rather have lived by himself, but that wouldn't happen for a while; and it was a fuck sight better here than at Paladin Mansions.

He made a mental note to ask Bryher what those little birds were called. And those large white shells strewn everywhere, like spearheads. There was rubbish along the high-water mark: plastic bottles, cans, frayed rope, timber, an unravelled cassette, a metal drum stencilled with a serial number, corporate logo and the name of a distant country. Out to sea, he spotted the islanders' fishing boat. It would be heading ashore, before the light failed and the fret closed in. He enjoyed knowing this. Enjoyed being away from the cottage. Taking off his boots, he worked his bare toes into the sand.

A movement at the edge of his field of vision. A figure, scrambling down the boulders beneath Tye and Qway's cottage. Finn shielded his eyes. It was the dark-haired boy, the tree climber. Jad. In his usual shorts and flip-flops, bare topped beneath a school sports bib: red, with the letters GA in black. He carried two plastic buckets on the ends of a long wooden yoke across his shoulders. The boy appeared to register Finn, but made no show of acknowledgement. The pails swung as he worked the tideline of flotsam and jetsam. Now and then, he stooped to gather something and tossed it into one or other of the buckets. Finn couldn't make out what these things were. As he drew closer, the boy came to stand beside the rock where Finn sat, as if that had been his intention all along. As if they'd arranged to meet there. He smiled and said hi.

'What've you got?' Finn said, returning the smile.

He set the buckets down. Washing-up gloves – pink, blue, yellow – sealed in clear plastic. The text on the packs was foreign; Finn didn't recognise the brand.

'So far, they're all mediums,' the boy said.

'How many've you found?'

'Nine pairs, on Gibbet.' Then aiming a hand beyond Tye and Qway's place: 'This morning, I got forty-six off Long Strand and nineteen off The Strand.'

'They all mediums as well?' The boy nodded, so earnest that Finn had to try hard not to crack a smile. 'You're Jad, yeah?' Another nod. Teeth, white against his tan. Sand coated his shins like long socks. 'I'm Finn, but you're not meant to know.'

'*Thin*, like *not fat*?'

'What's the GA stand for?'

'Goal Attack. It's for netball. I found it down in South Bay one time.'

The bib was too big. His arms, the colour of stained wood, poked out like the spindly branches of a sapling. Finn tried to recall how old Bryher had said he was. Twelve? The boy had spotted another pair of washing-up gloves nearby. He added them to his haul.

'Medium, again.' He said a merchant ship had probably been blown up. When he saw Finn's frown, Jad told him that sometimes stuff washed up from thousands of miles away. Other times it might be something you'd thrown in yourself just the day before, from a beach on another part of the island.

Then, matter-of-factly, he said: 'Can I see where you got hurt?' Finn raised his sweatshirt. By his expression you'd have thought Jad had seen plenty of knife wounds in his time and only wanted to confirm that Finn's was no different. 'You a soldier?'

Finn lowered the sweatshirt. 'No.'

'I thought you were.'

'I should've been, but I'm not.' Jad's gaze drifted to the debris still to be beachcombed. 'My brother was,' Finn said. He told the boy about Kurt losing both feet in an RPG attack. He didn't know why he'd said both feet. It just came out.

'What's an RPG?'

'Rocket-propelled grenade.'

The boy looked satisfied with this piece of information; another item salvaged from the shore, to be taken home and kept safe until he found a use for it. Not in any snide or calculating way; Jad gave the impression of being someone who collected things – objects, knowledge, conversation – not for personal advantage, but for the things themselves, and for the simple act of collection.

'Is he in a wheelchair?' Jad said.

'Kurt?' Finn hesitated, unsure how truthful, how explicit, to be. 'He died,' he said, finally. 'From the shock and from all the blood he lost.'

Jad took this with the same insouciance as the sight of Finn's wound.

In the early days, after Kurt signed up, Finn talked of his brother – the soldier, the squaddie – if the war came up in conversation. At work, wherever. Not boasting, but with pride and a vicarious glamour, as if Finn himself attained some kudos by association. Despite opposing the war, he'd done this. Here, talking to Jad, he was uneasy with making his brother into a topic of curiosity once more, using him to sharpen the boy's attention. He wondered why he'd spoken of Kurt now, to this child, when he'd said little about him so far to Bryher. Partly, he'd wanted to prolong the contact with the boy. It was good, sitting on a beach in the sunshine, talking. Also, it was easier, less complicated, to open up to him than to a woman like Bryher, about Kurt, even though – or maybe *because* – she'd her own loss to deal with. Finn felt adult and worldly in front of Jad; with Bryher, he felt like the know-nothing kid.

'You got any brothers?' Finn said.

'Sister.'

The boy pointed to the fishing boat, which had drawn in close to the shore. It would be heading for the pontoon quay down at The Strand, Finn supposed. He could make out a pair of figures on board, both neck to feet in yellow oilskins. Two women. One at the wheel, the other making brisk adjustments to the lobster pots stacked on deck. This one – the younger of the two, her hair the same bluey black as Jad's – spread her feet wide as she worked, bracing herself against the roll and pitch of the boat. She might've been at a funfair, riding the zigzag floor in the House of Tricks. Her hair had come loose and, as it ribboned across her face, the girl half-turned her head to let the breeze thresh it clear. Jad cried out and she looked up. Late teens, at a guess. She hesitated, then waved, and her brother waved back.

'What's her name?' Finn said.

'Amver. The other one's my mum.' She was waving now. 'Yué, she's called.'

Finn nodded, recalling the food she'd made him. 'Where's your dad today?'

Jad didn't reply right away. Then he said: 'He lives on the mainland now.'

Finn thought Bryher had told him this already, and was cross with himself for forgetting, for upsetting Jad. The boy was suddenly subdued. The girl continued to stare in their direction for a moment, then returned to work. In silence, they watched the boat until it disappeared behind the point.

'Where's your house?' Finn said, changing the subject.

'The other side of Wreckers Hill.' The boy nodded towards the slope behind Bryher's. He said it got its name from when folk kept

185

watch for wrecked ships on the outlying rocks. They'd row out and loot the cargo before the ship broke up – and if any of the sailors were still alive, the islanders killed them. That was hundreds of years ago. The boy sniffed. You could see the mainland from Wreckers Hill, he said. Jad and his sister were both born here and had never been to the mainland. Never left the island, or its waters. Finn was amazed, but Jad just shrugged it off.

'Amver wants to leave,' he said.

'But you don't?'

'Nah.' Jad rubbed at the sand on his legs. 'It's OK, living here.'

'Don't you ever wonder what it's like, on the mainland?'

The boy shook his head. 'Most of it washes up here sooner or later.'

Coming from someone older, this might've been profound. Something Lila would've said. From Jad, it was throwaway. As if he hadn't understood the question, or didn't give a fuck about it.

'You don't like the mainland, I guess?' Finn said, smiling. The boy shrugged again. 'What about mainlanders? What about *me*?'

'You're on the island, now.'

'And the other islanders, will they accept me so easily?' Bryher had sworn it was a communal decision, but he didn't believe in unanimity; not in a group of – what was it? – a dozen adults. 'If they come looking for me . . . well, maybe I'm not a good guy to have around the place.'

'Will they shoot you?'

'Not if I take you hostage.' Finn was pleased to see the boy laugh, to crack his shell of seriousness. He indicated the stranded launch. 'Who does that belong to?'

'No one,' Jad said. He corrected himself. 'Everyone.'

'Where d'you buy the fuel?'

'From Skins.'

'Right.' He should've figured. He asked if the islanders ever traded with Mr Skins for cigarettes. Jad shook his head.

186

'I could take you out in it, if you like.' The rope securing the boat to its buoy resembled a long snake in the sludge. For the first time, Jad looked shy. 'Go round the island or something.'

'Yeah, I'd like that. When I'm fitter.'

Finn asked about the shells shaped like spearheads, which weren't shells at all, Jad said, but cuttlefish bones. And those little birds were sanderlings. They were still talking when a sound silenced them. Distant booming; like thunder, but too rhythmic. It seemed to be issuing from the sea, at first, then from all directions at once; but, as he listened, Finn placed it in the island's interior. Fog horn? Drum? Bell? No, it was a gong. The resonant whoom of a large gong. In the cidery late-afternoon light, it might have been the cry of some gigantic bird come home to roost.

'What's that?' Finn said.

'A Gathering call.'

'A what?'

But Jad was already sorting the yoke, hoisting it on to his shoulders, steadying the load. The plastic buckets swung as the boy turned, grinning with those white teeth of his, walking backwards up the beach towards the track.

'See you, Thin.'

By the time Finn made it back, Bryher wasn't home. She'd left a note saying she'd gone to the Gathering. There was a PS asking Finn to sleep in the living room that night. Now that he was up and about again, she wanted her bedroom back.

The Gathering

Hobb broke the first silence. So, he had been the one to call the Gathering; now they would discover his reason. Bryher had considered the possibilities – concerned that Finn would be the subject, but hoping not. Surely it was too soon to discuss whether to let him stay? As Hobb spoke, her anxieties eased; he was talking about the trading arrangements with Skins. Evening closed in around the Gathering Hall and, encircled on the veranda, the islanders' faces loomed like Hallowe'en masks in the erratic light of the oil lamps. Some still had their eyes shut from the period of silence. Others, like Bryher herself, had settled their gaze on Hobb, or on the essential-oil burner in the circle's centre. An aroma of vanilla impregnated the warm night.

'Skins is proposing to alter the barter.'

Gravelly voiced, deliberate, Hobb set out the words like brush-strokes in a line of calligraphy. To Bryher, it was the intonation of an actor who'd narrated a bedtime-story tape she listened to as a child. Hobb detailed the new quotas – for fish, flowers, kelp – that the crocodile farmer intended to levy. Not a huge increase, but enough to require the islanders to work a little harder, be a bit more productive. Enough, too, to remind them of his authority. Skins' 'proposals' were usually non-negotiable. He was their sole supplier, but they were not his — which left them the more dependent. They had faced this many times, in many ways, but an awareness crept up on Bryher that there might be another, more disturbing, significance: the timing.

Effie was the one to pose the question that, Bryher supposed, must have been on all their minds once Hobb finished speaking. 'Is this because of the Incomer?'

'I asked if this was his "fee" for bringing the Incomer to us,' Hobb said. 'Of course, Skins said no. And, of course, he was affronted by the very suggestion.'

'Of course.' This was Zess. He was seated alongside Hobb, but directed his comment at the centre of the ring. Hobb raised his hands, a don't-shoot-the-messenger gesture. The palms were unnaturally white in the flickering illumination. 'So,' Zess said, 'it's just coincidence that a week after the Incomer . . .'

'His name's *Finn*. He isn't the Incomer, he's called Finn.'

Bryher's interjection surprised her as much as it did the others. The discussion of Finn in the abstract — his anonymity, his absence from the circle — had bothered her, but it was Zess's repetition of the term that brought her irritation to the surface. A hush followed her outburst. It had been an outburst, she realised; not angry so much as tetchy — yet shocking, even so, to cut across Zess, or any speaker, at a Gathering. Of late, though, there was a fund of sympathy for her to draw on; Bryher, the young widow, for whom allowances must be made. Now, she had been over-protective of 'the Incomer'; that too would be tolerated, over-looked, understood.

'Finn, then,' Zess said, at last. 'Sorry, Bry, I didn't know his actual name.'

Of course. How could he? She had been unreasonable in rounding on him. So, for all that the gentleness of his apology

189

added to Bryher's sense of being patronised, she apologised to Zess in return.

'You see the point I'm making?' he said.

'Uh-huh,' she said, quietly. 'I thought it myself.'

Yué spoke next; she was sitting to Bryher's left and smelled so strongly of the sea it was almost overwhelming. She and Amver had been last to join the ring, having barely docked with their catch when the gong sounded. 'We shouldn't be surprised by this, should we?' Her hair, black as her daughter's but self-cut into an approximation of a bob, cast her face in shadow as she leaned forward. 'Once Skins became involved he was bound to profit one way or another. At least it's out there now.'

'If this is the end of it.'

Tye. Bryher had been waiting for him to speak. At the last Gathering, he had been the firmest opponent of harbouring a draft-dodger, for fear of the penalty.

'You think he'll want more from us?' Yué said.

Tye looked at her. 'From us, or from the Incomer himself. From Finn.'

'Perhaps he paid up front.'

'No,' Bryher said. 'He was robbed. He arrived at Skins' place with nothing.'

Qway spoke now. Smiling. In that case, he suggested, they should get Finn fit again as soon as possible so he could be put to work – help them meet the increased barter rates. 'Is it too soon to have him lugging kelp?'

This brought laughter, followed by inquiries about Finn's progress. Bryher said he had made it down to Gibbet Cove that afternoon. She thought of the scene she'd witnessed from her bedroom window: Finn and Jad, talking. She hadn't meant to watch Finn for as long as she did, but once she had seen him make it safely to the cove, she spotted Jad heading down there too. When they'd fallen into conversation, Bryher continued watching, fascinated by the sight of them together. It had made her smile. When Finn raised his sweater, she'd let out a laugh, surprised only that Jad hadn't asked to see the wound sooner. Then the amusement turned to resentment, and Bryher failed to understand why. Perhaps it was as simple, as unfair, as the fact that Roop and Jad had been good mates, especially after Mor left, and it hurt to see Finn with the boy, filling that void. She hadn't been conscious of this association at the time, but it occurred to her now. With it came regret at writing such a terse note. She'd meant to discuss the sleeping arrangements face to face with Finn after his walk, but the call to Gathering had intruded. Vaguely resentful, still, she had scribbled something hurried and hard-nosed instead.

Bryher looked at Jad. Sometimes he played inside the hall, or at the end of the veranda, with the other kids; tonight, he had sat himself in the circle with the grown-ups (beside Sholo, typically). His head was dipped right down over his crossed knees and, for some reason, he wore a pair of yellow washing-up gloves.

The discussion continued. Respectful, reflective. Before coming to the island, Bryher had never known people to disagree with one another so politely, or for them to listen – to really *listen* – to opposing viewpoints. Somehow, consensus was always reached without grievance. This time, she was less sure of that. Some in the circle – Tye, Effie, Liddy, Zess – wanted to reconsider the decision to shelter Finn in the first place. Others – Nudge, Hobb, Qway, Amver, Yué – urged them to focus on Mr Skins' new quotas, and whether they had any option but to accept. Beneath the courtesies, Bryher detected an unfamiliar undercurrent of tension. There was more debating to be done. Sholo hadn't spoken; neither had Orr, snoring lightly, slumped against Nudge. Neither had Jad. It was Sholo's silence, though, that weighed heaviest.

Tye persisted. 'Skins has chipped away at our unity before,' he said. 'What we've done, by taking this Finn, is give the man another tool to do that with.'

191

'Please,' Yué said, 'let's not turn this into a rerun. He's among us now.'

'So is Skins, with his new quotas.' Tye gestured in the vague direction of The Strand. 'He'll be here again, with the next "proposition", and the next.'

Bryher looked at him. His tanned forearms and chest, through his open shirt, gleamed as though oiled. As he spoke, he pulled at the ring on the third finger of his right hand. He had lowered the trademark purple hairband and wore it loose round his throat. The same age as Qway, yet he seemed the older of the two, just lately. Since Roop, Tye had changed. Grown pessimistic, defensive; or, rather, she had the sense of him withdrawing into an interior space, an 'island' within himself, where the outside world – which had taken Roop – could not intrude. In this, his grieving was like her own. The difference was that Tye wanted to draw the rest of the islanders in with him, combined against those beyond; Bryher had gone in there by herself.

'If we don't resist Skins now,' Tye said, his tone measured, almost apologetic, 'we may not have another chance. And, with Finn here, how are we able to resist?'

This time, no one responded. In the ensuing quiet, Tye pulled the headband back into place, as if to indicate that he would say no more. She caught an exchange of glances between Tye and Qway; it was rare to find them on the opposite sides of a debate. Bryher suspected Tye was as divided by the Finn question as the rest of them. He wanted the Incomer gone yet he didn't *want* to want that. How else to explain why he helped Qway to carry Finn to her cottage that first day? He did it for her sake, he'd said at the time; in memory of Roop, too. And because Qway asked him to. Whatever he thought of the Incomer, or of the decision to accept him, Tye loved Qway, and Bry, just as he'd loved Roop; he loved the island, too.

When the debate resumed it became cyclical, stalling short of

192

agreement. The issue had at least crystallised: it was about Finn, not the barter. Having declared the new rates, Skins would most likely enforce them regardless of whether Finn stayed. If he stayed, though, the islanders were vulnerable to further exploitation; if he left, they weren't. Tye and his supporters had secured consensus on these points. The islanders had to decide whether to let Finn remain in any case. To help him. Because he needed their help, because sheltering him was the symbol – more than a symbol, the tangible expression – of their opposition to the draft, to the war itself. An 'articulation of our humanity', as Hobb put it. Would they take the risk, pay whatever price the crocodile farmer exacted, or would they let Finn return to his fate on the mainland?

Sholo, as so often, was the last to break her silence.

'Which of us has spoken to him?' she said.

A question, typically. Her gaze, grey irises whitened by lamp-light, swept the circle, pausing at each face in turn. Sholo's features were draped vertically in shadow, like strips of black cloth. Not the oldest islander, but she'd lived here three decades, since the start, and had attained the unconferred status of ma-triarch. Of earth mother. Even though she had no children of her own, she'd been midwife, teacher, surrogate grandmother to those who'd been born here. Bryher had come to think of the island's essential nature – the community's, too – as a reflection of Sholo's. It was a feminine land. A land of healing, unobtrusive wisdom. 'Which of us has spoken to him?' As ever her question held others beneath the surface. *Which of us knows him? Which of us, gathered here, is ready to reject a man before we have the measure of him, before we have exchanged even one word with him?* Apart from Bryher, only one islander had spoken to Finn. She watched Jad, waiting for him to declare himself; his head hung low over his knees, still, masking his face. The hush Sholo's question trailed in its wake left Bryher to wonder if Jad – secretive scavenger – would hoard his encounter on the beach with Finn. Or whether Sholo was no more expecting a reply than he was willing to offer one. At last he raised a yellow-gloved hand.

Sholo spoke his name and he lifted his head. After the adult speakers, Jad's voice was falsetto, but not childish. Jad never sounded that to Bryher.

'It's all right,' he said, nodding away to himself.

'What is, Jad?' This was his mother, Yué.

'Him. Thin.' The boy sniffed and swallowed. 'Having him here, and that.'

Like a Regular Couple

They became like a regular couple. Eating together, sitting in the garden, going for walks, picnics, down to the beach. Slipping into a no-rota-but-everything-gets-done routine around the house. They even bickered. But, mostly, they got along just fine. In the evenings, they'd share a meal and swap tales of what they had done during the day. Bryher would head off to her bed, and Finn would settle himself on the cushions on the floor downstairs. 'G'night. See you in the morning.' He didn't have a sister, but he figured this was how life would be if you crashed at your (widowed) sister's place for a while after the world had fucked up on both of you in some way.

Bryher had drawn him a map of the island. A ragged figure 3, with a quiff – less than three kilometres, top to bottom. Mostly heath, apart from a diagonal belt of dwellings and cultivation across the centre. She'd sketched in the tracks, coastal paths, strands and hills. No roads, because the islanders had no vehicles. The seven homes were marked, along with who lived in each, so Finn could visit, if he wished. But, at first, he kept close to home, or to the initial, easy slopes of The Down, the uninhabited headland to the north. As for Wreckers Hill, looming over the cottage, it was a while before he felt fit enough to take it on.

They went up together. The going was steep, in places the track disappeared and they had to wade through scrub. Finn had worn shorts, against Bry's advice, and his shins were scratched to fuck. But it was OK. There were plain blue butterflies the colour of eyeshadow and others patterned like exotic flags. He took off his T-shirt and looped it round his neck like a bandanna to let the sun at his back. When they reached the top, he used the shirt to towel himself down. There was a large water tank and the broken stone foundations of what he learned was a watch house, way back, in the time of a forgotten war. Just so many giant dice in the grass, now.

Finn, catching his breath, didn't speak. Bryher unhooked a water bottle from her belt harness and they took turns to drink.

Using the bottle as a pointer, she said: 'There's the mainland.'

A pencil line of greeny grey that, at first, seemed no more than a continuation of the horizon. At night, she said, you could see the lights of Skins' place. Already, the crocodile farm was a lifetime ago. Yet, hearing the man's name, Finn could've imagined himself still there – that, if he went to sleep right here in the grass, he'd wake to find himself among the Skins again. Lately, he'd been aroused in the night by pornographic dreams of Mrs Skins and, more disturbingly, of the girl. In one, he'd watched through the barred window of the unfinished offices while, outside on the boardwalk, Mr Skins had a blow job off his own pre-pubescent daughter.

'I don't know if I'll ever be free of that fucking place.' He took another slug of water. Couldn't tell her about the dreams. Or about his arrangement. 'I'm hauling the Skins around with me all the time. In my head. Every twinge in my side.' He jabbed a thumb at his ID tattoo. 'This.'

'Uh-huh.'

'When I think of the mainland, I think of *them* now.'

'When we came,' Bryher said, 'the first few months, it was . . . we were living in two places at once.'

'Both of you?'

'What?'

'It's just, whenever couples come out with this "we" stuff, I don't buy it. Two people don't feel exactly the same about things. Not things like that.'

It was the first time he'd challenged her on this way she had of talking about herself and Roop. Bryher took the bottle from him, drank, then screwed the top back. He couldn't tell if she was pissed off, or what she was thinking. At last, she said: 'It was me, more than him. Roop loved it here from the start, like he'd lived here all his life.' She paused, gazing out towards the mainland. 'So, no. Not both of us.'

He liked that about her. How she could concede something without it being a big deal for her; as if she was ready to look inside herself – or have someone else look inside her – and discover something she hadn't thought was there.

She ran fingers through her hair, spiky with sweat. 'I wanted to be with him, wherever that was. But he wanted to be with me *and* he wanted to be here – that was the difference between us. To begin with.'

Finn remembered something he'd been meaning to ask her. 'How come you don't have any photos of him around the cottage?'

'Never had a camera. This idea of capturing someone, a permanent record . . .' Bryher left the idea unfinished.

'Do you wish you had some now?'

'In case I forget what he looked like?'

He caught the edge in her voice. This was the other side of her; the side that let you see just so much, then closed you out. 'No,' he said, 'I'm just . . .'

They scored a line of quiet under the exchange. Finn pulled the map out and unfolded it. From Wreckers Hill you could see most of the island, and he tried to match it against Bryher's version. He identified South Hill, right at the bottom end; to the north, the broad hump of The Down concealed the tapering Down Head. This was the quiff, a knuckly finger pointing out to sea. It was spectacular, apparently; wild and rocky and bashed by the waves. According to Jad, there was a secret cave where a wise old hermit lived. A month or so back, Bryher had said, while Jad was beachcombing there at low tide, the boy had discovered a man's leather boot. He'd brought it to her in case it was Roop's. But it wasn't. It was just a boot. She'd kept it, even so. Filled it with potting soil; Finn had seen it on the kitchen window sill, with shoots of mint growing.

'How come the hedges are so high?'

He was looking down into the central part of the island, its neat, boxed-in plots of vegetables, flowers and fruit enclosed by walls of glossy green shrubs taller than a man. Windbreaks, she said, protecting the crops from onshore breezes and salt spray.

'Pittosporum, Euonymus and Veronica.'

He frowned over the map. 'So which house do those three live in?'

Bryher laughed. Easy with him again, now that the momentary awkwardness was behind them. They settled themselves on the grass among the ruins of the watch house and shared the apples she'd brought. Finn took in the view as he ate. The daffodils weren't in flower yet. The fields were brown still. Corrugated. It would be a while before the rows 'showed green', as Bryher called it.

A breeze had got up. He folded the map away. 'I could go anywhere, here,' Finn said. 'No getting hassled or mugged or beaten up. Folk stop and chat.'

'Even Tye?' Bryher was smiling. Teasing.

'Yeah, well.' Finn smiled too.

'He's all right, Tye. It's not you he dislikes, it's the situation.'

'You've got – what? – a dozen adults here,' Finn said. 'Not everyone's going to like me or want me around, whatever you reckon about *consensus*.'

Bry left that unanswered. She'd refused to tell him who had said what at the Gathering; who was on Finn's side, who was against. They didn't think like that, here, she said, but if he wanted to see it in those terms then they were all on his side against the draft. The question was, were they prepared to put themselves, their *community*, at risk by continuing to offer him refuge? So it wasn't about him, as such. It'd seemed to be about him, though, in the days after that Gathering. In ones and twos, the islanders had come to the cottage to introduce themselves. To welcome him. To talk to him. To suss him out, was how it felt. But this was just him, projecting. Bryher had told him about the barter, but none of them spoke of it unless he did. It was their decision to go along with Mr Skins, their responsibility. Not his. That was the party line. 'Anything happens to us, it's self-inflicted.' Tye had said that. It could've been any of them, but it was Tye. Finn didn't know what to make of him, or whether he meant it. He hadn't stayed long. Ten minutes, maybe less.

On Wreckers Hill, Bryher was picking absent-mindedly at the stitching on a repair job on her jeans.

'You lot don't wear clothes,' Finn said, 'you wear patches.'

'You're really quite shallow, aren't you?'

'Not beneath the surface.'

She laughed. 'Anyway, Amver always manages to look stylish in patches.'

The dark-haired girl on the lobster boat. That was still how he pictured Amver, even though she'd called at Bry's the day after the Gathering, sat in the garden with him; she was going to the mainland, to uni, and she couldn't wait, and what was such-and-such a town like and what was the Capital like? The way she'd been – poised, but restless – was just as she'd been when he caught that first glimpse of her on the boat. A balancing act. Balancing between what and what was hard to tell.

'That's her place.' Bry pointed to a partially obscured cottage at the foot of the hill, where the orchards began. There was washing on the line. 'Her, Jad and Yué.'

'What's the story with the dad?'

'Mor? He went back. Got a job on the trawlers a way down the coast.'

'Just upped and left?'

'Uh-huh.'

'How long had he been here?'

'Twenty years.'

He was conscious of Bryher, watching the remains of his apple spin away into the undergrowth. His thoughts drifted to Kurt, to the place where he'd been blown up. Finn had no idea of the location, the lie of the land, yet he imagined it had happened somewhere like this. A hill, the grass shifting in the wind, a grenade lobbed down – not lobbed, *propelled* – into an assault party. There was the oddest sense of *déjà vu*, as if it really had happened right here, on Wreckers Hill, not in some anonymous place halfway round the globe. It had been a while since he'd thought about Kurt.

Maybe the quality of his silence tuned her in; more likely, she'd been building up to this and it happened to come out now. The loss of people we love. Mor, Roop, Kurt. Dipping her chin, as if to set the words carefully on the ground between them, Bryher said: 'D'you miss him?'

He figured who she meant, but even so he said: 'Who?'

'Your brother.'

'Yeah. Yeah, I do.' Finn had told her some of it before; not much, but some. Now he let out the full story. Bry heard him without interruption. 'Jad probably told you all this already,' Finn said.

Bryher smiled. 'Most of it, yeah.'

'He dredged it out of me down at Gibbet Cove. Twelve going on forty.'

'Jad listens,' she said. 'I talk to him a lot. About Roop, about all sorts.'

'Does he ask you about when you were a nurse? The gory bits.'

'The more blood, the better.'

After a pause, he said: 'I lied to him about Kurt cutting off his own foot. Told him they'd both been blown off by the grenade.' Finn had been reclining on the grass, propped up on his elbows. He sat up again. 'I feel bad for lying to him.'

As he said this, he wished more than anything that he'd told Jad the truth – told him about the blood, the bone. The hacking. That a man – a soldier – could do that to himself. *You should've fucking seen it, Jad.* Not simply because he felt so bad about lying. But because, in the boy's response, he might've found the key to his own way of dealing with what Kurt did.

Bryher's forearms were folded across her knees, the sun picking out the tiny golden hairs; like a dusting of brown sugar. 'Was he afraid?' she said.

'Jad?'

'Kurt. Was he afraid of fighting?'

Finn went to say yes, then corrected himself. 'At first, I guess – when he signed up.' He rubbed at his chest with the flat of his hand. The sweat had dried on him and he could smell his own body odour. 'Then, after he'd been trained, and the longer he was in, it was, like . . . he was more soldier than civilian. He didn't seem afraid any more. In his letters. The way he talked when he came home on leave.'

'You think, what?' she said. 'Soldiers aren't afraid to fight, and civilians are?'

201

'It's what they do.' Finn tried to explain himself. 'I look up at a bloke on some scaffolding – a builder, fifty metres up – and I think: *Jesus, I'd cack myself.* But you do that every day, you don't cack yourself. It's your job. You do it.'

'Builders die. They fall off and die sometimes. Soldiers die.'

'Kurt reckoned the worst thing about being a soldier was boredom. Weeks of sitting around, waiting to fight. *Not* fighting, was what he hated.'

Bryher didn't respond. She'd tipped her head forward so her face was hidden. Her hair had two crowns. He hadn't noticed that before.

'Anyway, what do I know?' Finn said. 'I don't know fuck all.'

Her tone softened. 'Don't be so hard on yourself.'

'But I don't know, do I?'

'When someone you love dies, it's easy to hate yourself for still being here.' She glanced up at him, pursing her lips a little. 'If you let that feeling take hold, you can end up wishing you'd died as well.'

They stood up, ready to head back down. The ocean seemed bluer than ever. With no muddy rivers draining into it, there was no discolouring – just a brilliant blue glazed by sunlight. From the hilltop, the seabed was visible to a depth of several fathoms.

'Look,' she said. 'Porpoises.'

He saw them, less than thirty metres from the shore directly beneath them at The Strand – half a dozen, sleek, grey, arcing in and out of the water in single file. It was so quiet Finn could hear the spray hiss from their spouts.

'Fantastic,' he said.

She was pointing further out to sea now. A boat. White, slicing through the water at speed and raising weals of wake. A patrol launch. He'd seen one before, from the bedroom window at the cottage. Bryher had told him there was a naval installation forty or so K up the coast, and the patrols were a regular sight; sometimes they'd put ashore. The crew would nose around. Help themselves to fish, a basket of lobster. Maybe set themselves up with a crate of beer and a barbeque on one of the beaches. This patrol, though, was maintaining a steady course, following the channel to the east of the island's outlying rocks. Even so, a weight settled in his guts.

'No visit today,' she said.

'No.'

Finn's shoulders smarted. He pulled on his T-shirt. From up here, the beach at The Strand looked perfect as an iced cake. He decided to swim there that afternoon.

'He thinks you'll unsettle us,' Bryher said.

She meant Tye, she said. She'd do this – spin off from whatever she'd been thinking about, expecting you to follow. Perhaps the launch had triggered this one. If Finn wasn't here, the islanders would have no cause to worry at the sight of a patrol.

'Unsettle,' he said. 'Am I unsettling, would you say?'

Bryher wouldn't be provoked. 'We should cope with you. Someone in your situation, I mean. If we don't change, we stagnate – and, then, what's the point?'

'What's the point of what?'

'All this. If we can't reinvent ourselves we might as well do what Mor did.'

It struck Finn that she was really talking about herself. Or about him. 'The mainland isn't an alternative,' he said.

'Not for you, maybe. Not at the moment.'

'Didn't you lot come here to leave that place? Didn't you and Roop do that?'

'People came here for all sorts of reasons.'

Sometimes, arguing with Bry, he felt like the issues were too complicated for him. He didn't want her to think that. Her tease about him being shallow had got to him. 'I've never had a sense of

203

belonging over there, like the one you have here,' he said. 'Not *you*, specifically – all of you.'

'Are you talking about before the war?' she said. 'Before the draft?'

'Long as I can remember. I used to think: these aren't my people, this isn't my place. This isn't what I want to do.'

'What do you want to do?'

'That's just it,' he said. 'I've only ever known what I *didn't* want to do.'

'Roop used to say he was an islander trapped in a mainlander's body.'

'I don't feel that.'

She was plucking hard once more at the patched-up leg of her jeans. Her skin showed through. 'Me neither,' she said, quietly.

No disloyalty in this. Again, it was more complicated. Finn spoke of his alienation, his disaffection, towards his own country – its people, its culture, its attitudes. Not just the state. He used a Lila word – 'anomie' – surer of its meaning than he'd been back then. It was in him long before he was conscripted. Most of the time, you conformed, fitted in. Enough to live in that world. Enough to live with yourself. But, in your head, you were giving it the finger.

It was the longest time since Finn had talked like this with anyone. He felt loosened and stretched. Not just mentally, but physically – as though he was a lump of modelling clay, rolled out into a thin, springy strip.

'The war, the draft, what Kurt did to himself,' he said, 'they were just the final straw. It's . . . I guess it's to do with identity. Identification.'

'Uh-huh.'

'I'm not putting this very well.'

'Ask any of the first settlers – it took ages for the community to discover its sense of *self*. Same for most of us when we arrived. We were defined by what we'd left.' She paused. 'That's you. You're not an islander, you're an anti-mainlander.'

'But I didn't choose to come here, did I?'

'You're here, though. Aren't you?'

At the Hives

The day the patrol landed, Finn had been on the island six weeks. He wasn't at home when the crew came knocking; he'd gone to the hives to work with Qway. That was what he was today: a trainee assistant bee-keeper. Other days he was learning to milk the goat, or picking fruit, or cleaning out hen houses, or gathering kelp, or sea fishing, or mending nets and pots, or helping fix the roof on Orr's place, or digging vegetable plots, or unloading the supply boats Skins sent across once a week. The long period of enforced inactivity – confined to his quarters at the crocodile farm, then laid up in bed at Bryher's place – had left him brimming with energy. The more he did, the more he wanted to do. Finn had never relished work before. But, then, he'd never done these kinds of jobs before. Real labour. Working with his hands, his whole body. Keeping going even when you were knackered. It was as if he wanted not just to work but to test his limits of endurance – to punish himself, almost, for his weeks as an invalid and, before that, the years of screen gazing and keyboard pecking, sat on his ass in a poxy office. More than that, he wanted to give something back to this place that was his adoptive home, and to these people who'd put themselves at risk to harbour him. Bry was right: he may not have chosen to come here, but he was *here* now. He could choose how he lived. Displaced, snuck away in fear like a refugee, an asylum seeker, a fugitive . . . or right out there, living it large, like he belonged.

So Finn worked. He worked his fucking butt off.

That afternoon, as the patrol crew put ashore, he was climbing a seized metal gate into the place where the bees were kept. The hives, five of them, stood beside a corrugated-iron shed, which was arched like an air-raid shelter, in an overgrown meadow. Wild daffodils bobbed among the rough grass. The rattle of the gate drew a figure from the shed. Qway. He smiled, waving Finn over.

'You made it, then.'

It was hard to look at Qway, the dazzle of his white boiler suit in the sunshine. His head, cropped to a sandy-coloured pelt, gleamed. He was taller and bulkier than Finn. Chunky, freckly knuckles; clumsy looking. You could picture him ripping open a pack of rice and the grains scattering everywhere.

Qway gestured at the hives, the meadow. 'What do you think of my retreat?'

Finn looked around, nodding. 'I've been in worse dumps.'

'Come on,' Qway said, smiling, 'I'll show you my shed. There's cold drinks and candy . . . and a visitor who'll hog the lot, given the chance.'

The visitor could've been anyone; the islanders were fluid, moving where they were needed and showing up unpredictably; it was a pattern of sorts and, somehow, all the tasks got done. Inside, it took his eyes a moment to adjust. He made out a figure in a weird-looking chair. He'd imagined the shed to be hot and airless, oven-like; in fact, even with the candles, it was cool. The figure gradually became distinct. Female. Amver. In the candle-light, her long black hair appeared blue.

Sucking at whatever was in her mouth, she said: 'Welcome.'

The mood was druggy, den-like, furtive. Finn saw that Amver's chair was the type you use at the dentist, minus the anglepoise lamp and the vine of drilling gear. The girl faced a table laid with plates, tumblers, a pitcher; on the near side, a pair of regular armchairs covered with plain white throws.

Finn and Qway sat down. 'It's the sucrose,' Qway said, his knees jolting the table. 'She becomes all garrulous and affectionate. Don't take it personally.'

'Have some,' the girl said, leaning across the table to pass Finn a plate.

On it was a hard-looking white slab, chopped into cubes. Finn tried a piece. Flavour burst in his mouth like all the sweetness you've ever tasted. 'Mm. What is it?'

'Ambrosia, is what it is,' Amver said. 'Little squares of heaven.'

Qway was more practical. 'Half a litre of water to two and a half kilos of sugar.' Then, as an afterthought: 'White sugar, not brown, or they get dysentery.'

'They?' Finn said.

'The bees.'

'Imagine that,' Amver said. 'Bee dysentery.'

Finn frowned. 'I thought they lived on . . . pollen, and stuff. Flowers.'

'They're my babies,' Qway said. 'I spoil them.'

'Put it under your tongue.' This was Amver. Holding his gaze, she spoke softly. 'Don't chew, just leave it there till it melts . . . away . . . to . . . *nothing*.'

They talked. Mostly, the two men talked. Amver did her sucrose trippy thing, drifting in and out of the exchanges. Finn took in his surroundings. The 'living' area occupied the front portion of the shelter. A large rag rug and the table and chairs (the dentist chair had been salvaged from a container that broke up on the rocks at Dread Bay). The rest of the space was for storage: Qway's bee-keeping gear; then, further into the dark recesses, assorted junk and clutter. Finn noticed a pile of old backpacks, holdalls and suitcases. Dusty, cobwebby, mouldy. He asked about them. They were the bags the islanders had used to carry their belongings across when they'd settled here. Some were thirty years old. They could've burned them, dumped them, or put them to some other purpose; but here they were, decomposing in a dirty, undisturbed corner of a shack. Like their owners' attachment to the lives they'd left behind – not deleted, but deliberately memorialised by neglect. Finn suggested this to the others, that it was kind of symbolic. They laughed. Qway said no, the bags had been stowed there for want of anyplace else to put them.

'I feel like we're playing hookey when we should be working.' Finn nodded at the drinks, the candy. 'Like this is against the rules or something.'

Qway shook his head. 'There are no rules, here.'

Amver spoke then. Her first contribution for some time. 'Surely the absence of rules is a rule in itself?' she said. 'Rule number one: Thou Shalt Have No Rules.'

Finn smiled.

'It's repressive,' Amver said, and he saw that she wasn't joking. 'Having to do the right thing, live the right way. "Least harm, most good." Anyone ever told you that?' She'd draped one arm over the side of the dentist's chair, like she was in a row-boat, trailing her fingers in the water. Finn said no, no one had told him that. 'The island's ethos,' Amver said. 'Unwritten, of course. But everything we do or say has to pass the test.' She made a face. 'It's just *so* much crap.'

Qway cut in, his voice hard; the first time Finn had heard one islander use that tone to another. 'You'll be free of all that *crap* soon enough.'

Amver's eyes remained fixed on Finn, ignoring Qway but

answering him at the same time. Quietly, half-smiling, she said: 'One can only hope.'

Finn wondered how they squared the two: the absence of rules, and the least-harm-most-good rule. How they'd square it, if they found out what he was expected to do for Mr Skins, when the time came. He'd thought of telling Bryher. He could see himself telling these two, if it was booze and dope instead of candy and juice. The longer he lived among these people, working with them, immersing himself in this place, the more he wanted to confess. And the harder that became. Amver had zoned out again. Her face surprised him, flickeringly illuminated. Gothic pale. The slant of her cheeks, her eyes. The minutely freckled nose. Before dating Lila he'd noticed her, working in a book store he passed on his way to work. Each morning, he'd sneak a glance in the window. When he finally went in to talk to her, she looked different, across the counter, than she had from the street. A score of subtle details. Same with Amv. Her semi-detachment from the conversation, in the shed, seemed an extension of whatever game she was playing in her attitude towards him. Distant, then friendly; now, argumentative – inviting him to take sides. He wasn't sure what to make of her.

In the awkward aftermath of her spat with Qway, she produced something out of left field: 'You could *live* here,' she said, addressing Finn.

'In the shed?'

'Clear out the junk, put a bed in. Some lamps.'

'I already have someplace to live.'

Amver shrugged; in an instant it was as if the idea had gone from exciting her to boring her. She released her chair from semi to full recline, hands behind her head, legs crossed at the ankles. The insides of her arms were the colour of bleached bone in the candlelight. 'You look like someone who needs his own space, is all.'

Finn was irritated by her readiness to tell him about himself. 'I like living at the cottage,' he said, taking another piece of candy. 'You get used to people.'

Qway, in broad-brimmed hat and veil, made a clumsy job of cutting the last slab into pieces and taking the tray outside. But when he placed the candy in each of the hives, there was a transformation. Precise, gentle – as dexterous in handling the frame and positioning the food as a bomb–disposal expert defusing an unexploded device.

'You have to take care not to crush any of them,' he said.

Finn was standing back, unprotected. Amver had gone, leaving him to his first bee-keeping lesson. 'What,' he said, 'in case they give off an alarm to the other bees?'

'Well, there is that.' Qway half-turned to peer at him through the veil. 'Also, if you crush a bee, it dies.'

Finn didn't know how many bees were in there, but he hadn't appreciated that losing one or two would matter. This lot looked docile, dozy – not buzzing around so much as dribbling in and out of the hives. He thought it would make his skin crawl, but it didn't. When Qway was done, and had covered and sealed the candy stores – 'to keep wasps out' – he returned to Finn's side, removing the protective headgear.

'You don't wear gloves,' Finn said.

'Smell.' Qway held out his hands. 'Cider vinegar. Deters them from stinging. Anyway, I'm such a galumph with the gloves on.'

Finn raised his head. 'What is it with Amver?'

'It's since she lost Mor,' Qway said. Then, shrugging: 'I'm no psychoanalyst. I don't know why she's the way she is, but she's changed this past year.'

The way he talked, you'd have thought Amver had suffered a bereavement. They were standing close to the shed, toasted by the sun's heat radiating from the metal. Finn had removed his boots

211

and socks. Qway's boiler suit was unzipped, the sleeves rolled up. His arms were muscular, dense with gingery-blond hair.

'What was Roop like?' Finn said.

'Roop?'

'Bry doesn't talk about him much. Not to me.'

'He was way sexier than you,' Qway said, smiling. 'No offence.'

Finn laughed. 'None taken.'

'Roop was so fucking straight it made you weep.' Qway allowed himself a laugh too. Then, serious again: 'Seeing you in his gear.' He tugged at Finn's combat pants. 'I'd find that the toughest thing of all, if I was Bry – catching these glimpses of her man everywhere.'

'She still goes out looking for him. Even if we're just at the beach, walking, having a picnic, whatever – I'll catch her staring along the shoreline.'

Qway dropped his gaze down at their feet. 'I know.' After a long gap, he said: 'He grew impatient. Reckless. Wanting more of everything – of life, I suppose – and always pushing it to the edge.'

'How d'you mean, reckless?'

Qway hesitated. 'That wasn't the first time he'd stayed at sea in the fret for one last catch. Roop died, but he could've killed Nudge as well.' His tone remained even, unemotional. 'You can't make Nudge see the truth of that, of course. Or Bry.'

Finn was dripping sweat. The drone of the bees pulsed to the rhythm of the beating sun. 'I had him down as some kind of tragic hero,' he said. 'The great love and loss of her life.'

'Well, he was all of that too.'

They talked some more. About Roop, Bryher. They were still talking when a distant voice caused them to look up. A yell.

'Thin! Thin!'

Finn looked up to see Jad sprinting down the track. Waving

212

his arms, calling to him again and again. At first, Finn mistook it for the *watch-out-here-I-come* whoop of an exuberant boy. As he drew nearer – the jerk of his limbs, the quality of his cries – Finn sensed something was wrong. Jad wasn't excited, he was scared shitless.

The Patrol

She tried to convince herself it was routine. The patrol crew were heading out on foot from the landing jetty to Down Head and the path, as it would do, had taken them by her cottage. She'd been in the garden, and so they had stopped to pass the time of day. Roop hadn't been mentioned. They joked about the weather – 'raining again, then?' – and made small talk. All very flirtatious; this, in itself, reassured her. They were acting the way mainland men act when talking to a woman. The more senior of the two was the more self-confident; but the younger one – tall, athletic, his scalp stubble shorter than that on his face – looked the likelier to take his chances with her. Rumours had reached the island from other remote coastal regions of patrol crews raping civilians. Bryher searched this one's eyes for signs he might be capable. He was about Roop's age or older. A regular, not a conscript, she supposed. Too androgynously pretty to be a marine, which might explain the haircut, the hard-man expression. The pose would have been ludicrous, in different circumstances. Here, now, his air of menace didn't seem so fake. Also, he looked familiar. This was what troubled her, she realised: that he might've been here before.

Might have met Roop. It was unlikely, given that crews were assigned to coastal security for short-term stints, as respite duty, before returning to the front; and that patrols had put ashore only a dozen times or so in her two years here. What were the chances of seeing the same one twice? All the same, the young marine bothered her. She was just thankful he hadn't caught Finn at home.

Then the older of the two asked to use the bathroom. By the time he came back outside, Finn had appeared on the path that skirted Wreckers Hill.

'This is Roop,' she said, kissing his cheek.

Finn had joined her in the garden, facing the marines across the low wall. He seemed relaxed; that should've eased her own anxiety, but for some reason it didn't.

'Hi.' Finn smiled at the men. 'How you doing?'

They failed to acknowledge his greeting. The older one repeated, to Finn, what he had told Bryher: they were here to recce sites for the installation of a radio mast. A 'comms. tower'. They would scout The Down and Down Head this afternoon, then camp overnight and check out the island's other hilltops in the morning. The flirty edge had gone from his tone; he was serious, blokeish. Man to man. His manner, even so, implied an inequality – the squaddie, and the civvy. Their dress emphasised this. His hair in need of a trim, and wearing Roop's stained T-shirt and baggy combats, Finn was a beach bum beside the two men in camouflage kit, black boots and with the hardware that was clipped, hooked and strapped to them. If they'd had cause, they could have killed him in an instant. All Finn carried was a jar of honey in each hand, like a pair of pretend grenades. As if conscious of this, he set them down on the wall.

Bryher had kept her hand on Finn's shoulder after kissing him; she lowered it, taking his hand and interlocking fingers. He

215

returned the pressure. If she let go, she was sure her tremor would become obvious.

'How romantic.' This was the senior one. 'I must remember to hold my wife's hand, next time I get to see her.'

'You must miss her,' she said, acting as if his remark had not been sarcastic. Wanting them to go, but not for them to see that.

The officer looked at her. 'Yeah, well. Goes with the job, doesn't it?'

'How long you been in?' Finn said.

'Ten years.' He adjusted his ammunition harness. 'Only another eleven to go and I can take my pension and live somewhere like this. Sit on my ass in the sunshine all fucking day.' Then, evenly, to Bryher: 'If you'll excuse my language.'

Finn was smiling. Bryher squeezed his hand to shut him up, but he wouldn't. 'We've only been here a couple of years and my ass is worn out already.'

'Is that right?'

The younger marine, who had said nothing since Finn arrived – who'd barely taken his eyes off Finn – was watching him still. His expression blank, unreadable. He might have been staring at a TV programme that didn't particularly interest him, but none the less held his gaze. She tried to place him, to settle whether she recognised him or was simply alarming herself. But she couldn't. What was clear was that neither of the marines was in a hurry to go; she could conceive of them remaining there, talking across the wall, until dusk made their features indistinct. Standing, as they were now: cryptic, watchful. The younger one produced a canister from his pack, eyes steady on Finn as he drank. She watched his Adam's apple move as he swallowed. He shared the water with his partner. Bryher had to halt this. Before she could think of a way to break the men's hold over them, the older one spoke.

'Can I see your ID, please?' He looked at Finn, then at her. 'Sir. Madam.'

'Our ID?' Bryher said.

'Just routine. We'll be calling at all the residences while we're here.'

'Mine's indoors,' she said.

'Sir?'

'Mine too.'

'You're meant to keep it with you at all times. You do know that?'

Bryher went inside to get the cards. When she returned, Finn and the two men were as she had left them: on opposite sides of the wall, motionless and silent. They resembled actors, in position, waiting for the filming of a scene to begin. She surrendered their ID. Calm, deliberate. She suspected, even as she did it, that being too controlled might be as much of a giveaway as being too nervous. The desire for the marines to leave was so acute now it lodged in her throat like an obstruction.

The officer examined the cards in turn, glancing up at each of their faces as if to check them against their digitalised photographs. Addressing Finn, he said: 'Could you confirm your date of birth for me, please?'

They had practised this, but – in the beat between question and response – she tightened with the fear of Finn getting it wrong. He didn't. He reeled it off. Bryher, on the other hand, was so preoccupied she stumbled over her own birth date. The officer, though, seemed satisfied. Even so, he continued to inspect the cards – one forged, the other genuine – and she wondered if Finn's would pass this, its first official scrutiny.

'Roop,' he said at last. 'What sort of a name is that?'

'You want to meet my brothers,' Finn said. 'Hoop and Loop.'

The officer regarded his colleague. Deadpan, no trace of amusement. 'What we have here is a taking-the-piss type situation, wouldn't you say?' The younger one didn't reply. Turning back to Finn again, the first one said: 'Roop, Hoop and Loop.'

'When the three of us are together we're called Groop.'

Bryher dipped her head, trying not to laugh. The officer looked to be weighing up possible responses. In the end, he simply indicated the honey on the wall and asked if it was fresh. Finn confirmed that it was. At a gesture from his superior, the younger marine helped himself to the jars, stowing them in his pack.

'A home-made loaf would go nicely with that,' the officer said. 'Bit of butter. Some fruit. Maybe a lobster or a couple of crabs, if you've got any.'

'Milk,' the younger one said; his first word since Finn appeared. Still staring at him, aiming the syllable at him like a blown kiss. A *fuck-you* kiss.

The officer smiled. 'He likes his milk, this one. Milk and honey.'

Finn had fallen silent. Bryher was conscious of him, monitoring her comings and goings from the cottage. As she gave up each item, the younger of the two men ensured their hands made contact; she was aware of Finn observing that, too. She would have expected the marine's skin to be abrasive, but it was smooth, his touch as gentle as a caress. This unnerved her more than if she had been groped. Fetching the milk, the last of the provisions, Bryher set it down on the wall between them before he had a chance to take it from her. All this achieved was to leave him looking pleased with himself, smiling at the small triumph of causing her to do this. With his smile, came the recognition. Bryher found herself smiling too, privately, a spreading warmth within her. She recalled where she had seen him before.

Finally, the officer returned their ID cards, as though in payment for the food. They should carry them 'about their persons' in future. With that, the men left.

It was warm enough for them to eat outside in the failing light but, perhaps because the garden carried an after-trace of the patrol crew, they remained indoors. They sat in the living room, two half-eaten meals pushed aside. Their lack of appetite told its own story. Nevertheless, the ebbing of Bryher's adrenaline was drawing her anxiety away like sand in the backwash of a wave. The atmosphere in the room – cosy, the window mauve with the onset of nightfall, the candles distributing an amber glow – was one of relief rather than celebration. They'd got away with it.

'You were so cool,' Finn said.

'*You* were, you mean. I was a bag of nerves.'

'That's not how you came across.'

Bryher shook her head. 'Roop, Loop and Hoop – I nearly cracked up.'

They both laughed. Bryher was on the sofa, legs tucked beneath her; Finn, cross-legged on the floor, reclining against the armchair, the lower half of his face in shadow and the upper half splashed with candlelight. When he spoke she could barely see his lips move, but when he laughed his irises looked as if they contained glitter. The room was aromatic with onion from the unfinished omelettes. Also, with hot wax and smoke, and rosemary from the burner she'd set on the mantleshelf – its piquancy suiting the mood more beautifully than she could've anticipated. They had resumed the trawl of the incident, re-enacting parts of it line by line, Finn impersonating the officer with uncanny accuracy. It was good to enjoy the moment.

'We ought to get word to Jad that everything's OK,' she said.

'You should've seen his face.' Finn performed a mime of panic. 'Thin, they're here! They're here!'

'Don't. Poor kid.'

'Anyway, knowing Jad, he'll have found out by now that they've not come because of me.'

'What did you think, though, when you saw them outside the cottage?'

219

'I thought: that saves me the hassle of warning Bry a patrol has landed.'

'No bother, then?'

'Having to kiss you was the worst part.'

'You didn't kiss me, I kissed you.'

'Also, you grip too tight.' He flexed his fingers 'And your hands are sweaty.'

Bryher noticed the marks then. 'What've you done?'

'What?'

'Show me.' She leaned forward, reaching for his hand. 'These.'

'Stings,' Finn said. 'Jad turning up in a flap seemed to piss the bees off.'

The back of one hand was blotched with fierce lumps. Bryher fetched cotton wool and calamine and dabbed lotion on the stings. It was nothing compared to the injuries Roop had brought home; she'd sat with him, right here, suturing a gash at the base of his thumb. Finn's hands were cold, although they were warming from the contact.

'I've seen him before,' she said. 'The younger one. The one with his head shaved.'

Finn looked alarmed. 'Here?'

'On the mainland – when I was training.' She binned the last of the swabs and sealed the calamine. 'He'd come off a motorbike and fractured his wrist. I'd only been attached to A & E a couple of weeks and this was my first cast.'

'He was hitting on you out there,' Finn said.

'He hit on me *then*,' she said, laughing. 'Me, the woman doctor who examined him, the radiographer, the receptionist. Thought we were all drooling over him.' She wiped her fingers. The scent of the lotion had obliterated all the others in the room. 'He wasn't hitting on me earlier,' she said. 'That was all about power. Intimidation.'

'D'you think he recognised you?'

'I doubt it.' She sank back into the cushions, the drama of the day catching up with her in a wave of tiredness. Finn's sheet, blanket and pillow were stacked, not so neatly, at the other end of the sofa, ready for the nightly rebuilding of his bed on the living-room floor. Bryher stretched her legs, her feet resting on the pile of bedding. 'My hair's way shorter now, and the sun's bleached it. Also, I haven't got the spotty-faced, pasty mainlander complexion of a student nurse living on toast, pot-noodles and carbon monoxide.' She shrugged. 'And so what if he does?'

'I can't imagine you living anywhere before this. You and the mainland, you seem totally . . . *alien* to one another.'

That was the word: alien. Bryher felt that too. Or, at least, it was how she liked to characterise herself in relation to her former life. But then, encounters with patrol crews, or Skins' men, or other outsiders, always held a resonance of the mainland for her. Cracking the carapace she'd constructed around herself on the island. Even now, two years on. Perhaps especially now, with Roop gone and Finn here, the streetwise chancer from the Capital being lippy to a patrol crew.

'Living with you,' she said, then paused, seeking the correct description. 'It's like there's a piece of the mainland still stuck inside me. I'm different, around you.'

'I'm the one who's different,' Finn said.

'I get stressed. With you, myself. With *things*. I've not been like that for ages.'

'And you think that's down to me?'

'Partly, yeah.' Then, 'No, it's me. It's *in* me.'

'You don't think it's anything to do with the fact that you want Roop back, and I can't give you that?'

'I don't need you to tell me that.' Then checking herself, she said: 'Sorry.'

Finn exhaled. 'Me too.'

They fell quiet. A couple of the candles had burned out and the

221

room dimmed a little, the pattern of its shadows subtly altered. Finn clasped his hands behind his head. He looked restless. This, Bryher suspected, was one of what he called his booze-and-smokes occasions; except that, as usual, there were none to be had. She reflected on what they had said. There were other, less negative, aspects to Finn being here. She caught herself registering the silence: apart from waves striking the rocks in the cove, the odd creak of the cottage's timber frame, the putter of the oil-burner, there wasn't a sound to be heard. Several times, over the weeks, Finn had remarked on the quality of quietness here, and she had agreed with him; but only at this moment, attending to the hush, did she appreciate that she had come to take the island's tranquillity for granted. And that it had been Finn who'd helped her to recognise it afresh. Bryher would have liked to articulate this – to thank him for it, as well as for the other small sharpenings of her senses that had come with the seeing of this place through his eyes. To show that he didn't merely rekindle the mainlander in her. But the phrases she rehearsed in her head embarrassed her, and she left them unsaid.

When they turned in, Finn suggested he share Bryher's bed in case the patrol made a surprise visit in the night. A joke; she took it as such.

It was only as she settled down to sleep that Finn's words troubled her. Bryher thought of his bedding, heaped on the sofa, and how the older of the two marines had come into the cottage to use the bathroom. Although he was gone longer than seemed necessary, she hadn't made anything of it at the time. Now, she imagined him nosing around, discovering that this loving couple – with their hand-holding and affectionate kisses – slept apart. At the very least, it would strike him as unusual. And perhaps not straight away, but sooner or later, that sense of oddness might harden into suspicion.

The Men on the Hill

It was one thing to swim in the ocean, or to look out over it from the shore or from a hilltop, but it was something else to be riding it – bullied by wind and waves, soaked in spray – in a two-and-a-half-metre fibreglass craft piloted by a twelve-year-old joyrider.

'Do we have to go so fast?' Finn said, shouting to make himself heard.

'What?'

'*Slow down!*'

'This isn't fast.' Jad raised the revs. '*This* is fast.'

Finn grabbed at the sides. 'Fuck sake.'

Fun over, Jad eased off the throttle and the launch slipped into synch with the swell, skimming and steady and rhythmic. They were passing the cliffs of The Down. The boat was compact, pale blue with white trim. Jad sat in the stern, controlling the arm of the outboard motor, which was sleek, gunmetal grey, and hoarse as a bandsaw. The wind was against them. Finn's eyes watered, his hair all over the place, and he tasted salt and felt the skin tightening on his cheeks as the sea spray dried. This was OK, now they'd slowed. He let go of the sides and half-turned to watch Jad, whose red netball bib was straining at its ties. That familiar expression of a child trying out the face he would have as an adult. Gulls soared and shrieked overhead. Away to the left – *to port* – waves exploded against the jagged base of the cliffs; to starboard lay the blur of the mainland; ahead, relentless blue.

They put ashore at a narrow inlet where the waters calmed enough for Jad to secure the boat and for them to disembark safely. The boy wanted to show him The Shoot. Stepping across wet rocks, then a scramble to where the granite formed a broad shelf. They were making their way through a channel in the cliffs. This was the joint that connected Down Head to The Down, Jad explained, leading the way. At high tide they'd be spat right out of here by the sea, squirting through the gap; it was safe just now, he said, so long as they cleared out in good time. Finn felt like a character in a children's adventure story.

'The hermit's cave is up there,' Jad said, as the channel widened. It was less sheer here; you could clamber up out of The Shoot and on to the moorland that rose above on either side. The boy was pointing. 'Badplace Hill. The easiest way to the cave is on foot, from Bryher's, or over the rocks from the track above Dread Bay.'

Badplace Hill. Dread Bay. 'Who made up these names?' Finn said.

'Dread Bay was where most of the shipwrecks happened. In history, and that.'

They sat to watch the water in the narrow, lower cleft. White with violence. The blast from a hundred police water-cannons. If it was like that at low tide, he'd not want to be sitting here when the full force of the ocean came barrelling right through.

'I should be in school today,' Jad said.

'School?'

'At Sholo's.'

'Right.' Finn had seen the children there when he'd called in during one of his walkabouts. 'Is this going to get you in trouble,' he said, 'coming out with me?'

'You don't get in trouble with Sholo. You just feel bad.'

Finn understood that. Bry had that effect on him sometimes. 'I used to hook off all the time,' he said. He almost added: 'when I was your age', but stopped himself.

'Did you ever get in fights?'

Finn looked at him. 'Fights?'

'At school. You know, with other boys.'

Jad was watching The Shoot with a switched-off expression, as if he'd lost interest in his own question even before Finn answered. The dead spit of his sister in that instant. He uprooted clumps of moss and flicked them away on the breeze.

'Yeah, I had fights.' Finn had never had a fight at school. He'd been beaten up a couple of times (no resistance, he'd just curled up and shielded his head till they stopped kicking); one time, he'd swung his book bag at a kid. He said none of this. Twenty-four, trying to impress a boy half his age.

Jad sniffed and swallowed. 'I wouldn't want to go to school on the mainland.'

Finn thought of the differences; growing up here, or on the mainland. 'No,' he said, 'you wouldn't.'

The boy inspected his fingers, rubbed them on his shorts. 'Thin?'

'Yeah?'

'D'you have sex with Bryher?'

Finn gave himself a moment. 'No.'

'Why not?'

'It's not like that between us.'

Jad looked on the point of saying something else, but didn't. The sea water in The Shoot was already frothing over the rim of the lower channel. The rocks there were patterned with rust-coloured marks – ornately geometric, as if tools or pieces of

225

machinery had once been placed there to corrode. Finn figured the stains came from the rock itself. Or from its interaction with the sea or the salt or something. Whatever, they were beautiful.

On the boat again, Finn thought about Bry. About how it was between them. On the mainland, he'd have seen sex as a natural, almost inevitable, development in their . . . whatever it was. Relationship. Situation. Their arrangement. Two fit young people under one roof: they make love. It wasn't happening. The shadow of Roop, of Mr Skins, the patrol crew – and his expectation that if he slept with Bryher she would, sooner or later, have cause to hate him for it. In the two weeks since the patrol they'd been good, in that brother-and-sister way. They'd not seen the marines since; the crew didn't call again during their recce and hadn't returned to the island, despite Bryher's fear that the bedding had given them away. The incident had strengthened them, made them see they were in this together. At the same time, it had left a nagging anxiety. A tension, for all that they tried to persuade themselves they hadn't been suspected. If each passing day put distance between them and the marines, it also brought closer the day when the men might come knocking again.

They rounded the tip of Down Head and passed the cliffs on the far side of the headland, where there were puffins and guillemots high up on the face. When he got back, he would tell her about them. He would say that, but for her, he couldn't have identified the birds and maybe wouldn't even have paid them any attention. She would smile and be pleased by that. The wind was at their backs now, stronger, and the sea was more choppy. The western coast was angled full tilt into the insistent onslaught of the rollers that heaved in from another part of the hemisphere. Already, Finn saw that its cliffs were more tumble-down and eroded, debris piled up at their feet in truck-sized chunks, and that Dread Bay – the northernmost of the great bays on this shore – was gaping and hostile; a punched-in, broken-

226

toothed scream compared to the small, sweet smiles of the eastern coves and strands. Jad said seals hung out around here, but they didn't spot any that morning. The boy plotted a course well clear of the shoreline, rugged enough in itself, and guarded by rocks, only some of which ruptured the surface. If you didn't know the waters here you'd kill yourself. Finn felt safe with Jad. From his face, the way he conducted himself and the boat, you could see the boy was showing respect to this coast, that he knew what he was doing – and that, of the two of them, he was the man just now.

This was the kind of trip Finn had dreamed of taking with Kurt, the time they ran away to sea and got as far as the motorway.

'My brother would've *loved* this,' he said, turning in his seat. But Jad smiled and shrugged to say he couldn't hear him, and Finn faced the front again.

They picnicked on the beach at The Ear. A pair of oystercatchers were goose-stepping across the sand, peeping to one another. Here, the dunes were reinforced with granite blocks – from Purgo's time, Jad said; or else the sea would one day split the island in half across the low-lying neck where the crops and most of the daffodils grew. Finn finished eating, lay back in the sun and shut his eyes. He fitted the bay into the map of the island he held in his head. They must've been a few minutes' walk from Sholo and Hobb's place, a white-washed house out on a point. The time he'd visited, Sholo was in the garden, with the children working at easels. Kags, Peef and Jafe painting, Jad sketching in charcoal. They had been asked to make pictures of 'courage' and 'cowardice', Sholo had told him. Finn was curious to see how children, or anyone, would represent these; he saw they were doing no such thing – their pictures were of trees. She'd been teasing him, he figured. Or making an abstract point. You couldn't always tell, with Sholo. Jad's picture had been so good it raised hairs on your neck.

Finn remembered something. Sitting up, he reached into the bag that had contained his lunch and brought out a package, crudely enclosed in cloth and twine. He handed it to Jad; told him it was to say thanks for taking him out in the boat. Jad untied the bindings and pulled out a pair of washing-up gloves – yellow, still in their plastic wrapper. He raised his eyes to meet Finn's.

'Extra large,' the boy said.

'I found them at South Bay,' Finn said. 'When I was kelping.'

Jad examined the gloves again. He turned them over in his hands; they might have been an injured bird. 'I don't have any extra large.'

'I know.'

It was a solemn ceremony; neither of them smiled and, for a moment, Finn thought the boy was about to cry. But he didn't. He simply gave a nod and stowed the rubber gloves in his own pack and buckled the flap down tight. Jad's 'thank you' was so quiet Finn wasn't sure he'd said anything at all.

'Tell me about your brother,' Jad said.

They were both lying down now. Finn had been dozing. 'What about him?'

'About how he lost his feet.'

'I told you, I don't really know.' Finn hesitated. 'An RPG, is all I know.'

They were quiet for a while. The oystercatchers were still nearby; Finn could hear them. It sounded like crying. 'Make it up,' Jad said.

Finn propped himself up on his elbows. Jad's eyes were shut. The boy had managed to bury himself in sand up to his neck. 'Aren't you hot under all that?'

'Tell me.'

'You want me to make up a story about Kurt in the war?' Finn lay back down. 'Jesus, I don't know.'

228

'Go on.'

'I don't know if I want to do this. If I should.'

'Because I'm a *child*?'

Finn paused before answering. 'No, because he was my brother.'

Then Jad said, as if it was obvious: 'I'm your brother now.'

'A hill. A steep and grassy hill, the grass was waist deep in places, and the wind was blowing patterns in it and making it glittery so it looked like the sea. The men were at the foot of the hill, sheltering in some trees there. Kurt's unit, some other units. There were maybe sixty or seventy soldiers . . .'

'No maybes.'

'There were sixty-seven soldiers and they were looking up the hill but they couldn't see right to the top because there were false summits and dips and ledges and small valleys so that it wasn't just one slope but lots of slopes overlapping into one big hill. And there was a bunker at the top. The enemy was in the bunker. They had machine guns, grenades, RPGs. The allied troops had been ordered to make a frontal assault but the first wave had been decimated . . .'

'What does decimated mean?'

'Cut to ribbons. Mown down. The bodies were still up there in among the long grass – ten, fifteen men, it was hard to be sure with all the explosions and the shooting – and the wounded were down in the trees receiving treatment . . .'

'Were they bleeding? Were their guts hanging out?'

'Yeah, all of that. They were a mess. Some were dying. There were screams of agony and men puking up. Then it was deafening again because the allied artillery were shelling the enemy positions, to try to neutralise the bunkers, or the next assault would walk straight into a hail of bullets.'

'Why did they need to attack the hill?'

'There was an airfield the other side. They had to take control of the airfield.'

'Why didn't they come at the hill from the flanks, instead of front on?'

'I don't know, they just couldn't.'

'OK.'

'Anyway, the bombardment stopped and the order came through on comms. that they had to go up the hill again. Kurt's unit was one of those going this time. He was shitting himself after what'd happened before – the guy next to him was crying, saying he wouldn't go, but the sergeant said he'd personally kick his ass all the way up to the top of the fucken hill. You don't use that word. I didn't teach you that word.'

'The story.'

'They go. But it's just as bad – the shelling must've missed the bunker, cos the moment they reach the first crest they're being blasted and shot at and the guy in front of Kurt, something's hit him, cos his blood hits Kurt splat in the face, it's in his eyes and his mouth and he can't run cos it's too steep and the grass is long and it's hot and his lungs are bursting but he has to keep going and he steps over the other guy – the dead guy – and Kurt's putting rounds into where he thinks the bunker is . . .'

'What kind of gun?'

'Rifle. Semi–automatic. They can see me, cos the shit keeps coming and the guys to either side are dropping and some scream and some go down without a sound and there's smoke from the grenades and soil and grass spraying everywhere, and I've got earth in my right ear – *bam*, like a hammer to the head – and I think I'm deaf . . .'

'You said "I".'

'What?'

'You've switched from "him" to "me".'

'Have I? Sorry.'

'No, "I" is good. It's better. Also, you've started saying "is", not "was".'

'Is present tense all right?'

'Yeah, it's good.'

'OK, so I'm hit in the ear – mud, soil whatever – and I can't hear too well and my balance is fucked and then I see it. The bunker. I see the sun catch the nozzle of the machine gun and next to the gunner is a guy with a tube on his shoulder and it's a rocket-launcher and even as he aims it my way I keep running and shooting cos if I don't shoot him I'm fucked . . . but I'm not afraid, not even thinking, I'm just trying to shoot the cunt, take him out, but it's not happening and then I see it before I hear it. Smoke. The flame. And it's hit and I'm down on all fours facing away from the bunker, and there it is, I can see it. My foot. My boot with my fucking foot inside. I don't look at the end of my leg. I don't want to look at the end of my leg so I just keep on looking at the boot, my boot, and I think maybe if I could crawl over to it – it's right there, nestled in the long grass, like something someone's dropped – if I could just crawl over to it I could reattach it. But I can't. I can't crawl. It doesn't hurt, I just can't. And then I've gone. Blackout. When I come round, I'm not on the hill any more I'm on a stretcher-bed in a tent under a mosquito net and I'm hooked up to a drip. I think I'm OK. Then I remember. I look at my leg. I let my head fall back on to the pillow and shut my eyes. With my eyes closed I see the hill, the grass blowing in the wind, the sunshine, how beautiful it is. The most beautiful place you ever saw.'

'*Feet.*'

'What?'

'You said "foot". It's "feet". Both feet get blown off.'

'No, it's foot. One foot.'

Finn told Jad the story of the other foot.

★   ★   ★

As they cleared the southern end of the island and entered calmer waters, Jad swapped seats with him.

'Your turn, Thin.'

The boy explained the controls, the steering, how left was right and right was left, indicated the channel of safe passage . . . and Finn was doing it, piloting the boat by himself, maintaining a course between the sets of faded orange marker-buoys that looped them round South Hill. Gaining speed as he gained in confidence. And OK so they zig-zagged a bit, and every time they landed, smack, off a wave Finn's pulse thumped in his throat, and sometimes the boat felt as heavy as concrete and sometimes it skipped along like it was made of cardboard and would flip at any moment, but he was doing it.

He punched the air. 'Woo-hoo!'

'You're going to kill us both!'

'I know!'

Jad grinned and gave him the thumbs up. Buddies. Comrades.

Still in storytelling mode, Finn had a fleeting fantasy that he was at the helm of a landing craft about to put a deployment of marines ashore behind enemy lines.

They hadn't discussed the war story he'd invented just now, or the true one about Kurt's death. When Finn had finished, they'd simply lain side by side on the sand in silence. Then Jad disinterred himself, and they returned to the boat. The boy seemed content to leave it at that: he had demanded the story of Kurt's feet, and that's what he'd got. The war story was a scene from a movie, in fact – a video Finn had rented a year or so ago. Lila had begun watching it with him, but she'd gone to bed before it ended. He didn't recall the title. But that's all it was, his battle scene: a clip of made-up action, customised and retold. Even so, retelling it as Kurt's story had shaken him and he was glad to let it rest. To push the guilt and the unease and the confusion aside for the moment. Not to have to think about it.

Now, back at sea – exhilarated – Finn felt the surge of release.

They were still in the lee of South Hill, with its bald grassy pate and a skirt of neglected pasture and disused daffodil fields where the lower slopes petered out into the shingle banks of the shoreline. He spotted Orr's place above the old cultivation, off the track to the summit – a cinder-block and corrugated-iron prefab shrouded in vegetation, where the dark waxy green of rhododendron gave way to yellow gorse. Dilapidated, isolated, overgrown. If you hadn't helped re-roof it a few weeks back, you could believe the building had been abandoned, left to rot, to be reclaimed by nature. On the mainland – in Paladin Mansions, for fuck sake, or anywhere – Orr would've lived as an outcast. You'd have thought he did, here, to look at the place. But, Finn had been told, he'd picked the site, selected the materials and more or less built the thing single-handed, in the days when he could still manage that. The way he lived, Orr could seek out people, if he chose to, or keep to himself. But there wasn't a day went by when one or other of the islanders didn't pay him a call to check he was OK, to bring food, to sit with him and share whatever talk was possible. Or piss off again and leave him alone, if that's what Orr wished. Seeing his place from offshore, its connectedness and disconnectedness suddenly made perfect sense to Finn.

'Can we land there?' he called, on a whim. 'See if he's home?'

Jad didn't respond.

He had the binoculars out and was training them on the hill. Then Jad lowered them and pointed. There was something in the way he did this. Finn tried to get a fix on where the boy was looking; higher, where the path curved away from Orr's place. Finn saw them. The men on the hill. Five – no, six – in single file.

Jad joined Finn in the stern. He killed the engine. 'Here.'

Finn took the binoculars. In their uniforms, the two marines were easy to pick out. Four others: three in workmen's dungarees, the fourth – bringing up the rear – wearing a light-coloured suit.

233

A hat, too. He focused in on him. Just as Jad was saying it must be the gang from the mainland, come to start work on the radio tower, Finn identified the man in white.

Mr Skins.

He lowered the binoculars. As if this action had caused it, Skins stopped at that exact moment and turned in their direction. Stock still on the track. He might've been watching them, or gazing out to sea while he took a breather. Finn was wary – afraid, almost – of using the binoculars again. If he could see Mr Skins' face in close-up, then Mr Skins would be able to see his. That was how it seemed to him. So he kept the bins down. At last the figure in white turned and continued after the other men.

The Caller at the Cottage

Finn was pegging out the wash. The clothes flapped in the breeze that came directly off the sea, which was why he and Bryher always smelled faintly of brine. He'd been at work all morning, picking fruit, and had come home to a note – Bry had gone to the boatyard (where else, these days?) and please would he see to the laundry. His hands were raw from the scrubbing. Do this, then a swim. A nap in the sun. Then throw a bit of food together for when she got back. He saw less of her now she was helping Hobb at the chandlery. That was Bryher's latest job: assistant boat-builder. She always came home buzzing, tired. Ravenous. Finn liked to cook for her, listen to her talk of battens and tapers and midship moulds. The smell of sawdust on her.

If you forgot about Mr Skins for a moment, this wasn't such a bad existence.

He'd been waiting for the crocodile farmer to pay a call since catching sight of him from the launch. That was a week ago, and still Skins hadn't shown. Maybe the man hadn't given Finn a thought in the meantime; or maybe the delay was tactical, calculated to heighten Finn's anxiety. This, the not knowing, was a part of his hold over you – you were primed, so scared of your own shadow that all he had to do was *be there*, in the background, at the edges of your imagination. While he was at the orchard, he'd seen Skins' boat dock – seen the man himself disembark – and for the rest of the morning he'd been too distracted to think about much else. Probably, Skins was just checking up on the progress his men were making with the radio mast.

Finn hung trousers, two shirts. A sock fell into the turf beneath the washing line. Stooping to retrieve it, an image of Kurt's boot, on a grassy hillside, came with the clarity of an actual memory rather than a story he'd spun for Jad. All his life, he had mythologised his brother and he was still doing it now he was dead. What he held in his head, Finn realised – what he'd always held – wasn't Kurt but a version of him, an approximation. Maybe that was the most you could hope to have of someone. This struck him with the suddenness of a revelation, but also with the familiarity of a thing he'd known all along. He tossed the peg bag into the empty wash-basket and turned to go back inside. The line creaked as it took the strain. The gulls, who'd lined up on the flat roof above the kitchen to watch Finn, on the off-chance of food scraps, flapped away as he headed towards them. Then Finn saw that something else had disturbed them – a figure, emerging from the kitchen doorway into the back garden.

'It's a lovely age, isn't it?' Mr Skins said.

His trademark white suit shimmered as he materialised from the shadows. He removed his hat. He could've been a police officer calling with bad news; but he was smiling, looking first at the departing gulls, then at Finn.

'A lovely age, we live in,' he said. 'Where a man can join in the brutality of battle or attend to the laundry. The barbaric and the domestic.' It was disconcerting, seeing him close up again, and in bright sunlight, after the remorseless rain-soaked grey of the crocodile farm. Skins' smile broadened. 'You know, time was when men were regarded as being capable of only one of these.'

Finn made no reply. Conscious of the basket, balanced against one hip. Skins cast his gaze about the garden. Why was it, he wondered aloud, that the islanders, for all their *communality*, enclosed their own personal territory with walls and hedges?

'It isn't territorial,' Finn said, trying to compose himself. 'It stops the bracken encroaching. Stops the wind and the sea spray trashing the soil.'

'You see, you are one of them now.'

'I wouldn't say that.' Finn put the basket down, nodded in the direction of the southern end of the island. 'Your men have a big job on,' he said.

'Most of the contracts in these parts come my way.'

His tone suggested the demands made upon him were a nuisance, but that he was resigned to them. He'd crossed the lawn and seated himself on a bench shaded by a bank of pittosporum, placing the panama upside down in his lap like an alms bowl. In the shade, his suit altered from brilliant white to pale green. Although he'd come over by boat from the mainland, and hiked up and down South Hill, and all the way here from the bottom end of the island – and even though the suit was linen – his jacket and trousers appeared unblemished, uncreased. Even his shoes were clean; Finn supposed he'd tied plastic bags over his feet, as he'd done with his hands that time at the crocodile pens. That thought led to another: the hurling in of the dog. He didn't want to think about that. In his only hint at discomfort, Skins produced a handkerchief and dabbed at his brow, his neck, his upper lip. There was a brief smell of eucalyptus.

'But, yes, a big job,' Skins said. 'So I'm afraid my men will be sharing your island for a little while yet, before the blot on this landscape is complete.' He tucked the handkerchief away. 'We have to do our bit for coastal security, don't we?'

'Sure.'

'Perhaps you could do some labouring for me? Earn a spot of cash?'

'I don't need cash, living here.'

'How is that going, your life in exile?'

'I'm just trying to fit in.'

'The good neighbour. The loving husband.'

Finn let the remarks go.

'And where is your dear lady?'

'Working. And *yours*?' Finn said, before he could stop himself.

The crocodile farmer looked at him. 'As I left this morning, she was showing our daughter how to apply make-up.' He shook his head. 'They grow up so fast. A cliché, but none the less true. Just twelve years old but, you know, in some cultures I would have young men pressing their claims.'

Finn recalled the pornographic dreams he'd had when he first came here. The girl's face, her mother's face. The sense of them – of the Skins' compound – was so palpable you could've believed this garden was an illusion and that he was back there, at the crocodile farm. He moved into the shade of the hedge, but remained standing. 'Why did you have her dog killed?' Finn said. 'You didn't have to do that.'

Mr Skins ignored this.

'Is "exile" an apt word?' he said, picking up the thread of an earlier question. He appeared genuinely fascinated by the concept. 'Or what are you? A fugitive? An *émigré*? Or just another lost soul?' Then, changing tack. 'How are you, *Roop*, since your injury? I have to say you look in fine fettle. It must be all this sunshine, fresh air and home-grown food. Truly, *la dolce vita*.'

You'd have thought the crocodile farmer was the nervous one, filling the lulls in conversation in case he let in the words which, they both knew, were waiting to be said. The words the man had come here to say, that weren't preamble. Mr Skins wasn't done with that yet, though.

'They've put you to work, I believe?' he said.

'I've put myself to work.'

'You see, with the new barter – I imagine an extra pair of hands is welcome.'

'That was something else you didn't need to do.'

'There are the things we need to do and the things we do.' Skins dabbed at his forehead once more. 'Personally, I've always regarded that as a false distinction. We do things, and they are done, and life moves on. Life *always* moves on.'

'What did you want, Mr Skins?'

Skins folded the handkerchief away. He was sitting with his legs crossed, now, the hat perched on his knee. 'Want?'

'Or did you just drop by to see how I was doing?'

'I tend to think of your route to this island as a somewhat crudely assembled rope,' the man said. 'A set of sheets knotted together so that you might,' he made a hand-over-hand motion, 'effect your escape from a high window.' He paused. 'Each knot must hold fast, each sheet must remain unripped, or . . . the rope unravels.'

'The network,' Finn said.

'Precisely. The network, I regret to report, has been compromised.'

Finn swallowed. He hadn't expected this. He'd been bracing himself for the man to call in his 'fee' for getting Finn here in the first place. 'Where?' he said. 'I mean, how far along the chain?'

'As far as our friend Hano.' Skins retrieved the hat, brushing it, reshaping it. A trickle of sweat formed at each temple and rolled down his cheeks, as if synchronised.

'If they've traced me as far as Hano, then . . .'

'Ah but, you see, they've had no opportunity to question him

239

on account of the fact that, a couple of days before the IS arrived at the flood camp, Hano went on one of his hunting and trapping expeditions into the rainforest.' He paused, made his face solemn again. 'From which, unfortunately, he has failed to return.'

Finn didn't say anything.

'That was a week or more ago. Not a trace.' Mr Skins tutted. 'Of course I co-operated. Raising search parties. Helping the chaps from IS with their inquiries. A bit of financial assistance for the poor man's family – you met them, I believe?'

'Yeah.' Finn pictured Hano's wife, outside their tent that morning, doling out fish porridge. The silent, watchful kids.

'Which is odd because, when the IS ask them, they have no recollection of you whatsoever.' Skins faked a look of astonishment. 'But then, nor do I – and here we are: old chums, shooting the breeze.' He motioned with his hand. Dismissive. A scrub-that gesture. 'I won't waste your time with such matters.'

'There was a woman who took me to Tent City – have they caught her?' Finn said. 'She gave me my fake ID. She knows my new name, where I was headed.'

Mr Skins shrugged. 'My understanding is that Internal Security wanted a name from her. She gave them one: *Hano*.'

'That's all she told them?'

'*Please*.' The man's expression was that of a patient, indulgent parent.

Finn pictured the woman, being interrogated. Going to prison. Because of him. Her yellow eyes; the long hair they would have no doubt reduced to stubble by now. He thought of all those who'd helped him: Leander, the birdman, the owner of the safe apartment, Hano, Hano's family. Arrested or silenced because of him. Dead, it seemed, in Hano's case. Fed to the crocodiles, for all Finn knew.

'So many lives fucked up on my account,' he said, almost to himself.

'You spare these people a thought. That's good. But that's all you do – spare them a thought. Then you must forget about them.' Skins produced the handkerchief again. 'It's called self-preservation.'

Finn shook his head.

Mr Skins went on, 'Just like you must forget about all the men who are dying, even as we speak, in the war in which you chose not to participate.'

'I don't forget about them. I think about them.'

'Think about, then forget.'

'No.'

'If you're not a self-preservationist,' the other man said, 'why did you go on the run?' He spoke benevolently, sympathetically. He might've been helping Finn with a complicated piece of arithmetic. 'Isn't that the definition, the very essence of draft evasion? A new identity, a community of strangers, husband to another man's widow. All this, for what?' He answered his own question. 'To *preserve* yourself.'

'The people here, they're not strangers,' Finn said. 'Not any more.'

'You will have to make them strangers again. When the time comes.'

'What d'you mean, when the time comes?'

'What, you imagined you could truly become one of them? That you could live like this for ever?' Skins looked perplexed. 'As if I no longer existed. As if I was just a ship you'd passed in the night, never to see again. Is that what you imagined?'

Finn felt again the clawing claustrophobia of his incarceration at the crocodile farm, so many weeks ago. The pressure in his chest, his head, his joints. A narcotic rush so real he thought he'd faint; if he closed his eyes, he was sure he would do.

'I have to sit down.'

'Of course you do,' Skins said. 'You are happy, making new

friends, putting down roots, savouring your Arcadian idyll,' he indicated the washing line, 'busy with domestic chores . . . and then, suddenly, I turn up like this with bad tidings.' He patted the space beside him on the bench. 'Here.'

Finn lowered himself, instead, on to the ground. Made sure to keep his eyes open, to take deep, steady breaths. 'Will they look for me, here?'

'As it happens, they're still looking for Hano. Hano, it seems, is elusive.' Mr Skins looked slight, in the shade of the hedge, bathed in diffused light so that his skin was almost invisible – as if his suit were the greater presence, as if he wasn't there at all, but someone had draped his clothes on the bench to create the illusion of a seated man. 'Internal Security are following up a lead that Hano and the fugitive formerly known as Finn have headed into the interior – absorbed into the transient community of agricultural labourers who roam the land at this time of year.'

'A lead you gave them?'

'Not directly, no. But, yes, of course.'

'Another layer of debt for me to work off, then.'

'I'm a bad influence,' Skins said. 'We've been talking for only a few minutes and already you've reverted to the cynical mindset of the mainlander.'

Finn checked his impulse to come back at him. Whatever Skins was, however insidious, regardless of what he expected in return – the man had let the trail go cold on Finn. Let him disappear a second time. You took care what you said to a man who made trails go cold, and who could warm them again. It may have been a lie, this tale of the network, Hano, the IS – but how was Finn to know? Go to the mainland and find out for himself? Even if he fronted it out, called Skins' bluff, the man could bring the authorities here whenever he chose. He looked at him, sitting there. Cool as fuck. The breeze got up, snapping one of the shirts on the line like a whip. Skins glanced at the shirt, then turned his attention once more to Finn. He had put his hat back on and was straightening his suit, as though it was important for him to look presentable for what he was about to say. What he'd come here to say all along.

'Now,' he said. 'To business.'

The day after next, one of Mr Skins' boats would bring the island's regular provisions, along with the latest parts for the comms. tower; Finn was to make sure he was among those who helped unload it and haul the materials up to the site. At some point, a crew member would pass on his instructions: the day, time and location of *the delivery*. That was it, for now. Simple. Finn thought about Skins' earlier remark: that he'd have to make them strangers again. Bry, Jad, Qway, Sholo, Amver. All of them. In doing Mr Skins' bidding, Finn would betray their friendship, their trust; he would make them strangers again in his heart. How could you do it, otherwise? For sure, the islanders would make a stranger of him, if this deal became known.

'When I agreed to work for you,' he said, when Skins was through, 'I had no idea what kind of place I was coming to. What kind of people.'

'Naturally, you didn't. How could you have done?'

'I love it here.'

'Yes. I can see that. I can see why you would.'

'The way they live, the way they've treated me. I can't go behind their backs.'

'You see, if you tell them, they may try to compromise the transaction,' Skins said. 'I won't allow that.'

'This is their island, not mine. Not yours.'

The man stood up. 'Perhaps you'd prefer to put the deal at risk. Or renege on our agreement altogether. Stay true to your new friends.' Finn didn't reply. 'Except, of course,' Mr Skins went on, 'that would mean taking one or two of them down with you.' He paused. 'Bryher, for harbouring you.' Another pause. 'And that boy – Jad? Yes, Jad. The IS, I'm sure, would rigorously investigate any report that he'd brought you over here in that launch of his.'

Finn held his gaze for the longest time. The man came over to where he sat and laid a hand on his head. 'You're right, the island doesn't belong to me,' Skins said. His hand rested there. Gentle. Warm against his scalp. 'But I'm afraid you do.'

Finn remained sitting on the grass after the crocodile farmer left. He was still there a few minutes later, when he heard someone else approach from the cottage. He thought it would be Bry, home from the boatyard, but it wasn't. It was Qway.

He held a bulging pillowcase in each hand. 'I brought these for you.'

Finn looked up at him.

'You OK?' Qway said.

'Yeah, I'm fine.'

'I thought I saw Skins just now.'

'Yeah, he was here.'

Neither of them spoke for a moment. 'What'd he want?' Qway said, at last.

Finn told him. He said the crocodile farmer had come to warn him that IS had picked up his trail as far as the refugee camp, that they'd been at Skins' place asking questions. 'It spooked me, is all,' Finn said, managing a smile. But they'd gone away again – on a wild goose chase – and he was in the clear, and things would be all right.

The Burning

Bryher returned from another long day's work on the boat to find him in the kitchen, drizzling lemon juice over a baked sea-bass. He had his back to her, and hadn't heard her come in; she stood in the doorway, watching him cover the fish and set it aside, then turn his attention to a pan of rice. Steam lifted in gusts as Finn drained the water, still oblivious to her. She saw the clothes he wore. A bright yellow T-shirt, ripped at one shoulder, that she recognised as belonging to Nudge; Tye's purple cords – his *harlequin pants* – with their crudely stitched sky-blue patches; Qway's red sandals. He looked so strange, so unlike himself, that it startled her.

'What's with the gear?' She tried to sound curious rather than pointed.

Finn turned at her voice. Putting the pan down, posing for her, he smiled and said: 'What d'you reckon? Can I carry these colours?'

She calmed herself enough to smile, to collude, for now, in the pretence that this was what they were discussing.

'I have a whole new wardrobe,' Finn said. 'It's not all as garish as this.'

He was still holding the sieve of rice, milky spits of water dripping on to the floor. He placed it on the counter. 'I had a word with Qway the other day,' Finn said. He pointed at the garden beyond the kitchen window. She saw washing on the line. 'He came by earlier with two bags full of gear. Most of it his, but some from Hobb, Nudge and Zess as well.' He indicated the trousers. 'And Tye, would you believe.'

Bryher was no longer able to act as if this was a joking matter. There was so much to be said about the clothes she was unsure where to start. She guessed at the reason – the *timing*, at least. 'Is this because of Skins?'

'Skins?'

'I heard he was here this afternoon.'

'That's . . . yeah, he was, but what would that have to do with anything?' He gestured at the clothes. 'With these?'

'It's just coincidence, then?' Even as she spoke, the accusation made no sense to her; but she went ahead and made it, as if it was self-evidently true. Finn had been complacent at first, on seeing her, but he looked uncomfortable now – and she found that she wanted him to be. The fragrance of fish filled her nostrils. 'Skins shows up,' she said, 'and you decide you don't want to wear Roop's clothes any more.'

'Like I said, I spoke to Qway a couple of days ago. He just happened to turn up after Skins . . .'

Bryher dropped her shoulder bag, took two steps into the room; she thought, fleetingly, of going over to Finn, confront-ing him. Not that she imagined striking him – but crowding him, in his space by the hob, in those clothes, in her kitchen, with the components of the meal laid out like weapons in their argument. Craziness. But she couldn't stop herself from wanting to discompose him, as he'd done to her. She hadn't interrupted him, but her sudden movement stopped him speaking all the same.

She said: 'I'm just trying to work out, why do this? Why do it now?'

'Bry, don't.' Where her voice had sounded shrill, to her, his sounded mellow, soothing. 'Don't make this into something it isn't.'

Pushing her fingers into her hair, conscious of the tremor in her voice, she said: 'You don't do things for no reason. Not something like this.'

'Look,' Finn let out all his breath at once. 'Bry, sit down. Please.'

'I don't want to sit down.'

'OK. OK, fine, stand then.' He was trying not to be exasperated, she could tell. Trying to be patient. It occurred to her that this might be their first real fight, and that it was overdue. 'I've been thinking a lot about him just lately,' Finn said. 'Roop, I mean.' He glanced at the hob where a fry-pan of vegetables needed stirring, but left them untouched, sizzling. 'About you and him.'

'What about me and Roop?'

'Thing is, Bry . . . I don't think it's good for me to go on wearing his clothes any more. You know, looking like him.'

She waited for him to continue.

'Not for my sake. For yours.' He'd been avoiding her gaze, but he lifted his eyes to hers now. 'So you won't have to look at me, and see him.'

He knew how tough some of the others found it to be reminded of Roop, he said, whenever they caught sight of Finn; if it upset *them* so much, he had eventually come to realise, what must it have been doing to *her* all these weeks? He apologised. He should've done something about it sooner. 'But sometimes you . . .'

'Where are they?' she said.

'What?'

247

'Roop's clothes.'

'Oh. I put them all back.'

She caught herself nodding repeatedly. Without another word – trailing his query, 'Bry?', unanswered in her wake – she headed back out of the kitchen, climbed the stairs to the bedroom and opened the closet, the drawers, to check Roop's clothes were there.

The next day, straight after breakfast, she set off for South Bay. Her first thought had been to burn them in the kelp pit on Whin Hill; but South Bay was Roop's favourite spot on the island. The place where they'd first made love outdoors. Bryher decided to make a bonfire on the beach and feed each item into it, like offerings, until the clothes were all burned up. Reduced to smoke and scraps to be dispersed on the breeze.

'Like a cremation?' Finn had said, when she told him what she planned to do.

'No. Not like a cremation.'

He had offered to help carry them, but she said it was something she wanted to do by herself; in any case, all of Roop's gear, bagged up and slung over her shoulders, made a surprisingly light load. Easier than hauling kelp, anyway. Finn suggested she was acting in haste, as if the sight of him wearing clothes other than Roop's had been the starting point of her decision rather than the culmination of it.

No, she told him, she'd delayed too long as it was.

They were tentative, cautious with one another; Finn edging around her in their conversation at breakfast. Bryher wasn't so immersed in her own thoughts that she couldn't detect that a subtle shift in his own mood was about more than their spat in the kitchen the previous evening. Finn was distracted, subdued. She'd gone to bed early, without eating the meal he'd prepared; when she came down at first light she saw from the remains that he'd barely touched the food himself. He'd skipped breakfast, too, apart from tea.

So she had asked once again about Skins' visit to the cottage, this time more rationally. 'What did he want?'

Finn gave her the same answer she had heard from Qway, and which neither of them fully believed. It might well be true that the IS had been sniffing around the crocodile farm, but Skins was unlikely to relay the news to Finn without some other purpose. With Finn so out of sorts, so obviously reluctant to discuss the visit at all, Bryher didn't force the issue. More so than the other men on the island, he required time to open up to questions he preferred not to answer; she'd had to learn to be patient with him. And she didn't want another quarrel now that they were back, albeit with such fragility, on speaking terms.

In any case, there were more pressing matters. Roop's clothes. An unspecified tension had gathered in her shoulders and her guts, along with a more familiar mental white noise of anxiety she had grown used to in recent months. And a residue of last night's distress remained in her system; enough, at least, for her to stride off to the foot of the island with her load when she was meant to be putting in another shift on Amver's boat. That could wait. Finn could wait. What she felt compelled to do was obliterate Roop's clothes – all of them, immediately – before she changed her mind.

Leaving the track that skirted South Bay, Bryher scouted around for a suitable spot. The blonde, fan-like swathe of beach was so bright in the morning sun it made her squint. The tide was out, as she'd known it would be; the sea, becalmed, resembled a sheet of aluminium foil that had been crumpled, then smoothed flat again. She paused to stare for a moment – not thinking of Roop, especially, or of anything much, beyond a simple registering of colour and shape, the gentle press of warm air against her face, and how beautiful and beautifully sad this place was. The hours she'd

249

spent here with him were behind her thoughts but they were not precisely what she thought of in that instant. Thinking about Roop was never a simple matter. Sometimes the associations were specific, at other times – here, now – they were as general and persistent as the sunlight itself. The pervasive *Roopness* of her life, as she'd come to think of it. He was everywhere and nowhere. She might have stood like that for a long time, if she hadn't been distracted at last by the cry of a herring gull directly overhead. Bryher found it against the sky, riding a thermal, hanging in the air like a child's kite.

She selected a point above the high-water mark, where the sand was powdery, but far enough from the scrubby marram of the dunes so stray sparks would not catch. Using her hands, she scooped out a shallow pit and, after several trips, returned with enough dried-out driftwood and kindling to build the fire. The clothes burned slowly, smouldering for an age before properly igniting; the smoke was black, foul smelling. Bryher was used to fires, from all the kelp-burning, but she had imagined this would be different. Ritualised, respectful. She'd envisaged a moment of ceremony, of private contemplation, as she released each shirt, each pair of trousers, each sweater into the flames. She had expected to connect each item with Roop, or some memory of him. In fact, the burning quickly became methodical and practical – if she was conscious of Roop at all, it was only by default, by an awareness of her detachment from him.

Her initial reaction to seeing Finn in the gear donated by Qway and Tye and the others had been resentment. That it was an act of rejection – not just of Roop's things, but of Roop himself; Finn was shedding him as a snake sheds its skin. As if he was Finn's to shed. That he had supposedly done it for *her* sake – implying that she needed protecting from herself, and he'd assumed the role of protector. She'd gone to bed too upset to speak. Not until morning, once the shock of him looking so altered had faded, did she begin to see that Finn was, at least, entitled to choose the clothes he wore. Adapting to life here was hard enough for him as it was, without being dressed as a dead man. Bryher also saw, then, that if it made sense for him to rid himself of Roop's clothes, it made sense for her to be done with them too. Or else she would let the drawers and shelves revert to the shrine they'd been before Finn came.

So that was what she'd do; what she was doing. It was good and necessary. None of which explained why, as she watched each garment go up in flames, she felt no sense of catharsis whatsoever.

'Roop.'

'Yes, they were Roop's.' She had seen Orr, watching from the track, not long after the bonfire had been lit. His place was nearby and he would've seen the smoke. He'd waited until the last article of clothing had been added before approaching. She offered him a smile. 'I'm burning Roop's clothes.'

Orr stared at the flames. Despite the warmth, he wore a greatcoat that reached to his shins, buttoned up, and his flappy home-made hat. 'Roop's clothes,' he said.

'Uh-huh.'

'Smelly.' Orr had positioned himself downwind of the smoke, but it seemed not to bother him enough to move even though he coughed repeatedly.

Bryher nodded. 'I decided to burn them all.'

'The brown dungarees,' Orr said. 'The check shirt. The boots.'

Tears started in her eyes. These were the things Roop had been wearing on that final fishing trip, and which she could not burn and would never be able to burn. Orr remembered and was correcting her; not to upset her, she knew, but because he liked exactness. 'No,' she managed to say. 'Not all of them. Just those that were left.'

They stood, watching the fire. At last Orr reached into his pocket, producing a sandwich that looked as if it had been in there for some time and handed it to her. She bit into it – goat's cheese and tomato, a little warm and squashed but fresh enough. From his gestures, she saw that it wasn't all for her, that he'd meant them to share it. They took turns until it was gone. Then, as if his whole purpose in joining her on the beach had been to bring her this offering, Orr left. She followed his progress through the gorse-clad slopes towards his prefab. Not until he was a speck on the hillside did he turn to wave, in that manic semaphor of his, hollering inaudibly. She waved back. He had almost made her cry and now, in his ridiculousness, he had made her laugh. When Bryher returned her attention to the fire she saw that there was little left to look at. So she covered it with sand.

Although the direct route to the boatyard would've been to follow the track Orr had used, Bryher took the coastal path. If anyone had asked why, she would have said it was more scenic, and easier than trekking uphill and down again through gorse. But she knew the true reason. The ingrained habit of movement about the island that took her to the shore as often as possible, for fear that Roop's body – what remained of it – might be lying washed-up, undiscovered. It was a form of madness. As grief itself was. But she couldn't break the cycle of mourning and searching. She accepted that Sholo was right when she'd said that each time you relapse into an obsessive pattern (of thought, action, anything) you have to forgive yourself, draw a line, begin again. Yet within minutes of ridding herself of the clothes – the drawing of a line, if ever there was one – here she was, on another futile trawl of the water margins.

She picked her way among the humped ruins of the earthen battery at South Point, the relic of an ancient civil war, now

252

littered with modern debris. Frayed rope, food wrappers, cans, scraps of plastic. A bottle of Tabasco sauce, intact and with the tiny red cap still in place, yet empty; the moulded casing for a set of drill bits; a small tin – rusted, its blue-and-red decoration bleached to hints of colour – that might once have contained tobacco but which, she saw from the faded foreign lettering, had held liquorice pastilles. There was a dead shag, too; an elongated S in the grass, rotted and flyblown, its feathers intricately patterned in shades of brown. Jad regarded flotsam and jetsam as objects of fascination to be collected; while she shared his fascination, to Bryher the detritus belonged where it lay. As if, however minuscule the odds that a particular item should have ended up at this spot, on this beach, on this island, at this time, there was an inevitability that it would be here for her to find. It was one of the reasons why she went on searching for Roop – the idea that it might be *meant* for her to discover him. That was madness, too. But no more implausible than her discovery of that Tabasco bottle, that drill case, that tin of liquorice.

Rounding the point into the great curve of Long Strand, she heard the voices just before she saw the men. The marines and four of Skins' gang. They were playing volleyball, the court marked out with lines in the sand and a net fashioned from two poles and a cord draped with fishing net. Each of the men had stripped to the waist, even the patrol crew, their weaponry and ammunition-belts strewn on the sidelines, along with their clothes, a cool-box and a clutter of empty beer bottles. A CD player was pumping out. Bryher had been aware of this while she tended the bonfire, but had assumed the music to be coming from the construction site on South Hill. The men had set up their game on the exposed foreshore in a strip of flat, damp sand between two rows of rocks, the remains of Bronze Age field walls. Their calls and whoops and laughter, the slap of the ball, reached her on the breeze. None of them had noticed her. She could've

253

turned back, avoiding them and the remarks they would make; but she lived here and refused to be intimidated. Drawing nearer, she spotted a seventh figure: a spectator. Jad, intent on the game, his netball bib a red gash against the brilliance of the sand. Each time the ball bounced out of play he would scamper after it, punch it back volleyball-style, then settle back on his haunches at the edge of the court. Until she saw him move, Bryher had mistaken him for an item of discarded clothing.

Jad was the first to see her. But, by the time she reached them, all six players had stopped to watch her pass by. She said hello to Jad, then cast a general greeting at the men. One of Mr Skins' gang gave a low whistle. This didn't surprise her. What did surprise her was the younger of the two marines, telling him to 'shut the fuck up'. For a moment Bryher thought he was about to break away from the game and walk with her, like an escort. But he followed her with his eyes instead. Motionless and expression-less. His chest was so damp with sweat that the tattoo there looked as if its colours ought to run. It depicted a rampant lion, apparently clawing at the inked digits of the marine's military ID. Silence made a wake behind her. It wasn't until Bryher left the beach to join the track leading to the boatyard that she heard the sounds of the volleyball game resuming.

Seeing the marines unsettled her. Their casually strewn guns and uniforms — a reminder of other men in other uniforms, searching for Finn. How close they'd come to tracing him here, and how close they might come again one day. Just as Roop had done, Finn could be made to disappear with sudden violence, without warning. She had known this all along. It went with the territory of sheltering a fugitive. But Skins' news had sharpened her awareness of the danger, not just to Finn but to herself; to all of them, here. Now, so soon after the crocodile farmer's visit, the encounter with his gang (who knew about Finn) and the patrol crew (who didn't) had brought home to her just how tenuous

Finn's freedom was. How tenuous was the thread that connected her to him. Before this, imagining his recapture, she had never thought of it in those terms. In terms of loss. That she would be losing Finn, or that it should matter to her.

Beach Party

Finn was groggy with sleep as he stumbled along the track after Jad, barely able to see him. Cloud partially obscured the moon and, for once, there was no magnesium-white bloom of flood-lighting on South Hill to turn the land from black to silver. Skins' men weren't working through the night, as they'd been doing these past days; tonight, the place was its old dark self again, taking its regular night-time drenching. Not silent, though. Instead of the drone from the work gang's generator, a different rip in the quiet issued from the bottom end of the island. Music. The tinny pump of a portable rather than a sound-system blast, but plenty loud enough – here, in the dead hours – to reach Finn and the boy on the path that led from Bryher's. He recognised it. A dance track that had played repeatedly in the club on Draft Nite. As they neared the source, other noises came their way. The riff of laughter, of men's voices.

'Come see,' Jad had whispered, waking him.

'See what?'

But the boy hadn't answered, just jostled him awake and from his makeshift bed and out of the cottage, Finn stepping into boots and yanking on clothes as they went. 'Thin, come on.' He would say nothing more and they trekked wordlessly the rest of the way. Step by step, the rain in Finn's face and the cool night air shook the sleep from him. Jad was leading him, he realised, directly to the music.

It was all he could do to keep up, to keep his footing. His side was sore. A tugging, like the closure of a drawstring purse. Maybe he'd done some damage while he was out at sea that day, helping Yué to bring in the lobster catch. More likely the old pain resurfacing, not a new one. Finn prodded the flesh, the familiar numb patch of pins and needles. Bry had explained how the blade would've severed some small nerves. Nothing to worry about. Most of the time his side didn't ache at all, unless he overexerted himself; as he was now, trailing the boy in the dark like a drunk chasing a goat. By the time they stopped Finn was breathing hard and they were both soaked.

The din was insistent, close to. A rupture. A fissure of sound, split apart by the hissing lava-spit whoops of two of the men, dancing, lurching reddened and sweaty around the flames of a campfire that thrived despite the rain. The others were sitting under a rigged-up tarp with their barbecue deck and CD player, in the wash of light from a battery-powered lamp. Each with his can, taking steady pulls; one tending to the grill. A bunch of men skiving off their shift, drinking, smoking, talking, playing music, eating meat with their fingers and, now and then, finding something funny enough to laugh out loud. They'd set themselves among the dunes at one end of South Bay. Mr Skins' regular gang and the older of the two marines. No sign of the younger one. Finn spotted the guy from the crocodile farm – his escort, that first day; the one who'd pitched the dog to its death. *Rudy.* Rudy, pressing bread-wrapped sausage into his mouth between slugs of beer, his lips lipsticked with ketchup.

'Why are we here?' Finn said, barely speaking, mouth breathy at Jad's ear.

The boy had halted them a short distance inland, in a slight depression, hidden in the high scrub beyond the tussocky humps of sand. Out of reach of the light from the beach party, but able to observe, to eavesdrop. Not that there was much to see, or hear above the blare of the music. Jad shushed him, signalled him to watch and wait. Finn figured this was what the boy did with himself when he went walkabout these days. Dogging the men, spying on them, collecting whatever there was to witness or overhear, or merely collecting the sight, the fact, the curiosity of these mainlanders, camped out on the island. Even before work began on the radio mast, Jad had gone snooping where he pleased, when he pleased. 'On patrol', he called it. As if the island was his to guard. He would disappear altogether or show up out of nowhere, so that you could believe there were several Jads wandering about, or no Jad at all. Sholo reckoned it was common for him to skip classes only to pitch up at her place at night, demanding a lesson in some obscure topic. Or the boy would clear out of his home, without a word to Yué or Amver, and 'adopt' another family for a day or two – or sleep rough in one of his dens.

The nomad. Tonight, he was the spy, the voyeur.

Finn was about to ask again why he'd been brought here, when Jad tensed beside him, pointing towards a stand of stunted haw-thorns along the coastal path from the men's bivouac. A figure emerged from the trees and stood silhouetted against the grey-white band of the beach. Tall, gangly, unmistakably male. He paused to adjust his belt, then headed back to join the party. Not until he ducked beneath the tarp was Finn able to identify him: the second marine, his cropped scalp shiny in the lamplight. Back from a leak in the bushes, by the looks of things. As he sat down he placed a steadying hand on Rudy's shoulder. That was all; no words passed between them. Mr Skins' man shot him a smile. Placing his beer down, screwing the base of the can into the sand, killing his cigarette, pushing a last piece of hot dog into his gob, Rudy stood up and headed out on to the track, the way the marine had just come. He, too, became a silhouette, then vanished into the trees. Finn, damp and stiff and shivery alongside Jad, felt his chest tighten as they waited for Rudy to reappear. Nothing he could name, just a sense of wrongness. His gaze no longer on the men, but fixed on the blackened scuzz of hawthorn. Telling himself it was OK for a guy to take so long over a crap. All the while watching. At last, he heard a grunt – shrill, almost bestial, piercing the music – and the clump of trees altered shape and a piece broke away, as if one of the hawthorns had uprooted itself and lumbered off. The form became human, hurrying; then, a second figure, catching up. Before the pair drew into the lamplight for Finn to make out the face of the first one, he'd recognised enough – the hair, the swing of the arms, the hips – to know her.

Amver. Slim, boyish. Whitely naked and clutching clothes to her chest.

Rudy, trouserless, had her by the hair, yanking her to a stop, pulling her to her knees. She was screaming, clawing uselessly at him, but he pressed her face-down in the sand, ass in the air like a Muslim at prayer, and she was bellowing: 'No not that not that please don't', and still he went at her, trying to keep her down, keep her steady, as he positioned himself behind her, cock flapping thickly beneath his gut. Beyond them, the men continued as before – sitting, drinking, eating, dancing – gazing indifferently at the commotion, as though deciding whether it was worth watching.

Jad was first out of the hiding place, but Finn beat him to Rudy.

The surprise, along with the burst of rage, caught Rudy unawares and, for a moment, Finn had the better of him. Long enough to knock him off-balance, away from Amver, rolling him down the dune and getting in a punch a kick another push. The other men were up now. Moving in.

'Thin! Run, Thin!'

Rudy was up too, swatting away Finn's next wild swing and putting him down. Finn wasn't sure what he'd been hit with, or where, or who by, he was just down in the sand and the sharp grass and there was no breath to be had. Wet sand in his mouth, his eyes, his nose.

'Up you get.'

Hands under his armpits, and he was being hauled to his feet, marched back up the dune to the track. Rudy. It was Rudy, helping him. You'd have thought he was making sure he was OK, only as soon as Finn was steady again the guy leaned in like he wanted to kiss him and brought his forehead down smack into the centre of Finn's face. Finn lay there, then, on the track. Watching the guy's bare feet as he stood beside his head. The toes, black with dirt, each big toe as broad and flattened as if they'd been hammered out of shape. Finn breathed. He breathed some more, spat out blood. If he could just keep looking at those feet he would be all right.

Rudy's voice. 'Where's the fucking girl?'

'Gone,' someone said.

'Bring her back here.'

'Rood, she's gone. It's pitch black.'

'I want her fucking back here.'

They argued about the girl. Finn stayed put, trying to keep breathing, to figure out if he could move, get up. Watching the feet. The feet were gone. They were back again, in boots. Fingers lacing the boots. Only once the kicking started did Finn under-stand that Rudy had put his boots on just for this. Circling him. Naked from the waist down, except the boots – hairy legs, cock still flapping, still semi. You could laugh at how ludicrous he

260

looked, if he wasn't doing what he was doing to you. Circling, kicking. Placing the kicks: knee, shoulder, thigh, ribs. Talking to Finn, telling him how it was.

'So she'll take *kick* my fucking money, yeah? *kick* and then *kick* she'll *kick* fucking tell me which fucking *kick* holes I can and can't *kick* fucking put my *kick* fucking dick in. Yeah?' Kick. Kick. 'Take your hands away from your face.'

Finn's back was the worst. The sacrum.

'Take. Your. Fucking. Hands. Away. From. Your. Fucking. Face.'

'That's it. Leave it, now.' Another voice. The older of the two marines.

Hard, like he meant it. Telling him again to 'leave it, Rudy, he's had enough'. The music had stopped. When did that happen? Just the one booted foot, now, beside Finn's face. The first splash missed, splatted into the sand right next to him, then it was slapping against his fingers, between them, into his hair, his eyes, one of his ears and over his cheek, his chin, his lips, warm and frothy and beery, the sharp ammonia stink, and the pissing went on and on and then it stopped.

'Like old times,' Finn said, trying not to wince as Bryher tended to him.

'Knife wounds, bee stings, fights . . . you'd have been safer in the Army.'

Another time, this might've been a joke, a bit of nurse–patient banter – maybe it was, now – but her tone was flat, her mood, her body language more fatigued than you could blame on a curtailed night's sleep. They were in the kitchen, the window lightening with the rumour of daybreak. The marines had brought him from South Bay in the patrol launch, helped him from the shallows at Gibbet Cove to the door of the cottage and woken Bryher. She had cleaned him up and, one by one, was seeing to his injuries.

Scrapes and bruises, she said – nothing broken, not even his nose, despite the clots of blood in his throat if he sniffed. The strength and size and sheer fury of Rudy, it was as well the guy had been too drunk to do a proper job. That was what the older marine reckoned. When they'd gone, Finn told her what happened. *Why* it happened.

'Where's Amver now?' she said.

'I don't know – at home, I guess. She got away with Jad.'

Bry said she'd head up there, after. Check she was all right. The prospect appeared to add another weight to the scales of her mood. Finn must be done in, she said, though she might've been talking about herself. It was possible she hadn't slept much, even before he'd been brought home. The way she'd been, since the burning of Roop's clothes less than twenty-four hours ago. Distracted, switched off. Like she was the one who'd taken a beating. This, though, didn't explain why she seemed so unfazed by the news of what Amver had been doing down there, with the men.

'You knew?' Finn said. 'About Amv.'

'Uh-huh.'

'This wasn't the first time, then?'

'It's been going on since Mor left. Since Amver decided to go to the mainland herself.' Bryher was irrigating his nose with a moist cotton swab, slopping blood and mucus and sand into a small dish. Finn's eyes were watering. 'The men are her ticket out of here,' Bry said. 'That's how she sees it. The materials for the boat, a bit of cash to set herself up over there.'

Finn sucked in through his teeth.

'Sorry. I'm trying to be gentle.'

'What about Yué? What does she make of it?'

'She's her mother. She loves her.' Bryher binned the swab, started on the other nostril with a fresh one. 'It's Jad who takes it the hardest – wants to act the father, the big brother, protecting her. Defending her honour, you know?'

262

'Which is why he took me down there,' Finn said.

'I suppose.' She binned that swab too, roughed her fingers through her hair; as she straightened up he thought for a moment she might faint, but she steadied herself against the back of his chair. 'There,' she said, as if it hadn't happened. 'All done.'

'Bry . . .'

'Now, bed. A few hours' sleep, you'll feel a whole lot better.'

Sleep sounded so good. Then Finn remembered. This was the morning he was meant to be unloading Skins' boat.

The Boat (1)

This was where they'd first fetched him ashore, though he had no memory of it. Finn couldn't have said how many weeks ago. Time blurred, here. Its usual divisions didn't apply, and you learned to measure time differently. No watch or clock anywhere on the island, no diaries, no calendars. You slept when you were tired, ate when you were hungry, worked when there was work to be done, rested when there wasn't. A life in synch with the sun and tides. If you arranged to meet someone 'after breakfast' or 'at sundown' you might get there first and have to wait, or they might have to wait for you . . . and neither of you minded. If a cargo boat was due 'in the morning', you knew to expect it at, or near, high tide, when the channel to The Strand was navigable.

The tide was pretty much in. The end of the quay had disappeared, and water sloshed among the upper pontoons. Zess and Nudge were already there, facing out to sea; Orr was with them, and not with them – sitting with his legs over the side, letting the waves slap at his boots. Orr was the only one to see him coming. He waved. Finn waved back. This simple exchange sent a plumb line of anxiety into his gut. Of guilt and self-loathing. But he would go through with this. Even though he ached and his head throbbed and he limped and could drop with weariness, even though he sickened himself with what he was about to do, Finn would do what Skins wanted.

He crossed the beach, its crust broken by the prints of the other three. The sky was a pure cobalt, feathered with cirrus and rinsed in sunlight the colour of reflected butter. This morning, the scene was plastic. Too picture-postcard perfect. Qway and Tye would be along soon; the last of the gang of stevedores. When they greeted him, he would reciprocate. Act normal, as if nothing was going on. As he was, now, with Zess and Nudge, as they registered his footsteps on the boards and turned with their bright hellos. Their gazes caught on his damaged face, but neither of them asked what had happened, and Finn knew that word must've got round already. If he was out of sorts this morning, they would no doubt assume it was because of the fight.

'Looks like being a nice one,' Nudge said.

Finn nodded. 'Shaping up that way.'

You always said this. It was always a nice day, here, and this was the call-and-response ritual the islanders performed with one another, deadpan, like it was the best joke. Not so long ago, Finn had been chuffed when Hobb handed him the feed-line – the first time he'd been included in the ritual by someone other than Bry or Jad. 'Looks like being a nice one,' Hobb had said. Finn could've hugged him. Today, when he felt a fraud even for being with them, he delivered the punchline all the same.

'Is that broken?' Nudge said.

Finn sniffed, spat out some blood. 'No.'

'What's good for a nosebleed?' Nudge said, to Zess.

Zess grinned. 'A headbutt usually works.'

Finn didn't want this, the teasing. Not this morning. He went along with it, all the same. They spun it out a little, then switched

265

to serious. It was good, what he'd done for Amver last night; Finn took their praise, as he had taken their banter.

Qway and Tye arrived, similarly unsurprised by Finn's injuries. Qway asked if he was OK, and whether he was up to the job of unloading the boat. Finn said yeah, he was fine, he'd be all right. He flexed his arms, as though to demonstrate his fitness; in fact, he wasn't sure he could manage. His nose seemed to fill his entire face and the ache at the base of his spine was worsening, from standing around. As for *lifting*. Qway asked after Bryher, then. Her relapse, since the burning of the clothes, was as widely known as his own battered state.

'She's not so good,' Finn said.

'She's tough,' Qway said. 'She's opened old wounds, but they'll close again.'

'The wounds aren't so old, though, are they?' Finn said.

Qway didn't reply. Instead, Tye said: 'Is she by herself today?'

'She's gone to Yué's.'

The boat had come into view and the men on the quay fell silent, watching it draw close enough for them to make out the figures on board. Finn considered what Qway had said, about Bry being tough. She was. Also, she wasn't. Not always. Finn used to believe that to be tough you had to be tough all the time, but what you needed was the capacity to be tough when you had to be. Bryher had that kind of toughness. Finn wasn't so sure that he did.

The deal would buy him more time here, yet he couldn't shrug off the feeling that, somehow, this would be the beginning of the end. As if his time was expanding and contracting all at once: the sinuous timelessness of his new life stretched taut and about to snap under the strain of the old. These past months, Finn had begun to forget himself: who he was, what he was, how and why he'd come to be on this island. His *status*. Then Skins pays a visit and he's a dodger again. Like that defined him, was the sum of his identity; whatever else he was becoming, or could become, was wiped by that single fact. He wondered if it was possible to exist as a fugitive without having to *be* one, in your head, the whole time. Whether what you *were* could be severed once and for all from what you *might be*, given the chance to reinvent yourself. Living here as a dodger you were neither safe nor in danger, but suspended between the two – cross-beamed by the lure of this life and the drag of the one you'd fled, or tried to. Even as it seemed hopeless for him – here, in the shadow of Mr Skins – the island was the hope Finn clung to. He knew what Bryher would tell him. That he was thinking of exile purely in terms of place when it was also a state of mind. But Skins was there, too, in his mind: the man who could let him stay, or make him leave. To live life on the run was to be constantly on the verge of departure – even now, with an arrival in the offing.

The arrival of this boat seeped into thoughts of the other one that had ferried him to the same landing place all those weeks ago. Same boat, for all he knew. That time, Finn had been the cargo – stretchered ashore, along the track to the cottage, up the steep, narrow stairs to Bry's bed. He stood on the quay and, wishing it was then not now – wishing time could be made to cease – he watched Skins' vessel approach, low in the water with the weight of its load.

The boat docked. One of the crew clambered down on to the pontoon to fasten the mooring ropes. No Rudy, or any of the regulars – they would still be sprawled in their camp at South Bay, sleeping off last night. First they unloaded the general supplies, piling them above the high-water line. Orr busied himself: contentedly, needlessly, stacking and restacking the boxes. It was a big delivery. Rice, pasta, cooking oil, engine oil, fuel, paint, light bulbs, soap, detergent, shampoo, toothpaste, a bundle of second-hand paperbacks, engine parts for the fishing boat, timber, nails, screws, Effie's asthma drugs, school books, blocks of writing paper, pencils, condoms, toilet rolls. Hundreds of flat-pack cardboard boxes for the flowers that would be ready for cropping soon. Orr took charge of it all. The men, meanwhile, brought ashore the batch of materials for the communications mast. The base and foundations had been completed; now the crew needed help relaying the parts for the next section. Pre-fabricated steel rigging, brackets, bolts, rivets . . . an industrial-scale assembly kit. The islanders would lend a hand with the haulage. As Skins had put it: 'You want your provisions, you assist my men with their work.' The parts were divided into bundles so they could be borne on the shoulders with a man at either end. There were five crew aboard the boat. Four of them paired off with Nudge, Zess, Qway and Tye. The fifth was the skipper. Pointing at Finn, he said:

'You're with me – and don't fucking bleed over everything.'

He wore a black vest, black shorts, black workboots and a black cap with the peak reversed. Mirror shades. He produced a cigarette from a carton swinging from his neck on a clip, like a security tag, and lit up. With his long hair, he resembled a roadie for a heavy-metal band; but then, most of Skins' men did. Positioning Finn at one end, himself at the other, he gave the count of three for them to hoist their loads. One on each shoulder. There wasn't a part of Finn that didn't hurt. The load bit into the collarbone, such a deadweight you couldn't believe you'd make it off the beach, let alone to the top of South Hill.

The skipper waited until they were returning from the second trip.

As the men trekked downhill in single file among the head-high gorse, he engineered it for him and Finn to be last. They slowed. Stopped for a cigarette. All without a word so that, even though Finn was expecting it, the actual moment still surprised him. Skins' man tapped out two cigs, lit his own then went to light Finn's.

'I don't smoke any more.'

The skipper gave him a look. 'What happened to you?'

'Got hit by a boom,' Finn said.

The man indicated the cigarette. 'Just smoke it, will you?'

The smoking was a pretext to stop, Finn saw that now – let the rest drift ahead, out of eavesdropping range. He put the cig between his lips and leaned into the flame.

'*Don't fucking smoke.*' The other man laughed. The kind of laugh that leaves you in no doubt what a prick you've made of yourself. 'Nice one.'

'Yeah, well.'

It tasted even better than he'd imagined. One smoke. How many inhalations was that? Hardly any. He wouldn't have another for a while and this was good and sweet as he took it down in short, rationed draws. The two men smoked in silence, the sounds of the rest of the party diminishing. The skipper's bare arms were unevenly tanned – darker at the shoulders and forearms, paler at the biceps. The loads they'd carried had etched two raw, red epaulettes on his skin either side of the straps of his vest. Finn's own shoulders and neck were sore as fuck. He caught sight of himself, twinned in the other man's shades, his silhouette distended by the curvature of the lenses and speckled yellow from the reflection of the flowers in the gorse all around them. He watched the guy smoke. Drag, hold, exhale. No hurry. No talking. This was a mannered performance. Finn lowered his gaze to the ground at his feet. *Just do it. Let's do it and get going*. He kept this thought to himself.

The skipper took a last drag and spun the butt away.

As if sending a small child on an errand to the shops, he spelled it out for Finn: the delivery. Named the day, the tide, the place where the boat would put ashore with the merchandise, then got

Finn to repeat the instructions back to him. He was to make the rendezvous without any of the islanders knowing, then store the goods someplace they wouldn't be found. Sit tight and wait for further instructions.

'Mr Skins has *supreme confidence* in you,' the skipper said, finally. 'He asked me to make sure you understood that.'

The Boat (2)

Two days later the bleeding had stopped and the swelling had gone down, but his nose and both eyes, so he was told, were the colour of aubergine. Not so much pain, now, and at least he could move more freely. His arms, his legs, his back.

'You'll be fit for the cropping,' Bryher had said, matter-of-factly. Indifferent. She was pretty much getting through the days on autopilot. Still working on Amver's boat, but like it didn't matter to her a whole lot. Like nothing did.

Finn had meant to tell her. Each day, since Skins had paid his visit, and since the smoke with the skipper on South Hill – even tonight, before setting off – he had wanted to let her know about the delivery. Make her see why he had no choice – and not just for his sake. Swear her to secrecy. Bryher, though, was in no condition to hear this just now. Even supposing she was, there was no way she'd collude in keeping it from the community. No one kept secrets here. Except him. Most likely, if he'd told her, she would've called a Gathering right there and then and shafted the whole deal.

Lying to Bry was the worst.

The day of the burning of Roop's clothes, the two of them had talked long into the evening, outside on the bench she made, a blanket each, her clothes and hair still smelling of bonfire. The crying had begun out of nowhere – Bryher losing it, hands over her face, sobbing, the blanket slipping from her shoulders – and he'd wrapped her up warm again. Held her, to still the shaking. Made her stand. He'd led her – she had allowed herself to be led – indoors, to the living room, where they huddled among his bedding. All the while, though, Finn was aware of a separation – that, despite their snugness, their intimacy, he was a spectator at an episode that had nothing to do with him. The cliché would've been for Bry to raise her face to his, for him to brush away the tears, for them to kiss, to make love. She didn't raise her face. Pressed it into his shoulder the whole time, snot and tears penetrating his shirt. She needed not to cry alone, that was all. Needed holding. Bryher needed nothing more from him than that. Eventually, she'd untangled herself from him and, with a chaste goodnight peck, had headed upstairs to her own bed to sleep alone.

If she had raised her face to him? He didn't know. To have kissed and made love would've been so easy, if Bryher had made it possible. But she didn't. It was as simple and as complicated as that. The smell of her hair was what stayed with him most clearly from that night. Smoky, but sweet – like fresh-grated ginger. That, and the warmth of her body against his.

What he should do was *tell* her. Then, call a Gathering himself. Tell *them*.

Waiting for the delivery – 'the drop', Skins' man had called it – he'd had time to beat himself up over what he was about to do. To look in their faces – in Bry's face – knowing what he knew, was an act of deception in itself. An infidelity. When you have an affair, you're unfaithful each minute of each day, not just in those moments when you're in bed with the other. So, a Gathering. A confession. Agree to whatever they decided. Only, suppose they said no? Or suppose, tonight, he pulls a no-show – the boat comes, but no Finn to meet it? What then? He knew what. Skins turns him in, *cashes* him in; he's packed off to jail or to the front, a dead man walking. Easy as that. Bryher and Jad cashed in too, shipped to some shithole of a mainland prison; it could be years before either of them got to see this place, or their people, again.

No, you couldn't tell anyone. And you couldn't miss the drop. However much you longed to, you couldn't.

Finn snuck out the cottage well after dark, hushing the door shut behind him. Left his boots off, left the torch off, until he was well clear of any of the dwellings. He picked up the pace a little, then. It was a calm night, no trace of a breeze. The rain was lighter than usual, a mist so fine the torch-lit flecks of moisture gave the illusion of floating in perpetual suspension in the still air. As he cleared the rear slopes of Wreckers Hill and followed the path to the gate, the arched shack at the beehives ghosted out of the night – shadowy, formless against the blackened meadow. The door was solid enough as he let himself in, jumpy, startled by the scrape of corrugated iron on the cement floor. He aimed the torch at the clutter of tools and equipment along one wall. The wheelbarrow was rusted, its tyre flat and starting to perish, but it was intact and you could trundle it along well enough. Easing it out of the shed with as little noise as possible, he was on his way again, along the track that would take him to The Ear. There, it was a waiting game. Sitting among the shore defences, on one of the large blocks that looked almost luminous in the frail cast of the moon; listening, staring out to sea. Trying to think of nothing. Behind him, the island lay slumbering. Ahead, the ocean was placid, rain-pocked, steadily encroaching. He knew the tides well enough by now, but even so he was way too early. When the rendezvous took place, Finn was stiff from sitting for so long, his eyes ached

273

with looking and for want of sleep, and he might almost have forgotten why he was there if he hadn't been so wired with anticipation.

He never sighted the mother ship, at anchor out there he supposed. All he saw was the small launch that put into the bay, its engine cut some distance offshore, and two figures rowing hard into the shallows. He waded out knee-deep to help beach the craft and keep it fast. Between the three of them they unloaded the packages without torches, and without exchanging a word. The men wore dark oilskins, with the hoods up, and kept their heads bowed over their task; in any case there was so little light Finn couldn't have said what colour their skin was, let alone what they looked like. No orders were issued, but it was clear that the job had to be done quickly and without fuss, and that Finn was expected to muck in. They worked methodically, the one in the launch handing a package at a time to the second man, or to Finn, to be hauled to the dirt track above the beach. Finn had parked the barrow there, sure that once it was fully laden it would be impossible to wheel across the sand. The packs were heavy, like bags of sugar only bigger, and wrapped in thick plastic film. Too many for the barrow, so the rest had to be laid out beside it. As soon as the last was unloaded, the second man rejoined his mate and they pushed off and were away, rowing out to sea while Finn lugged the final package up the beach. He set it down with the others and watched the craft head towards the scattering of islets from which it had emerged. It disappeared before he heard the engine kick in. The men couldn't have been ashore for fifteen minutes. Alone again, Finn caught his breath. Surveyed the merchandise – so many bloated parcels, piled in the barrow or arranged in rows on the ground like a conceptual art installation. Their wrappers sweaty with raindrops. It was done, now. While Bry and the rest of the islanders slept, oblivious, Finn had brought these things among them. But it was done, and they needed shifting, so he hoisted the barrow on to its wheel and set off with the first load.

Dawn loomed before the gear was stowed in Qway's shack, carefully hidden in the dump of old bags and suitcases so that nothing looked to have been disturbed.

What She Found on the Shore

Alone in bed, with the brush of her bare skin against cotton, with that familiar, loose, liquid warmth inside, it would have been so easy to weaken, to let the fantasy play on in her imagination, to ease a hand between her thighs. But she didn't. Hadn't, yet, in all these months. Despite sometimes being filled with such an intolerable ache that she thought she'd have to strap her wrists to the bedframe to stop herself. It would be wrong. It would be like cheating on Roop. Bryher hadn't even been able to touch herself while fantasising about *him* – but to masturbate while imagining herself with *someone else*, as she was so close to doing now, would be just too appalling. And for what? One transiently satiating surge of pleasure that would leave her dirty, wretched.

Tonight, as on other nights recently, it was Finn.

If she caressed her nipples, if she stroked her clitoris, if she slipped her fingers inside herself, they would be Finn's fingers, not hers. Not Roop's.

Bryher threw the covers aside, stepped out of bed into the shock of cool air.

She always kept a fresh glass of water on the bedside table; she fumbled in the half-light and, placing the glass against her stomach, jolted herself once more with the cold. Her skin was goosebumped. She took a long drink. The bedroom was shades of grey, chopped into geometric shards by the play of light, what little there was, from the window. It was beyond midnight, she supposed. Bryher had come to bed early, then lain in bed reading. She'd heard Finn moving about downstairs, making his customary snack; but it had been quiet for some while and she could pretend she was alone in the cottage. She would do this, still, even after so long with him under the same roof.

Retrieving her robe, she wrapped it around herself, not ready to risk returning to bed just yet. In any case, she'd awoken herself and was suddenly alert, restless. She went to the window. The night rain had spread a silvery patina on the rocks at the end of the cove where the light from a half-moon lay fractured. Out to sea, as usual, the fret sprawled, bruised against a slate sky. She stood at the window for ages, emptying her thoughts, registering the slowing of her rhythms, watching the sea whiten at the base of Gibbet Rock, watching the waves flatten where the beach shelved. The tide was in retreat. Scraps of cloud overhung this scene like components in a collage. She yawned, rubbed her eyes. Her hands, for all that she'd bathed, were redolent of wood from the hours she had put in on the boat. It would be finished soon. In a week or two, Amver's boat would be built. Resting her forehead on the cold glass, she wondered if it was possible to fall asleep standing up like this, leaning against the windowpane.

At that moment, she noticed the body on the shore.

Not thinking to put on a coat or shoes, she ran outside into the rain, her eyes adapting to the lack of light as she went. The sand-drifts caused her to stumble, and the litter of shells, pebbles and cuttlefish bones sent spikes of pain into her bare feet. But she kept running. Her robe flapped about her and her breath burned her

277

throat. She didn't slow down until she drew closer to the body. It lay some ten metres away, in the shallows where the outcrop at the far end of the cove broke up into rubble. She halted, panting, then advanced again with tentative steps. The rain in her face felt like cobwebs. The rocks hereabouts were dotted with limpets that made the pitted surface of the granite appear diseased, yellowy grey in the moonlight. The body was slumped over one of the rocks, as though hugging it, or as though the figure had been trying to pick it up and had finally collapsed, exhausted. It lay half in the water, half out. Fat and bloated, bulging at each push of the sea. She could make out little of the face, just a pale shape where the head ought to be. It was hard to tell if she was looking at flesh or bone, or some putrid stage of decomposition. Or whether there was a head at all.

Bryher bent and retched between her feet.

Straightening again, she heard herself speak. 'Roop? Roop?' She continued to say his name as she approached, her voice unlike her own – whispering, like a child sharing a dreadful secret in the dark with a friend. At the same time her thoughts had become both disconnected from and acutely conscious of the act of placing one foot in front of another. That she was walking and watching herself walk.

'Roop?'

The smell. Then the sight. She knelt in the sodden sand beside the body, hands hovering above it as if summoning the figure to levitate. Petrified. Afraid of touching it, but having to. Having to confirm what her eyes and nose told her; to know this with her skin, too. The shock, the tangible fact of contact. She could let go of hope then; if she could only bring herself to touch the body, Bryher would know it for what it was.

What she'd taken for an arm was a section of torso, partially shorn off to hang from the flank like a useless limb. A second wound to

278

one side of the skull gaped wide, its surgical-neat incision ruptured by a gobbet of extruded brain. There were bloodstains around the muzzle as well. The seal hadn't been dead long; a few hours, perhaps. The odour – pungent, metallic, meaty, fishy, unmistakably animal rather than human – was fresh, not rotten, and not especially unpleasant. There was no sign of scavenging. The corpse had been carried ashore by the ocean and left by the tide's withdrawal. An offering, washed up for her to find. Damp, lit by the moon, the creature might have been sculpted in pewter. She smoothed her hands along its back, moving with the nap of the pelt and squeezing out excess water by the simple pressure of her fingertips. The skin was cold, rougher than she'd expected, the flesh beneath surprisingly firm. She touched the damaged places, too. A propeller would have done this. Or the keel of a speeding boat. She pictured the patrol launch setting out to sea, as it had done late the previous day, slicing the waves . . . the seal, surfacing directly beneath. The crew would not have spotted it; in the bump and pitch and roar of their craft, they wouldn't have been aware of the collision, or that they'd left a dead thing in their wake.

She didn't register Finn's approach. She'd managed to roll the corpse off the rock, but couldn't shift it far enough into the receding shallows to set it afloat. When Finn spoke she was close to despair, weak, rain-soaked, her gown unwrapped and trailing in the sea, her joints aching, feet abraded by the sand, her palms by the seal's salty hide, sobs of frustration snagging in her throat as she pushed. Weeping. Sinking uselessly to her knees in the water, cruciform against the creature's obstinate bulk.

'Bry?'

The tone of voice was the same as hers had been, earlier, before she'd realised her mistake. 'Roop?' she had said then. Bryher felt Finn's hand at her shoulder as she slumped over the dead seal. Not halting her, or drawing her away, but placed there. A simple gesture of contact. *I'm here*, he seemed to say. *It's OK, I'm here now.*

'They'll peck his eyes out when they find him,' she said. 'The gulls. I have to get him back into the water before it's light.'

'You're drenched.'

She tugged the gown closed, refastening it, as if he had told her she was cold rather than wet. The saturated towelling dragged at her flesh. 'If we both push . . .'

'Bry, please . . .'

She mimed the action. She *was* cold, suddenly. Shivering, her teeth clacking, her mouth unable to shape the words properly. 'If we rock him back and forth, we'll get enough . . .' but she couldn't manage 'momentum'. She braced herself, pushed again. Felt the pelt move a little beneath her palms, but that was all. 'If you help me.'

'Come on.'

She batted his hands away. 'They'll pick him clean!' Bryher imagined herself at the bedroom window, watching the seabirds strip him. Their squabbles. The chunks of ragged, bloodied fat, like slugs in their beaks. 'I can't see him like that.'

Finn's hands were there again, on her shoulders, and this time she didn't resist. 'Even if we roll him into the water he'll float,' he said. 'And they'll get him anyway.'

'I'm not going to leave him here like this.'

'Come inside.' Gentle, patient. 'Come indoors with me, and I'll sort it.'

They sat in the kitchen, talking quietly, as if another person slept upstairs and ought not to be disturbed. Bryher had dried off and was dressed, a blanket around her. The hob was on. Finn had made tea and toast. She left the food untouched, urging him to tuck in; eventually, he did. The room smelled of buttered toast, peppermint and a seawater stink that would linger for days, she suspected.

280

Bryher watched him eat. 'Why do you tear it?'

'Do I?'

'You tear each slice into strips and fold them into your mouth.'

Finn ate another piece, as if to test her observation. 'I never knew I did that.'

He had been back outside to retrieve an old tarpaulin from the garden toolshed and hauled it down to the cove to stake out over the seal carcass. It would serve as a temporary measure to keep off the gulls. In the morning, he'd said, he would get Tye and Qway to help remove the body before the tide came in. Finn, too, was dressed, his hair dishevelled and damp. Daybreak was still a way off. The window reflected the kitchen's candlelit interior – the pair of them, sitting opposite one another at the table that Roop had made in their first week. She inspected her hands. The palms were raw, smarting with the heat of the mug. She was calm; calmer, anyway. Aware, though, of the stirrings of embarrassment at what had happened.

'I lost it out there,' she said. 'I thought it was . . .' She broke off. 'Anyway, you can guess what I thought.'

'Some people have a thing for seals,' Finn said. 'It's cool.'

Bryher laughed. Laughter felt good after a few days in which she'd cried too much. Curiously, tonight, she didn't even feel close to tears. She thanked Finn for rescuing her. He explained that he'd been woken by the cold (she'd left the front door wide open) and had gone outside to investigate. Her thoughts drifted to the night of the accident, when she'd sat like this with Effie, finding things to say between long stretches of nothing, waiting for it to become light enough – for the fret to disperse – so that the search could begin. Finn spoke, drawing her from her introspection.

'It was like Kurt that time,' he said. 'Going out to look for you.'

She'd heard this story. The shed. She pictured him waking to find her gone, as he had found Kurt gone; heading off into the dark with that same dread. Finn looked disconsolate, like some-one made up to appear old. It had been an ordeal for him, too.

'Sorry,' she said.

'What for?'

'Putting you through all that again.'

He had finished eating and, seemingly at a loss for what to do with his hands, placed them on the table, as a clairvoyant might. 'It wasn't so freaky, really.'

'Right. Uh-huh.'

He poured the last of the tea – fascinated, it seemed, by the coils of vapour that rose from the two mugs. 'The middle of the night is when it gets to you, isn't it?' he said. 'You kid yourself you're doing OK and, most of the time you are, and then . . .'

'Then you're not.'

'It's when you're at your lowest ebb – mind and body switched to standby.'

Standby. She recognised that. The sense of loss had intensified again, lately, but the long-term problem – her chronic grief, as opposed to the acute – could be equally damaging. Her mind and body had been on standby for too many months.

Bryher set her mug down. 'The first couple of weeks, I tried to keep myself awake at night. Then I found I could dream about him. Nice dreams. Dreams he was still alive. It got so that I looked forward to bedtime because I knew I could bring him to me. The days were the times I dreaded – all those hours to get through.'

'D'you still dream about him?'

She recalled the erotic fantasy she'd had, and which had resulted in all of this. It was like an episode from a different night. She glanced at Finn's hands, his fingers. Though there was no arousal, she flushed and looked away. 'No. Not really.'

'Out there,' he said. 'It might turn out to be some kind of, I don't know . . .' He shrugged. 'Maybe things will be different for you, after this.'

'Different, how?'

'It's like a big thing happened – the kind that takes you to the other side of where you were before.' She let him continue. 'Burning the clothes seemed to make things worse . . . I guess I'm saying maybe this will do the opposite.'

'Help me to *move on*?' She couldn't keep the ironic edge from her voice.

'Just . . . take you someplace different. That's all.'

The seal episode had seemed, while it was happening, to be no more than a sequence of physical responses. From spying the carcass from the window to being ushered back indoors she had acted, or *re*acted, according to what she saw. Even the tears of frustration at her failure to set it afloat had felt mechanical, unemotional. She was unaware of having thought about what she was doing, and, reflecting on it now, she couldn't begin to see where this left her. Perhaps tonight would prove to be the breakthrough Finn suggested, perhaps not. It felt less climactic, more complicated – another stage in a process that had been unfolding within her. Towards absorbing Roop's absence into her life, instead of absorbing her life into his absence. It was a stage, though; she wasn't there yet. Bryher wasn't sure she believed in epiphanies.

She was sure of one thing. 'I won't stop hoping to find him on a beach one day,' she said. 'All the time I live here, a part of me will go on waiting for it.'

'And if that moment never comes?'

'The question isn't whether or not it comes. It's whether I can live like that.'

'The boat's almost ready,' she said. They were both eating toast, now, and a fresh pot of peppermint tea stood in the centre of the table.

'Yeah?' Finn leaned back, his chair creaking.

'Uh-huh. Couple of weeks.'

'You won't know what to do with yourself once that's finished.'

Bryher smiled. 'I could always go with her.'

The statement surprised her more than it seemed to surprise him. The idea was so new to her, and she hadn't planned on mentioning it to Finn, or to anyone else, just yet. Finn knew she was unsure about her future here, without Roop – but they hadn't spoken of it in weeks, so she might have expected him to react less calmly, however throwaway the remark. He folded his arms, then unfolded them. That was all. Bryher searched his expression, but it held no clue to his thoughts.

After a moment, he said: 'To do what? Nursing?'

'I don't know. Probably. Yeah, I'd have to I guess.'

'Is this because of what happened?' He pointed towards Gibbet Cove.

'What? No, of course not.'

'The way you said it, it seemed sudden, like it just occurred to you.'

'It's while I've been helping Hobb with the boat,' she said. 'Now it's nearly finished I've been . . . I don't know, I was working on it the last couple of days and, for the first time, I could actually picture it afloat, setting sail. You know?'

'And you saw yourself in that picture?'

'Kind of, I suppose. The possibility, anyway.' She sought a better explanation, for herself as much as for him. Talking about it like this, when she hadn't meant to, was pulling the idea into shape quicker than she was quite ready for. 'Up till now, the idea of leaving has been . . . *general*, I guess. Something vague and theoretical. The boat makes it more specific – something I could actually *do*, if I wanted.'

'Do you?' Finn said. 'Want to, I mean?'

Bryher swallowed down some tea. It was warm in here, now;

284

the windows were misting over. She had never done this with
Roop, talking deep into the night; even in bed, after making love,
they seldom spoke like this. The mornings were their times. Long,
lazy, sunny mornings. 'I was talking to Amver,' she said. 'You
know, the morning after your fight? I asked her why she wanted
to go to the mainland, and she said it was to do with living on an
island – being surrounded by all this water.'

'She feels cut off. She's told me that.'

'It's more to do with the idea of the voyage, I think. The way
she explained it. On an island, the tension between the possibility
of staying or leaving is much more obvious than it is on the
mainland. Over there, you move from one place to another and it
isn't so dramatic, so final. Here, the ocean – the boundary of your
existence – is staring you in the face every day, every time you
look at the horizon.'

'Like an invitation to leave,' Finn said.

'Uh-huh. Yes, that's exactly it. An invitation to leave.' Bryher
liked the sound of that phrase. She smiled across the table at Finn.
'I could manage some more toast,' she said, indicating the empty
plate.

Finn got up, seemingly relieved to have something to do. His
face had almost returned to normal, she noticed, the streaks of
bruising faded to a yellowish tinge that, with only two of the
original four candles still alight, lent him a particularly spectral
appearance. 'Burned or burned?' he said, slicing up the last of the
loaf.

'Burned, please.'

Watching him, reflecting on how he had been with her out
there on the beach, a tenderness towards Finn welled up, in stark
contrast to the feelings she'd had earlier, in bed. There was an
awkwardness of movement to him, here in the kitchen – aware of
being observed – that she found endearing, and not at all sexy.
The idea of *actually* sleeping with him seemed bizarre, now. Yet

285

she saw how close they'd become, their comfortable and casual intimacy. She hadn't believed this would be possible.

'I'm glad you came,' she said. Too abruptly, she could tell. Her thoughts had led her to this remark, but Finn was unprepared and looked at her, confused. 'To the island, I mean.' She offered him another smile. 'I was thinking, it's been good to have you around; you know, what with everything that's gone on. I wanted to say that.'

Finn busied himself with plates, butter. Unnecessarily checking the grill. Say something, she thought, please say something. But he didn't.

'So, there. I've said it.' She rubbed at her eyes with the heels of her hands; her palms were as sore as if she'd scalded them on the hob. A hush had assembled around Finn, like an aura. She didn't regret that she'd put her thoughts into words, but wished she had done so less clumsily. Despite herself, she yawned profusely. 'Pardon me.'

'You're exhausted, Bry. You should turn in.'

'Uh-huh.' She yawned again. 'I think I will.' Her chair scraped on the floor as she stood up. In the doorway, Bryher paused. 'Sorry about the toast.'

Finn said it wasn't a problem.

'Night, then. And thanks, for what you did out there.'

That wasn't a problem either. Then Finn threw her completely: 'When they come for me,' he said, 'it'd be best for you not to be around any more.'

She frowned. Puzzled, irritated. 'If I do leave, that won't be the reason.'

'I know. Yeah, I know that.'

Later, in bed – listening to him still moving about down in the kitchen – she tried to unpack his parting remark from its level, matter-of-fact tone. It was as if he had been the one to suggest she

286

should leave the island, and was simply taking her through the rationale. As if he hadn't listened to, or understood, anything she'd said about the boat or about the island, the voyage. Or as if he was implying that her departure would be a selfish act. In there, as well, however, was his use of 'when', not 'if'; his resignation to the inevitable: she would go; he would be recaptured. Bryher had lingered in the doorway, debating whether to press him. In the end she had decided she was too tired, too confused, and had simply said goodnight a second time and gone upstairs.

Flower Picking

They issued Finn with rubber boots (black, Nudge's) and gloves (pink, tight) from Jad's beachcombed cache. From a string belt around his waist, they hung the bottom half of a one-litre cola bottle, full of elastic bands. Every ten flowers, you fastened the bunch and dropped it on to the foliage. Not on the soil, or they got dirty. The daffodils grew in ridges that scored stripes down the field – vertically, with the gradient, rather than the contour. You picked each ridge from bottom to top, working your way uphill, so you didn't have to stoop so far. Coming back down, you gathered up the bunches. Oh, and it was called a *piece*, not a field. It wasn't picking, it was *cropping*.

Finn pulled on the boots, the gloves, and tried to take all this in. Hobb's spiel.

'Each daff. has to be around thirty cems – twenty-eight, minimum,' Hobb said. He gave Finn a thirty-centimetre rule, told him to measure from his fingertips and mark a line on his forearm. 'You crop *in* the soil, not above.' Hobb demonstrated. 'The stem is paler where there's new growth at the base. If you don't get that, you're cropping high.'

'What happens then?'

'Mr Skins rejects them.'

'Skins. That figures.'

'His buyers set the spec. The wholesaler, the supermarkets, the florists.' Hobb took in the piece with a sweep of his hand. 'Thirty-six hours from now, most of these will be laid on the graves of the war dead or at the doorsteps of the grieving.'

Finn thought of his mother fixing a wreath to her door, for Kurt. He couldn't recall if there had been daffodils; for all he knew, some of those flowers had come from here, picked by the folk he now lived with. 'So, what, if they're not thirty centimetres tall,' he said, 'it's not proper grief?'

Hobb shrugged. It was the way of things.

Finn surveyed the scene: the bustle and colour, the figures moving among the rows as if choreographed. In his time on the island he hadn't seen so much activity – so many people – concentrated in one place. So far as he could see, every islander had turned out. Even the children. Peef, Jafe and Kags were chasing one another along the field edge; Jad was helping Orr and Sholo assemble cartons from the cardboard sheets that had come ashore in the last shipment. Others were already fanned out along the ridges: Tye, Zess, Yué, Nudge, Qway, Liddy – trailing banded bunches in their wake. Effie was sorting out boots and gloves for Amver, who'd arrived even later than Finn.

One person was missing: Bryher.

Finn went over to the two women. Asked where she was.

Effie pushed her frizz of ginger fringe back from her face. 'At the boatyard.'

'She's not picking, then? Cropping.'

'There you go.' Effie was talking to Amver, making a final adjustment to the twine belt, with its pot of elastic bands. Then, to Finn: 'Doesn't look like it.'

Bryher had been a whole lot better since the night of the seal,

289

and her no-show was less worrying than it might've been before that. All the same, it was a surprise. A big communal thing was going on here, at the flower pieces, and Bryher wasn't taking part – away by herself, building the boat still. Hobb was there again, ushering him and Amver to the ridges, setting them up to work side by side.

'Keep an eye on him,' Hobb told Amv, then left them to it.

The piece was long and narrow – one of ten dividing the low-lying pasture of The Neck from the slope of South Hill. The incline, slight at first, sharpened towards the point where cultivation gave way to bracken and scrub. Finn straddled his ridge, as instructed: feet wide apart, knees braced, bent at the waist, cropping methodically, pushing his thumb into the soil to snap the stem with a twist. Shuffling forward after each bunch. Soon he was soaked in sweat, his back ached and his hamstrings were tight as fuck. But it got easier. Once he sorted out the posture, the actions, once he struck a rhythm, his muscles warmed and loosened and he became fluid. Started to enjoy himself. Finn thought he was working quickly but, glancing up, he saw the rest were way further ahead than when he'd begun and Amv was pulling clear of him too.

'How you doing?' she said, over her shoulder. Her hair had come untied and a few strands caught in her mouth. She tipped her head to let the breeze set them free.

He returned her smile. 'I'm doing OK.'

'Go at your own pace, yeah?'

She went back to her own cropping – brisk, seemingly careless. Finn watched her, stooping over the ridge. The unnaturally white heels of her bare feet, her calves – shaped by muscle – beneath the frayed hem of her skirt. Her top was streaked with damp, like ink stains. He thought of her, naked, prostrate on the track beneath Rudy. Thought of the men, taking turns at her. This whole place belonged to Skins and his gang and to the patrol crew – to mainlanders – to buy and sell, to fuck and fuck over, whenever they chose. Seventeen years old. Sixteen, she'd been, when it started. Fuck sake. Finn hadn't spoken to her since that night at South Bay. Not properly. Amv had come to the cottage to thank him, to tell him she was OK, but that was it. Not long now before she left, on the boat Bryher was helping to build. Whatever they thought of Amver's desire to quit for the mainland, whatever they thought of her prostituting herself to pay for it . . . she wanted to go, and the islanders were making it possible for this to happen in style. Sailing away, as her father had done twelve months ago. Yet seeing her like this, busy among these people, she looked so much a part of this place.

Amv dropped another bunch, straightened up, stepped forward, bent down again. His attention strayed to the columns of unpicked stems. Today and for days to come it was Paper Whites. Next week, Soleil d'Or – the principal crop – then Primo, Avalanche, Grand Monarch, King Alfred. He loved the names; more like butterflies than daffodils and narcissi. Cheerfulness, Fortune, Actea, Golden Dawn. In the next couple of months, Hobb had told him, they would crop 100,000 bunches for Mr Skins. Looking back along his own ridge, Finn reckoned he'd done about forty.

He worked without stopping for what must've been a couple of hours. Hobb toured the ridges, doling out water, measuring stems at random, especially Finn's. The labour was so absorbing in its repetitive monotony that Finn slipped into a groove. No longer aware of Amver, or the other croppers. Or the strain on his muscles, his joints. Or the sweat. Or the heat of the sun. Or the noise of the workmen, hidden from sight at the top of South Hill, as they put the final touches to the communications mast. No longer aware of the flowers he picked, just the point where each stem disappeared into the soil. For these hours, at least, he ceased even to think about the parcels he would hand over to Mr Skins, when word came. You could almost forget they were there, in that shack down at the hives; could believe that, if you looked for them, they would be gone, it would all be over and done with, your debt cleared, and you could continue to live among these folk as if nothing had happened.

Mid-morning, they all took a break. Finn sat with Amver at the top of the piece, away from the rest. From up there, The Neck's vulnerability was stark – a slight rise in sea level would split the island in two. Directly below, the ridged fields made a patchwork corduroy of greens and browns.

'It's your fingers and wrist.' Finn made and unmade a fist.

'Yeah,' Amv said. 'You'd think it would be your back, but it isn't.'

He held them out, palms down, like a pianist preparing to play. The left hand was steady, the right trembled, thumb and index finger involuntarily curling inwards. He tucked the hand in his lap to stop the tremor. 'How come the daffodils don't all ripen at the same time?' he said.

'The planting is staggered.' Amver pointed to one piece, then another. 'Each week, the next variety is ready to be cropped.'

She'd been sitting, but lay back now, raising her legs. Flexed each one in turn and rotated her feet. *Cramp.* Her skirt slid right to the tops of her thighs. She said the island's microclimate – sun by day, rain by night, no frosts, one year-round unaltering season – meant they could pretty much grow what they liked, when they liked.

'This place is a defiance of nature,' Finn said.

'You're telling me.' Amv rolled on to her front and began plucking the rough grass, as Jad had done with the moss that time at The Shoot. Out of nowhere, she said: 'If it was safe for you to go back, would you?'

Maybe she'd been thinking about herself, her imminent departure, and it had segued into a question about him. He told her he didn't know.

'You would,' she said. 'You don't belong here.'

'Thanks.'

She dropped bits of grass on to Finn's lap; childlike, all twitchy restlessness and animation. Beside her, he was a point of stillness. 'You don't, though, do you? Neither of us do, or how come we're sat here on our own?'

That had just happened, hadn't it? Nothing deliberate: they'd worked together then, at the break – lagging behind the rest – they'd sat together. Finn looked at the others, clustered in twos and threes further down. By himself at the foot of the piece: Jad, aiming stones at a fence-post; if anyone was isolated it was him. Or Bryher, who wasn't even here. It was Bry, in her absence, who seemed the more cast-off just now. They'd spoken again about her thoughts of leaving on the boat with Amv; he couldn't decide if Bryher was talking herself out of it, or into it, or whether she was just testing the idea out loud. *Don't go*, he'd wanted to say. By the end of their conversation, she still hadn't made up her mind. Now, with every last one of the islanders scattered about the piece, apart from Bry, there was a glimpse of this land as it would look without her. As if she was already gone.

There was something in what Amver had said, though. About him, and about belonging. He *did* feel cut off from them. Here they all were, working their butts off to keep Mr Skins sweet. Toiling away to protect his profit margins, and the remains of their way of being; to protect Finn, too, what with the new quotas. Amver, beside him, turning up late this morning because, for all he knew, she'd been up half the night again with Skins' men. Which was the paradox: that Finn should feel so estranged from these people when he was jerking at the end of the same set of puppet strings.

'I didn't belong over there, either.' He gestured towards the

293

mainland. Amver had stopped sprinkling him with grass. She was sitting up again, cross-legged.

'Where, then?' she said.

'I don't know. Maybe people don't naturally belong. Maybe they learn to.'

'Maybe not everyone wants to.' She was fiddling with a braided, rainbow-coloured ankle bracelet. 'I made this,' she said, locking on to the direction of his gaze. 'This too.' She displayed a second band around her wrist. They were fashioned from lengths of beachcombed cord Jad had given her, she said. Offering her wrist, Amver invited him to smell it. Finn was reminded of Qway, that time at the hives, his cupped palms reeking of cider vinegar.

Finn dipped his face, inhaled. 'Mm. Seaweed.'

'It's in my hair, too. D'you think it ever goes?'

'It's a nice smell,' Finn said.

'They call me The Mermaid.' She meant the men, he realised. He didn't know what to say, so he said nothing. Amver smiled. 'Couple of weeks to go. You know, I wish it was tomorrow.'

'Two weeks isn't so long. Not after seventeen years.'

The Mermaid. In another context, it might've been a term of affection. Maybe it was, even so. What did he know about the way things were between Amver and the men; he'd seen them with her once, that was all. He wanted to ask her why. Why she went with them. Was it because of Mor: his leaving, his absence? She would say 'for the money', probably; or she would tell him to mind his own business. Maybe Amver would've gone with the men this past year whatever her father had done. Finn hadn't yet made sense of his own absences – Lila, Kurt, his mother, his own father for fuck sake – so how was he supposed to understand Amver's? Or Bryher's for that matter.

'Why d'you want to leave so much?' he said.

'I want to live someplace where I don't know anyone and no one knows me. Where I can't walk from one end of the land to

294

the other in the time it takes to do a batch of washing. Where I can't see the sea everywhere I look.'

Finn followed her gaze. The ocean, implacable, to either side. Even the ribbon of pasture and flower-pieces was a swathe of silvery-blue in the sunlight – an illusion of water as lifelike as the sea, a premonition of how it would look under flood. Gulls spiralled above the fields as if they too had been taken in. There were times when the entire island seemed to be a mirage, a sequence of optical deceits that never displayed the same scene twice no matter how often you came upon it. He recalled what Bryher had said: that Amver saw the sea as a boundary to be crossed, an invitation to voyage. Finn wasn't so sure. What he got was an impression of infinite space in a land so tiny, so enveloped; the lightness and openness beyond its physical limits somehow erased those limits altogether. Not just the obvious limitlessness: the horizon, the ocean, the sky; it was the *possibility*. Living on the island raised the possibility of an existence outside the margins of anything you'd known. Amver imagined that when she went to the mainland she would leave somewhere small for somewhere huge; even though he'd travelled in the opposite direction, Finn had seen himself making the exact same transition. Only now, with the gear stashed away at the bee shack awaiting collection, was he beginning to glimpse the claustrophobia she described.

Finn smiled. ' "How can I be set free?" the traveller asked. And the guru replied: "Who is it keeps you in chains?" '

Amver looked at him, curious. 'What?'

'Nothing. Just something someone told me.' He changed subjects. 'You going to your dad's first?'

'Yeah.' She nodded, still looking at him. 'Sail down the coast and crash with him for a while, before uni. It'll be good.'

Mor, Finn knew, was working the trawlers in a port ninety kilometres to the south. The port, her father, they seemed to hold a mythic quality for Amver, the way she sometimes spoke of

295

them. A place she'd never visited, a father she hadn't seen in a year. She'd created a version of them so seductive it was hard not to taste their promise. He envied her, having somewhere to go – somewhere unsoiled by the slow seep of experience into expectation.

'Girlfriend?' Amver said. 'The someone who told you the story of the guru?'

Finn nodded. 'Lila.'

'You left her when you went on the run?'

'We'd more or less split anyway.'

'Split, or she ditched you?'

He laughed. 'She said I was too pissed off all the time.'

Amver had stretched out once more, on her side, head propped on one hand. Studying him. His shoulders were burned from working with his shirt off for most of the morning; he ought to put something on them, she said. Salve, or something. He thought she was going to touch his skin, but she didn't. She wanted to know, did he trim the hairs on his chest? Only it was like they were shaped, *styled*.

'When I got my call-up papers,' Finn said, 'I had this idea she'd fall in love with me all over again.'

'The hero thing.'

'I was the same as a kid. If there was a girl I liked I'd have these dreams about her watching me play football – blood on my face from a clash of heads and the coach wants to take me off, but I refuse to leave the field and then, in the last minute of play, with the scores tied, I go on this mazy run and win the game for my team.'

'And she's on the touchline,' Amver said. '*Swooning*.'

Finn brushed the grass from his lap, meticulously, until every blade was gone. Sounds from the boatyard reached them just then; the yard was lost from view beyond the scrubby trees huddled beside the track down to Long Strand, but they both

296

stared in that direction, even so. Thinking their different thoughts. Finn saw that the others were returning to the cropping. Amver was watching them, too, he noticed; distracted, as if they were people she recognised but couldn't quite place.

'I like it,' she said. 'The sex.' Her gaze stayed fixed on the piece. 'That's what none of them get, that I actually *like* it. Not that shit with Rudy – I mean, mostly, most of the time, I do it because I want to. Because I can.' She gestured at the straggle of stooped figures. 'They think I do it to piss them off, like it's some kind of statement. "There goes Amv, making a point." And so they build me the boat as a gift – a fucking *leaving present*.'

'Bastards,' Finn said, deadpan. 'You'll be well shot of these people.'

Even Amver had to crack a smile. Serious again, calmer, she said: 'When I'm around the men, I get such a buzz. Sometimes we don't even do it – I just sit and talk and drink with them. Have a laugh. Over on the mainland . . .'

She left the thought unfinished. Finn watched her, watching the croppers. That night, spying on the men – before it all kicked off – he'd been able to imagine himself among them, partying. Boozed up. The *buzz* Amv spoke of. He hadn't wanted to, but he wasn't as far from wanting to as he'd have expected, after his time here. Wasn't so different. If there was an affinity between him and Amver, it was this.

'Come on.' She jolted his leg with her foot. 'Only another 99,000 to go.'

'I'll catch you up,' he said. 'I need a piss.'

Finn was behind the windbreak, all buttoned up again and turning away to skirt back round to the ridges, when he saw him. Hadn't caught his approach at all. No glimpse, no sound, nothing. Yet, there he was – the younger of the two marines – just a few metres

297

away, sitting against a tumbledown wall, smoking. Waiting for Finn to spot him. Finn's first thought was the tattoo. He pulled the shirt from where he'd looped it over his belt and went to draw it on, but the marine told him not to bother.

The Young Marine

'"Thin", the kid called you. And I'm thinking: *"Thin", what's that all about?*'

The fight. Jad, calling out to him to 'run, Thin, run!'. And he'd figured it would be the pile of bedding on the sofa that gave him away, or Skins, or one of his men, or an islander – Tye, maybe – who didn't want him here. Or the tattoo. Even now, Finn thought he should put his shirt back on. He had followed the young marine away from the pieces, screened from view by the windbreak, then the curve of South Hill itself as they rounded its lower slopes towards Great Pool. Where they'd stopped, safely alone. Finn sat where he was told, on the turf beside the track; the marine settled himself on the opposite verge, laid his gun at his feet and took a moment to finish the cigarette.

'So I trawl through the APBs,' he said, 'and I come across a "Finn",' pointing at Finn's chest, 'tag code KD150/468C, last reliable whereabouts a refugee camp just a few K from Mr Skins' place.' It was odd, hearing him. Their first encounter, outside the cottage, he'd barely said a word; after the scrap, too, ferrying him home, the older marine did most of the talking. The young one had plenty to say now. 'But it checks out: "Roop". Your ID card. And the residency rolls: Bryher and Roop.'

'Is there a way we can do this without her being involved?' Finn said.

'So then I'm thinking, if she's passing this Finn guy off as her bloke then what the fuck happened to Roop?'

'You don't have to take her down as well.'

'No, seriously, this Roop – he just clears off and leaves his *wife* to you?'

'You've got your dodger.' Finn held his gaze, looking for a spark, something he could find hope in. Saw nothing. The marine had found his voice, but the eyes were blank as ever. Hard-man blank. 'You could settle for that. Take me back and leave her out of it – all of these people.'

'He died, is what I figure. But then he's not draft age, not joined up. So how'd he die?' He looked at Finn's chest. 'Cover yourself up, I'm sick of seeing that fucking tattoo.' Finn pulled the shirt on. It was still damp with sweat. 'I have to go back out there,' the young marine said. Quieter. Examining the spent cigarette butt between his fingers, as though surprised to find it still there. He flicked it away. 'Two weeks.'

'Roop drowned,' Finn said. 'He was on the fishing boat . . .'

'Poxy. *Fucking*. War.'

The venom in his voice; Finn couldn't tell if it was directed at the war itself, or at him, for evading it. Since his arrival on the island Finn had dreaded this moment. Exposure. Recapture. Now that it was here, he was calm. Almost relieved that the anticipation was over. It was happening. This was how it happened. He wasn't sure where to look, how to sit, what was expected of him. Beyond the marine, Great Pool shimmered like a huge disk of new-laid asphalt. Finn decided to look there, to wait.

'You a conchie, or what?'

300

It was so long since Finn had considered his motives the question threw him. He was a dodger, that was all. 'I guess,' he said.

'You *guess*.'

'Look, it doesn't matter what I am.'

'Fucking right it doesn't.' The young marine looked like he would gladly pick up the semi-automatic that lay on the ground between his feet and empty it into Finn.

The noise from the hill started up again after a lull; a dull clanka-clanka-clank. Finn had his own work to return to. His absence would've been noted by now; he'd have to come up with an excuse. With this thought came the realisation that he wasn't going back to the pieces. Any time now they would witness him being escorted to the patrol launch. That image – the islanders, heads raised from their labour to watch in silence as he was led away – was more shocking, more intensely upsetting than the fact of his capture. Their expressions. Amver. Jad. The marine was talking again.

'See, I have to report where I found you,' he said. The earlier flash of temper might not have happened, he was so neutral. So matter-of-fact. 'And there's no way the IS won't come after whoever sheltered you. Or want to know why I didn't bring them in too. So how can I leave her out of it?'

'What will they do to her?'

'You want to worry about what they'll do to you.'

'She nursed you,' Finn said. 'You broke your wrist one time, coming off your motorbike – she was the nurse who set it.'

The marine looked interested. Puzzled, then figuring it out. 'Was that her?'

'Yeah.'

'Fuck sake, yeah?' He almost smiled. His sleeves were rolled up; he turned his wrist one way then the other, as if searching for some mark or scar, but there was no sign that Finn could see to show it'd ever been broken. The marine glanced up at him. Blank, again. Flat and toneless. 'She doesn't look like her.'

'She recognised *you*.'

'So, she's a widow. And all the time I had her down as a wife.'

Finn watched him produce a carton of cigarettes from his tunic and light one. Smoke, bluish mauve in the sunlight. The air smelled of wild garlic and heat and tobacco and, now and then, of water, cool on the breeze that skimmed Great Pool. Finn was aware of himself making a mental impression of the moment, of this place.

'What about Skins?' he said. 'Does he go down for bringing me here?'

'D'you know what the reward is, for handing in a draft-dodger?'

Finn said that he did.

'Six months, it'd take me to earn that. Six fucking months.' The marine jabbed himself in the chest. 'You know what I'd get for you?' He didn't wait for an answer. 'Fuck all. It's my job – my *duty* – so I'd get a clap on the back and sweet fucking zip.'

Finn tried to square him with the earlier versions – outside the cottage, sullen and silent; after Finn's battering, quietly efficient. Difference was, he'd been working alongside the other patrol-man. The deference of rank, age, experience. Here, acting solo, he'd opened out. Become the man. But, also, less soldierly. There was the mood of the renegade about him, now he was off the leash; he could do anything, anything he fucking liked. Where was the older marine? That must mean something, him not being here. Unaware this was taking place, maybe. He would be here, if he knew. If it was official. So why wasn't he here? If there was a shred of hope, it could be this: the absence of the senior officer, the fact of the young marine sneaking up on Finn the way he did, bringing him down here, like this, instead of the handcuffs, the reading of his rights, the gunpoint march down to the quay, the boat ride back to the mainland.

Still, though, the guy sat there, smoking, volatile. Closed off to Finn.

'She'll get three years,' he said. 'Three, four, something like that. Some cunt doesn't want to fight, there's got to be a helper. No helper, no dodger. Yeah?'

Finn said nothing. A butterfly landed on the toecap of the marine's boot. Pale blue. Opened its wings, basked a moment, then lifted off again, letting the air take it. The two men watched it go.

'I heard your brother died out there.'

Finn hesitated. 'Yeah,' he said. 'RPG attack.'

'S'what I heard.' The young marine nodded, his face lost for a moment behind a thin drape of smoke. 'What regiment?'

Finn told him.

'Conscript?'

'No. He volunteered.'

The marine appeared to be digesting this, although there was no telling what impression it made. 'Mine's too young to fight,' he said. 'Seventeen. Last letter I got, he'd been arrested at an anti-war demo.' He laughed. 'Two brothers: the marine and the peacenik. You put that in a movie, no one would fucking believe it.'

'We could be in the same movie,' Finn said. 'Me and Kurt.'

'Kurt.' The marine killed the cigarette, half-smoked, and slotted it back in the carton. 'Know what I hope? I hope he fucking haunts you.'

Before Finn could consider a response, the other man stood. Straightened his kit, picked up the gun. Signalled Finn to stand too. Which he did, already starting to stiffen from the cropping. This was it, then. The entire episode, the sneaking off, the talking, was about nothing – a pointless prelude to the formality of his arrest.

'OK,' the marine said, 'what happens now is you take me to the place.'

'What place?'

'The place where you've stashed Mr Skins' gear.'

Gloomy as ever inside the shack, despite the blaze of daylight framed by the door. It took Finn a moment to find the matches and light the candles Qway left positioned about the place. The recent remains of a meal cluttered the table. Qway's breakfast, Finn figured. He would've come down here at first light, to see to the hives before making his way to the daffodil pieces. The candlelight seemed plenty, to Finn, but the marine snapped on his heavy-duty torch all the same and played it about the interior.

'Fucking dentist's chair,' he said.

Finn went over to the heap of bags and suitcases in the rear. The marine had said he wanted all the packages pulling out, so that's what he did. Laid them out on the floor in neat rows and let the guy count them.

'Couple of kilos each?' the marine said.

' 'Bout that, yeah.'

'Pure?' Finn said he didn't know. But the marine was nodding to himself, saying, yeah, he reckoned it was. 'Skins'll cut this himself, and then you're looking at . . .' counting again, a slow slow smile forming, 'fuck sake, you could buy the whole fucking island with this lot.'

Finn felt cold for being out of the sun. Shivery.

The marine said: 'What I'm thinking is, how many go un-noticed? One? Two? You think he's gonna notice if two parcels go missing?'

'I'd say so.'

'Maybe he'll believe you if you say the drop was short. Go after them, instead of you. What d'you reckon?' He answered his own question. 'Yeah, I don't reckon old Skins will miss a couple of these. Two bags is fuck all, is it?' The marine pointed with the torch. 'Pass me that holdall.'

Finn pulled a canvas bag off the pile of discarded luggage and handed it over. The marine opened it, stowed two of the parcels inside, and drew it shut again. Buckled the flap down.

'There. Nice one.' It hung easy from his shoulder. 'You ever use this shit?' he said.

Finn said he had, once or twice.

'The guys out there, they can't get enough of it. Fucking stuff that goes down, you need something.' The marine adjusted the shoulder strap. 'I go back there with this, I'm telling you, I'm Mr Fucking In Demand.'

'How do I know you won't turn me in anyway?' Finn said. 'Or come back and help yourself to the lot?'

'You don't,' the marine said. 'But you've only got another two weeks to find out.' Then, smiling, the smile contained in the lower half of his face: 'After that, I'm out of here and you just got Mr Skins to deal with. And, what I'm thinking is, there's nothing Internal Security can do to you that he won't.'

The Painting of the Boat

She painted the name last of all, precisely filling in the stencilled letters. In navy, to match the plimsoll line that separated the hull's white upper portion from its pale blue bottom. With that, the exterior of the boat was done. All that remained was for the paint to dry and for the vessel to be fitted out, stocked with provisions and equipment, ready for launch. Bryher stepped back to inspect the lettering. She'd done the painting herself, all of it, insistent on performing this act of completion. Although much of the construction – certainly the more complex tasks – had been carried out by others, the look of the boat would be hers; the colours, the name, had been her choice. Now it was finished, the activity of many weeks reduced to a single moment of cessation, she was aware of stepping back from herself, too; of gauging her mood, with the boat finally built and standing before her, on its chocks, smart, bright and sleek. The L formed by mast and boom; the dolphin-like curve of the bilge; the keel, flattened to stern like the creased edge of an origami fold. The boat should have pleased her. It was new and whole, and she was satisfied with it, so long as she didn't let herself dwell on the countless small irritations, botch-

306

jobs and compromises that had gone into the making. Looking at the boat was like looking at her own face in a mirror: she knew it too intimately to see anything but the imperfections. Bryher couldn't say how she felt about the completion of the boat, beyond that; apart from a vague restlessness, both nervous and physical – as though she had energy left for this work, but no work left to do. She busied herself, instead, in sealing the paint tins and washing the brushes and putting them away, and in tidying the yard.

This was how she was occupied when Finn came. He wore a T-shirt and jeans, stripped of the cropper's paraphernalia; but dirt, the sweat stains, the boots, and the inked line inside his forearm revealed where he'd come from. As did the basket laden with picked stalks. It was odd, him being in the boatyard. In all Finn's wanderings he had never been inside while she was working – though, once, she'd heard him pass by, pausing to talk to Hobb, who had been cutting planks outside on the sawhorse. It had been as if the boat was her private space and, while she'd never asked it of him, he had chosen to stay away.

'Nice colours,' he said.

'Thanks.' Bryher set the broom against a wall. The dust, from the sweeping she had been doing, was still settling around her like so many particles of sunlight. 'How's the cropping coming along?'

'Down to sixty-one rejects today. So far.' He raised the basket. 'For you.'

She smiled. 'Have you eaten?'

'What? Oh, yeah.' He aimed a hand in the direction of the daffodil pieces. 'This is an extended lunch break. Unofficial.' He was looking at the boat. *Raven*.

The 'a', she noticed now, was fractionally smaller than the rest of the lower-case letters. 'It's the colour of Amver's hair,' she said. 'Also, I like that word. It's a symbol of providence, the raven.'

307

Then, with a laugh, 'Or doom, depending which myths and legends you believe. I thought it suited Amver's ambiguousness.'

Finn set down the basket of flowers and approached the vessel, pacing slowly along its length, then stopping in front of the name. He seemed unsure of himself. As he examined the characters she thought he would reach out and touch, but he didn't.

'If she was mine, I'd call her *Paladin*,' he said. 'A knight errant, roaming the world in search of adventure.'

Bryher couldn't tell if he was mocking himself. 'Wasn't that where you used to live?' she said. 'Paladin Mansions.'

'It was *like* being on board a ship, sometimes. The noise, the wind and that. A vast ocean liner or something.'

'Uh-huh.'

Speaking so quietly she strained to hear him, he said: 'Have you decided to go with her, Bry?'

'Is that why you're here?'

'It's just . . . you've not been at the cropping again today.'

'I had this to finish.'

Finn nodded, looking down at the floor, at the boat, everywhere except at her. At last he said, 'You shouldn't have swept up before the paint dried.'

The midday heat made a furnace of the workshop and, though she had been painting all morning, only now were the fumes bothering her. Finn bothered her, too. She hadn't seen him like this before. Hesitant, nervous. Bryher pushed her fingers through her hair, realising too late that her hand was still tacky. If they were to talk about this, she said, they ought to go outside where it was cooler. They left the yard and cut down the track a short distance to Long Strand, where – despite the lack of shade – there was at least the slightest of onshore breezes.

'After what we talked about, I thought, you know, because of Roop and everything.'

Finn looked lost. He'd taken his boots off, drawn his knees beneath his chin, stubble rasping against his jeans as he spoke. They were sitting on the slipway, facing out to sea, the sunlight on the water casting a thousand filaments of electricity. A flask of tepid apple juice passed between them. Bryher tasted salt on her lips. It was good to breathe fresh air, after all the dust and paint fumes; she filled her lungs. This should have been the point when the contentment of completing the boat settled on her, but there was Finn to negotiate. She thought for a moment, then said:

'I didn't say I was leaving. Not for sure.'

'No. I know.'

'And now you come down here with fifty-one Paper Whites . . .'

'*Sixty*-one.'

'. . . sixty-one Paper Whites, and it's like I'm going to set sail any moment and you just got here in time to do the big farewell presentation thing.'

At that moment, they were distracted by the appearance of Skins' gang, a way down the beach, setting up another volleyball game. The two marines were there too, along with the obligatory cool-boxes. They were a couple of hundred metres away and seemed not to have noticed Bryher and Finn on the slipway; at least, they paid them no attention. She watched, tracking the ball back and forth. It *had* seemed real to her, the notion of leaving. The possibility that came with the boat, and with Amver's own imminent departure. She'd thought about little else these past few days, putting the finishing touches to the vessel. So when had she reached her decision? Just that morning, painting the name? While she cleaned the brushes? Yesterday? The day before? During one of the nights that separated her final days' work at the yard? Or not until Finn asked: 'Have you decided to go with her, Bry?' Perhaps the answer had been buried inside her all along. She couldn't say. What she knew was that there had been no snap-of-the-light moment when the decision dropped, fully formed, into her head. Nor was it a gradual realisation – a period of deliberation, of reasoning out what she would do. To leave. To stay. No direct line of thought connected one to the other. If anything, the resolution had come because she'd *stopped* thinking. As soon as Bryher no longer thought about leaving, staying became possible – floating to the surface, just as the idea of leaving sank to the bottom. It was that simple: leaving had been an option, for a time; now, it wasn't. It simply wasn't.

'I'm not going anywhere,' she said.

'You're not?'

'This is where I live. These are my people.'

It was the first time she'd tested these words out loud. They fell from her like fat stones she had carried around in her pockets and which she'd at last managed to cast to the ground. Finn asked when she'd made up her mind and, though she tried to explain about the floating and sinking of possibilities, she saw it made little sense to him. Finn was a man; for all his time here, a mainlander. He sought black or white, but she couldn't offer him either. Bryher told him that perhaps she'd needed to isolate herself like this, to work on the boat – right to the end, while every other islander was at the cropping – to discover whether her place was with the boat, or with them.

'Is that Jad?' Finn said. He was gazing in the direction of the game.

'He's the ballboy. Self-appointed.'

'Why did his dad leave?'

'Mor? He fell out of love with Yué. Actually, she fell out of love with him.'

'It wasn't any big mainland versus island thing?'

'No.'

'Would it have been, for you?'

'If I'd gone, no – it would've been because of Roop. But it is

310

one of the reasons I'm staying. I want to see if I can be an islander. See if I can do this, without him.'

Finn was quiet for a moment. 'Do you believe people *belong* somewhere?' he said. 'That there's a place where each of us belongs.'

'Do you?'

'I don't know. I talked about it with Amv yesterday, and I don't know.'

'I don't see it in terms of place. The place is you. The things you are, or could be. If you don't know that then you don't belong anywhere.'

'Maybe the "place" is other people,' he said. 'Or another person.'

'Well, yeah. Uh-huh. It was for me, to begin with. Roop was my place.'

Watching Finn as she said this, Bryher thought he might be about to cry. He'd been looking at her, but turned his head away again, back towards the men; their calls and the scuff of the ball carried to them on the breeze. Finn seemed different to her – gentler than she had known him, but also reduced in some unidentifiable way; at least, knotted up, tense. Constrained. She hadn't seen him for a couple of days: last night, expecting him home from his first day's cropping, he hadn't turned up until she was already in bed; this morning, he'd gone off to the pieces at first light, before she was up. Now, he seemed altered. There was the greater alteration, too, between the Finn who had been brought to her cottage so many weeks ago and the man sitting beside her on the slipway. He removed his socks. His insteps were distended by a delta of veins. She had washed those feet, had washed all of him. Tended to the wound in his side. He'd been a stranger to her, then, but now it was as if this Finn was the stranger. Unrelated to that version, the invalid, the Incomer; unrelated, as well, to the Finn who'd emerged from his sickbed to

311

stride about like a released animal marking out its territory. He was neither weak nor strong – it seemed to her, as they sat together – but between the two; as such, he was almost un-recognisable. Just a man. It always came back to that. Taking him into her home, she had feared becoming dependent on Finn, using him to help her recover from Roop's death. That hadn't happened. Even when he rescued her from the seal, it hadn't happened. Seeing him – now, like this – she didn't know how she could have imagined it ever would.

'I'm glad you're staying,' Finn said.

'So am I.' The paint on her fingers was mostly dry now. Bryher picked it off, letting the breeze take the flakes away.

'It's not easy, is it?' he said. 'Leaving.'

'*You* managed it.'

'Did I?'

'You're here, aren't you?

'It doesn't always feel like that.'

'How d'you mean?'

'There's a difference between leaving a place and leaving it behind.'

Bryher recognised that. For all that this place was imbued with Roop, she'd been ready to leave the island – to leave him – if it had come to it. But she wasn't sure that she could have left either of them *behind*. She would only find out by staying. By being herself, here. She hadn't considered herself free to do that until now.

Her attention was snagged by two herring gulls disputing possession of a food scrap. They squabbled in flight, a small metal-bright fish dropping to the sand; one of the birds swooped to retrieve it and took wing again, the other in pursuit. Long Strand was her least favourite beach, a mostly featureless arc that, due to its orientation, took the brunt of the tidal debris and washed-up junk. 'The mainland's waste tip', Roop used to call it. After the accident, she'd walked this strand more than any other, in the hope of finding him. She recalled the last time, after that other volleyball game. She hadn't returned since. Hadn't scoured any part of the coast since the night of the seal. That was a kind of progress. She still missed Roop more than she could bear. But she *was* bearing it. And she didn't want to miss out on the life she might have with him gone, or on discovering the woman she might become, by herself, in a land like this.

Finn had fallen silent, absent-mindedly rubbing his hand.

'Look at that.'

His thumb was jerking in spasm. It kindled memories of her own initiation in the pieces. Spreading her fingers next to his, the bones in the back of her hand like raised wires beneath the skin. Could he see the lump at the base of her wrist, from two seasons' cropping? He couldn't. She let him find it with his fingertips.

'Does it hurt?'

'If you really press it. But, otherwise no, there's no sensation at all.'

This might have been the last day of a vacation: two lovers holding hands at the end of a holiday romance. The final hours before they flew to different parts of the world, promising to stay in touch but knowing the messages would tail off, and that they would never see one another again. Or, if they did, they wouldn't recapture what they'd had here, at this time, in this place. This wasn't at all how things were between them, and Bryher wondered why it struck her in this way. Even though they weren't lovers, and she wasn't leaving, she had a tangible impression of a shared and intimate sadness, of something precious drawing to a close. No doubt this romantic tableau of leave-taking was rooted in the completion of the boat, in Amver's leaving, in the fact that Bryher had never said a proper farewell, or any farewell, to Roop. She was able to think like this, now, about him. Objectively, almost. This was another progress, of a kind. It felt like progress, anyway. She gathered these small progressions, just as Jad collected his beachcombed hoards.

313

'Fancy a dip?' she said.

Finn hesitated, let go of her hand. 'I should be getting back.'

'OK.'

She would swim by herself once he was gone. Not here, near the men, but at another beach. Take the remainder of the afternoon off. That would be good. The boat was ready and she was staying on the island. Simple facts.

'Six months ago,' Finn said, 'I'd have never imagined myself as a flower picker.'

'You keep cropping short, you won't be one for much longer.'

He laughed. He was staring down between his feet. She caught herself looking there too, studying the patterns in the dusting of sand on the wooden boards. Finn had seemed melancholy, almost morose, for much of their conversation, and she was glad to have made him laugh. Then he became serious again, turning his attention to her.

'You've paint in your hair.'

She fingered her fringe.

'Here, let me.'

Bryher tipped her head forward and his left hand, the good one, eased into her spiked-up mop and began plucking at a tuft of hairs. The paint would be almost dry by now, an encrusted fleck of blue; he was carefully working it loose without tugging. Then, slowly, he trickled the fingertips like warm water among the roots, massaging her scalp in a sequence of small rotations until his hand was at the side of her face, her ear, her jaw, soft slow strokes to her chin, her mouth – his thumb, tracing the parting of her lips. Brushing against her tongue. The grain of his thumbprint, the taste of him. To be touched like this after so long. It would have been the easiest thing to let him continue. For this to be the way of things between them from now on. To take all the love and comfort and consolation this would bring.

'Finn, no.'

314

Bryher lowered his hand, firmly, trapped in her grip; her other hand, a splayed halt-mark on his chest.

She lay among the dunes, naked, a towel beneath her, the water yet to dry on her skin. Above her, the marram grass swayed, etched like porcupine quills against a clear sky. She'd swum for an age; her limbs were still elastic with it. She closed her eyes.

They had headed back together as far as the pieces, where Finn rejoined the others and Bryher continued alone to The Ear. Before going their separate ways, he apologised. He hadn't meant to make her uncomfortable, hadn't meant anything by it; it was a small moment of intimacy, that was all.

'It's a while since either of us have known that, isn't it?' she said.

Finn nodded and said he figured it was.

They had slipped back into the small talk of parting, Bryher's mind turning to an afternoon on the beach, when Finn seemed on the point of saying something else. Something significant. But he said nothing. The awkwardness fitted with the way he'd been at the boatyard, and on the slipway.

'You OK?' she said.

'Yeah, fine. I'm fine. Just . . .' The inked mark on his forearm, his cropping measure, had run and faded with sweat, like a tear-stained streak of mascara; he fretted at it with his thumb, erasing it altogether. 'Just knackered, I guess.'

In a little while, once she'd rested, she would swim some more. By the time she dozed off in the dunes Bryher had stopped thinking about Finn, or anything much. When she awoke it felt as if she hadn't slept for long, but the day had cooled and the tide was out. She thought she'd dreamed the sound. There it was again, though. The plaintive boom of the gong. A lament for the sunlight slowly leaching from the day.

315

Finn's First Gathering

He had passed the Gathering Hall often enough. A small, wooden A-frame building, like a chapel or a village hall, in the days when the mainland still had village halls that hadn't been torched, or boarded up, or squatted, or vandalised to fuck. He'd even been inside, during his walkabouts – an echoey room, smelling of ripe timber, dust and emptiness; somewhere cool to rest up in the heat of the day. The kids went there, Jad had told him, to slide on the varnished floor. Its walls were pinned with the pictures they'd made in Sholo's lessons, and the place was always clean and tidy; otherwise there was little sign of occupation. Roop had erected it, more or less single-handed, just before he died. Finn thought maybe this had blighted it for the islanders – unsure whether to use it, or to preserve it as a memorial. So he'd heard, they hadn't once met inside, gathering instead on the veranda. Even though Roop had built that too.

Finn stood for a while in the dusk beside Great Pool, his back to the building, before retracing his steps to join the early arrivals. Effie, Yué, Nudge and Zess had already taken their places; others could be heard coming along the track. In ones and twos, they added to the circle of seated figures. Bryher was the last to arrive, a towel scarfed round her shoulders, her hair in spiky clumps, face the colour of gold in the light from the oil lamps that hung from the beams at either end of the veranda. She settled herself on the cushion between Zess and Liddy, directly opposite Finn. Smiled at him, and at some of the others. Nods and greetings.

She had no idea.

He'd dreaded Bry being here more than anything. But how could she not be? In a way, it was the point: her being here, for this. Finn looked at her once more, the gong, on its stand behind where she sat, framing her head like a huge halo. She'd been swimming, he remembered; her cheeks were reddened by the sun, the knuckles of one hand dusted with sand.

How close had they been to kissing? He didn't know. It hardly mattered, now. It hadn't happened. For sure, it wouldn't happen after this.

The circle was complete, with Bryher's arrival. The only ones outside it were the younger children. At one end of the veranda, Jafe, Peef and Kags were bent over sketch pads, a tub of crayons to share. Jad had joined the adults, flanked by Tye and Sholo. Looking small beside them, more childlike than Finn remembered; vulnerable, his slender brown arms glistening, one elbow sketched with a fresh graze. They made eye contact but the boy dropped his gaze, like he was shy. Only, Jad didn't do shy. Finn wanted him to glance up again, to smile, but he didn't. An essential-oil burner stood at the hub of the ring, its dish clinking, releasing a smoky incense of eucalyptus. From the balustrade that gave over Great Pool, breaths of wind agitated the lamps, casting shadows. But for the illumination, those nearest the balcony – Qway, Effie, Hobb, Orr – would've begun to blur against the backdrop of nightfall. Flecks of white on the pool's surface: the resident swans, some gulls. Further off, the swell of Ocean Hill, daubed in greens, purples and greys. Beyond that, the ocean. The

317

fret. The sunset sometimes stained it with colour, but this evening the mist was a haze of aluminium.

Finn sat, cross-legged, aching from another day's cropping, craving sleep; the hardness of the decking beneath the cushion. Conscious of Roop, like a reproach, each joist laid by him, each board planed and cut to size by him, each screw driven in by him. What right did he have to be here, with these folk, in this place that Roop built? Casting his eyes around what had been, a moment ago, a group of familiar faces, he saw nothing but hostile strangers regarding him with unforgiving scepticism. As if this wasn't just his first Gathering, but his first day on the island, and they were all waiting for him to prove himself worthy of their acceptance.

Stupid. Spooking himself with their sudden quietness, with Jad's moodiness.

He knew something of the procedure from Bry. So far as he could make out, the procedure was that there was no procedure. The no rules thing. No chairperson, no agenda, no minute-taking, no debating protocol – just people in a ring taking turns to speak, or say nothing. The silences could stretch, she'd told him. You couldn't even know for sure why an assembly had been called until 'the breaking of the first silence'. Only then would the gatherer be identified.

This was the first silence.

Finn adjusted his legs, his posture. Calmed himself. Focused on the flickering burner. Aware of others doing the same – hushing down, becoming still, regulating their breathing. Attuning to themselves and to each other. Even the children outside the circle seemed to quieten in the drawing of their pictures. Finn used a breathing technique he'd learnt from Lila: in through the nose, out through the mouth, mindful of the passage of air. Counting the breaths. He closed his eyes. A peace opened up around him. A bird call, the puttering of the lamps, the ticking of wood, the

318

creak-creak of Orr rocking on his cushion, Jad's trademark sniff-and-swallow, the muffled bash of the sea on the rocks beyond Great Pool, the scritch of crayons on paper. In the collective mood these became absorbed into the tranquillity, became soundless. From this silence, the first voice would come. It might not come for a long time; but – when the gatherer was ready – the voice would come. That was the way of things.

Finally, Finn was ready. He cleared his throat.

'I wanted to show you this,' he said.

He removed a package from his bag and set it down on the decking in front of him: fat, swollen, its plastic wrapper shiny in the light from the lamps.

There was no vote. Near the end, Finn asked if there would be. But Hobb said there hadn't been a vote at a Gathering for thirty years, since the first group of settlers first gathered, and – by a show of hands – agreed to make it their last ever vote. There was no concept of majority or minority here, he said – only consensus. Finn doubted that a group of human beings could function like that, and Hobb suggested he try living here a while longer. As if that might still be an option.

What was it, then? A debate? A discussion? A deliberation?

First one spoke, then another; the courteous taking of turns. There might be a pause – another of the silences – between speakers, or several people would speak in quick succession. However the comments came, whatever was said, the tone was measured, non-confrontational. A collective respect for one another, and a generosity of spirit towards Finn (though not towards what he'd done). Even Tye reined in his antipathy, at first. Patiently, they got Finn to explain the deal with Mr Skins: how and when it came about, why he agreed to it, what it entailed, why he'd kept it from them. Less upset by the deal, it seemed, than by his concealment of it.

319

You deceived us, they told him, in one form of words or another.

'Skins thought you'd try to block the delivery,' he said. 'He was going to turn me in if that happened. Turn Bry in, as well. And Jad.'

'Jad?' Yué said.

'He'd say Jad brought me here, in the launch.'

It was the crocodile farmer who'd threatened to take Bryher and Jad down, but the placing of their names in the circle made Finn feel as if he himself was responsible for endangering them. As he was, by being here. After this the atmosphere soured, the first traces of hostility surfaced.

'There are no secrets here.' Zess's voice. Cold, hard. 'We tell each other.'

He *was* telling them. He'd gathered them to do just that, hadn't he?

'Why now?' Tye said. 'Why leave it till now to tell us?'

'*You* trade with Skins,' Finn said. Was this so different?

They traded the produce of their own labour, Hobb said, and only what was theirs to trade. Tye, listing those things: 'flowers, kelp, fish' . . . unstated, each time: *not drugs, not drugs, not drugs*. Finn thought of adding 'sex' to the list – what about trading sex, what about Amver? – but he couldn't, wouldn't, defend himself by attacking her. Wouldn't make her out to be a whore, when he didn't regard her as one.

In any case, she saved him the trouble. 'Sex?' Amv said. Pointedly, to Tye. A challenge. A lone voice raised on Finn's behalf since the breaking of the first silence.

It was Hobb who answered her. 'We trade what's ours to trade,' he repeated. 'Communally, or individually.' Polite, composed, but making plain the distinction between Finn dealing in Skins' merchandise and Amver selling her own body. Hobb didn't spell out the island's ethos of 'least harm, most good', but the weight he placed on the word 'merchandise' left no doubt that

320

another distinction was being drawn. No trail of crack-heads or dead junkies would be left in Amver's wake. Nor did it need saying that she was an islander – Yué's daughter, Jad's brother, born and raised here, living among them these past seventeen years; Finn wasn't, couldn't ever be.

'This goes to the heart of our way of life,' Tye said. He was still wearing his twine belt from the cropping, minus the tub of rubber bands; sitting in half-lotus, the way Lila used to. For weeks, Finn had believed he was winning him over – with his work, his immersion in the island, his friendship with Bryher. He and Tye had never become comrades, but it was a while since they'd seemed like enemies.

Finn rubbed at his face, irritated, forcing himself to stay alert, to think. 'You people *trade* your way of life,' he said. 'You're as enslaved to Skins as I am.'

'More so, since you came among us,' Tye said.

Other voices, weighing in against Finn. Zess, Effie, Nudge. They'd given him shelter, put themselves at risk, worked hard to meet the new quotas . . . and look how he'd repaid them. It boiled down to an issue of trust, Hobb said. For this community to work, to survive, every member had to be trusted.

Finn said: 'You think Skins cares whether you trust each other?'

'That's the one place that man can't touch us,' Hobb said. Then, indicating the package: 'Couldn't, until now.'

The package. On the decking, where Finn had set it down. No getting away from that. Whatever he said, the fact of what he'd done, of what he still had to do, lay right there for all to see. Suddenly, he was sick of his own voice, of his self-serving justifications. He hadn't come here to excuse himself, but to confess. To lay himself bare before these people and let them see him, at last, for what he was.

Finn bowed his head, left the talking to them.

With the letting go, came the struggle to concentrate. Done in by his efforts at the pieces, and having barely slept in thirty-six hours since the marine had moved in. Finn caught himself zoning in and out, drifting. You have to stay focused. Don't yawn, don't close your eyes. Waves of fatigue, indistinguishable from the waves of words buzzing about him like so much white noise. A phrase broke through.

'Are you OK?'

Yué, sitting beside him, her hand on his shoulder.

Finn understood that he'd just fallen asleep, for a moment, chin on his chest, and she hadn't realised, but had assumed he was crying.

'Yeah, sorry, I'm just . . .'

Tye's voice again, insistent: 'Why tell us now?'

He'd asked that earlier, had he just asked the question again, as Finn nodded off? Finn snapped to attention. Yes, why? Why now? They had a right to know that. Their faces. A ring of eyes in the looming lights that moved with the wind, as though solid, as if the shadows cast the illumination rather than the other way round. How could that be? Finn told them about the young marine, unable to quite believe it was only the previous day that the confrontation had taken place. It might've been a scene from his past. The loss of the two parcels – which Skins *would* miss – had made Finn afraid. More than he was already. Afraid of the handover, whenever that would be, and of the counting, the weighing, and of what Skins would do when the shortfall was discovered. Afraid, too, of the marine. That he'd come back for second helpings, or would make his arrest after all. Finn was being exploited on two fronts, now – the crocodile farmer and the marine, both playing him like a fish they could reel in any time they fucking well pleased. Meanwhile, jerking him on the ends of their lines for the fun of it. Because they could. Because he could do fuck all but dance and thrash at each tug; or wait, hooked, for the next one.

There was another fear, though: Bryher. The dread of her disappointment in him. He'd gone behind the islanders' backs, that was bad enough – but deceiving Bry was the worst of this. The longer he'd lied to her, the harder it had become to tell her the truth. Just today, at the boatyard, and on Long Strand, and as they'd parted by the pieces, he'd tried and failed. The call to Gathering wasn't just a sudden telling, it was an accumulation of all the long weeks of his betrayal. He couldn't undo the deceit, but he could end it. Their fate – Bry's, Jad's, all of them – was tied to his. Finn, finally, had to tell them, tell *her*, what he'd done, and abide by whatever they decided.

So, there it was: he was afraid, but he'd had enough of living like this.

Bryher, who'd said nothing all this time, might've spoken now. But she didn't; she continued to sit there, as she'd done through-out, still and straight-backed, eyes fixed on the thin coil of smoke from the oil-burner in the circle's centre. Not once had she so much as glanced at him.

Finn had no idea how long the Gathering lasted. Might've been hours. It was pitch black beyond the veranda by the time they broke up; if he knew anything about the position of the stars he could've figured the time. Little Jafe had quit drawing before the end and joined the circle, going to Tye rather than Zess or Effie, settling herself in the cradle of his crossed legs. Sucking her thumb and letting him plait and unplait her hair. As if she'd sensed his anger and, by her action, was transforming his resentment into gentleness, into affection. Jafe's eyes had sagged and, at last, she'd fallen asleep on Tye's lap. Orr, too, had nodded off and was snoring softly. When the islanders had exhausted themselves as well as the arguments, a hush enclosed them again.

From all of this, a consensus of a kind *did* emerge. Though it was hard to say exactly what. Were they against him, or what he'd done, or what he intended to do? Were they being passive, indecisive – or actively resisting a judgement? Somehow, the Gathering adopted all of these positions, and none of them; their verdict, a non-verdict – punctuated, right at the end, by the briefest, subtlest of closing statements.

Sholo was the last to speak.

She'd said nothing until this point. For all that there was no hierarchy to these things, her prolonged silence had raised the stakes on what she would say. It was there in the prickle of anticipation as the circle fell quiet, waiting for her to speak. Her words, her pronouncement, would be the clincher.

Rising from her cushion – all elegance and poise and unhurried precision – she stepped into the centre of the ring, picked up the parcel from the decking in front of Finn and, with both hands, bent to place it in his lap. As though it were a gift. Or the gracious return of a gift that had been too valuable for her to accept. Her cotton skirt swung softly about her ankles; her hands were bird-like, long fingered, thin and bone-coloured in the flickering illumination. A pair of white doves.

In a clear voice, Sholo said: 'This belongs to you.'

That was all. Her words said little, but they said everything. They were the distillation, the essence of everything that had been said during the Gathering. If the package was Finn's, by implication it wasn't theirs. In laying it before them, he'd sought to place himself in their hands; he would do what they wished. Go through with the deal, or not. Remain on the island, or not. But she'd returned the package to him, along with the decision. 'This belongs to you.' His fate, her gesture said, wasn't theirs to determine. It was his. His alone.

Sholo withdrew to her cushion and, neatly, seated herself again. With this, a final quietness was drawn down. The Gathering, that had begun with the breaking of the first silence, ended with the sealing of the last words.

Moving Out

Finn moved out of the cottage the next morning, at first light. Bryher was still in bed. She'd left the Gathering ahead of him and was already upstairs, her door shut and her light off, by the time he'd made it back. She was still up there when he went. As soon as Finn awoke, he collected his things and some bedding and hauled them over to the hives. *His things*. The things that had become his. The bee shack would be his home, for now. He'd live there as best he could while he waited for news of the rendezvous with Skins. It was appropriate – the scene of his crime; and where better to see out his time here than alongside the bees? Their honey had kept him alive when he came to the island and they'd be his neighbours till he left, whenever that might be. He'd exist like Orr: among the islanders but apart from them. It would be OK. Looking into the days ahead, that was how he saw himself. A makeshift bed on an old dentist's chair, a standpipe outside for washing, bushes to piss in, whatever food he could scrounge, a few candles to see by at night – and the parcels, neatly stacked, pending collection.

Bryher might've come down, once she'd read his note. That

first morning, he half-expected it, even as he accepted that she wouldn't. She didn't. Mostly, he was glad; not sure what to say to her, not sure he wanted to hear what she would say to him. But, already, Finn missed her. Missing Bryher was something he'd have to get used to. In the time that remained, staying on at the cottage was impossible. For him to be there; for her to have him there. She'd blanked him so totally at the Gathering that he'd come to the decision, walking home by himself in the dark, that this must be his last night at her place. He'd spare her the trouble of asking him to leave.

He hadn't planned on cropping again. The last thing he felt like doing was spending another stretch of hours stooped over a ridge, fucking up his hand any more than it was already, having to see them all, and carry on as if it was OK, perfectly normal for him to be working among them once more. The easy thing would've been to stay away. Keep to himself. But Finn had no idea how long it might be before Skins got word to him. Could be hours, days, a week. Longer. The prospect of moping around the shack till then, or – what? – taking off on solitary hikes, like his early weeks on the island when he still had discoveries to make about this place, and about himself, which were now wrecked. You could feel sorry for yourself, living that way; might as well be in a cell, notching time on the wall, waiting for stuff to happen, doing nothing till you were told to. That wasn't him. That wasn't how he meant to finish his days here. Which was why, as soon as he'd moved his gear into the shack and made it halfway habitable, he headed off out again to the pieces.

That day, and the next, and for yet more days, Finn picked flowers. The others worked beside him (way ahead of him, mostly), accepting his presence as a regular team of croppers might tolerate a casual labourer, assigned to their gang for the week. They didn't shun him; the setting apart was of his own making. He cropped alone, but among them. When they broke for lunch, he would sit by himself, setting aside half his ration so he'd have something to eat in the evening. One or two spoke to him as they worked, or came over during the breaks – Yué, Hobb, Amver – but when Finn made it plain that he wanted to be by himself, they allowed him the space. All day, every day, he cropped and gave way to thoughts of the handover, and what he would do, until the two – the picking, the thinking – became so entwined that they seemed interdependent. The thinking, pulling him through the physical and mental monotony of the job. At times, though, he grew so distracted he'd lose the rhythm of his picking action altogether and come to a halt – catch himself straddling the ridge, staring down at the stems as if he'd forgotten how to snap them from the ground, or even why he was there, and without a clue how long he had been standing like that, immobile. If anyone noticed, they said nothing.

At dusk each day, Finn would make his way back to the hives, to his shack, to eat his meal alone and – slurred with exhaustion – go to sleep, unwashed, in his work clothes. His only visitors were Amver, who would sit and talk, or bring him fruit and fresh milk; and Qway, who came to attend to the bees, said as little as necessary, then left. The lifestyle suited Finn. The routine structured his days and the work filled it; being isolated, or semi-detached, most of the time didn't bother him so much. The worst of it was the waiting.

'You and me, we're both living in limbo,' Amver told him, one evening, and Finn saw that this was true.

Bryher didn't show up once at the pieces. He knew, from Amv, that she spent her days down at the boatyard, working on the vessel's interior – fitting out the cabin, installing supplies and equipment, carrying out safety checks – so that *Raven* would be ready for her maiden voyage. Finn suspected the boat was a handy excuse for Bry to avoid him. After the first few mornings, he more

327

or less stopped wondering if she would be there for the cropping. The other person to drop off the radar was Jad. This ought to have surprised Finn more, but the boy's unpredictability was predictable. He would be off on one of his disappearances; when that happened, Amver said, all you could do was wait for him to roll up again. Given the way Jad was with him at the Gathering and the fact that he hadn't been seen since, Finn might've worried that he'd made another enemy; but then, on the third day, he returned home to the shack to find a cuttlefish bone placed on the table. Two evenings later, it was a single washing-up glove, then a gull feather, then the hollowed-out husk of a crab the size of Finn's hand and missing one of its pincers. He began to look forward to these tokens.

Easy to lose track of time here. Finn reckoned it was nine days, or maybe ten, after the Gathering when he finally got word. Rudy was the messenger. He called one evening as Finn sat outside on an upturned crate in the last of the day's light, eating; from the guy's manner, the look he gave Finn, you'd have thought Rudy had come to settle the unfinished business from that night at South Bay. Finn set the plate down. Stood up. Useless gestures of preparation for a fight he couldn't hope to win. And which, in any case, didn't happen. Skins' man kept to the script. Day, tide, location. Delivered his lines, then left. Finn sat down again. It was a moment before he was steady enough to pick up the plate; when he did, he found that his appetite had gone.

Finn paid three visits that evening.

First he called at Yué's, to speak to Amver. Next he walked down to the white house on the point to see Sholo.

His third visit was to the cottage. To Bryher's. She should hear this from him. His decision. A light showed at the bedroom, but the rest of the place was in darkness. Not so late that she'd be in bed, though. Finn knocked. Bry's voice from the upstairs window

328

shouted to him to come in. The door, as ever, was unlocked. He went in. The narrow staircase, familiar yet strange. The cottage smelled differently to the way he remembered, even though it wasn't much more than a week since he'd left. It smelled strongly of paint. At once, he might've been back at the boatyard, taking her a basket of rejected Paper Whites the day the painting of the boat was done. In years to come, if he had years to come, he would associate her with paint fumes. Paint, and honey.

'Oh, it's you,' she said.

Toneless. Neither surprised nor disappointed, just stating a fact: she hadn't expected it to be him, but it was him, and that was all. Finn stood in the doorway. He couldn't stand anywhere else; the room was a mess of trestles, paint tins, plastic trays and tubs, a set of foldaway steps and, everywhere, a snowfall of shredded wallpaper. In the centre, the bed, the bits of furniture, huddled beneath grubby sheets. Bryher was the other side of all this clutter, painting the farthest wall. Or rather, interrupted in her painting. Orange. Not a bright citrus, but the blushed terracotta-orange of peach skin. She'd stripped off the paper and was painting directly on to the rough plaster.

'It's going to look different when it's done,' Finn said. 'Like a new room.'

'What d'you want, Finn?'

Bryher held the brush, poised, as if she might resume at any moment. Just turn away from him and carry on painting the wall without waiting for his reply. She wore navy-blue overalls that were way too big for her; mansize, but not Roop's, because all of his gear had gone, so he figured they must belong to Qway or Tye or someone.

'The handover has been fixed,' he said.

'Uh-huh.'

'I've got two more days.'

'You're doing it, then?'

329

'Yeah. Yeah, I'm doing it.' Finn searched her face for disappointment, for a sign that she felt let down, but her expression was neutral, unreadable. Most likely, Bryher had expected him to go through with the handover and this news was no news at all. He wanted her to ask: 'And then what will you do?' But the question didn't come.

Facing the wall again, painting, she said: 'Thanks for telling me.'

'Bry.'

'*What?*' She turned towards him, rounded on him. 'What is there to say?'

What was there to say that hadn't already been expressed by nine days', ten days', silence between them? All this time apart, on an island too small to avoid one another by chance. *If I'd wanted this conversation*, her face, her posture said, *I'd have come and found you by now.* What there was to say, was nothing.

'It's weird,' Finn said. Bryher just looked at him, motionless. 'I feel more of a stranger with you now than I did that first time, when I'd pissed the bed.'

The bed was there, between them, draped in dust covers.

'Do you?' she said.

'OK, I'm not expecting you to help me out here.'

'Finn, you know what? The others . . . no, look, let's stick to the goodbye bit.'

'The others what?'

Still, she gripped the brush. Paint had run down the handle, over her thumb. If she turned away again that would be it. 'The others are more forgiving than me,' she said. Hard as before, but she was talking at least. 'But they didn't share a house with you all these months. Get to know you like I did. Change you when you wet yourself.'

'No. They didn't.'

'So.'

'I know. You're not telling me anything I don't already know.'

'What did you think I'd do?'

'Tell the others.'

'And then what would happen? We'd turn you in? Strap you to a giant wicker effigy on Wreckers Hill and set it alight?'

'I hoped I could just do the deal, and you'd never need to know.'

'That's what you think of us. Of me.'

Standing there, across the room from her, deflated, as though his skeleton, his musculature, could no longer support him. 'Bry, there hasn't been a day since I left the cottage when I haven't wished I'd done things differently.'

She laid the brush on the trestle. Wiped the handle on a rag, then wiped her hand. He waited for her to pick the brush up again, but she left it where it was.

'How is it?' she said.

A gentler tone. Not her regular tone, but heading there. After so long to brood on her feelings towards him, Bryher might've had a week and a half's unspent anger to vent. But she seemed suddenly weary of it all, as though the sustained antipathy required too much effort. More effort than was in her nature; or than he was worth.

'How is what?'

'Living in Qway's shack.'

'It's OK. Pretty basic, but OK.'

'I couldn't have had you here,' she said.

'Yeah, I figured that.'

They fell silent. Bryher looked like she wanted to carry on painting, but felt imposed upon – required to be hospitable, despite or because of the fact it was Finn. It was hard to tell which. 'Are you doing the whole cottage, or just this room?' he said.

'Just this room.'

The room that had once been hers and Roop's; then hers; then

331

Finn's, briefly; now hers alone again. Finn spoke of the time his grandmother – his mum's mum – had come to stay for a few days; mum slept downstairs on the put-you-up and let Gran have her bed. The second night, the old woman died in her sleep. In the days while their mum was away at Gran's sorting her stuff, Finn and Kurt saw to the bedroom – painted it top to bottom, changed the position of the bed, the furniture, put up new curtains, new duvet cover, the lot – so she wouldn't be reminded of her dead mother whenever she went in there. They were thirteen and fifteen. Made such a mess of the decorating their mum had to fork out for it to be done again, professionally.

Bryher smiled, then checked herself. Grew serious again. Looked at the half-painted wall, did the hand through the hair thing.

'I was going to make myself a brew,' she said.

Finn said that would be good. He offered to make it, but she said no, it was fine, she'd do it. He watched her tidy up a little, put the brush in to soak, pick her way across the room; not looking at him. As she reached the doorway, he stepped back on to the landing to let her pass. 'Wicker effigy,' he said. 'Nice one.'

'Uh-huh, well, don't think we couldn't.'

They sat outside in the dark on the bench she made. It hadn't started to rain yet, but the clouds were already edging into position. Two mugs of mint tea perfumed the air. Across the way, at the far end of Gibbet Cove, lights blazed from every window at Tye and Qway's place. You could see them, moving about.

'I called on Sholo just now,' Finn said.

'Yeah?' Bry's response was hard to gauge, though she seemed more attentive. Borderline curious, at least.

'She asked if I was being kind to myself.'

'That sounds like the sort of thing Sholo would say.'

It was natural to be hard on yourself, Sholo had told him – to punish yourself, if you believed you deserved it. But you could punish yourself too much. More than was good for you. He thought she was referring to the deal, and to his betrayal of the islanders' trust; but as they'd talked he realised Sholo meant something else as well. She meant the guilt of dodging the draft.

He told Bry of that other time he'd pitched up at Sholo's during an art class, and she'd said the kids were painting pictures of 'courage' and 'cowardice'.

'I figured she was teasing me,' Finn said. 'Then I got to thinking the words were too pointed for that. Courage. Cowardice. It was like a challenge. Like she was challenging me to decide which one applied to me.'

'Does it have to be one or the other?' Bryher said.

'Is it courageous to risk your life running away from a war where other people are being killed? What does that make me: hero or coward?'

'Does it matter?'

'How can it not matter?'

'Finn, you're used to seeing courage and cowardice in those terms.'

'What terms?'

'The big adventure. Action. Wars. Wounding and killing. Heroism.'

Finn felt the first spits of rain, or possibly spray, carried from the cove on the breeze. He listened to the sea. In what remained of the moonlight, he saw that the fret had encroached almost to the shore. Thick, solid looking. The ghost ship of a vast barrage balloon, or the island's materialised shadow. He imagined Roop, dying in it. That naval ship looming out of a cliff of mist; maybe he never even saw the vessel, just the great smack of its bow-wave, then black water, then nothing. Not for the first time, thoughts of Roop segued into thoughts of his brother.

'I used to see Kurt as heroic,' Finn said. 'I hero-worshipped him, anyway. I don't know if that's the same thing.'

'Because he volunteered?'

'No, the whole time I was growing up. I had this . . . I guess, this *model* of what a boy, a youth, a teenager, a young man should be. It was my brother. If I could just be like him I would be OK. The trouble was, I wasn't Kurt and I never would be – but it took me till I was more or less grown up myself to realise that.'

'And then?'

'And then I didn't have a model any more.'

'You had – you *have* – yourself.'

Was that possible, to aspire to be yourself? Finn felt so unformed that he had no clear sense of himself to aspire to. He'd done a lot more growing up since going on the run; so far as he could judge, he was a much older twenty-four than when he'd left the Capital. Maybe it was his belated transition from adolescence to adulthood. If so, it was still happening. When he looked at Bry, who was younger than him, she seemed so together. So formed. So much more self-aware. All of the folk here did. Amver. Jad, for fuck sake.

'Why did you take me in?' Finn said.

'Me? You know why.' Bryher's face tilted towards him; greys and blacks. He could barely make out her features, but he pictured her frowning.

'Not *you*, all of you.'

'Because we're all dodgers too.'

Draft-dodgers in spirit, she said. United in opposition to the state conscription of young men to fight, regardless of individual will. Finn, though, glimpsed a second interpretation: that they were *literally* dodgers; fugitives from another life and from their own past. Like him, they'd fled from a land – a way of being – they no longer felt part of; like him, only to find that the waters dividing island from mainland also joined them. They were branded, just as

334

Finn's tattoo and the scar of his stab wound branded him, with the indelible mark of the nation they'd deserted, but still belonged to. Theirs, like his, was a life that must be lived in compromise and contradiction. The difference was, they'd learned how to live like that.

So, he wanted to know, where did you draw the line beyond which you were no longer prepared to compromise?

'Compromise,' Bryher said, as if the word was a morsel of food she wasn't sure she'd like. He felt her shift beside him; she was right, you couldn't sit on this bench for long. 'To me, it's more like living in ambiguity. Trying to establish a coexistence of contradictory states.'

'What does that mean?'

'Neither islander nor mainlander, yet both at once. I don't have a name for it.'

'You're comfortable with that?'

'What choice is there?'

'I think there's a choice,' Finn said. 'There has to be.'

'Ambiguity makes mainlanders anxious. You're so conditioned to choosing between apparent opposites that you believe, if you aren't one thing or the other, you must be nothing.'

'Isn't that just an excuse for the fact you can't cut loose from the mainland, no matter how much you'd like to?'

'You see, this is the line you talked of. It's so much simpler to look for a clear division between two sides. Then you can take definite, definitive positions – and this makes you feel strong and secure. It makes you believe you're right.'

Finn would miss these discussions as much as he would miss Bryher herself; he felt less stupid for talking to her, even when they disagreed. Of course, in her terms the discussions *were* Bryher, inseparable from all the other things that were her. She was made up of the coexistences she spoke of.

It was rain. No mistaking that now. Soon they would have to

335

retreat inside; more likely, Bry would go back indoors and he would be expected to return to the shack, conversation over.

'The reason I saw Sholo,' Finn said, 'was to tell her I'd be leaving.'

'Leaving the island?'

'After the handover. I can hardly stay after that, can I?' He didn't wait for her reply. He would still be in debt to Skins, he said – for being here, under his protection, and to the tune of two missing parcels; waiting for him to raise the next hoop for Finn to jump through. Or the young marine would bring the IS down on him after all, just because he could, and because dodgers were so much scum. 'And let's not even think about how I'd carry on living here, with you lot, after all this. Even if you'd let me.'

Bryher said nothing. There was nothing to say.

'You said it yourself, Bry: I'm a mainlander. Like it or not, that's what I am.'

'Where will you go? I mean, *how*. Skins won't . . .'

'The other person I saw tonight was Amver,' Finn said. 'Straight after I've let Skins have his gear I'm going with her, on the boat.'

Jad's Visit

At the sound of the gate, Finn turned.

It was Jad, swinging himself down from the seized five-bar gate and making his way across the meadow, casual as anything. Like he happened to be passing and decided to call in to say hi, like he hadn't been missing for however many days. Finn was washing at the standpipe, stripped to the waist. He shut off the water and towelled his torso, his hair, his soapy face, as the boy approached.

'You're back,' Finn said, smiling. Trying not to let his relief show. You're a boy in the role of a man, you don't want adults acting concerned over you.

'I wasn't gone,' Jad said. Sniff-and-swallow. 'I just wasn't where you were.'

Finn laughed. 'Fuck sake, Jad.'

'What?'

'*You.*'

'Me what?'

'Just you.'

The boy noticed Finn's sweatshirt, which had once been Tye's sweatshirt, on the ground; he picked it up, handed it to Finn. Finn

337

thanked him and pulled it on. Said he had a bit of food inside, if Jad wanted to eat. And some of Qway's candy he made for the bees. Jad gave a shrug; *yeah, OK.*

They went into the shack. A candle was burning; Finn lit a couple more.

'You been cropping?' Jad said. He looked incredulous.

'Yeah. Every day. I'm done in.'

'Why?'

'It's knackering, is why. Look at my hand.'

'No, I mean why go on working for them?'

Them. Since the Gathering, Finn had caught himself thinking of the islanders as 'them' again, but it was odd, hearing it from Jad. If the boy had been sulking all this time, maybe they were the reason. 'I've not been doing it for them,' Finn said, 'I've been doing it for myself.'

Finn put bread, cheese and candy on the low table and poured goat's milk into beakers. The bread and cheese were the remains of his lunch ration. The milk was hours old and starting to sour. He took one of the regular armchairs. Jad had claimed the dentist's chair and was messing with the controls; raising, lowering, reclining, returning to upright. Like the spaceship pilot in an animated TV serial Finn watched as a kid. He longed to ask where Jad had disappeared to, but knew better than to do that.

'It's the party tonight,' Jad said.

'What party?'

'On South Hill. They've finished the tower thing. The mast.' He tore off a strip of bread, dipped it in his milk and raised it to his mouth, dripping down himself. His chin. His netball bib. 'I saw them just now, taking all the beer up there and stuff.'

'Skins' men?'

'And the marines.' Chewing, chewing. 'Their tour of duty is up.'

Everyone was leaving. Finn thought of his own departure, less than thirty-six hours away. A night, a day, another night. Fleet-

338

ingly, he imagined himself staying on after the handover – living on in this shack, and fuck what they thought of him. The maverick loner, scavenging on the scraps of life here. Fetching sticks for Mr Skins each time Mr Skins whistled; waiting to be caught or turned in; seeing Bryher every day, working alongside her, talking to her, torturing yourself with that. Fooling yourself that this was a kind of belonging, that you had a purpose among them, or that this kind of existence made sense to you, or to her, or to anyone. No. They had plenty to give him, these people, but he'd nothing to offer them – Bry, any of them – in return; nothing he could bring to their lives that they lacked or wanted or wouldn't be better off without. They'd be glad to see Skins' gang leave, and the patrol crew; relieved, too, to see the last of Finn. To have the place back to themselves. From the moment he thought of setting sail with Amver, he knew his time among the islanders was spent.

'Have you been home?' he said.

Jad nodded. He was on to his third strip of milky bread.

'You see your sister?'

'Yeah.'

'She told you the news?' It was the reason why Jad was here, Finn figured.

'You'll get to meet my dad,' the boy said, matter-of-factly. Helping himself to cheese and a cube of candy, he began working them, pressing them together, shaping them into a pellet. 'Amv thinks I'm going to stow away with you.'

Finn wasn't sure if he was serious. His father, just a boat ride away. Carefully, he said: 'D'you want to see him again?' *Live with him*, he didn't say.

'Wouldn't be room for my stuff.' Jad meant his collections. He popped the pellet in his mouth and rolled it around, pulled a face. Goat's cheese and one hundred per cent sugar candy. After a long pause, he said: 'Anyway, it's OK here. With Mum and that.'

Finn saw how tough it had been for Jad to admit this to himself, let alone say it out loud. 'I'll say hi to him, for you,' Finn said.

'Yeah. If you want.'

Finn wondered if he would see Jad in his father; see the type of man Jad might grow to be. Mor was an unknown quantity. Another stranger in the chain that was taking him away from, and now back to, the world that had once been so familiar but which had become a bizarre memory. Finn didn't know that town or that part of the mainland; knew zip about working the big trawlers, or even if there'd be work for him. Mor would help him, Amver said. Mor was the last islander to leave and, for all that he'd quit this place and his family and gone back, her father was no mainlander. The sea was his place. Whether he got there from an island, or from a fishing port, didn't much matter to him. If his daughter pitched up with a friend, a dodger, Mor would help. Harbour Finn himself, if he could, if it was safe to; find him a job, if there was one. Or, at least, hide him away until he established contact with another cell of the anti-draft network; sell *Raven* to pay for another false identity, or to buy space in a safe house for the duration of the war. Somehow, he'd help.

He watched Jad. The boy looked half-starved, assaulting the makeshift meal as if it might be snatched from him at any moment. Finn was sure Yué would've tried to put some food inside her son when he turned up, but could just as easily picture him heading straight out again, unfed, on hearing the news. Coming down here, like this. For all his nonchalance when he arrived, his breath had been ragged from running.

'How come you're giving the parcels to Mr Skins?' the boy said, when he was done eating. Looking around as though the gear would be on show, instead of stashed neatly away in the two biggest suitcases, like so many gold ingots. 'Why not just go *now*? Take it with you, yeah? You could sell it yourself, on the mainland.'

Finn smiled at the simplicity of the plan. 'I do that, Skins comes after me,' he said. 'This way, I do the deal. I'm straight with him.'

'Apart from the two bags.'

'I'm hoping two bags won't be worth the hassle of tracking me down. The whole lot, there's no way he'd let that go unpunished.'

'Then do the handover, and stay.'

'Jad, you saw their faces at the Gathering. You heard what they said.' He let that register. 'And suppose I stay? I'm still working for that cunt.'

'Is that another word I don't get to use?'

Finn laughed. 'Absolutely.'

The boy had finished his own share of the food and was now making a start on Finn's, who was himself ravenous, but had held back on seeing Jad's hunger. In that moment, watching Jad's total absorption in eating, he loved him so much he had a glimpse of what it might be like to be a father, or an older brother. He would miss him as much as he'd miss Bry. A different missing, but a deep pit of loss all the same.

'You should go home,' he said. 'Get a proper meal inside you.'

Jad gave him a look. 'I eat. You think I don't eat when I'm gone?' He made a row of cheese and candy pellets and ate them one after another. 'I trap things. Rabbits and that.' He made a spear-throwing motion. 'I catch fish.'

Finn tried not to smile. He reckoned the boy raided his mum's food cupboards while she was out, or helped himself to fruit from the orchard in the dead of night, but the idea of Jad the hunter was more appealing.

'I'm going up there,' Jad said.

'Where?'

'The party.'

'You think they want any of us lot there?'

'Just to watch, I mean. Spy on them.'

341

'Bunch of guys getting pissed up,' Finn said, recalling their earlier spying mission. 'Sounds like fun to me.'

Jad frowned, put on his fortysomething expression. 'They just leave them lying around, when they're drunk,' he said. 'I could get one easy as shit.'

'One what?'

'Gun.'

'A gun. Right. Then . . . what? They wake up in the morning and one of their guns is missing, and they're just going to let you keep it. Add it to your collection.'

'I've seen them. The volleyball games, the beach parties – there's stuff all over the place. Radios, binoculars, guns, ammo, bits of uniform and that. They're too drunk or hungover after to find half of it.' Indignant, as if he wasn't being believed. 'I already got a set of handcuffs, a baton and a knife.' He shrugged. 'Anyway, they're leaving first thing. They'll be back at base before they even know it's gone.'

Finn stared at him. 'Jad, you really don't want a gun.'

'It's not *for* me,' the boy said. 'It's for *you*.'

'Oh right, sure, like a leaving present. Thanks. What would I do with a fucking gun? I don't even know how to use one.'

'It's piss-easy.'

'Jad.' Finn made sure to look directly in the boy's eyes, made sure to keep his voice hard and heavy and dead serious, spacing the words out. 'Listen to me, yeah: you are not going to steal a gun. OK?' He went on looking at the boy. 'OK?'

Jad was staring at the table, at the empty plates and beakers, like he couldn't work out where all the food had gone. Another shrug, another sniff-and-swallow; his top lip moist with milk in the candlelight. 'I'm just saying I could. If I wanted.'

Going to the Pieces

She washed and dressed early, before the windows had lightened. It was chilly when she entered the kitchen, but the heat from the cooking soon warmed her. On a regular morning Bryher would've eaten at the table, but today she took the food outside on a tray and ate as she watched the sunrise. The bench was still damp with overnight rain, but she didn't mind. She'd slept well enough, despite the boom of music from South Hill, but had woken way too early and been unable to get back off; excited, a little nervous, as if this was to be her first day's cropping rather than simply her first this season. How odd it would be to walk to the pieces, not the boatyard. But there was nothing more to be done to the boat (hadn't been, really, for a few days). Starting now, she'd have to learn to let go. Tomorrow, when *Raven* sailed, Bryher had decided she wouldn't be there to witness her launch or to watch her dissolve into the horizon.

After she'd eaten, she sat a while, collecting herself, gazing out over Gibbet Cove. Back inside, she washed the breakfast things and readied herself to leave. She would take the inland track, past Yué's place. It was still early enough for her to be the first to

343

arrive, which was her intention. Let the others come, in ones and twos, to find her already at work, as if nothing out of the ordinary was happening.

The last time she'd used this path it had been night-time, walking home from the Gathering with Tye and Qway either side of her, like bodyguards, a torch daubing paint streaks of sepia on the rough ground. None of them had spoken a word the whole way back until, as they'd parted by the cottages, Tye had taken her hands in his and said:

'We all brought him here.'

Bryher had told him that, yes, she knew that. It had been pitch-black, the sky filled with cloud. When she first came to the island the utter darkness at night unsettled her, after the pervasive light pollution of the mainland; but she had grown to love it. That night, she wouldn't have cared if Qway had switched off the torch and they'd walked home blind, only the changing terrain beneath their feet to tell them if they'd strayed from the track. Today, the awakening sky shifted through shades of grey to white. The track, the verge to either side, brushed with cobwebby light, slicks of mist pooling in the hollows of the crumpled landscape. It was another kind of beauty, but no more or less beautiful than absolute blackness, or the sharp rinse of sunshine that – during the morning – would anoint this place in brilliance.

Up ahead, she saw him.

Just short of Yué's, he must've emerged from behind a stand of rhododendron where the track to the rear of Wreckers Hill joined this one. But she didn't notice him until he was already on the path and so it seemed to Bryher as if he'd appeared like a will-o'-the-wisp in the creamy morning air.

She had known that, before he left, they would have to say their goodbyes – whether by chance, like this, or because one had sought the other out. So Bryher was both prepared and unprepared for this encounter. All the rehearsals she'd played

344

out in her mind undermined by the surprise of seeing him there for real.

Finn spotted her at the same instant and stalled, as she had done. He carried a large holdall over one shoulder. After a moment, they moved towards one another.

'You're up early,' he said.

'I like to start cropping while there's still dew on the stalks,' she said. It was true, she did. The fresh scent of the sap was at its strongest then.

'You're off to the pieces today?'

'I can't make the boat any more ready than she is.'

Finn smiled. 'The lost sheep returns to the fold.'

'Something like that.'

'How's the decorating going?'

'Yeah, good. Very orange.'

Finn indicated the bag. 'I was heading down to the yard, to stow my stuff on board. Amver said she'd show me round the boat.' He hesitated, looked not quite at her but past her. 'I was hoping . . . I guess, I didn't know if you'd be there as well. If you'd turn up while we were there.'

'No. I'm all done with that.'

'It's been a long time,' he said. 'A lot of work.'

'Uh-huh.'

He was looking at the ground now, the mid-point between her feet and his. 'If you hadn't turned up, I was going to come and find you. Say my goodbyes.'

'Yeah, I suppose we need to do that, don't we?'

For all that they'd talked a couple of nights ago − in the bedroom, outside on the bench − Bryher was aware of a residue of resentment towards Finn. More than a residue. She didn't like the sound of it in her own voice. After the Gathering she had wanted to be like this with him: terse and unyielding; hard. It wasn't how she wanted to *be*, though. If she hated him − she'd wanted to,

345

she'd wanted to hate him – it was for this, as much as for what he had done. For revealing a side of herself she thought she'd long since closed down. A meanness of spirit. It wasn't hate she felt towards him, though, it was disappointment. Living here had diminished her ability to hate. To despise, even to blame, others for the way they were, or the choices they made. The rights and wrongs of Bryher's own choices had never been simple; she had to suppose it was no easier for others. For Finn. If she had been in his situation – if she'd been him, the man he was, in his situation – she didn't know what she would have done. What began as anger had mutated into something altogether less toxic. In the days that followed the Gathering, she hadn't been sure she wanted to talk to him at all, or to listen; and so she had avoided him. As he had avoided her, by moving out. Then, he'd come calling. She had been hard on him that evening, but not as hard as she'd imagined. It wasn't in her. Yet it was – then, and still. Finn would be gone from here a long time, she suspected, before all traces of her disappointment in him had been covered over. Now, here they were. Talking again, perhaps for the last time. The morning was softening around them, the ocean turning almost imperceptibly from dull pewter to silver to greenish blue. Another perfect day in the making.

'I don't have a good feeling about tomorrow,' Finn said.

He meant the handover. 'How come?'

'I don't know. The two missing parcels. The way Skins is.' The holdall had slipped off his shoulder; he set it down at his feet. 'The way I've worked it all out – getting away from him, from here. It's too fucking easy.'

Finn's eyes, his pallor, his body – his whole demeanour – betrayed a lack of sleep. His work in the pieces, along with so many nights roughing it at the shack, the stress of the rendezvous with Skins – they had all taken their toll. He seemed almost as depleted as when he had first been brought to her.

'You're anxious,' she said. 'Thinking up ways for things to go wrong.'

He rubbed at his stubble. 'I just wish it was twenty-four hours from now, and it was all done and I was on the boat.' He aimed a hand. 'Out there, sailing away.'

'It doesn't seem five minutes since you came.'

He looked at her. 'No. No, it doesn't.'

Finn began to thank her for all she'd done for him, but she stopped him, said he didn't need to do that; he tried to say he would miss her – had already missed her, these past days. She stopped him again. It had done her good to be a nurse again, she said, so she should be thanking him.

'I didn't just mean the nursing,' he said.

'No, I know you didn't.'

'What I'm trying to say, I guess, is sorry. Thanks for everything, and sorry for everything.'

'Uh-huh.'

'Anyway.' Finn nodded to himself, gazing off in all directions as if taking a last look at the island, committing it to memory. He picked up the holdall, looped it over his shoulder. 'I'll be at the pieces later,' he said. 'After Amver's sorted me out.'

'What are we cropping today?'

'Rejects, mostly, in my case.'

Bryher laughed. She studied Finn, standing there so gawkily, pleased to have amused her. In another place, at another time, in other circumstances, in a different version of herself, she might've let herself like him enough to see where it took them. But there was only this Finn, now; there was only her, as she was now. Many stories were possible between two people, but time wrote the only, definitive one; this was their story – hers and Finn's – and it was drawing to a close. She hadn't seen much of life, although it sometimes felt as if she had seen too much too soon, but she saw that resolution came with the passing of time. Losing

Roop; her thoughts of leaving this place; the friendship with Finn – these had been the tales of her life, of late. Not one of them was unaltered by the drip-drip-drip of seconds, minutes, hours, days. She saw, too, that the alteration was internal, not external. It wasn't about people or places, but about herself. What had passed with time were the phases of the woman she'd once been . . . what remained was the woman she had become. So it would always be, over and over. This instant with Finn was just another reinvention of herself.

Bryher stepped closer, leaned into him; hugged him, holdall and all. 'Come on,' she said, releasing him. 'We both have places to be.'

As they turned to head up the track, they were distracted by the sound of an engine. A boat was setting out to sea from The Strand. It was the patrol launch, pushing out into the swell, steady at first, then raising a fierce wake as it gained speed in the deeper reaches of the navigation channel. Two figures on board, their heads and shoulders silhouetted in the wheelhouse; Bryher couldn't tell the younger and older marine apart from this distance. Watching them go, Finn told her they'd been recalled from their posting; she said she'd heard as much.

'I reckon that means he won't be paying me another visit,' he said.

He should have sounded relieved, but didn't. The young marine was too sharp a reminder of that other encounter still to come, she supposed, for Finn to draw much reassurance from the sight of him leaving the island for the last time. On that launch, too, stashed away somewhere, would be the two parcels.

'Skins' gang have gone as well.' Bryher pointed to the pontoon. The previous day, Skins' boat and the patrol launch had been moored there; now only the islanders' fishing boat remained. 'I'm amazed they're all on the move so early, after last night.'

'That sounded like some party,' Finn said.

'Come on,' she said once more, when the launch was a distant white blip.

They accompanied one another as far as Yué's. There, Bryher left him to give Amver a knock while she pressed on to the daffodil pieces. An exchange of see you laters, then a single, brief glance back to see Finn on the steps, refastening his bootlace. Amver was in the doorway, partially dressed, doing something complicated with her hair. They were talking, but Bryher was too far away to hear what they said.

Every last one of them was there already. Apart from Amver and Finn, every adult and child on the island had arrived at the pieces before her, which must have taken a deal of co-ordinating. It was early for them to have started work and, in fact, Bryher saw that none of them was cropping. They were standing at the foot of the ridges, spread out like statues arranged randomly in a sculpture park. Hobb, at the vague centrepoint; Qway and Tye, holding hands, a little to his left; Jad, by himself at one end, Sholo at the other. Yué, Liddy, Nudge, Zess, the little ones. Effie. Orr was there, near the heart of the grouping. All of them, there. Each facing towards the rise of land where she would come from, *was* coming from. Where she had drawn to a halt on seeing them, down below, waiting for her. Bryher had imagined she could be here before them, that by being the first she'd be spared the need to make any kind of an entrance. She had imagined they would allow her to do that – to return to them – without ceremony. Her people, gathered, motionless against the backdrop of daffodil pieces striped in green and brown, the yellow sweep of South Hill, the towering radio mast catching the sun's first frail rays, the sky's pale cloudless blue. She stood dead still on the track for what seemed an age, staring at the scene that lay before her, as they stood, gazing at her. She might have stayed like that for a long time, taking it all in. Then, at last, Orr began his wave. Flapping one arm in great arcs, bellowing her name so that it resonated across the slopes. Not waving, she saw, but beckoning. Bryher set off again on the final descent to the flower pieces.

Hermit's Cave

Jad helped him shift the gear to the Hermit's Cave. Finn had made a start on hauling the bags there himself when the boy pitched up at the hives. The wheelbarrow was good for most of the route, till the track across The Down steepened and disintegrated. From there, they carried them the rest of the way. It was good to be doing something. To act. When you acted, you could pretend you were in control of events. Early in the morning, at low tide, Mr Skins would come to The Shoot. To be sure of being on time, Finn planned to spend the night in the cave, a short distance from where The Down and Down Head were separated by the fierce tidal cleft. With the bags stowed, he'd take up bedding and food and wait for daybreak. Jad asked to stay with him, but Finn said no. He wanted to be alone in the final hours before the handover. Jad was cool with that. Solitude was a condition he didn't need to have explained.

'Thanks for lending a hand with the gear.'

'No one else would help you.'

Finn looked at the boy. 'Don't take sides with me against your own people.'

351

'I'm not taking sides.'

'Yeah, well don't.'

Back at the hives, Finn went to sort out the things he'd need for his night at the cave and Jad headed off, wheeling the empty barrow. Calling over his shoulder:

'See you tomorrow, Thin.'

Hermit's Cave lay among a jumble of rocks and boulders where The Down began its descent, narrowing to a finger that almost, but not quite, connected to the rugged bulk of Down Head, the island's northernmost headland. You climbed up through rough gorse and heather, then, as the ground fell away, the going became easier again: turf and moss, strewn with granite debris. It was dusk as Finn followed the grass track, his gear looped round his shoulders. The temperature had dropped and the breeze pushed against him and the things he carried. To the west, the first hint of the fret. Either side of the peninsula, the darkening sky had coloured the ocean deepest indigo – placid, although Dread Bay was foaming and raucous as ever down to the left of the path. Even close to, the cave was more or less undetectable. You'd to scramble up a grassy slope and go searching among the pile-up of stone blocks. According to Jad, the cave was the remnants of a Bronze Age burial cairn. The boy knew about ancient burial rites. You could tell it was Bronze Age, not Iron, he said, because it was typical of a chambered tomb or entrance grave: a central passage roofed with slabs, covered by earth and stones, built to store cremated remains. Iron Age people didn't burn their dead, they buried them; not in tombs, but in stone-lined cists. So, Finn's home for the night had once held the charred bones of folk who'd died thousands of years ago. Jad had described all this not with macabre relish so much as regret that there would be no human traces left for Finn to unearth.

352

The cave was formed by three great angular blocks of granite, propped against one another on the diagonal to create a kind of crude stone tepee. Access was via a triangular opening that caused you to shuffle through on all fours. Finn slung his gear in and crawled in after it. The walls sloped and there was no room to stand; the best you could do was squat, sit or kneel, or lie curled up on the compacted mud floor. He and Jad had arranged Skins' packages against one wall. They resembled a stack of sandbags. Setting his pack down in a dry corner, Finn cleared the ground where he would sleep; sweeping away loose stones and a curious clump of dried moss, possibly a nest made by a bird or small mammal. If the boy had stayed too, they'd have had to sleep sitting up, back to back. Finn spread the sleeping bag and sat on it with his legs crossed, settling in to his surroundings. It was sheltered in there, the breeze buffeting the path reduced to an occasional draught; although it was raining now, the angle of the slabs formed a natural flue that – as if by design – channelled the water away so that it didn't pool on the cave floor. Finn was neither warm nor cold, dry nor damp, comfortable nor uncomfortable.

He sat a while, watching his breath cloud and listening to the wind and the cries of gulls and the waves breaking against the cliffs and on the boulders down in Dread Bay. Soon it was black beyond the mouth of the cave and blacker still inside. Even so, he left the torch off for the time being. Just to sit in the dark, contemplative, calming himself. He understood why a myth had evolved about a hermit, a sage old recluse who lived here and would sit with you, hearing your troubles and dispensing wisdom. If you sat here by yourself quietly enough, for long enough, thinking deeply enough, you could become your own source of wisdom. He remembered something Lila had said, about sitting and waiting. How, if you sat for long enough beside a river you'd see the corpses of your enemies float past. But that was a river bank, not a cave. Anyway, what chance of that happening for real? What chance of Skins doing that? Drifting out of your life as harmlessly as a ghost of the Bronze Age dead.

Lila should've lived on this island. She'd have fitted in.

Wherever he lived, he ended up marginalised, alienated. Estranged. Maybe he carried his estrangement around with him like a backpack – you can never take it off, or put it down even for a moment, all you can hope for is to get used to the weight, to hauling it everywhere you go. Which meant you could live anywhere, or nowhere.

However long he'd remained on the island, he wouldn't have lived up to their expectations – Bry, Sholo, any of them. How he'd wanted to tell them: *I'm not doing it.* But, no. If it hadn't been this deal, it would've been something else. Something *in him* that, sooner or later, would've fucked up. By living here you learned how to live here, Bryher once said; but he'd lived here and hadn't learned. Not well enough. There had to be a piece of the island already inside you when you arrived for that to happen.

To see her on the path like that. Just half a day ago.

Finn snapped on the torch. Went outside to piss, then returned to the cave to eat and to drink tea from the thermos. The torchlight glinted on the plastic wrapping of the packages, and on the knife as he cut the loaf. They would be gone soon. The packages. By morning, they'd be gone. He looked at them. How simple it would've been to make a small incision in one of them with the knife, dip a moistened fingertip into the powder and run it over his gums. Just a dab would help. Help him through this. But he'd been clean so long the thought scared him. Another heightening of the apprehension that had built all day. Jesus. Finn killed the torch so he wouldn't have to look at the things any more and finished his food in the dark. Once he'd eaten, he removed his boots and got into the sleeping bag, folded a blanket for a pillow and lay down as best he could. It wasn't late but yet another day's cropping had exhausted him. If he slept he couldn't think. Could shut off Mr Skins and dream of what was to come after the rendezvous: setting sail on the high tide, on deck, the wind in his face.

He couldn't sleep. Apart from odd, delirious snatches that reminded him of being ill at the crocodile farm, and when he was first at Bryher's.

In the end he stopped trying and simply lay there, eyes open and straining to pick out detail in the dark-on-dark shapes of the cave. If he remained awake all night, so what? Finn prepared himself for that; the long haul till dawn. Almost as soon as he gave up on sleep, it claimed him; he slept fitfully, but he slept some. He woke for the last time in the half-light before sunrise. Tired, stiff, cold. Lying there a while, coming to. Refamiliarising himself with his surroundings.

It had stopped raining. The trickle of water in its natural gutter had ceased. Finn yawned. His face was close to the base of one of the sloping walls, its surface diseased with lichen the colour of cardboard, as though someone had chewed plugs of paper and flattened them on to the rock. Every joint ached. In the night, he'd stretched out so that he was now almost fully extended, feet and head hard up against granite. He eased on to his back. As he did so, something shifted against his feet and rolled to the floor. One of the bags. Others pressed down on his shins or were wedged between his ankles. Finn raised himself on to his elbows to take a look. The stack had partly collapsed; in stretching out in his sleep he must've caused them to topple. A pulse of panic that some of them might have split open. Sitting up properly, Finn bent forward to check they were intact, inspecting one parcel after another by the light of the torch. They were fine. It was then that he noticed another, tucked behind the rest. Wrapped not in cling film, but red cloth. Jad's netball bib. Not fully awake or making sense of this, Finn looked at the bundle for a moment before peeling back the folds of material.

There, resting on a single cuttlefish bone, was a handgun.

The Shoot

If she could've seen him now, high above The Shoot, splitting open the first of the parcels with the knife – like dividing a baked potato in half – and spilling the powder in gobbets that disintegrated long before they reached the sea; shaking the bag till it was empty, then letting the breeze carry the wrapper away. The second bag, the same. And the third. And the next. You could make believe you were scattering the ashes of a loved one. Kurt, Roop. That you were scattering their ashes into the air and on to the earth and down into the water far below. Where the sea frothed and spat and, now and then, a big one barrelled through even though the tide was out and you could scramble across, if you fancied your chances. If Bryher could've seen him. Doing this. Another bag. Another. It was so fucking easy: jab the knife in, cut, peel apart, shake, scatter and release. Some of the wrappers had become snagged, flapping on rocks or scrub, like giant mutant moths basking in the day's first sunlight. There was powder on his clothes and, he figured, in his hair. He took up another package and stabbed it once twice three times and aimed the thing at the place where the ocean shot through. It hit an adjacent ledge, soundless beneath the *fwoosh* of the waves, and made a paintball splat that the next wash swept away. Two more the same, until he landed one in the water, right in the fucking slot, and he gave a punch and a whoop, did a little jig.

By the time the boat came, there were only six bags left. Finn heard the craft before he saw it, the choppy drone of an outboard motor that made him think of Jad and that first trip in the launch. He was standing directly above the place where the pair of them had sat, talking, watching The Shoot. Another bag, punctured and hurled on to the rocks below. He caught sight of the boat, then – a red-and-white launch with two men on board: Rudy, at the tiller, and Skins in the prow. It came into view in the protected shallows beneath the cliff at the eastern end of the divide, where Jad moored that time. Finn ripped open another bag, then another, dispersing their contents. They were looking up at him now, and they'd have seen the powdery plume; like so much talc or flour, or the puff of smoke – *shazam!* – as a magician makes something vanish into thin air. They would be puzzled, at first, he supposed. Not sure, from a distance, exactly what he was doing but aware that, whatever it was it was odd and unsettling and then the sudden realisation that JesusfuckingChrist there was only one thing he *could* be doing. Finn saw this played out in their mannerisms, way down below, as Rudy slowed the launch to a halt and fixed the mooring ropes fore and aft, steadying the craft so that Skins could disembark on to the rock shelf. Neither of them appeared rushed or agitated at this point. Once both men were safely ashore and they'd looked up again to see one more bag scattered to nothing, they turned to each other, animated – an exchange of words, another glance up (another bag gone) – and their movements became jerky and urgent. Scrambling along the ledge above the gap; hurrying, as far as it was possible, towards the point where the rocks rose in Finn's direction. Rudy, agile, monkey-like; Mr Skins, in his cool-as-a-cucumber white linen

358

suit and panama, trying to keep up. Finn watched them. He took the final package, stabbed it repeatedly and lobbed it overarm into The Shoot like a grenade.

There. Job done.

Impossible for him just to walk away. From them. From this. No chance of merely being turned in, either; not now. They'd kill him, probably. Release his corpse to the authorities and claim the bounty; some small compensation for what he'd cost them. A captured draft-dodger who had tried to escape Mr Skins' custody and who, regrettably, they'd had no choice but to gun down.

But Finn was the one with the gun just now.

The gun meant possibility. The possibility of saying no to Skins. Telling him to fuck off with his drugs; the gimping, the gofering. With a gun, you could tell him to fuck off altogether. As soon as Finn had seen it, bundled up for him to find among the parcels, the possibilities opened up. What could Skins do about the gear, about Finn? What could he do about anything if Finn had a gun in his hand? What could he do to him, or to any of the islanders, if Finn aimed the gun at the man's face and fired? It would be easy to do that. To shoot Skins. To kill him. He'd only have to think of that dog, slung to the crocodiles; Mrs Skins' bruised face; their fucked-up daughter; how he'd let Finn almost die from his wound; Skins' hold over him since then, over this whole island; his men taking turns to fuck Amver . . . to think of how many people would be free of him. It would be the easiest thing in the world, to push the gun into his smug fucking mouth and shoot him. Rudy, as well. If he killed one, he'd have to kill both. Shoot them – *bang! bang!* – and dump the bodies at sea. Dump the gun. Let the tide take their launch so that when it was eventually found, empty, it'd look like an accident, like the two men had been swept overboard and drowned.

It reduced to this: the simple fact of the gun; the removal, once and for all, of Mr Skins. With a gun, Finn could do what the fuck he liked.

He let the knife drop to the ground. Clapped his hands, frisked his hair and dusted down his clothes. The sun had risen. Finn was warm from the exertion. Exhilarated. The fact of what he'd done burst inside him just as the gear had burst on the rocks, all his fear blown away by the sheer, euphoric thrill. He turned to face the men. With the detonation of the last of the packages, Rudy and Mr Skins had come to a stop on the final phase of the ascent, a few metres below where Finn stood. Sweaty and breathing hard, both of them. They were gazing down at the point of impact, even though any trace of the last parcel had already been obliterated by the waves. Rudy, in his heavy-metal roadie get-up, hands on his hips, his yellow vest striped with perspiration. Skins had taken off his hat and was mopping his face and neck with a handkerchief; his feet were enclosed as usual in plastic bags. The bags were ripped, one split right open and flapping about his ankle. He was the first to turn his attention to Finn.

'Spectacular.' Skins smiled. You could believe he hadn't just scampered up a steep rocky slope, or been the least flustered by what had taken place. Gesturing down into The Shoot, he said: 'You've put on quite a show for us this morning.'

The man patted Rudy on the back, indicating for them to complete the last part of the climb. Rudy raised himself, then extended a hand to help his boss. 'Some men lack imagination,' Skins said, to Finn. 'You are not such a man. Of all the resolutions to the story of the merchandise, yours was the product of a truly inventive mind.'

Finn had any number of remarks rehearsed for this meeting but, now that it was for real, he found himself with nothing he wanted to say to this man.

The pair stood a short distance away, stark against the bleached

360

sky. Skins was still breathless but Rudy had recovered. The belt around his shorts held a holster, with the handle of a knife protruding from it. No gun. Finn realised that if Rudy had had a rifle he could've picked him off from The Shoot before Finn finished dumping the bags, or had the chance to produce his own gun. This hadn't occurred to him till now. He was surprised by how little it troubled him. All the same, his breathing had tightened and he was shaky with unspent adrenaline. He watched the two men. Rudy, unshaven; so sleek with sweat, his jawline might've been spray-painted black. His bored expression was an attempt, maybe, to imitate Mr Skins' nonchalance; like a young boy assuming, but just missing, his father's posture.

Skins' attention had drifted, now that the climb was over and the parcels were gone. He appeared to be taking in the surroundings. '*This* is the place. Look at it.'

The Shoot, Dread Bay, The Down, Down Head. The ocean, on all sides. If you didn't know better, you could imagine yourself stranded on an uninhabited, desolate spur of rock in the middle of the sea, thousands of kilometres from anywhere.

'The drama of nature,' Skins said. 'To be up here when there's a storm – the rollers coming in, spray breaking over the headland.' He paused, as if to allow Finn to visualise the scene. 'What's remarkable about this end of the island isn't that it's so broken up, so *disfigured*, but that it hasn't been smashed into the sea altogether.'

'I'm leaving,' Finn said, aiming a hand in the direction of the interior.

His voice didn't sound like his own. The gun was under his shirt, wedged in the waistband of his trousers. He became more acutely aware of it, just then, pressing into him. If he hadn't been able to feel it, Finn would have begun to wonder if he'd dreamed it and that he was standing before them, unarmed and defenceless. Helpless. He felt oddly helpless even so.

361

Skins continued to gaze out to sea. 'You are a lucky man, to have all this.'

Here they were, like three hikers who'd stopped to pass the time of day. Finn zoned out, zoned back in again. Mr Skins, still banging on about what a wonderful place this was, talking about everything except what Finn had done and what would happen to him as a result. Coming at it in his own way, in his own time. Regaining control. Finn said none of the things he'd planned. But he didn't have to stand and listen to this any longer. The gun was right there, digging into his stomach.

'Your knife.' Skins' voice, confusing him. 'Don't forget your knife.'

Finn looked at the knife, lying where he'd dropped it. Rudy was staring at him. Poised. To bend over and pick up the knife would be a mistake.

Mr Skins seemed satisfied to have Finn's attention once more. 'I thought you might care to join us for breakfast,' he said.

Finn's mouth was so dry he couldn't swallow. The jubilation of a few minutes ago, watching the last package explode, had leaked from him. He had the urge to piss. This was it. This was the moment.

'I can't do that,' Finn said.

'Bacon and eggs. Pancakes. Hash browns. Fresh coffee. We weren't expecting you, but I'm sure Mrs Skins will be happy to get the cook to rustle up a little extra. I may be mistaken, but I believe there are brioches.'

'I'm not coming with you.'

Skins' smile had gone, he looked thoughtful. 'D'you mind where you sit? In the launch, I mean. I prefer to sit *for'ard*, as we say. The middle seat makes me a little queasy, though I have no idea why.' He spread his arms in a gesture of bemusement.

Finn reached under his shirt.

Immediately, Rudy made his move, just as Finn pulled out the

362

gun and raised it, meaning only to aim it at Rudy – let him see the gun, and that he shouldn't come any nearer. That was all, for now. He would display the gun, then say what needed to be said so that the crocodile farmer knew exactly what he was about to do; then he'd do it. Calm, controlled. The gun. The speech. Two clean shots. But although he had spent time that morning familiarising himself with it, the gun was strange and clumsy in his hand, his panicky, fucked-up, flower picker's hand, and – as he tugged it free from the waistband and raised it towards the oncoming Rudy – it discharged.

Mr Skins went down.

Not Rudy, Mr Skins. Like he'd been trying to hop and had lost his footing and fallen, smack, on his face. Rudy stopped. Gave a little hop of his own, an involuntary sideways skip. The sound of the shot appeared to come now. Then its echo. After that, Skins' bestial screams. It was as if the shooting itself had been silent and the noises that followed were unrelated to it, or to one another.

Finn looked at the gun in his hand. He'd thought that when the moment came he wouldn't manage to work it, or he'd fire and miss. Somehow, when he hadn't even meant to use it just yet – was aiming it at Rudy in any case – the fucking thing had gone off. Mr Skins, contorted on the ground, yelping like a dog knocked down in the street – clawing frantically at his thigh, as though he'd rip off his leg altogether if only that would stop the pain. His trouser leg was torn wide open. Where the knee should have been there was mush. Not a TV-neat bullet hole or stylised cosmetic bloodsplat, but a great, fucking, flapping gape of wreckage – as if the knee had been blown up. So far as Finn could tell, the kneecap had shattered to pieces, driven into what was left of the flesh and muscle and cartilage and ligament that held the joint together.

The man's shrieks were the worst of it. They appalled Finn. *Skins* appalled him, for making them. You could shoot him again just to shut him up.

363

Rudy hadn't moved since the gun went off. Like Finn, he was transfixed by the writhing figure of his boss, and by that place where the knee had been. It was as if neither of them could make sense of this version of Mr Skins. As if, at any moment, he would pull himself to his feet and resume the discussion about the seating plan for the launch. Or as if he was a movie director, demonstrating the getting-shot-in-the-leg scene to an actor before jumping back up and, with a clap of the hands, calling:

'Right, your turn. Places everyone.'

He just went on lying there. Dashing blood into the turf. Looking like he'd sooner die right there, that instant, than endure another second of this. He'd quietened a little, no longer thrashing around. The clawing action was the same, but less manic; as if his batteries were running down. His yells had become whimpers, groans; sharp, hissing exhalations. He was a swamp creature, beached and gasping for breath. Skins' hat had come off and lay a short distance away; even as Finn noticed it, a gust of wind took the hat up and carried it into The Shoot.

This was the man Finn had conceived of killing.

He'd found the gun and imagined shooting Skins with it. Putting a bullet into his head, and into Rudy's. That he could do it. That he could actually do it.

He had to, now. Had to see the thing through: use the gun on Rudy, then finish Skins. Because Rudy was still in shock – a bystander, stalled and out of commission – but he would come to his senses at any moment, shift back into bodyguard mode. So what Finn had to do was raise the gun again. Raise, aim and fire. Properly, carefully. Once, then twice. Just raise the gun. That was all. It was there, in his hand.

So, you raise it.

Rudy was looking at Finn. Weighing him up. For all the world like he was ready to take Finn down, regardless of the gun – finish what he'd left undone on the dunes at South Bay. Finn had raised

364

the weapon – had aimed it at those yellow-tinted shades – but he could see from Rudy's expression that the guy was still thinking about moving in on him, disarming him, taking a chance on whether this fucking jerk could or would pull the trigger. That was it: Rudy was the man, still; Finn, for all that he had a gun, was the jerk. The fucking jerk. The gun altered nothing. Except that Finn just went on pointing it right at Rudy – steady, unwavering – until Skins' man saw that he had no choice, for now, but to stand there, waiting to discover if he would die.

'Finish him,' Rudy said. He nodded at his boss. 'Do us all a fucking favour and put another one in him. You let him live, you're the dead man.'

Finn looked at Skins, kept the gun trained on Rudy.

'Go on.' Rudy's tone was emotionless; he wasn't pleading for his life, or even interested in doing that, it seemed – he was discussing the terms for Skins' execution, that was all. His manner was the same as the time he'd slung the dog to the crocodiles as if it was a sack of feed. 'We dump him, you walk away. No more Mr Skins.'

You couldn't think straight for him talking, talking. Telling you what to do. If he'd just shut up, you could concentrate.

Shooting a man, killing him, while he's on the ground with his leg half blown away, semi-conscious with pain and useless, helpless as a sleeping child; Finn wasn't sure he could do that. The shock of the first shot, of seeing what it'd done . . . then, to do it again, knowing that this time would be worse still. Worse than you could've ever imagined. Even so, Finn found the gun was now aimed not at Rudy but at Skins.

'Do it.'

The speeches. He had meant to make speeches. But there were no speeches in him. There was only the gun. Precisely, Finn took a half-step closer, extended his right arm, locked the elbow to keep his hand from shaking. Swung it towards Rudy.

Fired.

He'd expected Rudy's expression to change in the instant before the shot, but it didn't. He appeared neither surprised nor scared, nor especially concerned. Even as he went down, Rudy looked certain that Finn wouldn't shoot, as though the firing of the gun had been part of an elaborate bluff. The impact dropped him straight on to his back, one arm flailing out to the side like a fielder taking a catch. Or as if the bullet had flown wide and he'd dived to pluck it from the air. The recoil almost took the weapon from Finn's grip and he had no idea where Rudy had been hit until he bent over him. There. The chest, right where the heart would've been. Air escaped directly from the breach in his ribs, and from his mouth, in a pink mist that settled like measles on his shirt, his face, his throat, the lenses of his shades, then shut itself off.

Finn stepped away and vomited over his boots.

When he'd emptied himself, mopped his mouth as best he could, Finn went back to the two men. They lay side by side, though not quite touching, like lovers in bed, asleep, reaching out to one another. Rudy's outflung hand was arranged beside Skins' face, as though he was about to stroke his cheek with the back of his knuckles. Skins hadn't reacted to the second shot, seemed not to have registered it at all.

Finn composed himself. Checked the gun. Brief and simple. He had to keep it brief and simple, a simple set of actions. He pointed the muzzle at Skins' head, close enough that he couldn't miss however much the gun jumped. The crocodile farmer was as still as he'd been at any point since going down; murmuring, making small snorting sounds, his head twisted to one side. He was unrecognisable. Patches of yellow, white, grey; like a wax-work bust that had partially melted and reset. Finn forced himself to concentrate on the exposed temple, the pores, the sweat sheen, the creases of age, the faint red tidemark left by the hat, the single strand of damp hair that had become stuck to the side of the face and which twitched with each flutter of the eyelid.

Finn counted his breaths, shut out all the noise in his mind, shut out the words. The images. Thought of nothing.

With his eyes closed, he pulled the trigger.

Leaving

The thunder of the keel on the slipway, the *poom* the smack the jolt of water, a subtle re-gathering of momentum and they were pulling clear, away from the shore. Finn was soaked in spray, busily fixing ropes the way he'd been taught, avoiding the boom, obeying Amver's yelled instructions from the wheel. Having arrived on the island in unconscious oblivion, he'd imagined his leaving would be charged with detail, with impressions. But there was only the work. The crewing. He had been carried here, but he would have to carry himself away. Him and Amv, toiling as a team to put *Raven* to sea. The breeze bellying the mainsail, creaking the vessel into the navigation channel that would fetch them into deeper water, out into the ocean. By the time he was able to take a proper look back, the figures on Long Strand had become indistinguishable from one another. Some, he saw, had already begun to drift away.

They'd helped him. He hadn't asked or expected it of them, but all the same they'd helped: the hauling of Skins and Rudy down into The Shoot, into the red-and-white launch, and from there to the slipway; the unloading of the bodies; the towing out to sea of Mr Skins' craft so that it could be set adrift; the bringing of the tarpaulin and its conversion into a winding sheet, roped, taped and weighted; the loading of the dead men aboard Amver's boat. The burning of bloodstained clothes: Finn's, those of his helpers. The sound of the shots had brought them to The Down – Hobb, Nudge, Qway, Tye, Zess . . . the men of the island – where they'd found Finn struggling down into The Shoot with Rudy over his shoulder in a fireman's lift. From that moment, they had helped. In silence, apart from what needed to be said, the logistics of the task in hand. Hobb asked one question, indicating Finn's shirt: was any of the blood his? No, Finn told him; he was unhurt. They got on with it, then, having nothing more to say to him, or that they wanted to hear. If *Raven* was to be launched as planned on the high tide they had to work without fuss; Finn saw, too, that they were hastening the removal from the island of all traces of him, and of what he'd done.

Most of the women were at Long Strand, readying the boat and saying their farewells to Amver.

Not Bryher.

She'd set out in the fishing boat at first light, before the handover – as she had said she would, with no wish to witness the launch of the boat she'd helped build, or to repeat goodbyes that had already been said to Amver, and to Finn; they would both be long gone before Bryher returned to learn what had taken place that morning. His relief sat in his throat like a taste. When she'd told him she wouldn't be there to see him off, he was more upset than he'd let on; now, the thought of facing her, after this . . . Even so, her absence had cast her presence into the party gathered at the slipway and was shadowing him now, at sea, and would go ashore with him at the other end.

His only parting had been with Jad. Not even a parting.

The boy stood on the beach, watching the men secure the corpses inside the tarp. Sobbing, tracks of tears and snot down his

369

face; leaning into his mother's hug – she had tried to draw him away from the sight, but in the end she'd relented, simply held him and let him cry. Finn broke off to approach them.

'You didn't do this,' Finn said.

The boy was shaking his head, his words breaking among the sobs.

'Jad, forget about the gun. You didn't shoot them – I did.'

Yué pulled her son closer, stared Finn down. At that moment, Hobb called him back to the fastening of the tarp; his tone said: *We're helping, but this is your job, not ours.* He went back down the beach to rejoin them. The next time he searched among the people for Jad, the boy was no longer there.

The boat was out in open waters, clipping along, steadier in her rhythm as she eased into her course and into synch with the heave of the sea and the wind's persistence.

Behind them, the gradual diminution of the island.

'OK, this is as good a place as any.'

Finn turned at Amver's voice. She was standing on the deck, one hand holding the rail; at her feet lay the tarp's bulging, lumpen hulk, the thick white canvas criss-crossed with rope so that the thing resembled a deformed and mummified giant. He'd already hurled the gun into the ocean, now it was time to jettison the bodies. Amver couldn't leave the wheel for long, so Finn jolted into action. He took one end, using the binding as a handle; she did the same at the other end – knees bent, backs braced. One, two, three. No. Too heavy, too cumbersome. Instead, they dragged the load to the stern and, taking the same end, heaved and pushed it to vertical so that it stood propped against the rail. Together, with one shove, they toppled it overboard. Finn had expected a huge splash, or for the tarp not to sink right away, but it disappeared immediately beneath the boat's wake with barely a sound, or any sign of disturbance.

370

Even so, they remained by the rail, staring at the surface.

After a moment, Amver said: 'Why did you kill them, Finn?'

Because of the things they'd done, he might've said; the things they would've gone on doing, the *evil* in them. Because he could see no other way to be free of them, for the islanders to be free of them; because they deserved it; because he was scared of dying himself; because he panicked; because he wanted to be a hero; because, once Skins was wounded, he had to go through with it, or leave a worse mess than before; because he *could*, because the gun made it possible; because sometimes you have to kill; because of the dog, the girl, and the killing of Hano; because of Rudy kicking him, pissing in his face; because the world was a better place without them, and their tyranny; because he'd had enough; because he wanted to make a stand; because he hated them, he fucking hated them; because they made a beautiful land ugly.

Finn might have offered her any or all of these replies.

But in that moment, before turning the gun on Rudy – and again, before he finished off the crocodile farmer – he'd searched hard inside himself and found none of these reasons, these justifications. No rationale at all. You could try to justify it to yourself afterwards, convince yourself it was true or reasonable or permissible – that, despite bringing hatred and violence and death to a place of peace and love, you were not the same as Mr Skins, or Rudy. You could even delude yourself that, by killing them, you had killed off their kind. But, in the instant before firing the gun, when he still might've stopped himself, Finn knew it for what it was: an act of pure desire.

So, in answer to the question, he said: 'I killed them because I wanted to.'

Amver stayed beside him, looking out over the wake. She placed a hand on his back, between his shoulder blades, with the slightest pressure. Left it there a moment. Then she turned away and went back to the steering of the boat.

★   ★   ★

He didn't know what lay in store. Whether he would survive the war, shut away in an attic or cellar, or behind a fake wall, with hours, days, weeks and months of nothing stretching ahead of him; or if Amver's father would fit him up with a new name, a job on the trawlers; or if he'd be captured and jailed, or sent to fight after all. Whatever, he would have to learn to live the life that was to be his. And begin, all over again, the task of becoming a different kind of man; a mainlander, still, but one who'd caught a glimpse of himself as an islander. It wasn't much to hold on to, and it seemed slighter and more fleeting than before – but it *was* a glimpse, and it was all he had.

He lingered at the stern as the island receded into featureless-ness. The gorse in flower on South Hill, the bright strip of beach, the boatyard awning's reflective glint, the notch of the slipway . . . merging, blurring into one continuous, colourless sinew of land. With its undulations, it briefly resembled the surfacing of a giant sea-serpent, but now the coils of its hills were flattened and elongated; soon, the horizon would reclaim them altogether. He remained at the rail while there was still something to see that wasn't uninterrupted water or sky. If you stared hard enough, you could imagine you were approaching rather than departing, that the long white slick of the boat's wake was an unbreakable cord, slowly reeling you back towards shore, or that this was your first day on the island, not your last, and that a new world awaited you there and that, beneath these skies, anything was possible.

Allowing himself a final look, Finn left the stern and – braced against the roll and pitch of the ocean – made his way for'ard to join Amver in the wheelhouse, to see where they were headed.

Acknowledgements

The island is loosely modelled on Bryher, in the Isles of Scilly (although many liberties – geographical and otherwise – have been taken). Two trips to the Scillies were funded by awards from the Authors' Foundation, administered by the Society of Authors, and from Arts Council Yorkshire's Research and Development Fund – I am grateful to both organisations for their support.

The following publications were most helpful: *The Scilly Guidebook* by Rox Lyon Bowley (Bowley Publications Ltd, 2002); *Map & Guide to Exploring the Isles of Scilly* by Neil Reid (Cormorant Design, 2000); and *Bryher, Land of the Hills* by Glynis Reeve (Historic Occasions, 1994). Other works consulted for research purposes or as background reading included: *All American Boys: Draft Dodgers in Canada from the Vietnam War* by Frank Kusch (Praeger, 2001); *Northern Passage – American Vietnam War Resisters in Canada* by John Hagan (Harvard University Press, 2001); *Folk Medicine* by D.C. Jarvis (Pan Books, 1960); and *Island* by Aldous Huxley (Triad Grafton, 1962). The website of the McKinley Health Center, University of Illinois, contained useful information under 'Signs and Symptoms of Wound Infection'; other valuable Internet resources included: 'Honey as a Topical Anti-bacterial Agent for the Treatment of Infected Wounds', at www.worldwidewounds.com; and Jeff Davies's excellent site, 'Beekeeping the Natural Way', found via www.geocities.com.

I am deeply grateful to Mike Mann, director of Winchester Growers, of Winchester, Hants, and Pinchbeck, Lincs, for his time and expertise in explaining the rudiments of growing and cropping narcissi – grateful, too, to Thea Croxall and Paul Devey for putting me in contact with Mr Mann, and for their hospitality during my visit to Lincolnshire.

Finally, for their critical feedback on various drafts of this novel, I am greatly indebted to my agent, Jonny Geller, at Curtis Brown; Mike Jones, my editor, and Katherine Stanton, my copy-editor, at Bloomsbury; my friends and fellow writers Phil Whitaker and Martha Perkins; and, above all, to my wife, Damaris – for her thoughtful reading at every stage, and for lending me her confidence when mine ran low.

A NOTE ON THE AUTHOR

Martyn Bedford's previous novels – *Acts of Revision*, *Exit*, *Orange & Red*, *The Houdini Girl*, and *Black Cat* – have been translated into twelve languages. He teaches creative writing at Manchester University and is a fiction critic for the *Literary Review*. He lives in West Yorkshire with his wife and two young daughters.

A NOTE ON THE TYPE

The text of this book is set in Bembo. This type was first used in 1495 by the Venetian printer Aldus Manutius for Cardinal Bembo's *De Aetna*, and was cut for Manutius by Francesco Griffo. It was one of the types used by Claude Garamond (1480–1561) as a model for his Romain de L'Université, and so it was the forerunner of what became standard European type for the following two centuries. Its modern form follows the original types and was designed for Monotype in 1929.